Dolly Biters!

Dolly Biters!

The Vampire Girls of Victorian London

Paul Voodini

Many thanks to the following people whose belief and support made Dolly Biters possible! Luis Garcia, Jim Kleefeld, Aya, Jens Christian Rasch, Paul Noffsinger, Phineas Lane, William Gunderson

For all you little fingersmiths, in all your little bedrooms,
all busy exploring your magical kingdoms.

Don't Dilly Dally On The Way (The Dolly Biters' Song)
by Charles Collins and Fred W. Leigh, written in 1901

My old man said "Hop on the tram[1],
and don't dilly dally [2] on the way!"
Off went the tram with my old man in it,
but I was too slow and I didn't catch it!
I dillied and dallied, dallied and I dillied,
Lost my way from Whitechapel to Bow [3]!
Oh you can't trust those Dollies [4] and their Hounslow Heath
[5]
when you can't find your way home!

[1] Horse drawn and later electrical trams ran in London from 1860 until 1952.
[2] To 'dilly and dally' is an English expression which means to be slow, to dawdle, to be easily distracted.
[3] The Whitechapel to Bow horse-drawn tramway ran from 1870.
[4] 'Dollies' or 'Dolly Biters' was London slang for working class female vampires who lived in the East End of London, predominantly Whitechapel and Spitalfields.
[5] 'Hounslow Heath' is Cockney rhyming slang for teeth, and in this case is referencing the sharp teeth of the vampires, the 'Dolly Biters'. Humans tended to believe that they couldn't trust vampires, and that the lost or the unwary wandering the streets of the East End of London were likely to fall prey to vampires. Despite it being illegal for vampires to harm or kill humans, many humans believed that such laws were regularly broken and the crimes left unsolved by a police force unwilling to enter the dark maze of streets and alleyways that made up the East End in the mid-to-late 1800s.

...female children fall victims to the gross passions of natural-born vampires, when their tender age would have seemed to have put such dangers out of their way. When human girls and vampire

men are thrown promiscuously together, do you wonder that so many 'Dolly Biters' walk the streets of the East End at night...

Thomas Beames, *The Vampire Rookeries of London*, 1852. This book was banned in the United Kingdom until 1931, the ban being overturned once official sources reported that the last living 'turned' vampire had been burned at the stake in the grounds of Holloway Prison, London.

Introduction
Exhuming the Crypt

That vampires once existed in the London of the 18th and 19th Centuries is not in question. After all, it is this knowledge that has brought you here, to these streets, filled with fog and gas-lamps and alluring women with teeth too sharp and manners too coarse to belong anywhere else but in the old East End of London.

The streets that you are about to walk are streets that you will not recognise. They are not the Victorian streets of Christmas cards and biscuit tins and cosy televisual costume dramas. These streets are dangerous and dirty; they are filled with shit and shadows and at any moment, out of these shadows, death could appear in the guise of a thug's bludgeon or a prostitute's syphilis or a vampire's teeth. The truth of the matter, and it's a truth that you may already suspect, is that the streets of Whitechapel and Spitalfields were far more dangerous than you will ever truly comprehend. The average life expectancy in the East End of London was the mid-twenties (it was an extravagant mid-forties in wealthier areas such as Chelsea), with half of all children dying before they reached their tenth birthday. It was in this atmosphere that the vampires of Victorian London operated with all-but impunity. Death surrounded the mortals, and if it wasn't one thing that got you, well, it would be the other.

To the vampire girls of Victorian London, we soft, weak humans were nothing but food, to be preyed upon and taken at leisure. We may thank our Gods (should we have cause to believe in such fancies) that we live now in the 21st Century, and not in the 1800s. For if this were the 1800s we would by now, undoubtedly, be dead.

So enjoy these tales, these macabre tales of death and murder and lesbian sex. Slaver over them, let them haunt your sleep and benumb your waking day. Laugh and curse and thrill along with our dark heroines, safe and secure in the knowledge that if these girls still lived, if our paths should ever cross, they would despise us, spit in our face, and then feast upon our blood.

If my words seem harsh, then understand this: I only wish to impress upon you the dangerous times we are about to travel to, so you are prepared, so you are not shocked when you come face to face with the sheer depravity of their world and come running back to me, whining that I had not warned you sufficiently of the depths that you have been dragged down to. I have warned you. I have done my job. Now you may close this book and leave, or you may take my hand and let me lead you, safely through the medium of the printed word, into the vampire-infested streets of Victorian London. That choice is yours, and remember, you make it freely.

Paul Voodini, 2015.

Book 1
The Holmes of the Baskervilles

or the Fall & Rise & Fall Again of the Celebrated Heiress Miss Irene

Adler, Lesbian Vampire, Dolly Biter, and Infamous Trollop

London, 1866

The Royal Aeronautical Society is formed.

A cholera epidemic causes 5,000 deaths.

Elizabeth Garrett Anderson opens the St. Mary's Dispensary where women could seek medical advice from solely female practitioners.

Cadbury's first sell cocoa for drinking.

The General Post Office writes to all householders urging those without a front door letterbox to provide one.

Demonstrations in Hyde Park in favour of parliamentary reform turn violent.

HG Wells and Beatrix Potter are born.

Prologue
City of Dreadful Night

London, 20??

The door opens and I sense my prey immediately. I can smell her, smell the fear rising from her, a terrible perfume, as intoxicating as human fear always is. I can hear the blood pumping through her veins and the air being dragged in short, terrified bursts into her lungs. I can't see her, of course. My eyes had been lost during the Battle of Brick Lane back on New Year's Day, 1867; but my remaining vampire senses more than compensate for their loss, and during the intervening years they have been sharpened and heightened to such a state that I hardly notice these days that my eyes are lost. Some would say that I am blessed, others that I am cursed. I'm undecided either way. All I do know, these days especially, is that I am a survivor. I have seen the British Empire rise to unimaginable heights and then collapse again, I've lived through both of the World Wars that the humans fought against each other, and I'm still here, large as life. Still eighteen years old, as near as immortal as it is possible to be; still the handsome girl who turned the heads and bit the necks of the Poor Unfortunates down Spitalfields way. I am still here, minus my eyes of course. But I am still here when all the rest of the Spitalfields' gang have gone. Every last God-forsaken one of them.

The woman they have provided for me is trying to scream, but the gag they've put around her mouth is keeping her relatively quiet, save for little whimpers that serve to do nothing more than increase my excitement. My fangs, my dreadful, awful, pearly white fangs, extend in my mouth and the saliva begins to flow. On bare feet, I pad quietly up behind her. I do not think that she knows I am here. Perhaps she heard the door open and knew, instinctively, that it signalled her doom. But as for hearing me approach, no, I don't think so. You should understand that I am as quiet as the serpent when I want to be, a genuine snake in the grass. She does not know that I am behind her, but where, I ask, is the fun in that? I want her to see me, for her to know that it is I, this ancient eighteen-year-old relic of a by-gone age, that is about to feast upon her. For her to look at my face and know that my face, this face without eyes, is the face of her death.

The woman is tied quite securely to a chair, of course. The people who provide my food, who observe and record my every move, do not want to see the prey trying to escape. Personally speaking I think that I would prefer the sport of the chase, but the scientists, the observers, don't see it that way. I do not believe they want any undue distractions as they scribble on their notepads and push buttons on those machines that I do not understand. So she is bound to the chair as I sidle up behind her. I would have preferred the chase, but there is fun to be had in this game too.

I brush a hand through her hair, matted though it is with sweat and fear, and she stiffens at my touch. She is probably quite pretty. The scientists seem to get a perverse thrill from seeing me feast on pretty young ones, although, of course, they would never admit as much out loud. But I know humans and I know what makes them tick, and they cannot hide their dirty little secrets from me. I am too wise and too old and too full of sin for that.

"Don't worry, treacle," I whisper. "It will soon be over."

Her squealing begins afresh and she fights desperately against the ropes that bind her, the chair to which she is tied rocking backwards and forwards with her exertions. It is all to no avail.

I move around in front of her and sit on her lap, face to face, cheek to cheek, my legs straddling her. Her protests end and I imagine that she tries to beg with her eyes, beg for her life. I smile sweetly, like I used to smile close to two hundred years ago when this vampire life was new and there were adventures to be had. And then I bite down into her neck, deeply, mortally.

Her blood gushes in a torrent down my throat as her body convulses beneath me. As the convulsions subside I feel her life-force enter me, giving me sustenance, giving me strength, giving me life eternal.

I am not happy here, being watched and observed like some rat in a cage. But I am biding my time. Time. Time is my only friend.

Yes, I have seen empires rise and fall, wars begin and end, and through it all I have endured and shall endure again. This humiliation will not last, for nothing lasts forever save for myself and the ticking seconds of time. We endure. We are eternal. As eternal as the dreadful night. . .

Chapter One
The Vampire Girls
of Victorian London

London, 1866

The first thing I saw, coming out of the October darkness, were their eyes. First one pair, then two pairs, a dozen and more. Then their faces, the white faces of teenage girls, some older, some younger, as they emerged from the shadows and stood before me.

They were well-dressed compared to some of the humans who lived (well, more like *survived*) in other parts of London's East End, but even these vampire girls, these children of the night, looked dirty, dishevelled and hungry.

"Who are you?" asked one, as they approached. "What you doing down here?"

"Look at her ears!" said another. "She's one of us!"

"Of course she bleedin' is," said the first, "or I'd have eaten her by now."

The ears. Besides the fangs, the ears were always the easiest way to tell a vampire from a human. When a human was turned into a vampire, the body would go through a whole host of changes. The fangs were perhaps the most well-known change, along with the hunger for blood. But there were many other changes too; the skin became paler, the body cooler, the eyes redder. And the ears, they became slightly elongated and pointed, like pictures of an elf that you might have seen in a children's book of fairy tales.

These *elf ears* did not occur in 'natural-born' vampires (those born of vampire parents), but it always happened to humans that were turned into vampires. All of the girls now standing before me had these ears, regarded by the natural-borns as a disgusting deformity. Deformity or not, these girls all wore their hair high to accentuate their ears; a badge of honour, a deceleration of who and what they were. Turned vampires, the lowest of the low.

"Coo, take a gander at her pretty dress," said one of the vampire girls with a heavy East End accent. "She ain't from round here, whoever she is."

There were no boys. The only male vampires I had ever come across were natural-borns. Men could never make the turn from human to vampire; they all died, for whatever reason. So there were no boys here, just the girls.

"Who are you?" demanded the first girl, who seemed to be their leader. She appeared slightly older than the other girls, all of them suspended in time at the exact age that they were turned. Her hard, angry face glared at me with suspicion, red eyes piercing the darkness, and the other girls looked to her to gauge how they should react.

"Sisters!" I smiled, holding out my hands in what I conceived of as a welcoming gesture. I had a whole speech ready in my head. A speech about kinship and being amongst my own kind. Since I had been forced to flee from my family home I had been lost and alone, and although these girls were living in what was close to poverty, they were, at least, the same as me, the same breed as me. Humans turned vampires and abandoned by society and by those who they loved. Sisters, I said, hoping that I had found some kind of home where I would be welcome. I said sisters, and they fell about in fits of laughter.

"Fuck off, *sister!*" screeched one, and the laughter redoubled.

Well, as you can see, they did not take to me at first. I was too fancy, too West End for their liking. My accent was not the same as theirs, and I was far too quick with my *pleases* and *thank-yous*. But they allowed me to stay, gave me a roof over my head, and a blanket to pull over myself when the sun rose over the streets of Spitalfields and we were all forced to take refuge from the murderous day. After three nights, when my once pretty dress was almost as filthy as the other girls' dresses, and my face was smudged with dirt and blood, the vampire girls of Chicksand Street began to relent, their mood softened towards me, and they asked me to tell my story; the story of how a lady from the Royal Borough of Kensington and Chelsea came to be turned vampire and henceforth came to stagger into their midst looking for acceptance.

Chicksand Street lay smack bang in the middle of Spitalfields, running off Brick Lane. And running off Chicksand Street were half-a-dozen smaller roads, little more than alleys really; Ely Place, Luntley Place, all ruled over and dominated by the vampire girls. They called themselves the Brick Lane Irregulars. They weren't an organised gang as such, not like some of the human gangs that ruled over parts of the East End with an iron fist. This was more of a co-operative; I estimated them at three or four dozen turned vampires, living together for mutual protection. Alone they would be easy prey to those who would have rid the world of all turned vampires, but together they were strong. They hunted as a pack, and robbed their victims for good measure. Yes, *hunted*, for these were vampires and killers, make no mistake about that, and they feasted upon human blood, and from the pockets of their victims they stole whatever they could to make their lives a little easier. Money of course, but watches, shoes, even spectacles; anything that they could utilise, pawn, or sell to the fences of Brick Lane. The press called them vermin, the curse of the East End they said; but if they were such then it was only because circumstances dictated that there was no other way for them to live. To live and to survive. I had called them sisters and they had laughed, and now I saw the humour of it all.

Their leader, the girl with the hard, mean face, was called Raffles. On that third night she sat before me in one of the run-down terraced houses in Chicksand Street and said, "Come on then, darling. Tell us your story. You ain't from the street like the rest of us. How come you managed to get yourself turned?"

We were surrounded by a dozen or so older vampire girls, girls who had been in their late teens and twenties when they had been turned. The younger girls had their own house, next door to the one we were in, where they socialised and slept and called home. Sometimes their laughter and shrieks of joy could be heard through the thin walls and it would have been easy to forget that they were vampires and not simply mortal children, playing games and enjoying the innocence that their tender years should have afforded them. Other times their sobbing and cries for their mother could be heard, and the reality of the situation was almost too painful to bear.

Raffles looked across at the other girls as they sat on the floor or on the rickety chairs that were scattered around the room. "We want to hear her story, don't we?" she asked of them. The girls looked up at Raffles and nodded in agreement. A handful of candles stood flickering atop a crude wooden table, sending shadows dancing like drunken marionettes across the bare walls and meagre curtains. How had I been turned from human to vampire, from Chelsea lady to Spitalfields rough arse? I smiled a little sadly, and told them how.

* * *

My name is Irene Adler, you may have heard of me or at least you may have heard of my father's business, the Adler Shipping Company. Father dear had formed the company in his early twenties, and by the time I was conceived it had grown to become the foremost shipping line in the UK, transporting goods and people to and from the furthest flung corners of the Empire and beyond. Spices, cotton, tobacco, weapons, soldiers, people. Whatever, whoever, and wherever; the Adler Shipping Company transported them all.

I was my parent's only child, and I had been such a troublesome birth that my mother had been left incapable of bearing further children, a fact that was pointed out to me on more than one occasion when my behaviour had not been sufficiently ladylike or my appreciation of the worldly goods provided for me not appropriately gushing. Still, my parents were as loving as any other parents – do not let me give you the wrong impression about that – and I did, I fully acknowledge, receive a privileged upbringing. We lived in a sumptuous house in Chelsea, served by a veritable horde of maids and butlers and footmen and cooks, and I was schooled in my own private study by my very own school teacher, Miss Ainsworth, who was kind and gentle, with a loving heart, and who would later prove that kindness in the most practical of terms.

So there I was, the daughter and heir to Sir (yes, the Empire rewards its successful sons well) Adler. But a shadow hung over the household. You see, I was a *girl* and how on earth could I be expected to take over the reins of the business upon my father's retirement? There was also the question of propriety. It simply was not considered *decent* that Sir Adler's daughter, a female, should enter the world of shipping and commerce. That was considered the exclusive domain of the male. My place, it would seem, was sat upon a settee, indulging in a little embroidery or light reading, while organising the occasional ball or banquet with the maids, the better to further my husband's position. Ah yes, my husband. A suitable male would be selected whom I would marry and who would take over the helm of the Adler empire, and thus would the thorny issue of my unfortunate femininity be resolved.

But, as I have stated, my parents *did* love me and as such they found it difficult to find a suitable young man who lived up to their very high expectations. My life carried on as much before the decision to marry me off was made; schooling in the days (reading, mainly, with a little rudimentary mathematics), embroidery by candlelight in the evenings, with the occasional dinner party to add a little spice to my very orderly existence. My parents threw some lavish dinner parties, all in the name of business, and dignitaries from around the globe would attend, to be wined and dined and wooed into signing business contracts with father. I was blessed to have met cotton traders from the United States, silk traders from the Orient, ivory traders from Africa, and, to my recollection, two British Prime Ministers.

Many of those who dined at our Chelsea home were vampires. Not the sordid little creatures that could be found in Spitalfields, the ones I would later run to in desperation, with their grubby clothes and their pointed little ears. No, these were natural-born vampires, born of vampire parents and fully grown to sexual maturity when the vampire blood within them stopped the ageing process and they became, to all intents and purposes, immortal. Many in government and business were natural-born vampires, who having lived for centuries had managed to accrue great wealth and influence. To me, meeting a vampire was as common place as meeting an American or a Frenchman; the circles in which my father moved was full of them. Natural-born vampires held power, wealth, and influence, and oh! How they despised the 'turned' vampire girls that lived on the streets of east London. "They should be exterminated, like the vermin they are!" I heard more than one natural-born declare of his turned cousins.

And so it came to pass that at one of these glittering vampire-attended soirées I met my downfall, or perhaps it was my awakening. . .

He was a natural-born vampire and his name was Prince Wilhelm von Ormstein (a vampire and a prince, no less!) from the Kingdom of Bohemia, and I think I may have fallen a little in love with him at first sight. He was undeniably handsome, with his luxurious moustache, shiny hair, and ridiculously smart military uniform. Add to this his impeccable manners and mid-European accent, and I will admit that he set my heart all a-flutter. I wondered and hoped that he might not have been invited to dine with us as a possible suitor for myself, but it soon became apparent that his attendance was entirely a business affair, and perhaps not a terribly pleasant business at that.

One of the advantages of being a female in these situations is that the men will often talk quite candidly in front of you, almost as though they forget that you exist. We silly women are dismissed as being unimportant or as being incapable of understanding the subjects being discussed by the men, and as such I got to listen in on all manner of scandals and intrigues. Who owed money to whom, who was on the brink of bankruptcy, what shares were not worth the paper they are printed on, and even more earthy scandals such as whose daughter had been sent to the countryside for a nine month 'retreat' and who the cause of such an unscheduled *vacances* might have been. I enjoyed listening in on these little pieces of gossip, and it often struck me as amusing how like washer women these powerful magnates of business could be when they'd a few glasses of brandy or burgundy inside them. So it was on that fateful evening. There was a delicate issue being discussed between my father and the prince, and beneath the polite language and coded references, I sensed rage and anger on the prince's part and greed, I am sorry to say, on my father's.

There was a letter or a document or perhaps even a photograph that had fallen into my father's possession and which the prince wished to relieve him of. The prince offered my father money but my father waved this offer away. He wanted something far more valuable – the monopoly on all shipping conducted by the Bohemian government. The prince refused, and the dinner party ended with curt words and barely concealed hatred. But such matters were not of my concern, and with the dinner party at an end, and my head filled with silly romantic notions of the vampire prince coming to visit me in my chambers in the middle of the night to declare his undying affection for me (and how my heart fluttered at such a thought!), I kissed my mother and father goodnight for what would prove to be the very last time.

Oh, what childish fancies may enter the minds (and hearts) of mortal girls, for when the prince did enter my room, later that very night, it was a far more brutal and sordid encounter than my foolish daydreaming had imagined. I had been asleep for, well, who knows? An hour? Maybe longer? And then something awoke me and I sat bolt upright in bed, the drapes of the bed's canopy pulled tight and the room in darkness. But I was not alone, instinctively I sensed that there was someone, something, there with me in my chamber. Fear froze my body and though I wanted to cry out for help, I could not. My body, in terror, had betrayed me and there I sat, as helpless as a kitten before a rabid dog.

The drape beside me parted and by the light of the moon that now flooded from the window and into my meagre fortress, I could just make out the face of my sweet prince. "Miss Adler," he smiled, and the smile was evil and full of sharp teeth, not at all the face of the gentle suitor I had imagined in my girlish fantasy, "I do apologise for this unforgivable intrusion. But my, how beautiful you look by the light of the moon. Sadly though, I am here on a matter of business rather than affairs of the heart, and for this I do, once again, apologise. But the sad fact is, Miss Adler, that your father, a rather vain and arrogant man in my opinion, has something of mine and he steadfastly refuses to give it back to me. I have offered money and favours, and always he demands more, and, forgiving and reasonable though I am, I find myself at the end of my, how do you say it? The end of my tether? Yes, the end of my tether. He has something of mine and will not re-linquish it. Therefore, I find myself in the unenviable position of having to take something of value from him, to make amends, you understand?

"Now, what in all the world does your father value above every-thing else? Well, certainly his shipping line, of course. But surely there is something even more precious, more precious but also so terribly, terribly delicate? It is you, Miss Adler, that I fear I must take. I am forced to take you like a common thief in the night, so that your father may never know the innocence of your smile or the melody of your laugh ever again. To balance the books, as it were. It pains me, but I fear that it must be so."

"No," I managed to whisper by way of protest but that was all. I had no defence. I was an eighteen-year-old girl, he a centuries old vampire. I had no defence, and in a blink he was upon me.

There was pain at first as his teeth savaged the flesh of my neck, but the pain quickly subsided to be replaced by the peculiar sensation of my blood and my very soul being drained out of my body. I understand now that a vampire's bite produces a sedative of sorts that numbs the bite area and induces a sense of helpless euphoria within the victim. It is a strange sensation which, if I am to be honest, is not entirely unpleasant. I swooned beneath the prince's bite and beneath his grip and he drained the blood and the life from me. I was within seconds of being embraced by death when he stopped.

I looked up at him through watery, saucer-shaped eyes, and he looked back down at me, his eyes black pits of menace, my own blood dripping back down upon me from his lips and his teeth. "It is a singular gift that I bestow upon you, Miss Adler," he hissed down at me. "I leave you to turn. To become a turned vampire. The lowest form of life, reviled by both natural-borns and humans. You will have no place to call home, no friends to turn to, no sanctuary to seek. Enjoy your immortality, Miss Adler. I rather fear it will not last long."

In the room in Chicksand Street, the assembled girls let out howls of disgust. "What a rotter!" cried one, "I'd like to fix him good and proper!" cried another. Eventually Raffles hushed the outrage, and I continued my monologue of woe.

I passed out and awoke I do not know how much later. Whatever the time, I was surrounded by my mother and father, our local doctor, and several maids who scurried back and forth, dutifully carrying bowls of water and soiled towels and steadfastly avoiding my gaze. It was morning, or at least it was daytime, and light poured in through poorly closed curtains. The light pained my eyes and irritated my skin and, more than that, it offended me with its cheery brightness and its inane little message of hope. "Close those fucking curtains, you stupid cunts!" I screamed, spitting blood and fighting to sit up in my idiotically luxurious bed with its insipid comfort, plump pillows, and human succour. "You stupid fucking cunts!"

At my words mother dearest fainted, hitting the floor of my chamber like the veritable sack of potatoes, and my father, visibly shocked, slapped me across the face with the open palm of his hand. I rather suspect the blow hurt his hand far more than it hurt my face. I spat blood, my blood, the blood that had dripped down onto my face from the fangs of the prince, up at my father and began to writhe upon the bed. The light was hurting me, I felt hungry, I felt an itch deep down inside me that I did not know how to scratch, I felt hatred and anger and helplessness, and all I could do was moan and writhe and snarl.

"It is as I feared," said the doctor as he pulled my father away from my bedside. "She has been turned. She is a turned vampire."

The maids ran squealing from my chamber, taking my half-conscious mother with them. The doctor pulled the curtains tight across the windows, blocking out the light and providing me with a modicum of relief, and then both he and my father left the chamber also, locking the door as they went.

The hours passed and as twilight enveloped the house, my body began to relax and the distress caused by being awake in the day-time began to subside. I was increasingly hungry. I was not sure what exactly I was hungry *for*, but a terrible ache was making itself known in my stomach and I longed for sustenance. I tumbled out of bed and climbed to my feet unsteadily, and holding onto first the bedside and then a chair, I made my way across the room and towards the mirror that stood atop my dresser. I did not recognise the face that looked back at me. It was not the face of sweet, pretty, innocent Miss Adler. No, this was some manner of feral creature. My skin was pale and smeared with dried blood, my hair was dishevelled and matted, and my eyes were dark pits with glowing red embers deep within them. And my ears, my ears were pointed and elongated, and my teeth were white and sharp and dangerous. I picked up a perfume bottle and hurled it at the mirror. It exploded in a fountain of sparkling glass. "Bastards!" I screamed, at the prince and his teeth, at my father and his business, at the life that had been stolen away from me, at the whole sorry lot of them. What a shower of cunts they were, after all.

I had never used profane language before in the whole of my life! I had hardly even been aware of any four-letter words, and yet here they were, filling my mind and tripping off my tongue as easily as if I were a veteran sailor, used to swearing and cursing the whole day through. Where were these words coming from? Had I known them all along? I must have done. I must have known all these words and all this rage and all this anger before, but never acted upon them. Now though, now I truly was a little bundle of fury. Fury and hunger. The hunger, by now, really was quite intense. . .

The door opened and in walked the doctor, a white handkerchief held up to his mouth and his nose as though the little cunt thought this vampiric state might be contagious. He avoided my eyes, refused to look directly at me, rather he stared hard at the floor and blurted out a speech that he must have hastily concocted on the walk back up here, from the drawing room where doubtless my mother and father and the whole gaggle of them had convened, up the stairs and along the corridor to my bed chamber.

"Your father has decided that you must leave," he said, handkerchief still thrust up against his lips, giving his voice a ridiculously muffled sound. "He has disavowed you, disowned you. He cannot have a turned vampire for a daughter. It simply won't do. Your tutor, Miss Ainsworth, will be along presently to help you pack, and then you must leave. You should know that Miss Ainsworth volunteered to help you. Nobody else was willing." And with that the illustrious doctor slipped back through the door and was gone.

So that was it. My mother and father would not even come to say goodbye. Only that quack and my tutor, only they could bring themselves to enter my chamber to hasten my departure. Was I such a monster now as to be deserving of such treatment? Was this not all my father's fault, his avarice and his empire building bringing the wrath of the Bohemian vampire prince down upon me? I had paid a terrible price for his errors of judgement, and yet he would not even face me. I was truly damned.

Well if damned I was, then I was about to give them all good reason to damn me twice.

Miss Ainsworth was a handsome woman, in her mid-twenties, with a ready smile and pleasing countenance. She was a spinster, unmarried, as women with certain tastes in life can tend to be. My mother's sister was similarly a spinster, and I had often over-heard my parents discussing her choice of friends and 'companions' in less than flattering terms. It amused me to think that perhaps Miss Ainsworth secretly loved me. Certainly her teaching style was at times unconventional, and we would often laugh and make jokes at the expense of my parents or members of the household staff. We would discuss books late into the night, and on sunny afternoons walk arm-in-arm through the park, more sisters than tutor and pupil. If she really did love me she never declared this emotion or made any kind of overt gesture to express this emotion, but there was something in the glint of her eye and the tilt of her head when she regarded me that I liked to think spoke of secret wishes and taboo emotions. Perhaps, yes, perhaps we were in love, after a fashion.

I heard a key turn, unlocking the bed chamber door, and a tingling sensation buzzed across my mouth as my terrible fangs stretched and ached, yearning to reach out and violate human flesh. I turned to face the door as Miss Ainsworth entered. At the sight of me she took a step back, visibly shocked at the sight that befell her.

"Oh you poor, poor dear," she gasped, raising a hand to her lips. "Come, let me help you pack," she said, trying to regain her composure and focus on the task at hand. "I have some lady friends I can speak to. Perhaps we can find a place for you to stay."

Though tears were welling in her eyes, still she attempted to smile at me, attempting to reassure me that all would be well. She did not realise that I was beginning to come to the conclusion that all was well enough as things stood. My hunger had found a focus. She smiled at me meekly, tears in her gentle eyes, and I smiled back at her like a snake with a rat's tail hanging out of its mouth.

Catching sight of myself in the mirror, I was struck by how much I now resembled my vampiric father, the infamous prince.

I slid from the side of the dresser and quick as a flash made my way around the room towards the snivelling teacher. I tried to think of some words to say, perhaps an apology for what I was about to do, or a way of thanking her for her kindness, a way to perhaps even acknowledge her, *our*, unspoken affections, but at the sight of her neck and the smell of her sadness I could contain myself no longer, and I exploded upon her in a frenzy of hunger and passion.

My fangs clamped themselves around the back of her neck and my right hand reached around and clamped itself across her mouth, the better to stifle her screams. Under such exertions we tumbled to the carpeted floor, our legs and feet having become tangled in the teacher's voluminous dress, my breasts pushed up against her shoulder blades, her face pushed into the carpet, as I sucked her blood and waited for the natural sedative of my fangs to take hold and quell her vain struggling. It did not take long and soon she was subdued. I rolled her onto her back and slowly, luxuriously, drained her of her blood.

Her left foot, clad in a delicate pink heeled slipper, tapped rhythmically, involuntarily against one of my bed's wooden feet. Tap, tap, tap, in time with my sucking and the heaving of my chest. Tap, tap, tap. I tasted the summer walks in her blood, the books she had devoured, the laughter we had shared. It was all here, in her blood, and my mind exploded at the sweet taste of it. Her very life-force was here within her blood, and now it was within me, giving me life anew. I was reborn there in that bed chamber, writhing atop my dying tutor. Such a world this was for those few short minutes, a place of wondrous release and hellish passions. Tap, tap, tap, more gently now for death was upon her. I thrust my teeth deeper into her flesh and placed a hand upon her breasts, the better to know her fully, intimately, without sorrow or fear of judgement. We were joined at last as one, hunter and prey, with more intensity than any two lovers had ever known. And then, like the last bloom of summer, she was gone.

I sat up and leaned back on my heels. Miss Ainsworth was dead beneath me, and her blood still filled my mouth and my throat.

I raised a hand to my lips and fought back the urge to vomit. I was sitting in a lake of blood; it covered me and it covered the corpse, it was soaking into the carpet, and it had splattered across my dresser and my bed. So much blood. I dragged myself to my feet, my stomach bloated from the feeding, and knew I had to escape the house. If they found me here with the butchered Miss Ainsworth they would try to kill me. The authorities would be involved and they would hunt me down and burn me at the stake, the prescribed sentence for turned vampires that kill humans.

I pulled off my red-stained night dress, wiping my hands and my face as best I could on the soft linen, and then I quickly pulled on a dress that I found hanging in a closet. With no maids to help me I struggled at first to fasten the corset, but to my delight I found that being a vampire meant I was stronger now, lither, more subtle, and so what could have been a tricky job was accomplished in a matter of moments and I took a last look around my chamber. Nothing here to hold me back now, I decided. I had been abandoned, I had no soul, I did not belong with the living. "Cunts," I said of my family and the house and the doctor and the prince, relishing the way the word formed in my mouth and tumbled off my tongue. "Cunts." I had found my new favourite word.

There was one last matter to attend to before I fled. I knelt back down beside the ravaged body of Miss Ainsworth, my bloody hand-print now drying upon her breasts, and I kissed her gently upon the forehead. Dull, lifeless eyes looked back up at me. The spark had gone from them, she loved me no more. "*Au revoir, mon cheri,*" I whispered to her, remembering the time she had told me of her desire to one day visit Paris, a desire that now could never be acted upon, and then I stood, turned my back on her, and climbed out of my chamber window; it felt like I was eloping, but my love lay dead upon my bedroom floor and so I was left to elope alone.

London by night. What a sight! What a spectacle! Unmatched by any of the many wonders of the Empire! London is a jewel, and at night she sparkles with a ferocity to bring joy to the dourest of souls. I skipped along the streets of Chelsea with a spring in my step, feeling suddenly liberated, free from the shackles of conformity, and, perhaps most of all, supremely powerful. I was a vampire! A vampire, by all the saints! The teacher's blood coursed through my veins, intoxicating me, and I laughed out loud as I cantered through Chelsea and Belgravia and up towards the very centre of civilisation itself, Buckingham Palace. I had no plan in mind, no ultimate destination; I was simply enjoying this sense of euphoria. The night was beautiful, and I wished only to wallow in her dark radiance. I felt no sense of regret or remorse following the evening's gory events; my mind was focused solely on the here and now. My transformation was complete.

As a mortal, I had been a girl of privilege. I had grown up never having to work or want for anything. My life had been delivered to me on a silver platter, and whatever I had desired, within reason, had been mine for the asking. So, perhaps, I approached my new found vampiric status in a similar fashion. This was my new gift, my new toy, and I expected all around me, the mortals, to be impressed by the new me, to be afraid, to shrink from me or fall under my thrall. Well, I was soon to discover that a teenage girl with fangs, elf ears, and a blood smeared face (the night-dress had not been particularly effective at cleaning the blood from my visage), walking up Buckingham Palace Road as bold as brass, was not a sight welcomed by London's human populace. I had forgotten, in my excitement of the metamorphosis, that I was not regarded as a divine monster of the night. Rather I was a turned vampire, a filthy trollop, the lowest of the low, the scourge of the East End.

I first noticed a group of six or eight young men following me. I turned to smile at them, expecting I suppose that they were walking behind me in admiration or trance-like devotion. But when I saw them, saw their faces, I saw the truth. They looked angry, determined, full of bravado. "Watch out, love!" shouted one of these young toughs to a woman ahead of me, a nanny, pushing a baby in a pram. "We've got a Dirty Biter here! Must've wandered out from Spitalfields and got lost!" The nanny saw me, and quickly pushed the pram away from my path. As I passed her, she spat on the ground where I walked. The group of young vigilantes now numbered a dozen, maybe more, and with each step more men, older now, joined the throng.

Dirty Biter. It was the first time I had heard the term, and now these men were calling it again. "Dirty Biter!" they cried, warning others walking along Buckingham Palace Road to beware. And then they began to shout directly at me. "Get back to Spitalfields, you filthy slapper!" "Aye, sod off! You don't belong here!"

They had been keeping their distance, allowing me to keep perhaps twenty feet ahead of them. But as their number increased, so did their courage and now they were but a step or two behind me. I was unsure of my powers at the time, of course. I could have, if I had put my mind to it, killed them all – how many now, two dozen? – but this was still so very new to me, and I had never had cause to fight anyone before in my life! I was from Chelsea, for heaven's sakes, and these ruffians were, I hesitate to admit, quite intimidating. Five minutes before I had thought myself the Queen of the Night, Mistress of the Damned, and yet now I was hastening my step, on the verge of being chased by a rabble of righteous men, and the exuberance I had felt was now rapidly being replaced by fear.

An old woman, tottering along the middle of the pavement, saw the commotion and stepped unsteadily aside to let our dark parade pass. At the sight of me she hissed, "Filth!" and then to the men following, "Kick her face in, boys!" I could stand it no longer. I lifted up the bustles of my black dress and took flight. I was fast, amazingly fast, and I dodged between the mortals walking along the pavement, running at such a pace that I must have seemed like something of a blur to them. The men who had been following me attempted, for a short distance, to keep pace with me, but they could not. I ran and I dodged and I weaved, and I left them trailing in my wake. My exuberance returned; they could not hurt me, they could not even touch me!

I sprinted the rest of the way along Buckingham Palace Road, past the palace itself though I hardly registered it in my haste, and into St. James's Park where I hid amongst the trees and the shrubbery, catching my breath (not that I was terribly out of breath really), and making sure I had not been followed by any of those mortal ruffians. I hadn't. I was safe.

From my secret vantage point, I looked out at the human world carrying on around me. Here in the park I could see sweethearts walking hand-in-hand, the occasional gaggle of old maids out for an evening stroll, nannies pushing prams, a well-dressed city gentleman hastening along, perhaps having worked late and now heading for home. Here a young gentleman peddling along on one of those bicycle contraptions, here a smart soldier enjoying a pipe. What time was it? Perhaps half past eight? Yes, that would make sense. It was still early enough on this October evening for mortals to be wandering the streets in what they would regard as safety. I watched them and they had no idea that I was there. At any moment I could have leapt from my hiding place and ripped the throat out of them. Luckily for them I was still sated from the blood of Miss Ainsworth, my tutor, and so I only watched them as they strolled along. I watched them and I despised them, these humans who had chased me from their streets, who had spat on the floor as I passed, and who had called me filth. I suddenly felt a very real hatred for their warm-bloodedness, for their rosy complexions and their plump little cheeks. They were pigs, I realised. Pigs who walked on two legs and dressed in fine clothes, but pigs none-the-less. Pigs whose only true purpose in life was to serve as my food. I could stand being amongst them no longer; I needed to find my way to those like me, to my kin, to the so-called Dolly Biters. . .

How much did I know of these girl vampires, the pointy eared and sharp toothed trash of Spitalfields? Not much, I suppose. In the leafy avenues of Chelsea, such matters were not thought suitable subjects for discussion, except of course when one is entertaining at dinner parties and the wine is flowing.

I vaguely remembered one such dinner party, and oh how I wished I had paid more attention at the time! Again I think I must have appeared invisible to those sat around me, when business men, men of power, my father, were discussing these girls. I now struggled to recall what they had said. They had used words such as 'filthy' and 'vermin' when describing these turned vampires, they had said they lived in squalor, more animals now than the humans they had once been, preying on the unwary who wandered inadvertently into their lair, occasionally hunting farther afield, killing humans and drinking their blood and stealing their possessions. They were all females, most of them prostitutes who had been turned when natural-born vampires (the *respectable* vampires, the ones with the bloodlines and the ancestral homes and, perhaps most importantly, the money) had bitten them and infected them with vampire saliva during the throws of passion. Some of course had not been prostitutes. Some had just been unlucky enough to have crossed paths with a natural born of dubious morals. But all of them, all of these filthy East End Dolly Biters were shunned and detested by both human and natural-born society. Had it been a Prime Minister who had sat in our dining room and told my father that the situation was under control? That the female vermin had been contained in Spitalfields and that the government was working on a 'final solution' to the problem? Yes, I seemed to recall that it was.

Spitalfields. It was to Spitalfields that I must go. To go and find my sisters. . .

Having experienced how the humans reacted to a lone vampire in their midst, I took a moment to try and smarten my appearance. I pulled my hair over my ears, and in a near-by fountain, at an opportune moment, I quickly rinsed water over my face and teeth, washing away the bloody evidence of my earlier meal. I must still have looked a frightful state, but at least I looked marginally more human than before. I bowed my head, kept my mouth tightly shut, and hurried out of the park and down Horse Guards Road and towards the Embankment. I travelled along the Embankment and Thames Street, following the path of the great river, before, in the early hours of the morning, heading up Commercial Street into Whitechapel and hence to Spitalfields.

* * *

"Fuck off, *sister!*" screeched one, and the laughter redoubled.

* * *

"You were lucky to find us," said Raffles as we sat in that room on Chicksand Street. "A single vampire roaming the streets of London, well, it don't usually end so well. We have to stick together, watch each other's backs. I'm sorry if our welcome when you first arrived here was less than cordial. That weren't right of us. You're welcome here, Irene. I hope you knows that now."

"Thank you," I said and smiled, and around me all the other girls smiled too, a dozen or more pairs of fangs twinkling like shooting stars in the night.

Raffles put an arm around me and pulled me close. "Come here darling," she whispered, "let us welcome you into our little coven properly."

For the first few nights after my arrival on Chicksand Street, before the girls had properly accepted me, they had deigned to allow me to hunt with them. Each night we had set out into the dark streets of Spitalfields, and each night we had fed on the blood of mortals. But upon our return and during the daylight hours, I had slept alone, in a room by myself, very much an outsider in this tightly knit band of comrades. I had, during the daylight hours when blinds and drapes were pulled tight across windows to keep out the murderous rays of the sun, heard shuffling and giggles, the sound of people moving from room to room, and moans and wails also. I had not known what it all meant, but now, now I was about to discover the true intimacy of Raffles' coven.

Raffles put an arm around me and pulled me close. She began to kiss me on the neck, gentle little caresses that belied the awful power of her teeth and mouth. I heard the other girls breathing and was aware of them moving closer. I did not fight Raffles' attentions.

She stood me up and pulled my skirts up over my head, removing the dress from my body and finding me quite naked beneath save for my stockings and boots. I had still been wearing the dress

I had thrown on when I had vacated the family home, and having dressed in a hurry, under-garments had been sacrificed in favour of haste. Placing her hands around my neck and squeezing gently, she observed me with her face tilted to one side. Her lips were pulled back, like a snarling dog, and her fangs were elongated and dripping with saliva. Her eyes glowed a vibrant red, and around us were the eyes of the other girls, also glowing red. Their breathing sounded like panting, and their cold breath buffeted my naked skin.

I began to panic. Raffles' hands still squeezed me around the neck and her grip was growing tighter. Did she mean to murder me? Was this all some cruel joke? I tried to speak but found I could not. And then, and then just as tears began to roll down my cheeks, she released me. I felt insane desires take a hold of my mind, a feeling the likes of which I had never experienced before, and I had an overwhelming need to experience Raffles' tongue, long and lizard-like, caress my body and my breasts and my legs and...

I took a step towards her instinctively, but she manoeuvred me expertly, like a Spanish matador in those travel journals that I had read in my study with Miss Ainsworth, teasing the bull, tormenting the poor beast, before putting it to the sword. She laid me down upon the bare floor, and almost as though she could read my mind and understood my desires, her lips and her tongue devoured me. She devoured all of me, my neck, my breasts, my stomach, and my womanhood, until I exploded with passion, writhing on the floor, tears rolling down my cheeks, and all the while the other girls around me stroked my hair, kissed my forehead, and sucked upon my fingertips. Raffles had me, they *all* had me, and I was now a part of their coven. I had been blooded, and lay upon the floor with my hips still gently rocking as the girls and Raffles began to lick and tongue each other. It was an orgy and it lasted all night and into the following day.

Had I been a virgin before this encounter? Well, yes, of course. And, technically perhaps, I was still a virgin. I may not have been penetrated, but I had been devoured. Oh yes, I had been devoured. "Does it like the tongue?" Raffles had asked me in the throes of passion. "Oh yes," I had replied, "it does." She had called me *it*, and to be objectified in such a cruel manner had excited me more than I would have imagined possible. Poor, sweet, innocent Irene Adler was dead. In her place was the Vampire Irene Adler of Spitalfields, Dirty Biter, Brick Lane Irregular and, it would seem, Lesbian Trollop.

The next day, after the passions had subsided but while we were still forced to take refuge indoors from the sun, Raffles sat beside me on a battered old settee. "You'll be safe with us," she said. "Ain't nothing can hurt you while you're with us. No-one crosses the Spitalfields' vampires." But the way she spoke sounded more like, "Yewel be save wiff us. Ain't nuffink can hurtcha while you wiv us," and I smiled inwardly that this hard faced girl, this rough arse from the East End, was now my saviour and protector, me who had dined with Prime Ministers and European royalty! But at that moment, and now, more so now than ever, I would not swap Raffles, or any of the girls, not for all the royalty and lords and ladies in all the Empire, in all the world.

"You'll be safe with us," she had said. "No-one crosses the Spitalfields' vampires." Perhaps it was at that moment, that delicate instant, that Raffles inadvertently cursed us and brought the minions of hell down upon our coven. But that adventure was still yet to come...

So, over the next few weeks, my life attained some degree of normality, although it was a normality that would disgust and terrify the mortals. We hunted humans most every night, and during the daylight hours we rested, we hid from the sun, and we explored the most carnal of desires, swapping partners most days, and even swapping partners in the course of single days. I felt no guilt at engaging in such base appetites, rather I embraced these appetites, I enjoyed them, I craved them. I was liberated.

Chapter Two
1866 and All That

What was it like, you may wonder, to live in Spitalfields and to hunt humans and drink their blood? Well, let me tell you. But first I must explain a little about our situation, we vampire girls of Spitalfields. Although the human population of London may have referred to us as Dolly Biters, amongst ourselves and the other gangs of the East End we were known as the Brick Lane Irregulars. Irregular, you see, because we weren't normal, at least not as far as the humans were concerned. We were vampires – different, odd, *irregular*. We ruled Spitalfields, and Brick Lane was the shining jewel in our crown. The old East End was, of course, full of human street gangs, young men mainly, running riot, fighting with each other, picking pockets or snatching bags, doing over drunks and mug-hunting. Some of them, one or two, were more organised and dabbled in prostitution and poncing and extortion. There were the Yiddishers next door to us in Whitechapel, the Clockwork Oranges over in Aldgate, the Arabian Nights in Mile End, the Dicky Parrots in the old Jago, and coming towards us like an unstoppable steam train, the Holmes Boys of the Baskerville Estate. But more, much more, on those particular cunts later.

None of the human gangs, up to that point, bothered us and we didn't bother them back. We all knew each other's territories, and we respected the boundaries. For us, Brick Lane from Booth Street south to Old Montague Street and all the rat runs and rookeries to the east were ours, our main source of both blood and money. I estimated that there were three or four dozen of us all told, living in the terraced houses of Chicksand Street, some as young as twelve or fourteen with the eldest being perhaps in their early thirties, all frozen in time at the exact moment that they were turned, never ageing, constantly looking for blood and fearing the sun. Some, like Raffles, had been turned a hundred years or more ago, while most, like me, were more recent creations. The experienced looked after the new, showed them how the game worked, handed on knowledge and wisdom, and by such co-operation ensured that none were taken and killed by the mortals and their police and governments and churches. Despite what the Prime Minister may have assured my father all those months ago (and it felt like a lifetime ago to me), the vermin of Spitalfields were not 'contained'. They ruled it, just as assuredly as Queen Victoria herself ruled over the British Empire. Only a fool ventured into Spitalfields after dark, but venture they did, and we took them, and here is how.

During the daylight hours when we were forced to remain indoors, the humans had free reign of Brick Lane. But come sundown, the shops would all close-up and the mortals would hasten away; the shopkeepers, the shop-girls, the businessmen, the street urchins, all of them. It was quite a sight to see, a minute or two after the sun had dipped down below the horizon, the tardy ones scurrying along the streets like rats abandoning a sinking ship. That winter, the winter of 1866, the darkness fell by late afternoon. The humans of the East End lived in a constant state of fear. A cholera outbreak had already killed five thousand of their number in the summer, and now with us vampires preying on them, well, fear was etched all over their faces and dictated that they no longer amble along their merry way, but rather hurry from destination to destination, furtively looking over their shoulders, jumping at shadows and locking themselves away behind stout doors.

By 9 o'clock the girls would be getting restless for the hunt to start. The young girls from the house next door to us on Chicksand Street would come a-visiting, and all of us would be talking excitedly, laughing loudly, swearing at the top of our voices, and occasionally nipping, biting, and caressing each other. On reflection, the closest comparison to our behaviour in the evenings that I have subsequently heard about is the behaviour of a wolf pack prior to the hunt. Excitable, agitated, skittish. And then Raffles would clap her hands, and that would be it, the start of the hunt. We would tumble out of the house and onto the street, silent now, running barefoot, black dresses our camouflage, eyes and ears piercing the darkness. All of the girls wore black dresses and had bare feet, it was a uniform of sorts, and after my acceptance into their midst I had merrily thrown away my stockings and boots and acquired a black dress of my own.

Raffles would lead the hunt. The young girls would stick to the rear of the pack, with the older girls directly behind Raffles. Along Chicksand Street we would silently hurry, staying close to the walls and the shadows. The lamplighter did not, unsurprisingly, operate in our territory, and so the streets were murderously dark. Occasionally the hunt was easy and mortals were found close to home, but this was a rare occurrence, and normally we would either head east to George Street or, more often than not, west to our favourite stomping ground, Brick Lane.

With several dozen vampires to feed, the pack would need to locate several humans to feed upon. Sometimes we would hunt all night and only find one or two humans, and in that case we would share the kills, and every girl would get at least some blood. Other times we would hit the jackpot and we would find the night full of prey. On those glorious nights the girls would merrily hold hands and skip home, with full stomachs and hunger sated.

The hunt was all; it was the very reason for our existence. Everything else that we did, sleeping, talking, playing cards, laughing and joking and swapping lewd stories, even the lust we indulged in with each other, all of it was a distraction, a way of passing the time until we could hunt again. In the hunt the vampire felt truly alive, connected to the night, to her senses, and to the other vampires around her. It was an exhilarating experience, intoxicating and addictive.

Some of the girls preferred to catch a male human, but I preferred females. Of course all would happily eat any kind of human, even children, but we each had our particular favourites, our pet fancies. Mine was for the women. They were softer and smelled sweeter than the men. Their blood was like honey and their flesh like cream. Some preferred the ruggedness of men, the muscles writhing beneath them, the strength that was more of a challenge to overcome. But I was partial to the soft and the sweet and their delicate little voices cooing as I drained them of their life.

* * *

See her now, scurrying down Brick Lane breathlessly. Perhaps she was forced to work late or forgot the time or is on some kind of mercy mission, a relative lying ill at home and needing her attendance? Or perhaps she is from out of town and is unaware of the dangers of Spitalfields by night? Whatever the reason, there she is, holding up her skirts, the better to trot as best she can along the cobblestoned streets of Spitalfields.

I spy her first, and the girls to my side follow my lead. My bare feet pad along noiselessly but just as I am about to pounce on her she hears the rustling of the folds of my dress and spins around. She sees me and her eyes bulge wide in terror. What does she see that fills her with such dread? My pale skin, my red eyes, my wild hair, my fangs elongated and glistening, my nose wrinkled in a snarl. Her eyes bulge but there is no time for her to scream. I am upon her, biting deep and decisively into her neck, her sweet blood erupting like a geyser into my mouth and the back of my throat. At the taste of the blood, my mind explodes in a kaleidoscope of colours and emotions. Reds, yellows, greens, blues, love, hate, sorrow, joy, all exploding behind my eyes, making me reel drunkenly. We fall to the ground, the woman and I, and my legs wrap around her as we writhe on the cold pavement. My feet hook together and pull her close, fixing her in place, as her struggles lessen and the subduing chemicals of the bite begin take control of her mind, overcoming her, telling her to relax, to stop fighting, to enjoy this feeling of falling, falling away, falling away from life. With one hand I stroke her hair soothingly, while my other hand moves involuntarily towards her breasts, feeling her chest rise and fall, growing shallower, until at last she is still.

Two of the younger vampires, the two who had been at my side when I had spotted the woman, approach on all fours, crawling along the cobble-stones towards me and my prize. Their fangs are elongated and saliva drips from their mouths. They cannot have her, not yet. I growl at the youngsters from the back of my throat, my teeth still attached to the woman's neck, the effort of the growl spitting crimson blood across the woman's face, and they shrink back, hissing at me. I take more blood, feeling it slide down my throat, but the woman is dead and the initial euphoria has gone. I climb to my feet and step away, allowing the youngsters to claim their prize and drain her dry. I wipe the back of my hand across my mouth and lean back against a near-by brick wall, watching as the two girls drag the body of Miss Ainsworth away into the night, pulling her apart, limb from limb.

Miss Ainsworth? No. It was not Miss Ainsworth. But in that moment I realise why I am partial to female prey. I am searching for Miss Ainsworth, to relive the thrill of my first kill, my first night as a vampire when I murdered the teacher who was the only one who cared enough to come to my aid. Every night I go out and I kill Miss Ainsworth, over and over and over again.

My belly is full. I see Raffles and some of the other girls bowling down the road towards us, rushing and pushing and laughing. Their mouths, their faces, their hair is caked in blood. The hunt has been good tonight.

"What cheer, Raffles!" I cry.

She smiles, throws her arms around me, and kisses me on the forehead, leaving a bloody impression of her lips upon my skin. In the distance, my elf ears can clearly hear growling and flesh being ripped and torn. We are the monsters, we are the night, and later, as dawn breaks across London, this monster shall have the tongue and it will like it.

* * *

On Friday evenings, after the sun had gone down, an old pawn-broker from Brick Lane, a man with flaming red hair called Jabez Wilson, would come a-knocking upon our doors, come to pur-chase whatever knick-knacks we had managed to purloin during the week from our victims. Wilson, or the Pawn-Broker Man as he was more commonly referred to, was given safe passage to move amongst the girls without fear of being attacked. After all, he brought us money, and although we were aware that he sold us short for the trinkets that we gave him, still he was our only source of income other than taking coins directly from the pock-ets and purses of those we fed upon.

We sold him spectacles, cigarette cases, cigar cutters, watches and chains, rings, whatever we could find; even once, humor-ously, a 'bone-shaker' bicycle that some young man, in his cups, had thought it a good idea to ride down Brick Lane at gone ten o'clock at night. He had his bones shaken that night, and no mistake.

I sold the Pawn-Broker Man a Bible once. It was a very nice Bible with a leather jacket and gold gilt edges, with a touching dedication in the front declaring that the Book was a birthday gift to a darling daughter called Eloise. Being a member of the Salvation Army (or some-such), Eloise had ventured into Spital-fields alone one evening with the noble, if not foolhardy, intention of saving our souls. I found her hiding on Chicksand Street – in fact she had given me quite a start, emerging before me from some doorway where she had been hiding, and managing to look terrified, earnest, and determined all at the same time.

She told me, in a voice that only quivered a little bit, that she loved me, that God loved me, and that the Bible, which she held out before herself, was her armour. I took the Bible from her grasp, it had not proven itself to be particularly effective armour after all, and she had fallen to her knees in prayer. I lifted her up by the hair and ripped out her throat, before stealing the little money she had about her person, the gold crucifix around her neck, her boots, and of course the Bible. The following Friday I sold all of her possessions to the carrot-top Wilson for five shillings.

I do believe that she welcomed my dark embrace with open arms, perhaps expecting her God to save her right up until the end; or expecting Him to welcome her into Paradise, once my teeth had extinguished any hope of divine intervention on Earth. I too had Faith once, but that seemed a long time ago now, before I had my eyes opened to the true nature of the world.

The police almost never ventured into Spitalfields, and when they did it was during daylight hours and only for a cursory glance, a quick look around, and then scarper back westwards to the warmth and safety of their stations. But after I had fed on Jesus' little rainbow, the one that had come to save me, the police visited in force and they brought guests of honour with them!

The girl had been part of this Salvation Army malarkey, headed up by some Methodist priest called William Booth. When he heard of the cruel fate that had befallen one of his flock, he insisted on the police escorting him to the scene of the, *my*, dastardly deed. Here he prayed for some time while wary looking policemen guarded over him nervously, and then he talked to any mortals who happened to be around and who didn't mind answering the Holy Man's questions. The mortals in the East End had their own code of conduct, and snitching, narking, and telling tales to the authorities was frowned upon in the severest terms, even if the questions were coming from a man of God. I imagine that most humans would have kindly declined the offer of a chat with William Booth, and would have instead hurried along their way.

His visit occurred during daylight so he was reasonably safe from attack by the Biters, but some of the girls saw him and his entourage through cracks in the curtains, saw him praying on bended knees and no doubt tut-tutting at the dreadful state of affairs.

A few years later Booth and his Army would march through Spitalfields and Whitechapel banging drums, blowing on trumpets, and declaring that salvation was on its way. At least he had the balls to strive forth; that was more than could be said for London's glorious police force, unless they were mob handed and the battle already over, as we shall see as my tale progresses.

* * *

My life then, in the dying months of 1866, was like this. All blood and murder and carnal desires. It was the good life. But then on Boxing Day everything, *everything*, would change. Our paradise would be a paradise lost.

Chapter Three
The Holmes of the
Baskervilles

Like many of the girls in Spitalfields, Raffles had no idea what date her birthday fell upon. She had a vague notion that she might have been born in 1750, but that was as specific as she was able to be. It was for this reason that Raffles decided that, like Queen Victoria, she rather liked the idea of having two birthdays each year, and for this purpose she had chosen Boxing Day (or, as she called it, St Stephen's Day) and, a little bizarrely, Pancake Day. Therefore, Raffles celebrated her birthday on both December the 26th and the Tuesday before the first day of Lent, the exact date of which changes each year depending on when Easter falls.

Because she celebrated two birthdays a year, when I enquired after her age during that December of 1866 she replied with 232, rather than 116 which would have been technically the more accurate answer. This was Raffles, the hard faced killer and leader of the Brick Lane Irregulars, ripping out your throat one moment and then telling you that her birthday was Boxing Day *and* Pancake Day the next. Looking at her, I estimated that she must have been aged around twenty-four when she was turned, a native East End girl, full of the wisdom of the street but sorely lacking in any kind of education (she had laughed out loud at me when I told her that the Earth was round - "How comes we don't all just fall off then?" she had asked in earnest), working as a prostitute when she was turned by 'some toff vampire'. A remorseless hunter on the outside, a little girl on the inside, with, I might add, a positively indecent tongue. I looked at my own tongue one day in a mirror we kept in the drawing room of our house. It seemed longer than I had remembered it being as a mortal, but it was a far cry from Raffles' tongue, a singular *monster* that had carnal knowledge of every curve, bulge, and crevice on and in my poor body.

I didn't love Raffles, not at all. I feared her, I respected her, I pitied her, and I fancied her. But love? No. I wasn't even sure at that point that I, as a vampire, was capable of feeling something as human and weak as love. I would spend some days in Raffles' embrace, but other times I would be entertained by one of the other girls. Sometimes we would even swap partners during the same day, girls running naked from bedroom to bedroom, even from house to house along Chicksand Street if the hour was dark, giggling and smiling. Nobody was in a serious relationship with anyone, nobody, as far as I could tell, had a special beau who they were devoted to, we all shared, there was no jealousy.

Christmas had arrived and with it my first pangs of remorse at being away from my family. I had adapted seamlessly into my life as a vampire, almost as though it was a fate that I had been waiting for during all my years as a mortal. I had barely given my home and my parents a backwards glance as I had left, and not once had I wished myself back in the family home, or had thoughts of returning to visit. I was not like the young ones that I would hear in the house next door, crying themselves to sleep each morning and calling out to their mothers in their sleep. Maybe because I was slightly older, at eighteen, than the youngsters, I was more mature and able to deal with the seismic changes in my circumstances, or maybe I had never truly been happy in the place I had called home, or maybe this vampiric state had made me as hard as Raffles. But still, with Christmas upon us, something pulled at my heartstrings.

As a mortal I had been used to lavish Christmases, with decorations and gifts and banquets. We used to have a huge Christmas tree in our hallway, the type popularised by Victoria and Albert, and beneath its branches would be placed gifts of fruit and nuts and even jewellery and ear-rings for mother and I. Aunties and uncles and nephews would visit, and carollers from the local church would sing for alms upon the doorstep and father would invite them inside the house for mince pies and warming brandy.

Before the Christmas Day banquet, we would entertain ourselves by singing carols around the piano, which mother played well, and by the pulling of so-called 'crackers' that were full of *bonbons*. The pinnacle of the feast itself would be the goose, prepared by cook and served at the table by maids who, though they were working on Christmas Day, seemed cheerier and happier than on any other day of the year. Father joked, half-seriously, that they were all 'at' the sherry downstairs in the kitchen, which they probably were. Such sweet memories of candles flickering and log fires roaring and the snow falling outside.

I lay on my back in the dark alleyway with the woman struggling on top of me and snow pushing up into my ears and down the neck of my dress. "Fucking hell!" I screamed, and threw the woman off me. "Oh Lord ha' mercy!" she managed to whimper before I jumped to my feet, strode over to her as she floundered in the snow, and broke her neck in one easy double-handed action. It was Christmas Day, 1866, and my appetite had quite deserted me.

"You seem distracted, sweetie-pie," said a voice at the end of the alleyway. It was Raffles, leaning jauntily up against the wall. By her side knelt a woman, Raffles holding a firm grip of her hair. A sweet pink bow that at the beginning of the evening must have looked quite charming, now hung limply from the woman's hair and would, I thought, fall off soon if someone didn't take a moment to tighten it back up again. Blood was streaming down the woman's neck, and was, I noticed, dripping onto the snow beneath her from the cuff of her dress' sleeve. I imagined the journey this river of blood was taking; from her neck, under her clothing, over the skin of her shoulder, down the arm, all the while much of it being soaked up by the fabric of the dress, until eventually flowing across her wrist and dripping out into the night air and onto the snow that lay on the cobble-stones of this dirty alleyway. "This one's quite tasty," Raffles indicated down at the beaten and bloody woman who seemed to be in a trance-like state, hovering somewhere between life and death, whispering nonsenses to herself about a horse named Billy and her dear pig Clara. I had long since stopped trying to make sense of human death-throes. The mortal soul is a thing of infinite wonder, and when it is being ripped from a body it is capable of creating within the mortals such sweet delirium. Add to this the chemicals, the *venom* one could say, introduced by the vampire bite and well, it's a wonder we didn't hear more talk of horses and pigs with names like Billy and Clara. "Come on, darling," urged Raffles, "take a bite, to keep the chill out. You really ain't being yourself tonight."

"Oh Raffles!" I wailed. "I can't help it, I miss Christmas!" And with that I ran over to her, threw my arms around her neck, and cried onto her shoulder. I may have inadvertently stood on the dying woman, but neither myself nor the dying woman noticed and neither myself nor the dying woman cared.

Because of my outburst, and because it was one of Raffles' self-appointed birthdays, it was decided, by Raffles, that on Boxing Day night we should frequent a dancing room, in order to dance, and have fun, and, doubtless, eat something that came from a place other than Brick Lane. On the morning of Boxing Day, a few short hours after we had returned through the snow to Chicksand Street following the débâcle in the alleyway, I opened my eyes to find a sprig of holly and some mistletoe hanging over my bed. A little note was affixed to this greenery, and in childish handwriting were scrawled the words 'Happy Birfday to me, love Raffles'. I could not help but smile.

Along with myself and Raffles, a few of the other girls from our house decided to accompany us on our merry night out. It is with shame that I must now admit that I cannot recall their names. I lived with them, I killed with them, I had carnal knowledge of them, and now, all these years later, their names have slipped from my memory. But there were three of them, and perhaps one was called Marcy or Janey. Two of the younger girls from the house next door, upon hearing of our plan, asked if they could accompany us. At first Raffles said no, they were too young, the doormen probably wouldn't let them in to the dancing room, it wasn't a place for youngsters; but they persisted in asking and begging and pleading for several hours until, in desperation, Raffles relented and agreed that they could come along with us. I remember *their* names. Oh yes, I could never forget their names.

One was called Elsie and the other Frances. They were aged fourteen, and they were the youngsters who had approached me as I ate that woman on Brick Lane, the ones I had growled at to keep them away but then had acquiesced once my belly was full, and they had dragged the corpse away into the night between them. Elsie and Frances were not sisters, but to see them next to each other you would swear that they were, indeed you would probably insist that they were twins, so alike did they look. They were petite, black haired, with skin as white as communion candles, and they did everything together. You never saw one without the other, usually holding hands or whispering into each other's ear. It was nice, I thought, that they had each other for support and friendship, with them being so young and with all eternity stretching out before them.

So on that fateful Boxing Day night we all got dressed in our best dresses (we often stole them from our victims, Raffles had a wardrobe full that she never wore), we brushed our hair long to cover our ears, made sure to wash any bloody residue from our teeth and lips and faces, and even deigned to wear shoes! Something that we simply never did!

"Fucking things!" exclaimed Raffles as she tried to place a dainty pair of silk slippers upon her feet. I had no idea how many years it had been since she had last worn shoes. I knelt down before her and tied the laces for her. "There," I said with a smile, "you're a proper lady now!"

Once Raffles, myself, and the other girls from our house were ready, we called next door to collect the girls Frances and Elsie, who Raffles referred to as 'the terrible twins'. Another young girl, younger even than Elsie and Frances, answered the door. I had never seen her before, at least I didn't recall having seen her before, and I was quite taken aback by the youth of her and how small she looked.

"Sorry miss," this little waif said to us all with a curtsey, "but begging yer pardon, Frances and Elsie ain't ready yet. They had a fight wiv some other girls and it's quite put them behind schedule. As it were. Miss."

Raffles looked haughtily down at the girl who looked back up at her, all dirty face and tiny fangs and a dress that was little more than an old sack. "Well," said Raffles, pulling gloves onto her hands, "tell the little buggers that they will have to meet us at the venue. They know where we are going. And tell them not to get in to any bother on the way or I'll murder them myself."

"Yus miss," said the little girl and curtseyed again. We turned on our heels and walked away, the girl watching us from the doorway as we went. "You all look proper smashing!" she cried after us. "You could almost pass for human!" Raffles waved a hand in reply, a little like Queen Victoria as her carriage passes the gathered masses on the Mall. But then Raffles tottered on her heels, and being unaccustomed to wearing such things I had to catch her to save her from falling. Behind us we heard the tiny vampire girl laugh raucously. "Little shit," hissed Raffles.

Our destination was the Diogenes Rooms, a dancing room of note, and a certain reputation, located on Windmill Street, not far from Covent Garden. We had a little money, purloined from our meals, and so took a cab to transport us from the dear old East End to the glittering heart of theatre-land. The Diogenes Rooms had a reputation for being a place where gentlemen could find women of easy virtue who, for a price, might be willing to bestow their favours upon them. Or as Raffles had put it, "It's full of trollops who'll drop their drawers for a shilling."

I had heard of the Diogenes Rooms before, when I was mortal and was living with my parents. Again, it was likely to have been on one of those occasions when the men, engrossed in their tittle-tattle, had spoken over me as though I wasn't there. When I had heard that it was full of women of ill-repute, I had imagined that it must be a most vile place, dirty and rough with sawdust on the floor. Imagine my surprise then when I walked in through the doors to find myself in a room that looked like it had come straight from the Palace of Versailles!

In the middle of the room was a vast wooden dance floor, surrounded by rows of glass-topped tables at which sat ladies and gentlemen dressed in their finery. If I had expected the women, these trollops, to be rough arses like us, I was sadly mistaken. They all looked adorable, bejewelled, perfumed, and dressed in the latest styles. They would not have looked out of place at one of my family's balls or banquets. They sipped at glasses of champagne and tittered politely at the amusing conversation of the men come to woo them. A thick maroon carpet surrounded the dance floor, and it was upon this carpet that the tables sat, and on each of the four walls were placed dozens of large mirrors, reaching from floor to ceiling, encased in gold frames, and lending the room the illusion of going on forever, an optical illusion that made it impossible to really tell where the room started and where it ended. Bronze gas lamps blazed on the parts of the walls not dominated by mirrors, and a small orchestra played waltzes of a gay nature. We walked into the room and I stopped dead in my tracks, mesmerised by it all. "Alright 'ere, innit?" asked Raffles. "Yes," I gasped, "yes, it is."

The five of us sat down at a table and a waiter came over to take our order. Raffles ordered a bottle of champagne, but when it arrived we knew better than to drink it. Being vampires, blood and perhaps a little raw flesh was all we could stomach. If we had partaken of the champagne, we would have thrown it all back up again, so we ordered it, played with the glasses, and simply made a show of being human.

"Do you think the youngsters will get in?" I whispered to Raffles, of Frances and Elsie.

"Dunno," replied Raffles. "Probably best if they don't, to be honest. They'd only start a fight or something. Little buggers, them two."

"Who was that girl who answered the door of their house? I don't think I've seen her before."

"The little one? Mary, I think. She don't leave the house often. I think the other girls take care of her, bring back bits of food for her."

"You mean bring back humans for her to eat?"

"Yeah, or rats, that kind of thing."

"Rats?" I asked, disgusted. "I can't imagine they taste very nice?"

"Beggars can't be choosers, darling," said Raffles. "You'd be surprised what we have to do to survive sometimes. Eaten my own share of rats, and worse, in my time. The day will come when you'll gladly eat rat too, mark my words," and she smiled at me and patted my hand.

"She seemed very young," I said of Mary, the girl who answered the door.

"There's no end to the wickedness of the natural-borns," said Raffles, "and yet it's us who's called vermin. Money'll buy you anything, darling, and if there's one thing the natural-borns have got, it's money. But listen to us! Let's not be maudlin! It's me birthday! Let's enjoy ourselves. Talk about something more fun!"

And so we did. We laughed and we joked and we smoked cigarettes and we even danced, with each other you understand, the men in the room steering well-clear of us, almost as though an in-built radar, like the kind of thing bats use, told them to stay away from the pale girls in the black dresses and concentrate instead on the sweet smelling ones in the pinks and the blues and the yellows.

After an hour or so, I looked out across the room and my heart stopped. A girl, a woman more like, at a table on the opposite side of the dance floor to us, was chatting amicably to an older looking gentleman, and at the sight of her my heart fair missed a beat. She was the most captivating, ravishing thing I had ever seen. I do not know if it was hunger or lust, or some strange combination of the two, that drove me, but I could not for a moment tear my eyes away from her.

Her blonde hair fell in ringlets over her neck and her shoulders, and freckles played upon her cheeks and her nose. Her eyes were blue and her lips were pink, and she struck me as the summer to my winter, the daylight to my eternal night, warmth to my cold. She was everything I was not and everything I could never be again. She epitomised the humans; the pink, warm humans who I thought I despised, and yet, here I was, lusting after the one who was the pinnacle of their kind.

I watched her breasts rising in the cleavage of her dress, saw the veins of her creamy neck, watched her lips as she spoke, and her tongue as she drank. Raffles' voice caused me to jump from my reverie. "We can kill her later, if you like, when she leaves. Kill her and drink her dry. A fitting end to a merry night."

"Oh," I said, "I don't want to kill her! No, no, I just want to, you know..."

"Fuck her?"

"Well, yes, I think. I mean, I suppose so. Do you think she's a trollop?" I whispered the question, still feeling strangely puritan about the idea of women selling themselves for money.

"She's a trollop all right, darling, but there's one thing you need to understand. You and I may be what is often referred to as sapphists. All turned vampires are, must be something to do with the fact that men can't be turned, something happens to us, and suddenly as well as drinking blood we're lusting after the ladies. But most human women aren't like that, you understand? Most human women like men, they want to be with men, not women. And even these trollops, even if you offer them money, they'll most likely laugh you out of the place or scream blue bloody murder at the thought of having relationships with another woman. You want my advice? Let's kill her. Satisfy your needs that way. But we must be careful. Let us wait until she leaves, and then we can all take her and her friends in an alleyway, away from prying eyes. It'll be a jolly wheeze."

But I didn't want to kill her, and I had money, and I was giddy from the dancing and entranced by her beauty, and so when I saw her stand from her table and make her way to spend a penny at the ladies' conveniences, I stood up and I followed her.

The conveniences consisted of half a dozen cubicles and half a dozen sinks, the place lined, like the dance room, with mirrors and with gas lamps giving the surroundings a warm orange glow. As I entered, I heard a cubicle door close and lock, and then the sound of her passing water. There was no-one else in the place. I stood in front of her cubicle and asked tentatively, "Hello? Are you in there?"

I was going to wait until she emerged from the cubicle, but it suddenly seemed easier to talk to the closed door, rather than her radiant face.

"I'm sorry," came the reply, "are you talking to me?"

"Yes," I said. "Listen, this is all very awkward, but I couldn't help but notice you out there. I wonder, well, I wonder if, you might. . . " my voice trailed off, and then I blurted out, "I have money. I can pay you!"

"Pay me for what?" asked the voice cautiously from behind the door.

"Can I lick you?" I asked, remembering Raffles and her monster and how it had brought me so much pleasure. I longed to bring this pleasure to her, to this creature of the sun.

There was silence. Then the sound of the skirts of a dress being rearranged, and then the toilet being flushed. Finally, the sound of the lock being drawn back, and the door opened and I was face to face with the delightful woman. I smiled.

"Sod off," she hissed at me, "you blooming pervert!"

She attempted to push past me. I grabbed hold of her. "No," I said, "you don't understand! It's nice! I'll do it nicely!"

"Get off!" she screamed, but I pushed her back into the cubicle. We fell backwards onto the toilet, inadvertently pulling the flush again. The sound of gushing water filled my head and made my ears pound, and I realised that I had my teeth buried deep within her neck. I kicked the door closed with one foot, and continued to suck the blood out of her neck. Had she struggled at all once I'd clamped my mouth around her? I don't think she did. I took her blood while my hands ripped at her dress and her undergarments, revealing her breast and her stomach, freckled as sweetly as her face, but now with her precious blood dripping all over them.

I drained her dry and then went to work on her breasts, licking the blood from them. Although quite dead she was still warm, and I smelt the sweetness of her perfume and marvelled at the small downy hairs on her arms. I ravaged her, fully, completely, and then I staggered back against the toilet wall and realised the enormity of what I had done. I had killed her, and I had killed her in a public place, in the middle of the human world. This wasn't Spitalfields after dark, this wasn't some invisible alleyway, this was Covent Garden. We were five vampires in the centre of London, miles from home, surrounded by humans.

I fell out of the cubicle and pushed the door closed behind me, attempting to hide my crime. I caught sight of myself in the mirrors that were placed above the sinks. I seemed to be all blackness and red, my eyes burning with murderous desire, my fangs elongated, blood smeared over my face, my hair now pushed back and revealing my ears. No-one would be fooled now. I was the killer they all feared, who they all wanted eradicated, and I was in their midst, in the midst of the mortals. I staggered past the sinks, heading back into the dance room.

Hiding my face behind my hands, I ran over to Raffles and the other girls.

"Oh my God, girl!" exclaimed Raffles at the sight of me. "What have you been up to? Quick, come on, scarper!"

The girls stood up from the table, sending champagne and glasses spiralling, and we all pushed our way out of the room, into the lobby, and out through the doors. Howls of outrage followed us, at first because we were pushing people from our path, but after a few moments I heard the first cry of "Vampires!" and then more cries taking up the same accusation, and of course the inevitable call of "Dolly Biters!"

Once we hit the relatively open spaces of the pavements and the roads, our vampire speed helped us to take flight from our accusers, and we soon left them and their outrage behind. We tumbled into an alleyway, I don't recall where, to gather ourselves. Raffles put her hands on my shoulders and looked me in the eye. "Bleedin' hell, you daft twat!" she said, but she was laughing, and the other girls laughed too, and then I started to laugh as well. "I killed her!" I said. "In the latrine of all places! I can't believe it!"

"You can't believe it?" asked Raffles. "You're a vampire, darling. Of course you killed her. That's what you do. That feeling you get in your head and your stomach when you look at a human? Don't ever confuse it for love or even lust. It's hunger, darling, plain and simple."

I nodded and laughed again, but I can still see those freckles and those blonde ringlets, and I can still feel my tongue upon her breasts. She comes to me still, sometimes, in my dreams, and I don't know if she visits me in lust or in hunger, or whether the difference between the two is much of a difference at all.

* * *

Our journey back across town to Spitalfields was more or less uneventful, the other girls acting as my shields, walking in front, behind, and to the side of me, hiding me and the evidence of my crimes from sight. But as we walked I heard a girl scream, just once, somewhere in the distance. Who had screamed or for what reason I had no way of knowing, but the sound confounded me, as though the scream had been a premonition of something terrible that was on the verge of ripping us all apart. I tried to tell myself that this sudden feeling of doom was because of the drama in the dancing room, but it was more than that. This was more than a drama, this feeling was profound and doom-laden. I didn't tell the other girls, but I walked home with a sense of dread eating away at me, and oh! Would that this odd premonition had missed its mark. Would that I had been wrong and the only cloud hanging over me was the body in the toilet in the Diogenes Rooms. But alas this sense of foreboding was not wrong. Doom had visited us all right, doom and destruction and woe.

* * *

We arrived on Brick Lane intent on heading straight for Chicksand Street, but as soon as we turned the corner it was apparent that all was not well. Dozens of girls, vampire girls, were milling around, hugging each other, crying into each other's shoulders. It was dark and difficult to judge, but there seemed to be more girls than I had thought lived on Chicksand Street, but that thought was pushed from my mind by the immediate concern at hand, namely what the Dickens was going on?

At the sight of Raffles, several of the girls came running over, all sobs and wails, and they dragged Raffles across the road and to the side of the pavement were Elsie, of Frances and Elsie, the terrible twins who hadn't turned up at the Diogenes Rooms, was sat, surrounded by more girls.

Raffles knelt down beside Elsie and asked, "What's wrong, darling? What's going on?" Her tone was soft and gentle, not the brisk and dismissive voice she usually used with the younger girls. She knew that something was terribly wrong.

Seeing Raffles, Elsie threw her head onto the older girl's chest with a sob and began to cry. "I'm sorry," she managed to say between sniffles, "I'm so sorry."

"Will someone please just tell me what's happened?" asked Raffles, looking up at the other girls who stood around us.

"Frances is dead," said one girl. "She's been murdered."

"What?" asked Raffles. "How?" This was unheard of. We may have been referred to as vermin and scum, but the brutal fact of the matter was that we were the top of the food-chain, especially in Spitalfields, our own stomping ground. Nothing could hurt us here, let along *kill* us.

"Elsie better tell you," said another girl. "She saw it all."

"Elsie, darling," said Raffles, "tell me what happened."

Still clinging to Raffles, Elsie looked up and began to speak. But rather than look at Raffles, she looked directly at me. She told the story to me, and all my concerns about the Diogenes Rooms vanished in an instant.

"We was hurrying along Chicksand Street," said Elsie, tears smudging her cheeks and her eyes puffy from crying, "trying to catch up with you, because we were only a minute behind you and we thought we'd be able to catch up with you. But it was difficult in the snow, you know, and we weren't used to wearing shoes, but we was so excited to be going out with you, with the big girls, that we wanted to make sure we caught up with you. We never thought that Raffles would let us go out with you, we thought she'd say no, but she said yes and we thought it was going to be the greatest night ever!"

There was another bout of heavy sobbing, and the poor girl fought to control her breathing. After a moment or two, she continued.

"We wanted to catch up with you coz we weren't sure where we were going, we'd never been as far west as Covent Garden before, so we ran along Chicksand Street and out onto Brick Lane, and we thought we'd see you there, but you was gone. You must've caught a cab or something, coz we was only a minute behind you. And then he was there, this bloke, this bleeding great big bloke was standing there in front of us, and he had another bloke standing behind him at his right shoulder, and he says, 'Where d'you think you're going to, you little fucking whores?' and we're kind of shocked because he's a human and he's talking to us like he's our better, and no human ever talks to us like that because we'll just rip out their sodding throats, wouldn't we? But he don't care, and the bloke behind him don't care neither, and they just look at us, and he asks again, 'I said, where are you going to you little fucking whores?!' And Frances, well you know Frances, she can be a little bastard when she wants to be, so she bares her fangs at him and hisses like, and normally that's enough to send any human running for the hills, but not these two blokes. One looks at the other and he says, "Well, looks like we've got ourselves a fighter here!" And they laugh and then say something about them having a fighter of their own, and from out of the shadows comes this fucking great werewolf, I shit you not. A great *fucking* werewolf, and it comes lumbering out of the shadows, stinking of shite and piss, and it growls at us and I almost wet my pants, miss, coz it sounds so loud and so terrible."

"Wait, wait, wait!" said Raffles. "A *werewolf*?"

"Yes, miss," said Elsie. "A werewolf, I swears it. Ten feet tall he was! I seen it with my own eyes!"

"Jesus," said Raffles.

"Well, then the bloke at the front, he hits Frances with his fist, and he knocks her to the ground," continued Elsie. "Now I ain't never seen a human hit a vampire before and knock them to the ground. It just don't happen, do it? They ain't strong enough. But this bloke, he hits Frances and she goes flying across the pavement. While she's down, he kicks her in the stomach and she's rolling around on the floor in agony. Well, I ain't shy about having a bit of a scrap, 'specially when it's my Frances that's getting hurt, so I leap at this bloke and try to bite him, but the other bloke, fast as a shot, grabs hold of me and wraps his arms around me and he's so strong that I can't get away. I fight and struggle, but he's stronger than me. You ever hear of such a thing? A mortal bloke stronger than one of us? Coz I ain't never heard such a thing. It ain't natural."

All the girls around us were tut-tutting and shaking their heads.

"While I'm trying to escape, this other bloke is giving Frances a right old kicking. He's punching her and booting her and knocking seven bells of shit out of her. She's trying to get to her feet but she's slipping in the snow, and he just keeps on beating her.

"In the end, she holds up her purse, and she opens it, and she tries to give him money. She must've thought it was a mug job or something, that they was after our money. We'd been saving up pennies and farthings that we'd been nicking from the humans we'd killed, and we thought that tonight, you know, at the dancing rooms, we'd need some do-ray-me to look the part, like we was ladies. So Frances had some coins in her purse and she tries to give them to the bloke. She's on her knees, her face all beaten up and covered in her own claret, and she's trying to give him her sodding money, and the bastard just knocks it away. Her money goes flying across the pavement, into the snow, and then she's on all fours trying to pick it up again, and he stamps on her back, kicks her in the head, and throws her to the werewolf. The werewolf gets her head in its mouth and rips it off her body. Off her body, I tells ya! It's a huge stinking thing this werewolf, and it just pulls her head right off.

"Then the bloke comes over to me, I'm still being held down by the other bloke, and he says to me, 'We worship God in this country, not Lucifer and all his vampire whores. You've got six days to get out of the East End, get out of London, and leave all God-fearing people in peace. It took God six days to make the Heavens and the Earth and everything in it. Think you can get your scraggy little arses out of London in the same time it took our Lord and Saviour to create the universe?' Then the other bloke punched me in the stomach, and I ain't never been punched like that before, and I doubles over in the snow.

"The blokes stand over me and they tell me that they're the Holmes Boys from the Baskerville Estate, and they're on a holy mission to rid London of us Dolly Biters. He says they've got the blessing of the Vatican, that the Vatican's paying them, and that if we don't disappear they're going to kill us all."

"The Vatican?" asked Raffles. "What the bloody hell are they doing round here?"

"When I pull myself together, they're all gone," said Elsie, "the blokes and the wolf, and there's just my Frances' head and her body on the pavement, but she'd burst into flames, like what we vampires do when they die, and before my eyes she's fizzing and popping away, turning to dust and to ash and to shit. My Frances! She just died and then went away, and I tried to hold on to her, tried to stop her going, but there was nothing left to hold on to, just ashes and smoke.

"I got her purse. I picked it up and put her pennies back in. But she's gone. What am I going to do without her? How can I carry on without her? You're posh, miss," she looked me dead in the eye, "you come from a good family, not like me and Frances. Can't you do nothing? Can't you go to the Queen or the police or something? Tell them who you are, miss? Tell them they've got to stop these bastards from hurting us, tell them to bring Frances back?"

"I'm so sorry, Elsie," I said, and didn't know what else to say. What was there to say? The poor girl's heart was broken into a million pieces.

"They let me live, so I'd come back here and pass the message on. But I don't want to be alive, miss," she said to me, "not if my Frances ain't here. She was a little bastard when she wanted to be, you know? I seen her kill a baby once and drink its blood. But that weren't her fault. Sometimes, you know, us young 'uns, it's more difficult to get food. The bigger girls, they don't always share as much as they should, and we was always hungry miss, always." I thought of the night I had growled at the two of them, warning them away from my kill, and if I could have blushed in shame, I would have done. "So it weren't her fault she killed a baby. She was just hungry, is all. And I loved her like a sister. She was like me sister and me mam all wrapped up into one. How can I carry on without her? You're posh, miss. Can't you make it right? Can't you do nothing? Oh miss, do you think God will be angry with her, you know, coz she killed a baby?"

"I'm sure that if there is a God, Frances will be up there with Him right now, living in Paradise," I lied.

"I hope so, miss," said Elsie. "Least she ain't hungry now, eh?"

I couldn't help it, I knelt down beside her and I cried like a baby. What a bastard world this was, that made monsters of such as we.

Eventually, as dawn threatened over Spitalfields, some of the younger girls took Elsie back to their house on Chicksand Street, and me and Raffles headed to our home next door.

"We should go and parley with these Holmes bastards," said Raffles, "you and me, find out what the hell they're up to."

"Me?" I said. "I'm new to all this. I've no idea how all this works."

"Yes, but Elsie's right," said Raffles. "You've got the accent, you've got the etiquette, perhaps they'll listen to you where they wouldn't listen to a piece of East End trash like me."

I felt a tide of anger rise in me which I fought hard to suppress. It had been one hell of a night, what with the girl in the Diogenes Rooms and then poor Frances and Elsie, and now this. Was I being held accountable for all the ills of the East End simply because I had been lucky, or unlucky, enough to have been born on the other side of town? "I don't think I'd be much help, sorry," I said curtly, and went to bed. Nobody had any tongue that night, except for the blonde summer girl in the conveniences at the Diogenes Rooms, and she had been dead.

* * *

The following morning, December the twenty-seventh, broke cold but bright with an intense sun blazing from a clear blue sky. A frost had settled on the snow, and the world appeared frozen in a single moment in time. In her room at number fifty-three Chicksand Street, Elsie rose from the bed that she had once shared innocently with her friend Frances, and sat before the upturned tea chest that the pair had used as a make-shift dresser.

She wore her hair piled high with pride, showing off her elf ears, and she was barefoot because that was the way we ran, barefoot and silent. The dress she was wearing was not the fancy one she had worn the night before, when she had been excited at the prospect of visiting the Diogenes Rooms, but rather it was her plain black one, the one she felt most comfortable in, the one that was as dark as midnight and rendered her almost invisible as she hunted. If you had looked closely enough, you would have noticed that it was stained with the blood of a hundred dead humans.

She picked up Frances' pretty purse with the pennies still inside, the pennies that they were going to spend on their night out, and then Elsie walked downstairs, and still weeping for the loss of her Frances, she stepped out of the front door and into the glare of the killing sun.

She did not catch fire at first, it took a few seconds, long enough for her to step gingerly across the snow on the pavement and onto the cobble-stoned street. She had not seen the sun, not like this, for over fifty years. A smile of recognition began to break on her lips as she remembered a childhood once spent in the warmth of the sun, but then suddenly and terribly, she burst into flames. There was no time for her to scream, she was consumed by a mighty fireball, and she sank to her knees and burned. The flames, at last, dried her tears for Frances and took away the pain of immortality.

Her remains continued to burn for most of the day, a black plume of smoke billowing high into the winter sky, scattering embers and ashes across Spitalfields and beyond. We could not go out to her. The sun kept us prisoner in our homes, and all we could do was watch and mourn her and hurl abuse at the crows and the cats that came to take any flesh from her bones that was still edible once the flames began to subside.

By mid-afternoon we heard the young girls next door singing a song; a sad, lamenting song about kissing your girl by the factory wall and this being a dirty old town. I did not recognise the song and asked Raffles what it was.

"You don't get out much to the music hall, do you miss?" she replied. She'd never called me *miss* before, only the youngsters had ever called me that. I knew why she called it me now and although I was aware that I was being played like a fiddle, something about the way she had said it stung me more deeply than a silver blade.

"Very well," I said with a sigh, "let us go and meet with these Baskerville cunts and see what the hell they want."

* * *

By six o'clock in the evening, the remains of Elsie had been reduced to ash. I went outside with a broom and brushed her into the gutter. A gutter for a grave.

Chapter Four
The Dragon's Den

Raffles and I slipped out of our house and headed along Chicksand Street. The moon was full and bloated over-head, and the night eerily quiet. I imagine that for the mortals, hurrying about their business elsewhere in London, the night must have been bitterly cold, but for us vampires this was not an issue; we were cold of heart enough.

"I've seen an awful lot in my time," said Raffles, breaking the silence. "This world can be a hard, dreadful place. When I was a mortal I discovered that. But since I've been a vampire, well, I've been happy to be the hardest, most dreadful thing that walks these streets, to be honest. Nothing fucks with me now. Not like they used to fuck with me when I was human and soft and weak. But this werewolf thing, it ain't right. There ain't been were-wolves in England for bleedin' centuries. Something about this ain't right, darling, I tell you. I ain't felt scared, not really scared, for over a hundred years, but I can feel it tingling in my stomach now. Fear. And I bleeding hate it."

We headed north along Brick Lane, and for a moment I was aware of other girls near-by, other vampire girls. It struck me as odd; I hadn't noticed any of the other girls leaving Chicksand Street this night, but there they were, for a fleeting moment, prac-tically invisible in the shadows and the darkness. I did not have much time to ponder this odd little puzzle before we turned west onto Black Eagle Street and approached the Baskerville rookery. The Baskerville area was made up of Great Baskerville Street, which ran east to west from Brick Lane to Commercial Street, and all the streets and side-roads that ran off it; Baskerville Road, Baskerville Court, Baskerville Way, Vine Court, Vine Square, Vine Lane, dozens of small roads, courtyards, and alleyways. A maze in which the Holmes Boys held sway. We had no idea where to go to find the actual Holmes boys, the two brothers who headed-up this particular gang, but we needn't have worried. They soon found us.

Along Great Baskerville Street they came marching, about twenty or thirty of them, young men, part of the Holmes Boys gang, their breath rising above them on this chill night, catching the light from the gas-lamps. Spitalfields was always dark as the grave. The Baskervilles were lit up like one of Queen Victoria's Christmas trees. As they approached us I noticed that they all wore identical frock coats and top hats, and carried clubs barely disguised as walking sticks. Many of the more organised gangs wore uniforms like this, and here they were, the Holmes Boys, a private army hidden away down here in the bowels of the East End.

We stopped and stared at them, and they stopped and stared at us. One or two of them swung their clubs and patted them into their open palms menacingly. We could have killed them all, of course, but that wasn't the point. Beyond these boys playing at being soldiers lay the two men, the Holmes brothers, who had laid low two vampires with their own hands, and the werewolf that had dispatched Frances. We had to play nicely, to get to the real quarry.

"Parley!" shouted Raffles. "We represent the Brick Lane Irregulars, and we come to parley with the Holmes brothers."

"We know who you are, slag," said one of the men. "Follow us."

The men surrounded us and marched us, like two prisoners of war, deeper and deeper into their rookery, past pubs and gin houses full of human revellers, past prostitutes chatting up men and swearing at each other, and past policemen who respectfully tipped their hats to the gang members as we passed. I was not used to witnessing such life and frivolity in the night, and had all but forgotten that as Spitalfields fell silent of an evening, so the other areas of London came to life.

"We really must come hunting here one night," I said to Raffles. "We'd have a field day."

"Too right, darling," she replied. "If we get out of this jam, I promise you, a-hunting we will come."

At last we came to a house with more frock coated men standing outside it. Gas lights blazed away inside, and the occasional shout and roar of laughter emanated from within. We were led inside, a door opened, and we found ourselves in a drawing room with four men sat around a table playing cards. Behind them was placed a fifth man, a small man who stood as stiff as a board and with his hands clasped behind his back, like he, at least, had once been genuine military. At our arrival, the men stopped talking, laid down their cards, and turned to look at us.

One of the men, with a huge bushy moustache and greased down hair looked right at us, pointed a finger, and exclaimed, "Babylon the Great! The Mother of Harlots and Abominations of the Earth! You've got some balls coming down here!"

He turned to the man sat next to him, a man with a full beard and long hair, and they both roared with laughter. "I like their brass, brother!" laughed the man with the beard. "You've got to admire their brass!"

With the wave of the hand, the two men who had been seated playing cards with the brothers disappeared, and we were left face-to-face with the Holmes brothers and the funny little military man standing behind them.

"I'd offer you a drink," said the moustachioed brother, holding up a tumbler full of whisky or brandy, "but I fear it's not alcohol that you two harlots are used to drinking!"

"Indeed," agreed the bearded brother. "Did the little whore from last night not pass on our message?"

"She did," replied Raffles, "but she wasn't a whore."

"Oh, she was a whore all right!" said the bearded one, and in a flash of rage, smashed his glass down upon the table. "A whore with fangs for teeth who feasts upon the living! With whom the High Borns of the earth have committed fornication, and the inhabitants of the earth have had their blood turned into wine for her fornication!"

"What my brother Mycroft here is trying to say," said the moustachioed man, "is that you now have five nights left to get out of London, or you will be slain like the little one was slain last night." He looked us up and down and smiled slyly, like a dog sniffing its own shit. "I'm Sherlock Holmes by the way. Maybe you've heard of me?"

"Why are you doing this?" I asked. "We haven't strayed into your territory. Why do you come seeking a war?"

Sherlock Holmes roared with a humourless laugh. "Your territory?" he cried. "Your territory? Let me tell you something about *your territory*, and while you're listening you would do well to thank whatever heathen deity you bow down before that I don't kill you right here and right now!"

He picked up his glass of whisky or brandy, gulped it down, and spoke.

"There was a time when all of this territory belonged to the Holmes family. One hundred and sixty years ago, all the lands that we now call Whitechapel and Spitalfields and Brick Lane and Mile End, all of it, from the Thames up to Bethnal Green, belonged to the Holmes family. My ancestor, the great Hugo Baskerville-Holmes ran our family, our gang, with an iron fist. We controlled the alcohol, the tobacco, the silks; anything that passed along the Thames or was moved along the streets of the East End had to pay tribute to us. And with great wealth comes great power. Hugo Baskerville-Holmes was made Lord Mayor of London. Imagine that! Lord Mayor of London! Quite an achievement for a Catholic man in Protestant England. And of course, his name was forever attached to this particular corner of the East End, Great Baskerville Street and all its subsidiaries being named in his honour.

"One day a High Born from Central Europe came a-visiting Hugo, ready to pay tribute for the ship full of silks and spices he had moored on the Thames."

"What are these High Borns?" I asked.

"Natural borns," said Raffles. "What we call natural borns."

"But while he's visiting Hugo," continued Sherlock, "this High Born is smitten by a serving wench in the employ of Hugo. He offers Hugo a purse full of gold in exchange for the girl. So Hugo, being a man of business, kidnapped the girl and hid her away, ready to deliver her to the vampire. The girl though had other ideas about this little arrangement, and she managed to escape into the East End, eventually hiding out in Spitalfields. When the vampire discovered that the object of his lust had escaped, he flew into a rage and followed the girl into Spitalfields. He found her, ravaged her, and then, rather than kill her, he bit her, passing on his vampiric attributes and creating the first human-turned-vampire, the first Dolly Biter, the mother of all you whores. She was the first, the original, and she was called Lilith.

"Why am I telling you all this?" asked Sherlock. "Because I want you to understand the seriousness of our threat and the enormity of your predicament. You whores are the Curse of the Baskervilles. You multiplied and flourished in Spitalfields, fornicating like dogs and reproducing like rats, eventually forcing our ancestors out and away into this corner of the East End. Hugo himself was killed by a Dolly Biter, and each of our successors has met his doom at the hands of one of your kind. Well now, at last, the tables have once more turned in our favour."

"How so?" asked Raffles.

From beneath his collar, Sherlock revealed a multitude of crucifixes on silver chains and rosary beads hanging around his neck. Beneath Mycroft's collar I could see a similar collection. "Gifts from our new friends in the Vatican. Specially blessed and endowed with great power. Some of these little trinkets date back to the crusades. Quite apt, would you not say? These relics give us strength and protection and wisdom."

"And then there's this," said Mycroft, holding up a small glass bottle. "Vampire blood. *True* vampire blood, from the High Borns, donated to the cause. A sip of this and we are blessed with all your power, strength, speed, and more."

"What the hell have the Vatican and the *High Borns* got to do with all this?" I asked.

"Oh, you little harlots have pissed off a lot of very powerful people over the last century and a half. Both the Vatican and the High Borns see you as an abomination, to be eradicated from the face of the earth. There are some factions within the Holy See who believe that you are the Whore of Babylon, prophesied in the Book of Revelations. We tend to agree. And the British government, well they just want peace and order on the streets, they want business to thrive again in Spitalfields, they just want you to go away. If we can provide that small service for them, they will be eternally grateful and who knows, maybe in a few years me or my brother, or perhaps the both of us, will be invested as the Lord Mayor, and our family shall be returned to its rightful position of influence and power."

"You don't scare me, with your baubles and necklaces and tiny little bottles of blood," said Raffles.

"Me neither," I added. "No matter how strong you are, there's only two of you. We've dozens of vampires on Chicksand Street. In an all-out barney, we'd kick your arses."

"But you're forgetting our werewolf," leered Sherlock, leaning towards us over the table. "May I introduce to you Sergeant Major John Watson, late of the British Indian Army."

The small man behind the Holmes brothers snapped to attention. In any other situation the sight of this silly little man standing stiff as a rod might have been amusing, but not here and not now. Now it simply seemed *bizarre*.

"You would have heard of the good Sergeant Major, if you could have been bothered to read any of the reports in the newspapers regarding the Indian Mutiny of 1857. He was known by the local rebellious Muhammadans as 'The Devil's Dog', such was his ferocity in battle and his skill with the sabre. He almost single-handedly retook Lucknow from the darkies in 1858. A formidable fighter. Because of this he was cursed, not by the Muhammadans but by the Thuggees. They cursed him with their ancient magics and heathen incantations, cursed him to be the very devil dog after which he was named. Every night, if he finds himself out of doors, he miraculously transforms into the most fearsome werewolf. Isn't that right, Sergeant Major?"

"Oh yes, sir," said Watson. "Why, if I was outside now I'd be ripping the throats out of these two little slags, sir."

"Still feel confident that your whores would win in a pitched battle?" asked Mycroft, stroking his beard.

"Fly away, little birds," said Sherlock, dismissing us with a wave of the hand. "You have five nights to leave London, or God's Own Vengeance will reign down upon you and all your ilk. Tick tock. Tick tock."

I took Raffles by the hand and pulled her away. As we left, one of the brothers, it was impossible to tell which, cried after us, "And I saw the women drunken with the blood of the saints, and with the blood of the martyrs of Jesus! No more, whores! No more!"

"Cunts," I whispered to Raffles as we left the house. A guard of Holmes Boys escorted us out of the Baskerville rookery, only abandoning us when we reached Brick Lane and our own little piece of Sanctuary.

Chapter Five
Madame Moriarty and the Bitch Moran

"Why are the natural-borns giving their blood to those sods?" I asked Raffles when we were safely entrenched back in our little house on Chicksand Street. "I mean, I understand that the natural borns don't particularly like us, but to give their blood to those idiots, to betray other vampires like that, it beggars belief."

"It all stinks to High Heaven," said Raffles. "A whole conspiracy's formed behind our backs with the sole intention of wiping us out. The Vatican, the natural borns, the British. They all want us dead."

"Well bugger them!" I said. "We're vampires, we'll fight them and we'll win!"

"The Vatican? The natural borns? The British Empire? Have you any idea the power that those three wield? Come on, Irene darling, you know better than I do what they're capable of. And now they've turned their malice directly on us, providing the Holmes Boys with everything they need to destroy us. And we're just *us*, just *us*, down here in Spitalfields. I'm really scared."

This was the first, and only, time I had seen Raffles like this. Her normally hard continence had crumbled, and I could see the young girl beneath the Dirty Biter. I put my arms around her, and that day we slept together, wrapped around each other. No tongues, no lust, just comfort.

The next evening the Raffles of old had returned. She was brisk and off-hand with the youngsters, she scowled at everyone she came into contact with, and she told me that she had a plan.

* * *

What is it like to drink human blood? Blood is more than just sustenance, of course. First and foremost, yes, it is food, but it provides me, as a vampire, with more than that. When I ingest the blood of a mortal, I take in their soul, the very essence of their being. What does that mean? What is the soul? Why is it so difficult to describe something that to me is so second nature? I take in the blood and I take in the soul. Again I ask, what is the soul?

The soul is everything the mortal has been, all of its memories, its happiness and its sadness, the summer days and winter nights, Christmas and birthdays and Easter, home and school and tears and laughs, the tender sighs and gentle kisses, mother, father, everything that up to that point has made the mortal the creature all that it is. But more. It is more. . .

The future. All it could be. The homes it could live in, the husbands, the wives, the children. The memories of the future, the possibilities, the hopes and dreams, desires, wishes, all the promises of the years that are yet to come. The grandchildren and the old age and the blessed relief of the final breaths in a plump bed surrounded by family and children and friends, and the knowledge that all of that is stolen away when I take its blood and take its life; stolen away, yes, but looked after, like treasure, like jewels, stolen away but not frittered away, no, more than that; stored with my own memories and hopes and dreams, stored with my own treasure and my own jewels, accepted into my fold, into my family, into my life. The soul is a gift that I take gladly, but not to squander, not to gloat over, but to accept as a gift, to place away in my own heart, to relish and to celebrate and to say 'here you are safe, here we shall live together, and everything that you have dreamt about and hoped for, all of that together we shall search for, we shall find, and we shall achieve'.

That night, that night I found Miss Ainsworth again. Again and again, for futures that remain always out of reach and unobtainable, always, always, Miss Ainsworth. For what could have been. I take the blood for it helps me to dream of what would have and what should have been, and what now could never possibly be.

* * *

With four nights left before the Holmes' ultimatum ran out, Raffles took me to one side and told me of her plan. . .

* * *

There was a woman, Raffles said, who lived in Marylebone. She was a vampire, a natural-born, and she worked as a private detective, assisting other natural-borns in criminal cases that were perhaps a little too sensitive to entrust to the local human authorities. Missing persons, stolen property, bribery and corruption, she investigated them all, for a fee, and was renowned in natural-born society for both her ruthlessness and her ability to see through the lies cast by others. In the past, Raffles informed me, she had given the turned vampires of Spitalfields some assistance in a matter relating to the disappearance of one of the Brick Lane Irregulars' younger girls. It transpired that the girl had been murdered by a human mob and there was little more help the detective could offer, but she had looked kindly on the turned girls, and Raffles thought that perhaps she could help us in our plight. Speak on our behalf with the 'High Borns' who were helping the Holmes Boys, even warn off the Holmes Boys themselves. Her name was Madame Moriarty and she lived at 221b Baker Street.

Being a vampire, Madame Moriarty's office kept vampire hours meaning that her business was closed during the daytime but open for visitors from dusk till dawn. So that evening, without further ado, we set off for Baker Street.

We wore bonnets on our heads to hide our ears and pulled shoes onto our feet for the second time that week, and we, that is Raffles and myself, arrived at the Madame's office a little after midnight. A gas-lamp burned in the window, indicating that the occupants were at home. After knocking on the door and waiting for a minute or two, the door opened and we were met by an elderly mortal butler with a wrinkled face and a world-weary countenance.

"Yes?" he asked, peering at us through eyes the colour of cold dishwater.

"We've come to see Madame Moriarty," said Raffles.

"Do you have an appointment?" asked the butler, suspiciously.

"No. I hope that isn't a problem?" said Raffles.

"Madame Moriarty, you say?" asked the butler.

"Yes," sighed Raffles.

"And you have no appointment?" asked the butler.

"No."

"Hudson, you insufferable old fool, let them in and bring them through to me before I rip out your worthless throat and feast on your revolting old blood!" a female voice bellowed from within the bowels of the house.

The butler physically flinched. "This way," he said, stepping back to allow us to enter. "Madame is expecting you."

We were shown through into a drawing room where, behind a large oak desk, Madame Moriarty sat, resembling for all the world like a queen holding court.

"Well, well, well," said Madame Moriarty. "Dolly Biters. What a rare delight. And look, you're wearing shoes! How uncommonly civilised of you."

Madame Moriarty was an impressive woman. She stood, I estimated, well over six feet tall, with jet black hair pulled back tightly into a bun. Her nose was prominent, what mother would have called 'Roman', her lips were thin and seemed to be stretched across rows of teeth that resembled nothing so much as small white daggers. Her eyes were black and reptilian. without a hint of the red tinge that affected turned vampires, and her ears, of course, were small and curved, pinned back close against the scalp. It struck me that while natural-borns and the turned were both classified as vampires, we were a race apart, in many ways as different to each other as we were to humans. Her long black fingernails drummed on the top of the desk as she examined us.

"Pray tell, how can I be of service to girls such as yourselves?" she asked, in a tone that may or may not have been mocking.

Raffles began to explain the predicament that we found ourselves in, but the wind had been knocked out of my sails and I was no longer listening. All I could hear was my blood pumping in my head and my world being turned, once more, upside down.

Standing on Moriarty's right was what I initially took for a young boy dressed in a black tuxedo, black trousers, a stiff collared white shirt and black bow tie. However now, as I looked closer, it began to dawn on me that *he* was in fact a *she*! This was no young man, this was a young woman – a young woman with short slicked brown hair, the colour of nutmeg, wearing male clothes and dragging from a cigarette. I was scandalised, outraged, and yet fascinated and aroused. I felt like my brain was melting! I couldn't tear my eyes away from this captivating image before me; the shape of her breasts pushing against the stiffness of the shirt, the way the trousers clung to her waist, her hips, her thighs. Her plump lips, her cute button nose, and the way she stood, cocky, self-assured, pretending that she was indeed a man, a *lad*, the salt of the earth. *Her cute button nose*! So at odds with her arrogant countenance. I felt my heart being pulled from my chest.

I heard my name being spoken as though through a fog, one of the London Peculiars, thick, deep, impenetrable. "Irene? Irene? Irene?" The sound came closer and I jumped as if disturbed from a dream. "Sorry?" I said. "Miles away."

"Do tell," said Raffles, her voice dripping with sarcasm. "Put your fangs away, darling. Remember what happened last time you fell in love?"

"Verily you can take the Dolly Biter out of Spitalfields," said Madame Moriarty, "but you cannot take the Spitalfields out of the Dolly Biter. What's your name, vampire?"

"Irene," I replied, hastily wiping my mouth with the back of my hand. I appeared to have been drooling, which often happened when my fangs became excited. "Irene Adler." The tom boy, as I later discovered her kind were called, looked at me in a smug manner, as though she was used to capturing the hearts of passing lesbian vampires.

"Irene Adler?" exclaimed Madame Moriarty. "The Irene Adler of the Adler Shipping Company Adlers?"

"Yes," I replied. "That's me, or at least it used to be. I rather think I've been disowned by now. I left the family home under something of a cloud, you understand?"

"But my dear," said Madame Moriarty, standing from her seat and extending her hand for me to shake, "I fear I have done you a huge disservice. I know your father quite well, we have discussed business on several occasions. You probably aren't aware of it, being ensconced in the depths of Spitalfields, but your turning was quite the scandal. It is still the gossip of polite society. I must congratulate you, you appear to have adapted very well to your new *condition*, to say that you came from something of a privileged background."

"Irene's a fighter, ma'am," said Raffles with what I took for a tinge of pride, like an older sister speaking of a sibling.

"Poor little rich girl, more like," said the tom boy scornfully in a thick Cockney accent, stubbing her cigarette out in a cut glass ashtray.

"Ignore Moran," said Moriarty of the tom boy. "She has a deep mistrust of the ruling classes. It can be a little annoying at times. What are we this week, Moran? An anarchist? A socialist? It can be so difficult to keep up."

Suitably admonished, the tom boy slunk back against the wall and fumed. It made her even more fascinating. My heart was still entrapped, despite the fact that she clearly did not care for me.

"So the Holmes Boys are causing problems for you and making wild threats? Well, they are an unruly bunch of humans, I will grant you that. And they claim to be aided in their endeavours by some High Borns? I shan't lie to you, girls. There are elements within High Born society who would gladly watch while Spitalfields burned and with all of you girls in it, burning too. However, I do have ears to the ground in all areas of the capital, and I must admit that I have heard nothing of such a plot. I rather suspect that the Holmes Boys may be fabricating the truth somewhat, trying to scare you."

"Well it's worked, ma'am," said Raffles. "They killed one of our girls and they've got a werewolf!"

"Have you seen this werewolf for yourself?" asked Moriarty.

"Yes ma'am," said Raffles, "well, it was in human form at the time. A little man called Watson or something."

"In human form? So you haven't actually seen the wolf in the flesh? Seen it for yourself?"

"No," I said, "but Elsie saw it, she told us about it, and then she killed herself. The Holmes Boys are up to something, they're getting their power from somewhere, and it isn't all simply bravado."

"Oh, I have no doubt of that," said Moriarty, "and please, don't misunderstand me. I did not mean to sound as if I was doubting your word or your judgement. There is certainly a threat, and a threat that I shall investigate on your behalf and free-of-charge, one vampire to another and as a personal service to Miss Adler, but try not to let fear take a hold of your judgement. Are the Holmes Boys dangerous? Yes. Can they wipe out the vampire girls of Spitalfields? Of course not. Let us maintain our common sense."

"But you will investigate for us, ma'am? Find out what the truth is?" asked Raffles.

"Of course, and in the meantime I would recommend that you tell your girls only to travel in packs, stick together, keep to the shadows," said Moriarty, "just to be on the safe side."

"I wish you would come back with us, ma'am," said Raffles. "See the lay of the land, reassure the girls. For them to see that you were in our corner, ma'am, it would reassure them no end."

"If what I uncover warrants a personal visit from me, then you have my assurance that I shall attend. But you must understand that I currently have several high profile investigations which require my immediate attention. At the present instant one of the most revered High Borns in England is being besmirched by a blackmailer, and only I can stop a disastrous scandal. So, unless the situation warrants it, it is quite impossible for me to visit Spitalfields."

Raffles nodded her head in resignation, "I understand, ma'am, of course. And thank you for your help. Me and Irene are very appreciative."

Moriarty held up her hand to hush Raffles. "I do, however, feel it would be highly advantageous to have eyes and ears on the ground in Spitalfields. May I therefore recommend that Moran here accompany you back to the East End? Moran is my personal assistant, among other things, and would, I feel, prove to be helpful in this matter. She may report back to me daily, and any instructions I feel should be carried out may be passed on from me to her. Is this agreeable?"

"Yes!" I said a little too eagerly.

"Hold your horses!" said Moran, pulling herself up from the wall that she had been slouching against. "Don't I get a say in all this?"

"Not really," said Moriarty. "You'll do as your told. Unless you want a spanking."

Both Raffles and I grinned wildly and were forced to stifle sniggers, while Moran simply raged impotently. "Seems I've got no choice, then," she said.

"Indeed," said Moriarty. "Now hurry and pack a bag, there's a good girl. You need to be back across town before the sun comes up, or have you forgotten that these two ladies are vampires?"

"I ain't forgotten," hissed Moran. "I knows only too well exactly what these two *ladies* is."

"She's a good girl really," said Moriarty as Moran disappeared to pack a bag for her stay in Spitalfields. "She's from the streets like you and your girls, she's a tough little scrapper for a human, and she has proven herself a very able spy for me on more than one occasion. I am sure that she will serve us both well. But remember that she's human. Don't break her."

And of course all I could think about was how exactly she could serve me, if only I could woo her!

* * *

It was raining cats and dogs when we left Madame Moriarty's establishment in Baker Street, which proved to be a blessing in disguise; the lateness of the hour and the inclement weather meaning that the streets were all but deserted as our strange party of Dolly Biters and a cross-dressing tom boy made our way across town. Arriving back on Chicksand Street, Raffles said that I should secret Moran away into one of the abandoned, unused houses in the rookery, and make sure she was safe from being inadvertently eaten by one of the girls, who coming face to face with a human in their midst might decide to not look a gift horse in the mouth, as it were. "But make sure *you* don't bloody eat her, neither," said Raffles. "I saw the way you was drooling all over her. She's off limits. Keep your fangs to yourself, or you'll have old Moriarty to answer to."

I told Raffles that I would behave myself and that, of course, I wouldn't bite Moran or do anything silly, but I could hardly contain the skip in my step as I escorted the tom boy into an abandoned house on Ely Place, which ran off Chicksand Street. I felt giddy, like Moran was an old friend who was coming to stay with me for a few days' holiday, the thought of the adventures we would share rendering me quite light-headed. But it was clear that she hardly shared the same enthusiasm for our little enter-prise. "Fucking shit hole," she said of her temporary home.

She was right, of course. The house was a shit hole. It hadn't been used in years probably, not since the occupants were killed,

I imagine, by the Dolly Biters, and a thick layer of dust lay on everything. The house was furnished to a small degree, there were tables and chairs in several of the rooms, and a single bed in one of the bedrooms, but nothing had been touched in a very long time. On the drawing room wall, a clock had stopped at just before two o'clock.

I closed the front door and placed a chair up against the handle to deter visitors, then I ran around the house making sure that curtains were drawn across all the windows, the sun being more-or-less about to rise.

"We'd better stay in the same room today," I said, hoping that Moran did not detect the slight quiver of excitement in my voice. "Just until Raffles gets word out to all the girls that you're off the menu. Don't want you being sucked dry on your first day with us, do we?"

There appeared to be sexual innuendo in every word I used.

Moran regarded me with suspicion. "I fucking hate you," she said.

"Yes, well," I said, "I'm sure you'll come to like me, once you know me better."

"You're a Dolly Biter and a toff," said Moran. "Your family exploits the working classes, and you yourself is an insult to the High Borns. Please don't be entertaining no thoughts of me ever liking you. I'll always hate you."

"Well, that's nice" I said. "Shall we retire to the bedroom? I mean, you know, go to bed? To sleep. Just to sleep."

Moran picked up her bag. "Keep your filthy little fangs inside your filthy little mouth," she said, and with that we climbed the creaky old stairs to the bedroom.

Moran took the only bed in the room, there'd been no discussion about that, she'd simply taken it, leaving me with an old wooden chair to sit on and attempt to sleep on. The tom boy sat on the side of the bed and took some sandwiches, wrapped in a tea-towel, out of her bag, and a ceramic bottle of beer. In silence she worked her way through the sandwiches and guzzled on the ale. I hadn't eaten that evening. My stomach growled and I hoped that

Moran hadn't heard. After eating, she stood up and took off her clothes. I nearly fell off the chair.

Her neck, her shoulder blades, her arse, her legs; what a wonderful, lithe creature she was, and the thought entered my head that she seemed to be more elf than human. If she had ears like mine, I thought, she *would* be an elf. I felt my fangs stretching in my mouth and turned my head away to hide my shame. "I like your hair," I managed to mutter, as though making stupid, futile conversation. Moran said nothing, and when I dared look back again she was under the dusty covers with her eyes closed. She was, I supposed, quite used to keeping vampire hours, and so the daytime was when she would naturally sleep.

The daylight hours dragged by painfully; sometimes I dozed, but mostly I sat perched on that wooden chair as my backside grew increasingly numb. Eventually I must have fallen asleep, for I dreamt I was back in the family home, human once more. I was in my old study and Miss Ainsworth was reading a fairy tale to me, about an elf who was lost and was far away from home. But Miss Ainsworth was Moran, and as she read the story she licked her lips with a bloody wet tongue, and the blood smeared around her lips and her teeth. "Kill the elf," she said to me in a voice that was more like the hiss of a snake. "Kill the little lost elf."

I awoke with a start, and for a moment felt quite disoriented, until I remembered that I was in this unfamiliar bedroom because I had Moran to keep safe from the other girls. I looked across the room and saw Moran in the bed, but she had rolled over on to her back and in doing so the sheets had pulled back, revealing her naked breasts and stomach. I groaned audibly. This torment was too much to bear.

I stood from the chair and knelt down on the floor, looking at the wall like a naughty school-child. I tried to focus on the wall, tried to keep my eyes on the dirt and the cobwebs and the flaking paint. But like a magnet, the naked torso of Moran kept dragging my eyes back to her, back to her nipples, erect in this cold room, and the goosebumps on her skin. To the shape of her neck and shoulders and collar bone, cruelly exposed by her short boyish hair. I needed to kill someone or find some release elsewhere, otherwise I would go quite mad with desire and hunger and do, once more, something stupid.

One of my hands found my breasts and rubbed them angrily, feeling my own nipples pushing back against the rough fabric of my black dress. I was helpless to resist the call of my own desires, and my other hand worked its way underneath my skirts, along the length of my bare legs, and thrust itself up against my womanhood, where it began to rub. I turned to face Moran as she slept, and there in the dust and the dirt of this run-down old house, I masturbated over the tom boy. It did not take long for me to reach my pleasure, and stifling my moans, I rocked backwards and forwards on my heels, and felt my fingers become damp and then wet and then drenched. "I can see you, you know," said Moran, her eyes wide open.

I cried out in horror and disbelief. Moran sat up in bed and looked at me. "Dirty little slag," she said. I wailed and crawled away into a corner of the room and wept.

"I'm sorry," I said.

"I'm going to tell Madame Moriarty," said Moran in a voice that suddenly sounded almost cheerful. "Let's see what she makes of your little exploits."

"Please don't," was all I could say, to which Moran made no reply, and I spent the rest of the day in the corner, not daring to turn to look at my tom boy tormentor.

* * *

As darkness fell, there came a-banging upon the front door of the house. It was Raffles. There were now three nights until the Holmes' ultimatum expired.

"It's all right!" cried Raffles from the street. "I told the girls not to eat your girlfriend!" And she laughed, and I heard some other girls, out in the street, laugh too.

In the bedroom I turned hesitantly to look at Moran. She was half-dressed, quickly buttoning up her shirt and pulling her untied dickie bow loosely around the collar.

"Please don't say anything," I begged, climbing to my feet, wiping at the dried tears on my face with a grubby hand, the grubby hand that had brought about my downfall.

Moran only smirked at me and then trotted down the stairs whistling some music hall ditty; salt of the earth, Jack the Lad, fucking bitch. I tumbled down stairs after her, and followed her out into the chill night air.

"Come on then, Moran," said Raffles. "Let's introduce you to Spitalfields, show you our territory, and then I suppose you'll be wanting to report back to Madame Moriarty."

"Oh yes," said Moran, "I shall most certainly be reporting back to Madame later tonight. I have much to tell her." And she looked over at me and winked, like she was flirting with me, but she wasn't flirting with me. No, it felt like she had a wooden stake in my heart and was twisting it, just for the pleasure of seeing me squirm.

"Nothing out of the ordinary happened during the daytime, did it?" asked Raffles. My heart sank. Would Moran say anything to Raffles? Shame me to the closest thing to a friend I had?

"There was one thing," said Moran. "Dear Irene had to sleep on the floor, and I could hear the poor thing tossing and turning all day long. Would it be inappropriate of me to let her sleep in bed with me tomorrow? Just so she can get some rest? I feel so rotten about it. She must be exhausted, the poor thing."

"Oh," laughed Raffles, "I'm sure Irene would like that, wouldn't you Irene?"

I was flabbergasted and didn't know what to say. "Of course, yes," I managed to stutter and gave Moran a quizzical look. Behind Raffles' back she silently mouthed, "Fuck off," at me. What game was this damned girl playing?

Raffles took Moran with her on a circuit of Spitalfields. I needed food, and didn't need telling twice when Raffles suggested that I went out and hunted while she escorted Moran. I ran as fast as I could on to Brick Lane but it was deserted, so I ventured further afield, towards the gas lamps and the gin houses of Whitechapel. This was a dangerous thing to do, especially on my own, but I was hungry, and hungry for more than just blood.

In an alleyway behind a gin house I took a prostitute and nearly ripped her head off, so ferocious was my bite. I closed my eyes as I fed and pretended that the woman was Moran.

When I returned to Chicksand Street a rather large gaggle of vampire girls were hanging around outside the house that Raffles, myself and the older girls shared. There seemed an awful lot of them, more than I thought actually lived on Chicksand Street. And yet, here they were, peering through the windows, climbing on each other's backs to get a vantage point, even trying to glimpse through the crack in the door. I'd just feasted, so my eyes were glowing red and my mouth and chin were probably covered in blood and as such I imagine that I must have looked quite a fright, so when I shouted, "Come on girls, shift your arses!" they quickly backed away and allowed me to pass. I slipped in through the front door and slammed the door shut behind me. As soon as the door closed I heard the sound of the girls pushing up against it again. I was a little befuddled from feeding and confused by the girls outside and was still worried about what Moran would say to Moriarty about my masturbation, so when I walked into the drawing room to find Raffles and Moran sitting there, I must have looked like I was in need of answers.

"Your friend here is causing quite the stir," said Raffles, looking over at Moran. "They can smell her."

"Did you tell them that she's off-limits?" I asked.

"Yes," said Raffles, "but they're hungry and she'd make quite a banquet. They listen to me, they'll even do as I tell them, but hunger can be a strong motivator. I'm worried we may have a rebellion on our hands. If they decide they're coming in, we won't be able to stop them."

"Christ," I said, "I had no idea."

"She'd best go back," said Raffles. "I'll slip out the back door with her and escort her back over to Baker Street."

"No!" I said, and to be honest I'm not sure why. I should have been glad to be rid of her after the way she'd treated me. But still, despite it all, I wanted her to stay. "Let me take her to the abandoned house we used last night. We'll climb over the back wall, they'll never know we've gone or where we've gone to."

"Yes, let's do that," said Moran. "I should stay. What kind of spy would I be for the Madame if I went running back to Baker Street at the first sign of trouble?"

Raffles relented, so Moran and I slipped into the scullery and out of the back door. The wall of the back-yard was high, perhaps eight feet tall, which was no problem for me but was insurmountable for Moran. I placed my hands around her waist and lifted her up, feeling the warmth of her flesh against my fingers. She scrambled and heaved and managed to pull herself over the wall and dropped down into the alleyway on the other side. I hopped over the wall in one easy motion and landed face-to-face with her in the dark alleyway. Most of the snow had gone by now, but it was still cold and I noticed that Moran was shivering. She no longer looked like my mocking nemesis. Her smart suit was wrinkled and there was dirt on the knees of her trousers. Her short hair was no longer expertly groomed, but was ruffled and dishevelled. She looked lost and more than a little scared. I heard the voice from my dream urging me to kill the little lost elf.

I ignored the words in my head. "Come along," I said, taking her decisively by the hand, "let's get you out of this cold." She said nothing but kept hold of my hand and followed.

Back in the bedroom that we had used the previous evening, Moran climbed under the bedsheets fully clothed. "Jesus," she said in the dark, "it's cold enough to freeze the balls off a brass monkey!"

I said nothing but looked out of the bedroom window. The street below was deserted. We were quite safe. I hadn't lit any candles, and the front door was barred with a chair. "Try and get some sleep," I said. "The sun will be up in a few hours. That'll warm you up a little, and perhaps you can get some more clothes to-morrow?"

"Come to bed with me," said the voice of the elf. "After all, I promised Raffles that you could."

As a vampire I could see in the night as well as any human can in the daylight. I looked across the room and saw her big eyes searching for me through the darkness of the bedroom. I padded over to the side of the bed, unfastened the back of my dress, let it slip down my body, and then climbed under the covers. I could feel her clothes, the clothes that had so excited me when I first laid eyes on her in Madame Moriarty's drawing room the previous evening, pushing up against my body and the heat from her hands and her neck and her face made my skin ache.

All at once our lips were pressed together and we were kissing. I had never kissed like this before, what was known as *French kissing*, certainly not as a human girl and not even with Raffles and the vampire girls. The sex with the vampire girls had been all tongues and licking and snarling like beasts. We had never kissed; this pressing of the lips against each other seemed a very personal and human interaction. My fangs felt too big for my mouth and occasionally they would knock against Moran's teeth. Imperfect kisses that seemed more passionate and honest because of it. We kissed for what seemed a long time until I felt Moran's bottom lip get caught momentarily behind my fangs. I realised that if I inadvertently cut her, if even a drop of her blood was spilled, I would probably not be able to contain the animal that raged within me. I pulled my lips away from hers, though it took all of my will-power to do so, and we laid face-to-face, panting, with Moran's warm breath rising like a mist above us. Perhaps she read my mind for she whispered, "Please don't kill me." I held her close and cried tears of longing as my fangs burned in my mouth.

At length I managed to whisper, "Did you speak to Madame Moriarty?"

"Yes."

"Did you tell her?"

"Course not, treacle. I was never going to tell her!"

"Then why were you acting so mean to me?" I asked.

"I don't like toffs," she said, "and Madame Moriarty hates Dolly Biters. You know that, don't you? She hates you. So I felt it was my duty to hate you too. But when I saw you frigging away last night, well, it was just the sweetest thing. You fair melted my heart."

"You could have said something!" I whispered. "I've been in turmoil all night long!"

"Oh, I was just teasing you," she said. "Winding you up like a jack-in-the-box." Her hands ran over my face and stroked my cheeks. "Winding you up and winding you up until you're ready to pop," she sang the words like they were a child's lullaby. "You are ready to pop aren't you, Irene Adler of the Adler Shipping Company Adlers?"

"Yes," I shuddered.

"Then stay right there, treacle-pie, and prepare yourself to be popped."

She jumped out of bed and de-robed in about ten seconds flat, then she clambered back under the covers and climbed on top of me, naked as the day she was born. She kissed me on my neck, and then on my breasts, and down onto my stomach, and my thighs, and then finally between my legs. I placed my hands on the top of her head, running my fingers through her short boyish hair, as her tongue pleasured me. I popped all right, and then I popped again, and then I popped a third time, just for good luck.

As the day broke over London, that woman, that dirty, filthy, awful little tom boy, took me to places that by rights should exist only in poetry and pornography. She exhausted me, and fucked the hunger out of me. By midday, my fangs had retracted and I slept like a baby. The sleep of the innocent.

Chapter Six
In Which My
Relationship With
Raffles Becomes
Somewhat Strained

It was, I suppose, early afternoon when Moran roused me from my slumber to tell me that she was popping out to find warmer clothes and food. I stirred on the bed and smiled at her. Her lips had dried blood all over them. The blood that had been on my lips from that prostitute in Whitechapel was now on her lips. Unbeknownst to us both, in the darkness she had kissed my lips clean.

"Your lips," I said.

She smiled, told me to go back to sleep, and then she disappeared into the day, the one place where I could not follow her.

I must have dozed for a few hours, and at length the door to the bedroom flung open and in stomped Moran. As well as her suit and shirt, she was now wearing a bowler hat, long overcoat, and a scarf. She really could have passed for a boy. She was also covered in snow, which dropped off her in big clumps to melt on the floor.

"Bloody snowing again!" she said.

"So I see," I said, "and you have new clothes."

"Yes, I'm quite the Bobby Dazzler, ain't I?" she smiled.

"Yes," I said, "yes you are."

Out of one of the coat's pockets she pulled a small bundle wrapped up in newspaper. Sitting on the edge of the bed, and still wearing the overcoat and hat, she carefully unwrapped the newspaper to reveal a hot pie, steaming in the cold air.

"You look like a little boy unwrapping a gift on Christmas morning," I said softly.

"Do I?" she said. "Ain't never had nothing to unwrap on Christmas." But she said it with a smile on her face, with no sense of malice or regret. She pulled off a piece of pie with her dainty fingers, red from the cold, and popped it into her mouth. I noticed that her nose was running slightly and her cheeks were flush.

I laid there in the bed and watched her devour the pie, piece by piece. We didn't speak, yet the silence was not uncomfortable. In fact it was a delightful silence, a silence in which I could observe her, observe every nerve and sinew on view; observe the stiff collar pressing harshly against her soft skin, and her hat, damp from the snow, beneath which peeped her sweet nutmeg hair. I observed the action of her jaw as she ate, and the twinkle in her eye as she looked into the middle-distance. With the pie finished, she delved into an inside pocket and produced a bottle of beer which she gulped down in one easy action, her throat throbbing in and out as the deep brown liquid slid down.

When she had finished her make-shift meal, I smiled at her and asked, "Is that better?"

She smiled back at me, her finger-tips greasy from the pie and with flecks of pastry upon her lips. "Mmm," she replied with another smile.

She then spent the next ten minutes creating a fire in the bedroom's hearth. She broke up a chair from downstairs, and with the help of a box of Lucifers and the crumpled newspaper that had once housed the pie, she soon had a fire roaring. Happy with her work, she stepped away from the hearth, took off her hat and coat, and sat back down on the edge of the bed.

"I don't suppose you feel the cold much?" she said.

"Not so much," I said. "Not these days."

"You're lucky, it's bloody freezing."

I sat up in bed, naked beneath the dirty sheets. "I know a way to warm you," I said.

She leant towards me and we kissed, French kissed. "I imagine you had lots of gifts to unwrap on Christmas Day?" she said, a few minutes later, breathlessly.

"Yes," was all I could reply.

"What was inside? Inside the wrapping?"

"Bonbons," I said, "jewels sometimes, books, even the Bible once, with my name inscribed inside."

"You can unwrap me if you want," she said. And so I did. I undressed this clever boy girl who knew how to make fires, and ate pies out of newspaper with her fingers like some street urchin, and wore bowler hats as bold as brass. And then I pulled that shivering little body of hers beneath the bedsheets and I licked it with my vampire tongue. Like I had wanted to do to the summer girl from the Diogenes Rooms if only she hadn't been so stupid and resisted my kind offer.

By the time I'd finished with Moran, she was quite exhausted and night had fallen. It was my time now to leave the room and take care of business. I climbed out of bed and by the light of the embers of the fire I pulled on and deftly fastened my black dress. As I did, an odd thought entered my head.

"You talked to Madame Moriarty last night, then?" I asked.

"Mmm," Moran replied, sleepily.

"What did she say? Has she found anything out about the Holmes' gang and the werewolf?"

"No, nothing. She said not to worry. None of her informants had heard anything. I reckon it's all a bit of a storm in a teacup, if you ask me."

"How did you manage to talk to Moriarty?" I asked. Something had been niggling me all day, and now it dawned on me. "You couldn't have had enough time to travel back across town, not in the time it took me to go out hunting and come back?"

"Secret," said Moran, yawning lazily.

"Secret?" I laughed. "Do tell! You see, now I'm intrigued."

"Pass me my bag," she said, rolling over onto her side and leaning up on her elbow.

I did as she asked. She opened up the bag and pulled out a small glass vial, a small glass vial that was very similar to the one I'd seen in the possession of the Holmes brothers.

"Madame Moiety's probably skin me alive if she knew I was showing you this," said Moran, warily.

"Don't worry," I said, looking at the small bottle suspiciously, "I can keep a secret."

"Well sees that you do," she said. "This here is Madame's blood. I sip a few drops of it, no more than a drop or two really, and then it allows me to speak to her directly, from my mind to her mind kind of thing."

"I'm sorry," I said, "come again? Speak to her mind to mind?"

"That's right," said Moran. "Tele-paf-ikly I think Madame calls it. It's like we're in the same room, even when we're miles apart. Clever, innit?"

"Telepathy!" I exclaimed. "Yes, I remember my tutor reading me an article from the newspaper about the phenomena once."

"You had a bleedin' tutor?" asked Moran.

I ignored her and continued, "The Spiritualists claim to be able to do something similar, don't they? Communicate psychically?"

"I wouldn't trust them Spiritualists, treacle-pie," she said. "Frauds and charlatans, the ol' lot of 'em. But this," she held up the vial, "this is the proper stuff. But you mustn't tell no-one. It's a secret, a secret that the High Borns keep to themselves."

"Don't fret," I said, walking over to her and kissing her on the forehead. "My lips are sealed."

There were now two nights until the Holmes' ultimatum expired.

* * *

With a hop over the wall and a skip down the alleyway, I was soon back on Chicksand Street. The snow had stopped falling but a heavy frost had settled on the snow that lay on the ground, and Chicksand Street twinkled of its own accord, like the setting for some fairy tale about a Snow Queen and an Evil Witch. The sky was clear, the moon bright, and the stars shone from above. Fucking Moran had given me a hunger, and so I headed to Raffles' house to participate in that night's hunt.

I found Raffles in high spirits. As I entered the house, she smiled at me slyly and slithered over to me through the throng of girls who had gathered in anticipation of the hunt.

"The human says that Moriarty ain't worried," she said, speaking of Moran. "She reckons it might've all been blown up out of all pre-porshun. That's a relief, ain't it?"

"Raffles!" I said, exasperated. "They killed Frances! And you saw them, the Holmes brothers, they're bastards, they want a scrap. And don't forget that bloody wolf of theirs!"

"Yes," said Raffles, "but we never actually saw the wolf, did we? All we saw was that daft little bloke. He was daft, weren't he? Imagine him a werewolf? Not bleedin' likely, I say!" And she laughed boisterously.

"Elsie saw him!" I said. "Elsie saw him kill Frances!"

"Listen darling, thing is, Elsie was young, weren't she? And she'd been in a bit of a scrap, taken a few blows to the head like, you know what I'm saying? It's very sad and, yes, the Holmes Boys are bastards, but maybe, you know, maybe there never was a werewolf, excepting in Elsie's befuddled head."

"No, I don't believe that," I said. "Something's going on here, I can sense it. Something's not right."

Raffles lent in close and sniffed the air around me. The room was packed by now with excitable girls, laughing loudly, pushing each other in jest, licking each other's faces. They were winding themselves up for the hunt.

"I can smell her on you," said Raffles, looking me in the eye. "I can smell her cunny juice. It's all over you, like you been bathing in it."

"Raffles," I said and then didn't know what else to say.

"Maybe I should fuck her too?" she said. "See what all the fuss is about?"

My heart leapt as she said those words and I felt anger and jealousy rise in me.

"Leave her alone," I said. "I'm looking after her."

"No, I don't think so darling," said Raffles, whispering in my ear now. "Let's both fuck her? And then kill her? We can blame it on the young 'uns? Say they got carried away, apologise on bended knees to Her Bleedin' Majesty Moriarty, and carry on with our lives? Come on, let's eat the little slag's blood. You know you want to."

"No!" I shouted, but no sooner had the word left my mouth than Raffles had me by the hair. She pulled me off balance so that I was down on my knees, and she began to drag me across the room. "This one needs teaching a lesson," she screeched, "about who's in charge around here!"

The other girls in the room cheered their approval, and moved back to create a circle around us as I writhed on the ground with Raffles above me. She was stronger than me, a lot stronger. I hadn't known at the time, but as a vampire grows older, so their strength increases. I had only been turned a few months, Raffles a century and more. I was no match for her, especially with the rage that was coursing through her veins at that moment.

She thrust a hand against my throat and squeezed tightly, like she had done on my third night in the coven, the night I had told my story and then had the tongue. With a tight grip on my neck, she pinned me back-down to the floor, and with her spare hand she pulled the skirt of my dress up and over my breasts. I was naked beneath the dress. The girls around us were whipping themselves up into a frenzy. "Fuck her!" cried one. Through the tears that had welled in my eyes, I could see that some of the girls were rubbing each other's breasts and arses and some were licking the necks of others, their tongues indecent, elongated, and forked. I hadn't noticed before, but some of their tongues were forked.

"Raffles, don't," I managed to wail, though her grip around my throat made it almost impossible to speak.

"Shut the fuck up!" she hissed back at me, baring her fangs.

She pulled her own skirt up around her belly. She too was naked beneath. She wrapped her legs around my left leg, like a snake wrapping coils around its prey, and she began to rub her cunt up against me; a bitch-dog on heat, fucking anything that moved.

I was crying, the girls were roaring their approval, Raffles was hissing and drooling over me, her wet cunt sliding up and down my leg, and all I could think about was Moran back in the house on Ely Place and how she'd think it was me returning home when the door opens and Raffles comes to plunder and murder her.

How long was I pinned to the floor while Raffles took her pleasure? I honestly don't know. The minutes, perhaps the hours, blurred into a single moment of noise and terror.

At last Raffles shuddered, sagged down on to me, and placed her cheek against mine. "Oh my sweet," she sighed, "that was nice." Then she kissed me gently, almost *lovingly*, on the bridge of my nose, and stood up. "Now I need to kill something!" she exclaimed, at which the girls roared their approval and in a mass of fangs and red eyes and black dresses and spit, they were gone, out onto the streets. I laid on my back, the skirt still up around my neck, and I sobbed. They were beasts, monsters. I had thought them friends, but they were animals. Beneath the tiniest veneer of civility, the truth was, of course, that they, *and I*, were monsters. And these monsters, these vampires, were just as quick to turn on their own as they were to turn on those they feasted upon.

Had they gone for Moran? The thought of those creatures bursting in on my little tom boy focused my mind like ice-water flushing away shit. I dragged myself upright and ran barefoot through the snow, back to Ely Place. I found the house in darkness, the front door intact, and Moran asleep in our bed. She was snoring and I had to stifle a laugh that grew hysterically inside me. I sat down next to her on the bed and stroked her nutmeg hair. "Oh Moran,"

I whispered, though I knew she could not hear me, "what the Dickens is happening to us?"

My hunger had deserted me, and so I slipped out of my dress and climbed beneath the sheets of our bed. There I lay with my arms around Moran, protecting her, not daring to close my eyes for fear of hearing the girls, like a pack of hounds on the scent of a fox, breaking down the front door and rioting up the stairs. Only when the sun at last crept above the horizon did I allow myself to relax and bury my face in Moran's hair.

That morning we lay in bed, limbs wrapped lazily around each other. Moran smoked cigarettes and I placed my head on her chest like she was my bloke. I said nothing of the previous night's terrible events.

"How well do you know Moriarty?" I asked.

"Well enough, I s'pose," she replied. "Probably as well as anyone."

"What's she like?"

"She's a High Born," she said, a lilt in her voice, "what do you expect she's like? Snobbish, haughty, impatient, don't suffer fools gladly. Typical High Born behaviour, I suppose. Do you know her story? The story of how her family came to be vampires?"

"No," I replied, looking up at Moran. "Do tell."

"Well," said Moran, a smile on her lips and relish in her voice, "this is what I heard..."

Chapter Seven
Just Who Does
Madame Moriarty
Think She Is?

"Once upon a time," said Moran.

"You're enjoying this!" I laughed.

"Once upon a time," insisted Moran, "back in the 1400s, there was an old, old vampire who lived in a cottage near the Black Forest in Germany."

"What do you know about Germany and the Black Forest?" I asked.

"This is the story as it was told to me," said Moran impatiently. "It don't matter if I don't know where the bleedin' Black Forest is, does it? I imagine it's a forest and I understand that it's in Germany. Would I be right in making such a presumption?"

"Yes," I said. "Yes, you would."

"Then will you kindly shut your cake hole and let me tell the story? Or would you rather I didn't?"

"No, no, please continue," I said. "You have piqued my interest."

"I *will* peak your interest in a minute, young lady," smiled Moran. "Now, where were we? Oh yes, once upon a time there was an old, old vampire who lived in a cottage near the Black Forest in Germany.

"His name was Peter and according to the local gossip, he was so ancient that he had fought the Mohammedan hordes in the Crusades. There was a long tradition of High Borns, for such he was, serving the Roman church, and the vampire Peter had served them well. Now, however, he had grown tired of blood-shed and killing. He had retired himself to the Black Forest to, I suppose, die. He lived a quiet life, never bothering the few humans who lived locally on farms or in simple cottages. His newly found disdain for blood-lust meant that he could no longer bring himself to take human prey. Rather he existed on rats and mice and the snakes that slithered upon the ground.

"Such a diet was killing him. Vampires need human blood in order to grow and thrive. Animal blood, especially the blood of low animals, will keep them alive, but only just, and so Peter began to age, to whither, no longer the strapping young man who had fought for his king in the East, but now an old man, wrinkled and weak.

"Now, near-by lived a young family comprising of a mother and father and their two daughters, Heidi and Elsbeth. Heidi was the youngest of the two, being sixteen, while Elsbeth was older by two years. And my! How she lorded it over her younger sister, bullying her and teasing her and never giving the poor younger girl a moment's peace. The parents thought it was just the hijinks of youth, but really it was a deeper emotion that drove Elsbeth to torment Heidi, for as Elsbeth was dark haired and pale skinned, so Heidi was blonde and as fair as a summer's day. Elsbeth was terribly jealous of her sister's fair countenance, and so decided to make her sister's life hell.

"One evening Heidi was sent out into the woods by Elsbeth to find strawberries. 'Don't come back without any', said Elsbeth, 'or I shall beat you.' Now Elsbeth knew all too well that it was not the season for strawberries, being the middle of winter, and she pushed Heidi out of the cottage door in the sure and certain knowledge that she would, upon her sister's return, be able to administer her a thrashing.

"Oh, Heidi was so sad," said Moran. "She wandered the fast darkening woods, unable to find any strawberries but too afraid to return home for she knew what fate awaited her."

"Poor Heidi," I said.

"Oh yes," said Moran, "but it gets better."

"As Heidi wandered the forest," she continued, "she came across a small cottage with a candle burning at the window. Unbeknownst to Heidi, this was the cottage of the vampire Peter. She was so cold and so lost that she walked up to the door and knocked on it. The old, wrinkled vampire answered and invited the little blonde haired girl inside."

It will come, I am sure, as no surprise that as Moran told the story, Heidi, in my mind, became the summer girl from the Diogenes Rooms.

"The vampire stoked up a fire in the kitchen and allowed Heidi to warm herself by the flames. 'You do know who I am?' the vampire asked Heidi. Heidi replied that she did not, and so Peter told her that he was an ancient vampire, come to the forest to repent for past misdemeanours and so to die. Heidi was not afraid, which pleased the vampire, but rather she said that she was delighted to meet so brave a man who had fought so valiantly against the dark hordes of the East.

"Quite taking a shine to Heidi, Peter asked her if it would be possible for him to taste her blood. I suppose being so close to a young, tasty human had quite made the old rapscallion forget his vows of only eating rats! Perhaps he'd seen something what he quite fancied!"

"The old rapscallion!" I laughed at Moran's choice of words.

"The old pervert, more like," she whispered into my ear and we both rolled with laughter on the bed.

Once we had composed ourselves, Moran continued, "But he didn't want to bite her, oh no, for he knew that if he bit her he would turn her into a vampire."

"Don't I know it!" I exclaimed.

"So he gave her a knife and asked her to cut the palm of her hand and so allow a small amount of blood to drip into a goblet."

"Oh well, that's alright then!" I said sarcastically, and we rolled with laughter again.

"Now, once the vampire had tasted Heidi's sweet, young blood, he was suddenly quite restored. His ageing was reversed, his wrinkles faded, and there standing before a shocked Heidi was a handsome vampire knight."

And here, yes, I imagined the prince who had bitten me back in my old family home.

"Peter was so thankful to Heidi that he gave her a purse full of gold and escorted her safely through the woods back to her cottage."

"How come none of the blokes who bit us Dolly Biters were nice like that?" I asked.

" 'Cause none of your blokes was bleedin' vampire knights!" said Moran.

"Mine was a prince," I said.

"Yes," said Moran, "well, yours would be, wouldn't he?"

"Oi!" I laughed, pushing her away, and then we tussled on the bed for a bit and kissed, before Moran regained her composure and continued.

"Well, Heidi's parents were so thankful for the gold coins that the girl brought back with her, and they told her that she was without doubt the best daughter in the whole wide world. Elsbeth, as you can imagine, was not quite so delighted. In fact she fumed all night long, getting angrier and angrier, and the following evening she took it upon herself to visit the vampire herself and demand that she receive a purse full of gold too.

"When she said as much to Peter, he informed the girl that her sister had been very kind and had donated some of her blood to him in return for the gold. Elsbeth was shocked and spitefully told the vampire that there was no way in hell that she was giving the vampire any of her blood. No, she just wanted her gold and then she would be on her way. Well, such a display of impudence upset the vampire knight and so he decided that rather than give her a gift of gold, he would give her a different kind of gift altogether."

"Oh!" I shrieked, putting a hand to my mouth. "That's what the prince said to me! He said 'it is a singular gift that I bestow upon you'! The exact words!"

"Yeah well," said Moran, "this was Peter the vampire knight, not your lah-di-dah prince, so let's not get our knickers in a twist, alright?"

"You brute!" I hissed at her, though we were both giggling.

"So the gallant vampire knight, who was much nicer than any vampire prince could ever be, bit Elsbeth and drained her blood, though not all of it, for Peter did not want to kill Elsbeth, oh no. The following night Elsbeth did return to her family, though not with a purse full of gold as she had intended, but rather as a turned vampire!

"Now, Peter was a good man, and soon he regretted his actions. And so the following night he made his way to the cottage and proposed marriage to Elsbeth. He said that her blood, and that of her sister no doubt, had revived him and he wanted to make Elsbeth's life as a vampire as comfortable as he could. Her parents agreed, I think they was probably just glad to be shut of her, and it also appealed to Elsbeth's pride and arrogance, for to be married to a knight and hero of the crusades was something to be proud of, is it not?

"And so they were married and their union produced one off-spring; a daughter. And that daughter was," Moran paused for dramatic effect, "Madame Moriarty!"

"No?" I screamed, jumping up on the bed.

"Apparently so," said Moran. "That was back in the 1400s or something, so I reckon that makes her four hundred years old or more. So you can imagine that she's a little haughty in her attitude and will quickly slap you down, both figgeritively,"

"Figuratively,"

"Yes, that, and physically."

"And that story is true?" I asked.

"True? Who knows?" said Moran. "It's what I was told. I've no reason to doubt it, and it would explain a lot about her, about the way she is. But, whether it's true or not, she's always been good to me. She saved my worthless backside, good and proper."

"Saved your backside?" I asked. "How so?"

"Shan't tell," said Moran. "I'm done with telling stories."

I lent up to look at here. "Shan't tell?" I asked. "Why ever not?"

"You don't need to know," she said, "and I don't want you to know."

"Young lady!" I said, only half in jest. "Tell me this very instant!"

"Shan't," she said, and she meant it.

Quick as a flash I jumped up and straddled her, pinning her to the bed. "Tell me!" I said, flashing my fangs and pretending to nip at her neck. I had meant it as jest, but as I saw her eyes bulge in terror I knew that I had made an awful misjudgement. "Don't kill me," she pleaded for the second time in our short acquaintance.

"No, no, no!" I said, rolling off her. "It was a joke, I was merely teasing, I'd never kill you, darling, never!"

"You're fucking frightening," said Moran, her eyes still wide. "You know that, don't you? You're fucking frightening."

I pulled her close and wrapped my arms around her. "No, no, no," I said. "No I'm not, no I'm not." And I kissed her gently again and again on the forehead.

At last she relaxed and began to lean into me as I held her, and then, at length, she said, "Can I touch them?"

"What's that, dearest?" I asked.

"Can I touch them? Your fangs?"

I smiled. "Of course you can."

I laid back on the bed and opened my mouth. Moran lent over me and placed a finger against my fangs. She pushed them. They were hard and unyielding, and at her touch they grew, yearning to taste her. Bad thoughts entered my mind and I forced them away. She smiled at me, still prodding my teeth. "They're so funny," she said. "Like a bloke's knob, I suppose. They get bigger when you play with them."

"And what do you know of blokes' knobs?" I asked jovially, but she looked away. There was silence for a moment or two, and then she spoke and opened up her poor heart to me.

"Couple of years ago I was a Judy, a prostitute, used to work the streets up the Chapel. I only used the hand, sometimes the mouth, and it was only as a means to earn a bit of moolah, like. I ain't like you Irene. I ain't posh. I had to do some awful things to get by. You won't hold it against me, will you?"

"Of course not," I whispered, putting a hand to her cheek.

"Tell you what, seeing all them knobs fair put me off blokes for life. Reckon that's why I turned out, you know, queer like."

"Well I'm glad that you held all those knobs in your hands if it meant that it made you queer," I smiled, but she hadn't finished opening up her heart just yet.

"Then one night," she continued, "I was working in Whitechapel and a gang of Dolly Biters, no offence, jumped out on me. They had me pinned up against a wall and was about to top me when out of the shadows comes Madame Moriarty. At the sight of her, the Biters all scarper and she picks me up, brushes me down, and takes me under her wing. We did *it* once, you know, had sex, just the once on that night. But ever since then she never laid a hand on me. Bought me all me clothes, gave me a job, said that I knew the streets of the East End better than most, and that in her line of business such knowledge was invaluable. From being a Ladybird doling out hand-jobs to a private detective earning more money than I could have dreamt about in the space of one night! Goes to show, don't it? You never know what's around the corner."

"That's truly amazing," I said. "She saved your life."

"That she did."

"But why? She's a natural-born. Why did she get involved?"

"I told you, Irene. She hates you, hates turned vampires, really she does."

"Then why is she helping us now, with the Holmes Boys?" I asked.

"Dunno," said Moran and then fell quiet. "Come on," she said at last, "I need warming up." And she placed her lips around one of my nipples and began to gently suck, like a baby suckling at its mother's tit.

By mid-afternoon Moran was hungry for more than simple carnal desires. "I'm starving!" she exclaimed, jumping out of bed and beginning to dress herself.

"Another pie?" I asked.

"Maybe fish and chips today," she smiled, "from Malin's."

I shook my head. "Fish and chips? Never tried it. Too late now, of course."

"Well take it from me," she said, "they're sugar and spice!"

"Sugar and spice?" I laughed, and then watched her as she placed her bowler on her head and wrapped the scarf around her neck. "What was it like?" I asked. "Working on the streets?"

"It weren't no holiday," she said, buttoning up her coat, "but it could've been worse I suppose. Better than the Bastille, at least, and you could always guarantee making at least some money. Some of the girls were nice and friendly, others were right old witches. But it's funny, working in Whitechapel, well, it's an odd kind of place. People just disappear sometimes, you know? There'd be girls that you'd see every night, and then one night they wouldn't be there, and they'd never be there again. I suppose been so close to Brick Lane, maybe the Biters came and had them." She stopped herself and looked away. "Sorry," she said. "I wasn't implying. . . "

"It's alright," I said. "The Biters probably did kill most of those that disappeared, take it from me." I didn't mention that just two nights previously I myself had feasted on a prostitute in Whitechapel. Wheels within wheels. Stories within stories.

It was only when Moran had left to find her fish and chips that I realised how hungry I was. My stomach grumbled and moaned, and I regretted not feeding the night before. I sat on the side of the bed and looked towards the window, drapes drawn against the sun. There were still a good few hours until nightfall. I was, really, quite hungry. And then I spotted it, in the corner of the room. Moran's bag. It was open and inside, I knew, was the vial of Moriarty's blood. What was Moriarty's game? What was she after? Why was she helping the Dolly Biters if she hated us so much?

Telepathy. Like the Spiritualists.

It was never a conscious thought, never a planned decision; it happened almost of its own accord, like fate had decreed this course of action at the dawn of time and all I was doing was playing out my part. I stood up, walked over to the bag, found the vial of Moriarty's blood, took it out of the bag, and sat back down upon the bed. A voice, somewhere deep inside me, tried to warn me off, tried to change the course that I was traversing, but it was too late. I pulled the stopper from the bottle and took a swig. Just a drop or two, Moran had said. I took a swig. I took a swig and my mind exploded.

The blood was harsh and bitter on my tongue, very different to the sweet liquor that was human blood. It burned my throat and made me cry, like father's whisky that I had once secretly sipped on Christmas Day. My head was filled with a bright light that devoured my world. My mind flew away from Ely Place, away from Spitalfields and away from the East End. It flew away to the mind of Moriarty, and like water being absorbed into a sponge, so my mind was absorbed into hers.

I instinctively knew everything.

Moriarty, and it was difficult to separate myself from her now, was old, as old as Moran's story implied. I saw myself in the court of Queen Elizabeth, counselling the Virgin Queen, part of the establishment, directing the course of world events, presiding over the birth of the Empire. Moriarty and I had been joined and there were no secrets she could keep from me, nor I from her. When I thought of Moriarty I was thinking of *me*, and when Moriarty thought of me, she thought of herself. Was she aware of me within her, *my*, mind? Unless she was sleeping at the time, then I can perceive of no reason why she would not be aware of the fact. If she was asleep, and I could only hope that she slept deeply throughout the daylight hours, then I would surely have been there in her dreams.

Her secrets were my secrets and I knew them all. The Dolly Biters had been duped. Moriarty had marked them all down for death. Moriarty and the High Borns, the British government, the

Vatican; they intended to wipe the Dolly Biters from the face of the Earth. Eradicate the pestilence, destroy the heresy.

For the government, the motives were simple. Get rid of the turned vampires and rebuild the East End, knock down the rookeries and the slums and replace them with glittering towers of commerce, a testament to the Empire on which the sun would never, metaphorically, set. No more monsters in the darkness. They would send their policemen to fight the Dolly Biters alongside the Holmes Boys.

For the High Borns and the Vatican the cleansing of the Spitalfields streets had an even more sinister motivation – religious fervour. Both the High Borns and the Vatican believed that the turned vampires were an abomination, and although the High Borns were certainly no Christians, this mutual hatred for the girls of Spitalfields was enough to unite them on the battlefield, as it had done with the Muslims during the Crusades. The High Borns and the Vatican gave the Holmes brothers a werewolf, High Born blood, and the Christian relics to destroy the turned vampires.

"For no man has ever been turned vampire, only women who are weak of spirit and wallow in their baseness. You are charged with their destruction, for their dishonourable passions and unnatural hungers are an insult to the Creator."

And Moran. Moran. I became aware of the truth before I consciously searched for it. Moran knew the plan, she knew this was all a trap to ensnare and murder the Dolly Biters. When Raffles and myself had turned up unexpectedly at Moriarty's office, using that scheming intellect of hers, she had sent Moran to spy on us, to reassure us, to tell us to stay where we were. She was indeed a spy, a snake in the grass, Moriarty's eyes and ears in the East End. How had I been so blind to her true intents, to her connivings? She had been here for just two days, more or less, and not only had I not seen through her charade, I had fallen for her, had given my heart to her. Was this not the oldest tale ever told? Was

I not a female Samson betrayed by a short haired Delilah? What a fool I was. What a damned fool.

There was something else there too, something just out of reach. Something else that was just on the tip of my tongue. . .

I awoke on the floor of the bedroom, the vial upturned in my hand and the last of Moriarty's foul blood spilling across the floor-boards. That was that, then. There could be no pretence that I did not know the truth of the matter. Moran would find the empty bottle and would deduce what had happened here. I had to strike first.

Tears still streaking my cheeks, I crawled across the floor and dragged myself onto the bed. And there I lay in wait for that little fucker.

The minutes passed painfully and begrudgingly became an hour. As darkness slowly closed in on the city, my mind began to doubt itself, to wonder at the motivations of Moran, to wonder, perhaps, if she was not as much a victim of Moriarty as the Dolly Biters. She had been genuinely frightened by me at times over the past few days, and had on two occasions asked me, in all earnest, not to kill her. If she could be intimidated by me, imagine, my mind asked, how intimidated she would be by the fearsome Moriarty?

She was a young girl, eighteen years old, a girl who had worked as a prostitute in the rookeries of Whitechapel, experiencing the fear and trepidation that such a career carries with it as a matter of course. A young lesbian, confused by her desires, opting to wear men's clothing in an attempt to discover who she really was. Then to be taken in by a vampire, a *High Born* vampire, and put to work as a spy, a snitch, an informant. The girl's life, it would appear, was built on foundations of fear and confusion. Could I truly kill her for her betrayal? Had there even been a betrayal in the first instance? Perhaps - and oh! How my heart gave a glad little leap at the thought of it - perhaps she had fallen for me in a manner which was not part of Moriarty's plan? Perhaps she hadn't taken to my bed in order to better win my trust and the trust of the other Irregulars? Perhaps her kisses and her fingers and her tongue had been true.

We were both lost, I realised. Moran and myself. Rudderless ships drifting in the London night. I could save her. I could still save her in a way that I had failed to save Miss Ainsworth and the summer girl in the Diogenes Rooms.

Chapter Eight
The Cat Kissed

"Dark as the grave in here," said Moran as she opened the bedroom door and stepped inside. "Give me a moment, treacle, and I'll light a fire."

"I know," I said to the darkness, though I could see her well enough in the gloom, standing there in her bowler hat and overcoat, with fish and chips wrapped up in newspaper in one hand and a bottle of beer in the other.

"Sorry?" she asked. "You all right? You sound far away."

"I fucking know," I reiterated. "I know Moriarty's little plan, I know you all want us dead, I know you're a lying piece of shit."

She stopped in her tracks half way across the room, fish and chips and beer still in hand.

"What you talking about?" she asked with forced joviality in her tone. "You been on the gin?"

"I was going to kill you," I continued, ignoring her, "as soon as you opened the door. I was going to kill you."

"Darling," she said, a tremor in her voice, "you're scaring me." But this time, this third time, I was glad that I was scaring her. "Tell me what's happened. Who's been blabbing?"

"No-one's been *blabbing*!" I screamed, scornfully. "I drank Moriarty's blood, I saw it all! The Vatican, the Government, but most of all Moriarty being behind it all and you being sent along as a little spy, to feed us false information, and all the while the clock is ticking and the Holmes Boys and a werewolf, a *fucking werewolf,* are about ready to march down on us and kill us all. Will there be soldiers too? And policemen? I suppose there probably will. And you knew, you knew, and said nothing, and you kissed me and held me tight and still you said nothing."

Moran sat down on the side of the bed, still holding the food and the drink in her hands. "Well that's torn it," she said. "She'll kill me now, as likely as not."

"Who will?"

"Moriarty o'course. She's not very forgiving of them what lets her down."

"It's not your fault," I said, suddenly scared for my little tom boy. I should have been angry, should have said I couldn't care less if Moriarty sliced her up into little pieces and threw her remains into the filthy waters of the Thames. But I couldn't. I couldn't hide my feelings. She still, despite it all, was mistress of my heart. "She can't blame you for me drinking her blood."

"Shouldn't have left my bag here, like that," she said. "It was very lax of me, weren't it? Very lax. But I didn't think. I was so wrapped up in you, so enamoured by you, that I stopped thinking I s'pose. Only thing on my mind was fish and chips and getting back into bed with you." She laughed a little and wiped her nose on the sleeve of her coat. She looked very sad. "Silly me."

"Darling, no!" I said. "No, no, no! You have no idea how much you mean to me. These last few days with you have been the best days of my life. This isn't you fault, really it isn't. You're as much a pawn in all this as the rest of us." I placed an arm around her and pulled her close. She dropped her fish and chips to the floor and put a hand against my breasts. She was quivering beneath her coat.

"Listen," I said. "Let's run away. You and me. We can go any-where we want, just get away from the East End. There's going to be a war down here tomorrow night, with the Holmes Boys sozzled on Moriarty's blood and that sodding werewolf in tow, not to mention their gang and the police. It's going to be bloody carnage. We're better off out of it. What do you say? Let's just up sticks and go."

Moran lifted her head from my shoulder and looked up at me. "Just exactly how much do you know?" she asked.

"What do you mean? I know everything. Moriarty, the Holmes boys, the government."

"But it's you, Irene," she said and my blood, already as cold as damnation, ran colder still. "It's all happening because of you. You're the Cat Kissed. That's what Moriarty called you. The Cat Kissed."

"The Cat Kissed?" I asked. "I don't. . . oh. You mean the catalyst?"

"Yeah, something like that. She said you were the Cat Kissed that made all this happen. I thought you knew, when you said. . . ," her voice trailed off.

"Why? Why me?"

"Coz you're posh, treacle," she said. "You're the daughter of Sir Adler! It was all well and good when the Dirty Biters was just prostitutes and street girls from the East End. When it was just girls that nobody would miss. When the Dirty Biters was nobodies, they could be ignored, see? Brushed under the carpet, as it were. But you, you ain't nobody. You're the daughter of a knight, a sir. They couldn't allow that to happen. They couldn't allow posh ladies to get themselves turned into vampires. That wouldn't do, would it? No, they had to stop it, stop it all. That's why it's happening now and didn't happen years ago. What? You thought it was just a co-incidence that you arrived and then all this shit happens? You brought the shit here with you, treacle. And you can't leave or run away coz the shit will just follow you wherever you go. They've got to deal with you and kill everyone you've tainted. Me too, I suppose, now I think about it."

"It wasn't my fault," I said, the exact words I had used to describe Moran's actions. It wasn't your fault. There we were, two faultless angels who'd never harmed a fly in our lives! "He was a prince, a High Born prince. What could I do? I didn't ask to get turned!"

"No point crying over spilled milk," said Moran. "What's done is done."

"So what do we do now?" I asked. "Just sit here and wait to be killed tomorrow night?"

Moran leant forward and picked up her fish and chips. In darkness she unwrapped them and started to eat. "Like as not," she said, her mouth full of food. She had absolutely no manners. "Wonder what it's like? Being dead?"

I looked at her eating and remembered my own hunger. I could save her.

Putting an arm around her, I gently turned her face to mine. She smelt of warm grease and chips. "I can't let you die," I said. "Not like Miss Ainsworth and the girl in the toilet." And though she didn't know who Miss Ainsworth or the other girl was, I think she understood the implication for she dropped her food and opened her mouth to say something.

When I had been sixteen years old, Miss Ainsworth and I had spent a delightful summer's afternoon in Regent's Park. The day had been hot in a very un-English manner, and we had spent most of the day ambling along the gravel paths, picking daisies, and cooling ourselves with vanilla ice cream, known as Penny Licks. We even giggled together at the more forward young gentlemen who tipped their hats in our direction. As the afternoon wore on we decided to rest our aching feet, and sat beneath a tree looking out across the lake. Miss Ainsworth and myself had been laughing and joking, and she had been telling me fascinating stories about her friends and her family and her life outside of the Adler household. It was not unusual for us, on such occasions, to hold hands as sisters might hold hands, and so it was on that day. We sat beneath the tree holding hands, a smile never far from our lips, and in the heat of the day I found myself gently nodding off to sleep.

I can only have been asleep for ten minutes, no more, but when I awoke I found my head was resting on Miss Ainsworth's bosom, while she gently stroked my hair. I remember thinking that this was the most perfect moment of my life. The sun was warm, I felt so drowsy, the birds were singing in the trees, the swans were swimming on the lake, and Miss Ainsworth's gentle affections felt like the embrace of an angel. What harm could ever come to one so blessed as I? What harm?

I tried to pull Moran close to me so that I could kiss her and bite her at the same time, so she would know that this was no act of violence against her person, but an act of love. I would hold her close and stroke her hair as Miss Ainsworth had held me close and stroked my hair on that day in Regent's Park; that perfect moment. I could give such a gift, such a memory to Moran, a perfect moment of love and protection as I saved her life and turned her into a vampire like me.

But she fought back. She fought back with more strength and tenacity than I could have imagined. She punched and kicked and ripped at my hair, as I tried to embrace her and shush her and tell her that all would be well. Had I fought so intensely against my prince? Had I fought this hard for my humanity? Moran became a hell-cat, scratching and punching at me, pushing me away, fighting me with every last ounce of her strength. It did her no good, of course.

My teeth tore into her neck, her blood squirting across my face and across the room. I bit down deeply, ravenously, with hunger and love and affection, and still she fought my attentions. Why did she fight me so? Why did she resist? Miss Ainsworth had not fought like this, nor my summer girl. They had surrendered to my attentions. And yet here the one girl that I wanted to save, that I had no desire to kill, fought and she fought, and even when my fangs had pierced her neck and her blood was flowing and the venom should have been soothing her, still she fought on with punches against my back that grew weaker and weaker until with one last pitiful effort, they stopped.

With her sedated, I laid her on the floor and stripped her of her clothing, of her suit and her waistcoat and her shirt and her undergarments. She moaned incoherently as I took off my dress and laid upon her, both of us now naked, and continued to take the blood from her body. Laying upon her, I could feel her heart beating, fast and strong at first, angry and outraged, but slowing, becoming fainter with the passing of each second. At the last moment, when Death came to steal her away, I rolled from her and laid on my back, panting, looking up at the ceiling. Her heart continued to limp on, still alive though deep in coma. Her breathing was shallow and laboured. All I could do now was wait.

I clambered back onto the bed and watched her, my belly swollen with her sweet blood. Outside of this bedroom, cold night reigned and Raffles and the girls of Chicksand Street would be preparing themselves for the hunt. Here in the filthy bedroom on Ely Place, I laid on the bed all night long and waited for the miracle of rebirth to occur before me.

Her body was quite still and the colour had drained from her cheeks. Though the room was bitterly cold, no goosebumps rose on her skin. She was as a marble statue, a deathly replica of her former self. Within her veins, the vampire infection was spreading, multiplying, taking ownership.

Perhaps I should have picked her up then and taken her in my arms to the bed, so that the first thing she knew when she opened her eyes as a vampire was my love. But I felt strangely detached from myself now that the deed was done, now that the gift had been given, and all I could do was watch her from across the room. A strange malaise spread through my bones and soon I was asleep, while on the floor of the bedroom slept my little tom boy. Spitalfields' own Sleeping Beauties, waiting for Love's True Kiss to wake them.

I had not realised it, but it was the evening of December the thirty-first. Tomorrow was January the first, the first day of a new year, 1867.

* * *

Day broke over London Town, and across the frozen capital a cold sun burned from an ice blue sky. I awoke to a stinging in my eyes. A thin shaft of sunlight had broken through hastily drawn curtains and had illuminated the room, a small pool of light coming to rest not two feet from my beloved. This shaft of light resembled a thin finger, pointing towards Moran. Did this finger accuse me? Did it point out the awfulness of my crime? Or was it an acknowledgement from another, very different, Creator, who saw my craftsmanship and approved? Whether accusation or approval, the rogue shaft of light stung my eyes and I was forced to gingerly adjust the drapes, lest the sunlight burn my darling girl. With the curtains closed, the room fell into a dusty twilight. I knelt down next to Moran. She had not yet re-awoken, but during the course of the night she had drawn her body up into a foetal position, and had placed a thumb inside her mouth.

Her short, boyish hair was no longer the sweet chestnut colour of the previous day. The hair had grown several inches overnight and was now jet black interspersed with flashes of silver grey. Her ears were pointed and her short fingernails had grown in length and now resembled claws, as her fingers cupped her nose. With her thumb in her mouth, her lips were drawn back and I could see her teeth, white as ivory now and with two dangerous fangs clearly on display.

I reached a hand out to touch her, but drew it back. I dared not place a hand on her. She looked so different now. Was this still my Moran? She looked more like Moriarty now than the cheeky, street-wise East End tom who had toyed with my affections so. I simply sat beside her, both of us still naked, through most of the day and into the afternoon. Why did she not wake up? Why did it take so long? Had I, in my fit of passion, drained too much blood from her? Was she destined to die?

By mid-afternoon, I suppose it was, I had my answer. The fingers cupped around her nose began to twitch and the thumb fell from her mouth. Then a shudder spread through her body, like the ripple caused by a stone being thrown into a lake. I stood up, backed away, and sat down upon the bed, mesmerised.

Her eyes opened, twin points of red light in the fast gathering gloom of this winter's afternoon. I wanted to say something, to greet her, to ask her how she felt, but my voice failed me and besides, my words would have been pitiful and futile in the face of such dark wonder.

Her red eyes darted hither and thither for a full minute, perhaps trying to make sense of her surroundings, to understand where she was, as one might when waking from a dream, or a nightmare, that had seemed particularly real. Then her limbs began to move. She rolled over on to her side, and then up on to all fours like a dog. The black and grey hair that had grown so much overnight hung over her face, but through this hair I could still see her eyes blazing. She began to retch, terrible heaving sounds coming from her body, and then she vomited onto the floor the remains of last night's meal, her final supper of fish and chips.

"Oh my darling!" I cried, finding my voice at last. "It's all right! It's all right!"

She tried to stand up, but her limbs seemed longer than before and awkward to control. Her thin legs struggled to balance, a baby animal fresh from its mother's womb, and she fell back to the floor, slipping ungainly in her own expulsions.

I moved from the bed to offer her assistance, but as I approached she held out an arm, not to accept my help but to warn me away. She did not want my support, rather she struggled on alone, determinedly trying to find her balance.

At last she stood on two feet, and hunched over she looked around the bedroom. I placed an arm around her. Even to my vampiric touch, she felt cold and clammy. "Oh, Moran," I said, "it's all right. You're safe now. Nothing can harm us now, you'll see."

"You," she whispered.

"Yes, my darling" I said, "it's me. It's Irene."

"Done," she whispered.

"Done?" I said, not understanding.

"You done," she said, fixing me with her red eyes.

She was still confused, I decided. She needed more time to adapt to the change. "Shush now," I said, comforting her. "You just need some rest. Come, let us lie on the bed."

She pushed me with both hands in the chest, catching me by surprise and sending me sprawling across the room.

"What have you done?!" she screamed.

And suddenly, instantly, although I had perhaps known all along, suddenly and instantly I knew the true extent of my crime. I knew that what I had done was wrong, so terribly, terribly wrong. I sank to my knees. "Oh no, my darling," I said. "Don't be like that. We'll be all right. We're both vampires now. We can get away and live forever."

"What have you done?!" she cried again at me.

"It's for us," I said, "so we could be together forever. I can't lose you Moran, not like I lost Miss Ainsworth and the other girl. I need you to stay with me. Now we'll be together for always, can't you see?"

"You stupid bitch!" she cried, and fell to her knees also. We were both kneeling, facing each other, like we were part of some demonic prayer ritual. Her hands ran over her face, exploring her hair, her eyes, her pointed ears and fanged teeth. At each fresh discovery she gasped and sighed in disbelief. "No," she muttered to herself, "no, no, no."

"It's all right," I tried to console her, holding my hands outstretched to her but afraid to move towards her. "We'll be together, you and me. We'll leave London. Perhaps we shall go to Paris?"

"Paris?" she spat back at me.

The idea had entered my head, Miss Ainsworth had always wanted to go, and I had spoken the words immediately, without really thinking about them. But was it so insane? To leave London, make a fresh start in a fresh capital in a fresh country where nobody knew us and nobody wanted to kill us? I said as much to Moran, but she hissed back at me, "Fuck Paris and fuck you! What have you done?"

She looked down at her hands and noticed her fingernails. "No," she whimpered again. "Oh no."

Clambering unsteadily back up onto her feet, she staggered across the bedroom and rested herself up against a wall. There she proceeded to smash her head against the brickwork in a series of sickening thuds. I ran over to her, wrapped my arms around her, and dragged her down to the floor. She fought and struggled against my attentions, but I was the master of her and kept my arms and legs wrapped around her until, as the minutes passed, her fighting ceased to be replaced by pitiful tears. She cried into my shoulder, and she cried and she cried as though all the sorrow in the world was being channelled through her.

As night fell, she pushed me away gently and I acquiesced. Still naked, she stood and looked down at me. "I'm hungry," she said, simply.

"Oh yes," I replied, looking up at her as she stood over me, "you will be. Let us go out together, and we shall find you some food."

I began to stand up but she pushed me back down to the floor. "I'm leaving," she said, "on my own."

"But I can help," I protested.

"I don't want your help, Irene Adler," she said. "I don't want anything from you, not now, not ever. It's all over. Whatever it was that we shared, it's gone. I hate you. That's all. I hate you."

Calmly she walked over to the window, drew back the curtains to regard the night, and then, opening the window, she leapt from that upstairs bedroom and was gone. I rushed over and looked out, but she was nowhere to be seen. "Moran!" I wailed into the night but there was no reply.

Chapter Nine
The Battle of Brick Lane, January 1st 1867

I let her go. I let her disappear into the darkness of Spitalfields, and the surrounding alleyways and streets, alleyways and streets that she knew so well and I, hardly at all. In my stupidity and my blindness and my desire to create some manner of happy-ever-after for myself, I had turned Moran into a monster and in doing so, had lost her forever.

I looked around the room, at the dusty old bed that we had shared, at her clothes strewn on the floor, clothes that now lay limp as though the girl herself had simply vanished while wearing them, causing them to tumble forlornly to the ground. And there too, my dress. I picked it up and dressed myself.

There at my feet was Moran's vomit and blood and the un-opened bottle of beer that she had brought back with her food last night. I knelt down and dipped a finger into a small pool of her blood. It had thickened, become almost jelly-like. I tasted it. It tasted good. I dipped my finger in it once more and sucked the blood from my fingertip. I licked my lips. Her blood was still on them from the previous night. A final kiss, perhaps. A final kiss good night.

I felt so sad and broken that I had forgotten what night it was. It was the night that the ultimatum from the Holmes brothers expired. Now I heard shouts and cries from outside, and I remembered. I ran again to the window, the window from which Moran had leapt not ten minutes before, and looked out onto Spitalfields. I could hear gruff men's voices on the air, although it was difficult to tell exactly what was being shouted, and from the direction of Brick Lane a red glow in the darkness, as though fires had been lit. The war had started.

Leaping from the window, I sprinted down the alleyway and out onto Chicksand Street. Chaos reigned. Out of the doors of the few houses where the Dirty Biters lived tumbled dozens of girls. At the head of the street, emerging from Brick Lane, marched the Holmes Boys; top hats on their heads and clubs a-swinging. The girls rushed at the gang, which stood shoulder to shoulder like the Roman legions had done in the history books that I had read with Miss Ainsworth. As the girls leapt at them, the gang members swung their clubs, catching the girls on their skulls and in the face. The blows would have been lethal against humans, but these were vampires. The shuddering blows slowed them, but did not stop them. The girls slashed with long fingernails and ripped with their teeth, slowing the march of the gang, killing the first row of frock-coated thugs, and then the second.

From out of windows leapt more Dolly Biters, into the midst of the gang. Panic started to spread in their midst, and some of the blokes started to turn tail and run. The narrow Chicksand Street suited the girls more than it did the Holmes Boys. The panic spread and became pandemonium as the men backed away, turned and ran, pushing over their comrades, trampling on the wounded in their haste to escape, and all the while pursued by the wailing, slashing teeth of the Dirty Biters.

I saw Raffles and she saw me. She had blood dripping from her mouth, a strip of flesh hanging from her teeth. We looked at each other and an understanding passed between us. Whatever had happened over the past few days was history now, at least while we dealt with this threat. When push came to shove, we were still sisters, still the Brick Lane Irregulars. I ran at her side as we pushed the Holmes Boys back out into Brick Lane.

That had been a mistake.

Brick Lane was twice as wide as Chicksand Street, and here the Holmes Boys could regroup and reform, and there were their masters, Sherlock and Mycroft, urging them on, and beside them the werewolf. The werewolf. My God. I remembered Elsie trying to describe how big it was, but the words of that poor girl didn't do the beast justice. It was huge and its breath came off it in huge jets of steam, and it stank of death, and its eyes bore into you and seemed to steal away your very desire to live. At the sight of it, many of the girls stopped in their tracks, their courage deserting them, and began to back away. The impetus had been lost. Out here on Brick Lane the gang had more room to move and to yield their wooden clubs. I hadn't noticed before but the handles of the clubs had been sharpened to a point so that they resembled crude spears or stakes. Perhaps there had been no room to use them in the tight confines of Chicksand Street? But here on Brick Lane, now there was room aplenty.

Reforming into their Roman columns, the remnants of the Holmes Boys advanced on the girls, the clubs held out as spears so the whole contingent resembled some demonic hedgehog, spikes a-bristling. At the edge of the column marched the brothers, urging their men on with oaths and curses, their eyes black and dead and their muscles bulging from the High Born blood they had doubtless ingested. Moriarty's blood, I assumed.

And speak of the devil, there she was too, standing alongside the Holmes brother, advancing on the Dolly Biters with her own teeth bared. With her lifeless black eyes and her hooked nose and her talons for finger-nails, she looked like nothing more than a spider that walked on two legs.

The massed ranks of the Holmes Boys clashed with the Brick Lane Irregulars and the night was lit up with flashes of light as phosphorus flames engulfed the girls who had been struck in the heart with the sharpened wooden clubs. A stake to the heart a sure way to kill a vampire. The dying girls lit up the street like beacons in the night, urging the other girls to fight to avenge them.

If it had just been the gang members with their make-shift stakes, we might have prevailed. But the Holmes brothers and Moriarty and the wolf were ripping through the girls like mincers grinding beef. I saw Raffles being clubbed to the floor by at least six gang members. I ran over to join the fray, to engage in battle, but as I reached the spot where Raffles lay prone, the gang members backed away and left me alone. I could not understand what had happened; had I terrified them so much? I pulled Raffles to her feet. She patted me on the cheek as a way of saying thank you, smiled "What cheer, Irene!", then leapt back into the fray. I tried to join her, but each time I advanced, the Holmes Boys backed away, left me along, would not engage with me.

I stood in the middle of Brick Lane, a circle of emptiness around me as the blood-letting continued. No-one would fight me. If I moved backwards or forwards, the circle of emptiness followed me.

From the bottom of Brick Lane I heard whistles. It was the police. Rows and rows of police. I have no idea of the correct terminology; was there a battalion, a regiment, an *army* of them? I don't know, but what I do know was that there were dozens and dozens of them, perhaps a hundred or more, all advancing up Brick Lane. In their hands they carried not truncheons but wooden stakes. These police were not here to keep the peace, but to kill the Dirty Biters. The police reinforcements were too much, and together with the remnants of the Holmes Boys they began to push the girls back up the street, flashes of flames continuing to light up the night. No such fanfare heralded the humans' deaths; they died as dully as they had lived, their blood and guts spilling out of their fleshy bodies, over their nice frock coats and their smart blue uniforms.

By the sheer weight of numbers, the police and the Holmes Boys were owning the night.

I wanted to fight, but no-one would stand before me. "Fight me!" I bellowed angrily. "Fight me!"

"It must be awfully frustrating," said a voice behind me. I span around to find Moriarty, all six feet plus of her, towering over me, "but you see, none of these idiots would dare to fight you. You're far too valuable."

I had no idea what she was referring to, but here at least was a fight! I threw myself at Moriarty, intent on biting out her neck and sending her bitter blood spilling out onto the cobblestones of Brick Lane. She side-stepped me with ease, and as I lurched past her, she grabbed my hair and pulled me back, flinging me to the ground.

"Tut tut," she said, mockingly, "such a temper."

"Bitch!" I screamed, and launched myself at her once more. This time she caught me by the neck and lifted me off the ground. My feet kicked impotently against her.

"Where's Moran?" she asked, a genuine touch of concern in her voice. "What have you done with her?"

"Ha!" I laughed bitterly though it was difficult to speak. "Wouldn't you like to know?"

Moriarty threw me to the ground. "No matter," she said. "Plenty more where that one came from."

She turned on her heel and headed back into the battle, ripping out the throat of a Dolly Biter as she went. There weren't many girls left now. They were losing badly, and though the bodies of the Holmes Boys and the policemen littered the street, the werewolf, Moriarty, and Sherlock and Mycroft were making short work of the remaining Biters.

I saw Raffles kneeling in a corner, by the window of an old deserted bread shop. She was covered in blood, from head to toe or so it seemed, and it was impossible to tell which of the blood belonged to slain humans and which was her own. Her eyes were burning red and her fangs were elongated to such a degree that it almost gave her a comical look. The werewolf saw her and advanced on her, snorting through its snout, bloody saliva drooling from its gaping mouth. I climbed to my feet and launched myself at the beast. *It* would fight me, I was sure. I jumped on to its back, grabbing lumps of fur in my hands, and ripped off a mouthful of flesh from its shoulder. The beast roared in pain and its flesh tasted good. But at that moment hands ripped at my back also. It was Moriarty again. She pulled me from the beast and threw me clear across Brick Lane. "No!" she screamed. "Not you!"

My shoulders and the back of my skull crashed against a brick wall on the far side of the road, and I collapsed to the ground. I saw the wolf holding Raffles in its mouth, ragging her backwards and forwards like a terrier with a rat. Then it bit into her neck and Raffles disintegrated in a flash of fire and blood. Raffles was gone, most of the girls were gone, it was nearly over. I laid on the pavement and tried to get to my feet, but the wind was knocked out of me and my world was spinning.

I saw movement in the corner of my eye. Something was coming, emerging, from the boarded up shops and houses of Brick Lane, from the alleyways and darkened doorways. Something was coming. It seemed, at first, as though it was a giant creature that had been lying in wait behind the shop fronts and tenement façades. A giant creature with a hundred heads and arms and legs. But as it emerged out into the moonlight, the truth became apparent. It was girls, vampire girls, hundreds upon hundreds of them, emerging into the night air from the buildings of Brick Lane. I had always assumed that there were but a few dozen vampire girls living in Chicksand Street; that this had been the extent of the turned vampires in Spitalfields. But the truth had been there all along in clues I had half perceived during my stay in the East End. The Dolly Biters did not number dozens, they numbered hundreds, perhaps thousands. Chicksand Street had been but one aspect of the East End infestation, perhaps the more civilised (for want of a better word) aspect, for here came a hundred or more truly feral creatures.

They were young and small and thin, wearing rags for clothes. Pale spectral creatures, they looked emaciated, starving, and why shouldn't they? Oh, I had been blind all right. The young girls in rags that I sometimes saw, Raffles telling me that she'd eaten rats and worse on many occasions, Elsie telling me that it was difficult to eat if the big girls didn't share as they should. Here then were the dregs of the Dolly Biters; those too small and too weak to hunt humans. Those who lived on rats and mice and things that scurry about in the dark. Their bodies wasting away, their faces filthy, their hair matted and dropping out in clumps. But here they came now, oh yes, here they came now.

Encouraged by the sweet smell of fresh blood and, hopefully, a sense of sisterhood with the dress-wearing upstarts of the Brick Lane Irregulars, they came at the remaining police and Holmes Boys in an unstoppable wave. They were small and weak, but they were many. They pulled the last of the men to the floor, and it was difficult to discern which were the screams of death and which were the screams of victory. And still they came. They came and they took down the Holmes brothers as an army of ants might take down larger, more powerful prey. And they took the wolf, dragging him by their teeth up Brick Lane and back down again until they pulled off his legs and his arms and, finally, his head.

Moriarty tried to flee. Using her great strength and those talon-like fingernails, she began to climb up a wall, heading for the roof tops. But a little girl, filthy and half naked, grabbed the Madame's booted ankle and slowed her escape. Then a second hand joined the first, and a third and a fourth and a fifth, until Moriarty could resist no more and fell backwards into the baying mob below. I never saw her emerge again. But oh, there were such screams as could haunt even Lucifer's dreams.

I rested on my knees watching this wondrous, terrible sight. It was over. There were no men left, no Holmes Boys nor police; the Holmes brothers themselves had been ripped apart along with Moriarty and the wolf. Rivers of blood ran down the side of the road. The vampire girls had won, but I recognised none of them. These feral creatures had carried the day. But I, I was the only girl left on Brick Lane wearing a black dress with my hair piled up high. I was the only one.

And then there were more shrill whistles tearing apart the night air. More shrill whistles and more men, marching up Brick Lane. Would this night never end?

It was the army. Soldiers in uniform but wearing full-face helmets and metal gauntlets, carrying rifles the likes of which I had never seen. Their rifles spat fire, great waves of fire, and they sprayed this fire indiscriminately on all who stood, knelt, and laid on Brick Lane. They burned the bodies of the men and they burned the feral vampire girls as they fed. Any little vampire who had the wherewithal to fight back, found no way past the metal helmets and the metal gauntlets and the flames. They burned Brick Lane, all of it, to rid the city of our plague.

I was quite prepared, there and then, to die. I fully expected to die. It seemed only right that I should perish alongside the Chicksand Street girls and those other filthy little street vampires who had emerged from the shadows. The flames that surrounded me and the black pall of stinking smoke that served now as my sky spoke only of an ending to my adventure, a closing of my particular story book. I decided to stand up, to meet my fate as a lady.

"Hello treacle," said a voice behind me, and before I could turn around she had her hands around my throat. I do declare that I had more hands around my throat in the space of those few days than during the rest of my long, long life!

"Moran?" I tried to say. I threw my arms behind me and felt her. She was wearing a dress, like the ones that I wore. No suit, no overcoat. She was wearing a dress. I looked to the floor and caught sight of her feet, bare like my own.

"Look at what you've done!" she spat into my ear. "Look at it! This is your fucking work, you daft little bitch! This is the doom what a posh lady like yourself can bring down on the poor folk of the slums. Well, take a last look at it all, coz it'll be the last thing you ever bleedin' well see!"

I remember the scene so vividly. Thick smoke hung overhead, blotting out the night sky. The buildings all around us were on fire, blazing away, windows cracking and wood collapsing, while on the pavement and the street the bodies of men were burning; it seemed they had not died so dully after all. Rivers of fat were now running down the street where a few minutes earlier it had been rivers of blood. The flames generated a terrible heat. In the midst of an English winter, Brick Lane was hot enough to melt the lead in the window panes. If there was a hell, surely this was it.

And stepping through this madness, the soldiers with their fire guns, steadfastly avoiding us for some reason.

I remember it all. This scene is seared into my memory, for, you understand, it was the last thing that I ever saw. Moran dug her fingers into my eyes and she plucked them out, and so intense was the pain that, vampire or no, I fell to the ground in agony, and writhed amongst the flames. She took my eyes, the little bugger. She took them away with her, and she left me there to face eternity blind and alone.

* * *

"This is her, sir."

"Well, I'll be blessed, so it is! It's Sir Adler's daughter, sir!"

"'Ere, what's happened to her eyes?"

"Stone the crows, she ain't got no eyes, sir!"

Voices around me, men's voices, young men's voices and then an older gruffer voice. "Well don't just stand there, man. Call for the ambulance cart. Let's get her out of here."

"Yes sir. Right away sir."

"She looks a right old state, sir. Think she'll live?"

"If she one of those vampire creatures then I'm sure she'll pull through. Although I can't say the same for those medic johnnies if they don't hurry up with that blasted ambulance!"

"Quite a night, sir."

"Yes, corporal. Quite a night. Not experienced anything like it since Bombay in '57."

* * *

I've had many years to replay in my mind the events of that night, and to try and decipher who knew what and who was ultimately responsible for the massacre on Brick Lane. When I try to make sense of it all, I find that I cannot. The only explanation I can come up with that satisfies me is that they were all a bunch of cunts. Every last cunting one of them.

* * *

I was taken initially to a military field hospital that had been set up in Whitechapel. Here they sedated me, stitched up the holes where my eyes had been, swathed my poor battered head in bandages, and sent me on my way. The sweet smell of human blood had been strong in that place.

My next stop, still that same night, was Colney Hatch Lunatic Asylum in Barnet. This place did not smell so sweetly of blood, rather it stank of bleach and carbolic soap and tears. The asylum was to be my home for nearly a century and a half, where they prodded and poked me, took endless samples of my blood, electrocuted me, tried to drown me in ice-cold water, drilled holes into my brain, and, on occasion, raped me. All, I'm sure, in the pursuance of science.

I was moved from room to room, from laboratory to laboratory, in a specially constructed cart that I was strapped into, with a muzzle around my mouth and a straightjacket restraining my arms. They were terrified by me, mesmerised by me, intent on unlocking the mysteries of my existence, yet afraid that at any moment I would strike them all down dead. Since I was captured (or perhaps that should be *rescued*?) and taken away, I have spent twenty-three of most every twenty-four hours with a muzzle strapped around my face. I am eighteen years old, blind, lost and alone, and yet still they fear me so.

It was my name, that and my father's money, that saved me, I have no illusions regarding that. I am sure that during his lifetime he made some very generous donations to the asylum, and even after his death perhaps he left behind a legacy to ensure that I was kept alive, while the endless tests conducted on me no doubt aided the Empire's war effort, helped to combat human diseases, that kind of nonsense.

Then in the mid-1990s, the asylum was closed and I was moved to a new building in the heart of London. Here things took a rather delightfully sinister turn. I had, up to that point, been fed bottles of blood. Where the bottles of blood had originated from, I never asked nor did I care. Those who looked after my needs and experimented upon me seemed more concerned with how my body worked and what my abilities were. My feeding was a dirty little side-show that they tried not to concern themselves with. But in my new location, the feeding was *all* they were concerned with! They fed me live prey for the first time in one hundred and thirty years, and they recorded it on machines that I am led to believe can capture real life and replay it over and over again. They monitored my heart rate as I fed, took samples of my venom, and measured how long it took for the prey to die.

I knew nothing of their science and their machines. I knew only of love. And on that subject I kept my lips tightly shut, more tightly shut that their muzzles could ever hope to keep them.

In my new location, the Gherkin or Cucumber I believe it is referred to by amused Londoners, the scientists were not so much concerned with aiding mankind and combating disease. They appeared more concerned with how to create more of me. Create an army of me. It made me smile. I could still vividly remember those feral little vampires emerging from Brick Lane. I could still remember Raffles and Elsie and Francis. They didn't strike me as the kind of creatures that took orders from scientists with clipboards. I tried to tell the scientists this, but they never listened. They were too full of their own importance and their own intelligence to listen to an old Victorian relic like me. After all, what could I possibly teach them?

Epilogue
City of Dreadful
Night 2

London, 20??

I stand before the huge plate glass window that looks out over the great city of London and I wonder where she went. Where did Moran run to with my eyes? Did she live, did she survive, is she still out there somewhere, cursing me, loving me, wishing we could still be together so that she could kill me or love me and spend the rest of eternity with me?

Is she dead or does she still live?

I stand before the huge plate glass window that looks out over the great city of London and I wonder, I wonder of many things; not just Moran, but of the world, of the universe. Of London.

I cannot see, of course, the scene that is laid out below me. But if I place my hands against the glass, I can *feel* it. London vibrates below me. She prickles and dances with this thing called electricity. I lick my lips, savouring the sumptuous blood of the woman who sits quite dead on the chair in the middle of the room, the ropes that bind her now superfluous to requirements. The scientists will be here momentarily, to spirit the body away, give me my sedative, remove me back to my room.

But for now I stand before London and I wonder what the great city must look like. From conversations I have had with my captors, and I have been quite friendly with some of them, *particularly* the female ones, there are now horseless carriages that traverse the streets, electric lights that replaced the gas-lamps of my day, magic lantern machines that talk in the corners of every room in every house, and other such machines that contain the sum of all human knowledge but are used, in the main, for more frivolous purposes. All of this I do not, and cannot, truly understand. My only concern now, and it is a strange concern that catches me unawares, is not escape or revenge nor to find out what happened to Moran and French kiss her once more upon the lips. No, my only concern now is that we, the Dolly Biters of the old East End, are not forgotten.

I am told that the streets have changed so much, I wonder if Chicksand Street or Ely Place even still stand? Does the house still exist where Moran and I stayed, to keep her safe from the unwanted attentions of those unruly Biter girls? Where she ate pies and fish and chips and where, ultimately and predictably, I ate her? Or our little home on Chicksand Street? The home where Raffles gave me the tongue that I liked, and, less pleasingly perhaps, where she humped my leg on that awful night. It makes me smile now to think of her humping away on my leg in front of the other girls. At the time it seemed so horrific. Now it simply makes me smile.

The Diogenes Rooms. Does it still stand? Is there still a toilet cubicle where I killed the summer girl? Is there a plaque on the wall telling all of the terrible deed that was committed on that spot during the Christmas season of 1866? Or has it been knocked down, demolished, cast aside in the name of progress?

Did they rebuild Brick Lane after the fire? Are we forgotten? Do your history books speak of us? Do mothers frighten their children with tales of the Dolly Biters and their fearsome ways? Or are we as nothing? Erased from the memory? Specks of sand scattered to the horizon by the winds of time?

Questions without answers.

I cross the room and stroke the hair of the dead woman. She smells so nice, like honey and cream and lazy afternoons spent in the park. She smells so nice. She smells like Miss Ainsworth. But then, they all do.

Book 2
Miss Katie Bell, Victorian Vampire

or A True & Accurate Account of my Crimes & Adventures as a

Lesbian Vampire in the Spitalfields & Whitechapel Areas of

London, in the Year of Our Lord 1888 & Beyond

A Word From the Transcriber

Katie's language is terrible. She swears incessantly and the form of English that tumbles from between her ruby red lips would be unintelligible to most English speakers in the 21st Century. For the most part she speaks a combination of Cockney rhyming slang and Polari. The reader may at least be aware of the existence of Cockney rhyming slang, whereas Polari may be a complete unknown. Without getting into too much detail, Polari was a form of slang much favoured by homosexuals, criminals, and theatrical types throughout the latter Victorian period and up until the 1950s. Elements of rhyming slang found its way into Polari, elements of Polari have found their way into spoken English, and a true ne'er-do-well of London's East End would have been able to 'mix-and-match' rhyming slang, Polari and English with ease; the idea being, of course, to create a form of spoken English that would be a mystery to any law enforcement officers who just happened to be listening in on their conversations.

I remember asking Katie to slow down her speech on one of the first occasions that I met her. She smiled a little sadly and said that the only people who really understand her these days are some of the old girls in the markets 'up East' (by which she means the East End of London). I was suddenly struck by how sad her plight is. She is a relic, a fossil almost, from a by-gone era, who, due to the nature of her condition continues to traverse the years like a demonic time traveller. Always on the outside looking in, and yet entirely reliant on the human population around her who serve as her food supply.

Her language is archaic, her clothing antiquated, but even so there is a rare beauty to her. To the casual observer of course she looks 18 years old, it is one of the trademarks of her condition. And yet her eyes are old. She has an old woman's eyes. And her skin is pale, so pale, and puts me in mind of fine bone china, so delicate that at the merest touch you worry that it may shatter.

Like all vampires (for that is the condition that afflicts Katie), she has the ability to mesmerise with her gaze and her words. Many-a-time I found myself falling under her thrall as she spoke, and this even with all the *effing and blinding* (as she would call it) and the rhyming slang and the Polari. To hear her speak this half- forgotten form of English with her native East End accent is a rare privilege indeed.

Which brings me back to my original point, a point I seem to have wandered somewhat from (this happens a lot when I talk about Katie – I find myself meandering as though still under her thrall). No, my main point is this: I have 'tidied up' her language to make it intelligible for you, dear reader. However, I do hope that I have managed to maintain some of the original charm and, yes, innocence of her spoken language. A flavour, as it were. Just so you understand that Katie Bell is a girl from the Victorian slums of London, and not the bleedin' Queen or nuffink.

Paul Voodini
London, England. December 2013.

London, 1888

26th January 1888, The Lawn Tennis Association is formed.

13th February 1888, the first edition of The Financial Times goes on sale.

3rd April 1888, London prostitute Emma Elizabeth Smith is brutally attacked and killed by three men in Whitechapel.

June 1888, Annie Besant organises the London match- girls' strike.

7th August 1888, the body of London prostitute Martha Tabram is found; a possible victim of Jack the Ripper.

31st August 1888, the mutilated body of London prostitute Mary Ann Nichols is found, perhaps the first victim of Jack the Ripper.

8th September 1888, the mutilated body of London prostitute Annie Chapman is found, possibly the second victim of Jack the Ripper.

27th September 1888, the 'Dear Boss' letter signed by 'Jack the Ripper', the first time the name is used, is received by London's Central News Agency.

30th September 1888, the bodies of London prostitutes Elizabeth Stride and Catherine Eddowes are found. They are considered to be Jack the Ripper's third and fourth victims.

2nd October 1888, the dismembered body of a female is found in three separate locations around London.

9th November 1888, the heavily mutilated body of Mary Jane Kelly is found. She is considered the fifth and final victim of Jack the Ripper. A number of similar murders take place over the following months, but police attribute these to copy-cat killers.

17th December 1888, The Lyric Theatre opens in London.

Part One: "Poppy"

Chapter One

The first I knew of the vampire was his filthy great hands all over my mouth and around my waist, his fangs digging deep into the soft flesh of my neck. I struggled of course, tried to scream, but I knew right away that the game was up. It was my own bleeding fault for wandering up a darkened alleyway at eight o'clock at night, and that's exactly what I told myself as he dragged me to the floor and straddled me. 'Katie my girl,' I thought, 'you've no-one to blame but yourself. What will your mam say when she hears you've been walking up alleyways on your way home from work, when you knows all too well that she always says to stick to the pavements and the gas lamps?'

So there I was, lying on my back on the cobblestones, my pretty winter coat getting covered in rain water and mud and goodness knows what else, with this bloke, whoever he was, biting and sucking and licking away at my neck, and all I could think about was what my blooming mam was going to think of me. No sense of priorities me, and I've always been the same. Everyone I've ever known has always said so; the school teachers with their shouting, the headmistress with her cruel whipping of my outstretched palm as she told me that I spent too much time away with fairies; my dear old parents too, God love them, scalding me for not doing my jobs around the house and finding me instead lying on my bed looking at some picture book that I'd found discarded at the roadside. Away with the fairies, that was me all right, and maybe that was why I hadn't even noticed this particular sharp toothed gentleman until he was quite literally on top of me.

Mind you, in a funny kind of way, it was precisely my mam's fault that I found myself in such a predicament. See, it was down to her that I got the job in the hat shop, or *milliner's* if you prefer to use the fancy title, in the first place, and if it weren't for having that job I wouldn't be needing to walk home at such a late hour through such a darkened alleyway.

So you see, it wasn't really my fault. It wasn't really my fault at all.

But here I am, babbling away, and we ain't even been properly introduced as yet. I do apologise. If you'll permit me, I'll start again. Hello. My name is Katie Bell, *Miss* Katie Bell, although everyone nowadays just calls me Snow, for reasons I shall explain as we goes along. I'm eighteen years old and I'm a vampire. But I wasn't always a vampire, as you've probably already gathered. I used to be human, just like you, and I used to work in a hat shop, but that was before that fateful night in the alleyway when I was walking home from work.

The job in the hat shop was all right I suppose, and yes, I know, I was lucky to have a job at all that didn't involve climbing up chimneys or slaving away in some factory somewhere. But even so, being a general shop girl was no laughing matter. I had to be there at eight o'clock in the morning and didn't finish again till eight o'clock at night, and add on to that the twenty-minute walk either way and you can begin to understand why my blooming feet didn't half ache when I finally got around to taking off my boots and pulling off my stockings at the end of the day.

And while I was at the shop I had to bow and scrape to the customers, take their hats and coats, offer them a cup of tea, show them through to the fitting room, sweep and dust round twice a day, and then look after the needs of the ladies in the back, the actual hat makers. If they needed a cup of tea, I had to make it, if their floor got covered in bits of twine and material off-cuts it was down to me to sweep it all up and separate the waste from the off- cuts what could be used again. And woe betide me if I did anything wrong; if I didn't hurry up with someone's cup of tea or if any dust was spotted on any shelves or, worst of all, if I'd put any usable off-cuts into the waste bin. Then you can guarantee I'd be walking home in the dark with a flea in my ear. So you see, when that vampire grabbed hold of me in the alleyway, there was a very silly and wicked part of me that was quietly pleased. 'This'll show them,' I thought. 'When they find my body in the morning, then they'll all be sorry for the way they treated me!' And of course, while he was sucking and guzzling all over my naked neck, it gave me chance to put my poor aching feet up.

Now I know what you're thinking. How can I be so bleeding blasé about it all? After all, a young girl like me, a tender and in-nocent little eighteen-year-old, being jumped on by a great hulk of a bloke in a darkened alleyway is no laughing matter, and you'd be right of course, it is no laughing matter. But, and now I'm talking after years of experience and looking back on the situa-tion through a very different set of eyes, fear and terror can play funny games with the human mind, and at that particular in-stant I wanted to do nothing more than pet his head and say 'Slow down sweetheart, no need to rush'. That's awful, isn't it? I'm clearly what my mam would have described as a 'nasty piece of work'. Well let me tell you, I was to go on to do plenty more awful things after that night, and awful things that would make those evil thoughts seem positively saintly by comparison.

And so, with pleasant pictures being painted in my head of the drama and sorrow the discovery of my poor lifeless body would induce, I blacked out and knew nothing about anything until I awoke again in the morning, still lying on the filthy cobble-stones, surrounded by a pool of my own blood.

I reckon he meant to kill me, to drain me dry and leave my empty husk lying there in the alleyway, but for whatever reason I survived. Maybe he got disturbed while he was going about his business, or maybe he wasn't as hungry as he first thought, his eyes being bigger than his belly. Whatever the reason, I survived and by the morning the old mortal me was long gone. No more

Paul Voodini

working in that hat shop for me, thank you very much. That old life had died in the alleyway, even if I hadn't. I was now a vampire, the vampire infection or germ or virus or whatever it is being transferred to little old me by means of a frank and informative exchange of bodily fluids, namely his saliva and my blood. Of course I didn't know all of this at the time; I'd go on to learn the hows and wherefores and how's-your-fathers later on. For now, I had enough on my plate waking up in that alleyway, dishevelled, filthy, and confused.

The sun was rising and it blinded my eyes and hurt. I knew instinctively that the sun was bad for me, so I dragged myself into the darkest corner of the alleyway, curled up into a ball, and waited for evening to arrive. What folk passing by in that alleyway must have thought of me, I've no idea. They probably thought I was just some old lashings sleeping off the gin from the night before. The old East End was littered with lost souls, down on their luck, and I suppose I must have fitted right in, what with my pretty winter coat now all dirty and my dainty little neck covered in dried blood. I ignored the sound of passing footsteps, and tried to sleep as best I could.

As the evening started to arrive and darkness spread across the city, my senses began to come alive. I climbed to my feet to find that my body didn't ache, my mind was alert, and the wound in my neck had healed. I think I was more than a little confused, and who wouldn't be? I was unsure about what had happened to me, that's true, but at the same time a sense of elation the likes of which I'd not experienced in a very long time began to come over me. I wanted to run, to laugh, to jump. I felt full of energy, like I could run a mile, and my poor old feet didn't ache no more. I positively skipped out of that alleyway and onto the main road.

There were plenty of folk around and those what noticed me had a look on their faces like they thought I was off my rocker. They all took a wide berth around me, perhaps imagining that I was contagious or something. I can't in all honesty say that I blame them. My clothes, as you already know, were dirty and torn, my hair must have looked a right old mess, and I was, as I said, caked in blood. Well, that might have been the first night that I'd walked the streets of London caked in blood, but I promise you, it wasn't to be the last.

My first thought was to head home to my mam and my daddy. I still lived at home with them, and so I suppose it was perfectly natural for me to want to go home, to tell them I was all right, and to make amends for making a right old mess of my best work clothes. As I said, despite the euphoria, I was still confused. I didn't know what it all meant. Home was all I knew, and so towards my home I headed.

A light drizzle began to fall from the fast darkening sky and I remember how cool and sensual it felt against my face. I'd never known before, or never noticed more like, that rain could feel so good. It was a miracle that those around me, the people hurrying by, just didn't seem to appreciate – perfectly formed globules of moisture falling from the sky above and landing on my face, in my eyes, my hair. What a wonder! Why ever had I not noticed this before? And the smell – a gloriously clean, refreshing smell, like the heavens were cleaning the very air around me. I stopped walking and laughed. With my head tilted upwards, I let this wonderful rain, little more than drizzle really, fall onto my skin, and with this moisture, some of the dried blood around my cheeks and lips began to loosen and drip down into my mouth. The blood fell onto my tongue and I fell to the pavement, screaming my little head off in agony and in ecstasy.

My mouth exploded in pain as though a dozen wasps were stinging at my gums, and my mouth filled with saliva enough to make me gag. I didn't know it at the time, but it was my fangs extending for the first time. My stomach cried out in torment, and I felt a hunger like I had never felt before. I was overtaken by the desire to feed, a desire so strong that I was powerless to resist it.

I smelled to air. I was surrounded by prey. They were all around me, looking at me, pointing, or hurrying passed. But these were just people, men and women. What was I saying? They weren't my food. Were they?

I listened intently. I was sure I could hear their hearts beating, the blood rushing through their veins, the air being sucked into their lungs. My stomach cried out for sustenance. I heard a heart beating, smaller this time, faster. Sniffing the air, this one was different, it didn't smell like people. I glanced around. The side road opposite. The heart was beating in the side road opposite.

Springing to my feet, I legged it across the road causing the driver of a hansom cab to swear and curse at me. My own turn of speed astonished even me. I had no sooner got the notion of running across the road into my noggin, than I was there in the very side road, and there was the small beating heart that smelled different from the people around me. It was a cat. It saw me, its eyes wide, and it stopped what it was doing and froze. It seemed to be trying to decide whether to flee or stay put, so I pounced on it and put the matter to bed. I had it in my hands, it struggled but I was superior in all aspects; speed, strength, tenacity, and teeth. I bit into its neck. It wailed once, like the wailing of a bleeding lost soul it was, and then its body went into convulsions as I began to drain the blood from its body.

The hot, sticky blood poured down my throat and my own body entered a spasm, but a spasm of vitality and of ecstasy. I felt the life force of the cat enter my body, physically felt its soul combine with mine to create something new and strong and divine, and I felt insanely alive and indestructible. Detaching my jaws from the now dead cat, I lifted my head up to the sky, the drizzle still falling upon me, and I screamed in elation, "Fuck me backwards!"

There was a very respectable young woman standing not ten yards away from me and she was screaming. At her feet lay her husband, or maybe he was her beau, and he'd fainted dead away at the sight of dear old me. I opened my mouth to tell the young lady to hush, to tell her it was all right, nothing to concern herself with, but as I parted my lips, blood poured down my chin and down the front of my already filthy coat. I looked at myself, blood soaked, filthy, hair all over the place, holding a dead cat in my hands, and I thought to myself, 'Well Katie, there's no real surprise that this respectable young lady is screaming at you.

You must look a right proper sight and no mistake.' So I threw the cat at her, which only caused her to redouble her efforts in the screaming stakes, and legged it down the road as fast as a whippet.

I hid in another alleyway and waited for all the fuss to die down. Alleyways were to play, as you'll soon gen for yourself, quite a large part in my life from that moment on; whether it be hiding up them or chasing prey down them, there always seemed to be a darkened alleyway involved somewhere along the line. So I hid up this particular alleyway, and eventually, after a minute or two, the screaming lady stopped screaming and staggered off, back towards the main road, leaving her poor husband still sparko on the cobblestones. Another two minutes passed and then he finally came to his senses, climbed to his feet, and wandered off like he'd had a skin full of gin. Then just as I'm starting to think that it may be safe for me to emerge from the alleyway, and with my still grumbling stomach making my eyes look favourably upon the warm corpse of that cat, a brace of coppers come running down the road, blowing their whistles and making a right old racket. So I took a step or two back into the shadows of the alleyway and waited till they'd passed.

Then I heard a voice behind me. "You're new." That's all she said. "You're new." I span around and there were six of them, all girls, and all, by the looks of it, around the same age as me. Well, I'd heard all the rumours that were circulating about gangs of girls roaming the streets, robbing people just like they were blokes. Gangs with names like the Forty Elephants, and I thought to myself, 'Katie my girl, out of the frying pan and into the fire'. I was just about to tell them that I didn't have no money for them to purloin and certainly no jewels to speak of, and I was also starting to wonder why dear old filthy and blood soaked me hadn't given them the willies, when the first girl piped up again, "It's all right, my darling girl. You're among your own kind now. We can help you. Come with us."

And she was the most beautiful girl I'd ever seen in my life.

Chapter Two

Her name was Poppy, and in her white dress and white shawl and with her blonde hair clipped short she looked like nothing less than an angel, come to deliver me from the sheer bloody madness that my life had become over the last twenty-four hours.

"Not another mouth to feed?" said one of the other girls, a girl with long, curly red hair.

"We can't just leave the sweet thing here," said Poppy. "She's one of us and if I'm not much mistaken, she's only been turned a day or two. If we leave her here she'll be dead by this time tomorrow, I promise you. Remember what condition you were in when I first found you, Little Red?" Little Red, the girl with the long curly red hair was Little Red, although to look at the amount cleavage poking out of the top of her dress, 'little' didn't seem like a particularly accurate description. "So of course she's coming with us, aren't you darling girl?" Poppy turned to look at me with compassion in her eyes and I just started to cry. It all caught up with me and it was too much to bear; the vampire in the alleyway, the elation and the wonder and the fear of the changes within me, not having been home since I left for work yesterday morning (was it just yesterday? It seemed so long ago), the dead cat, the screaming lady, the police and their bloody whistles, and now this, this angel come to take me away to safety. I just cried and Poppy took me in her arms and I rested my face on her shoulder and blood from my mouth smeared her pretty white dress and she didn't mind one bit, not one blooming bit.

They lived, all six of them, in what was rather grandly known as a lodging house on Flower and Dean Street in Spitalfields. It was called a lodging house but it was really just a doss house, a run down terraced affair owned by an old shyster called Mr. Baginski who assumed that all six girls in his establishment were prostitutes. This suited the girls just fine because as long as the rent got paid on time old Baginski turned a blind eye to any odd goings-on in the house, of which there were plenty as I'm sure you're able to imagine. The lifestyles of the local prostitutes, and all the houses along Flower and Dean Street were filled with prostitutes and their pimps, fitted in perfectly with the needs of the six girls who were, in case you haven't already guessed, all vampires. Like the local three-penny-uprights, the vampire girls I'd fallen in with needed to sleep all day and be active all night. It was the perfect alibi, six vampires hiding in plain sight amongst the dregs of humanity.

And of course Spitalfields in those days *was* full of the dregs of humanity; vagrants, down and outs, lushingtons, the lost and the lonely. The perfect food, I would soon discover, for this little vampire coven. Spitalfields was overflowing with people who would not be missed, and for whom a quick death at the hands of a pretty young female vampire was, in all honesty and without wanting to sound overly flippant, a blessed relief.

That first night they took me to the lodgings on Flower and Dean Street and tucked me into a meagre little bed comprising simply of a mattress on the floor and a few linen sheets. Poppy unbuttoned my dirt and blood splattered dress and pulled it tenderly from my suddenly very weary body. Poppy said they'd sort me out with new clothes the following evening, but for now I should rest. Wearing just chemise and drawers I climbed beneath the cool sheets, and felt no shame for these perfect strangers seeing me dressed so immodestly.

It may have been on the top floor of a rotten dive in the arse-end of the British Empire, but nothing had ever felt so welcoming before in my entire life, I swear, as that filthy mattress and those meagre sheets did on that night. I allowed my body to sink into the thin mattress and let all the worries, thoughts and concerns drift out of me. I handed my welfare over completely, instinctively, to Poppy. My stomach was still grumbling, but Poppy said that it would have to wait till later, and that for now I needed rest and recuperation more than anything else. I trusted her. She was right. She knew what to do.

While I lay in bed, Poppy sitting by my side, cleaning up my face with a damp cloth and gently stroking my hair, the other girls left again. The night was still young, and as I learned later, there was hunting to be done. Poppy stayed by my side though, humming a lullaby, and watching over me, blood from my mouth still staining her pretty white dress like a careless kiss upon her breast, and her ruby red lips smiled at me occasionally.

"You're so pale and your hair is so black," she whispered. "You're like little Snow White. And there are seven of us now that we've found you, just like the little men in the fairy tale, so I suppose it's all quite apt. Perhaps I think I'll call you Snow White from now on. No, not Snow White, just Snow. That's it. That's you. My dearest Snow. Sleep now my dearest Snow and let me watch over you."

And so I drifted off to slumber, a new vampire in a new home with a new name. And to think, twenty-four hours earlier I'd been sweeping and dusting and making cups of tea for lady hat makers. I certainly hadn't seen this coming. Talk about a change in circumstances. What would my mam say if she knew? Nothing good, I'll wager.

While I slept I had the strangest dreams. I dreamt that I was a pearl diver like the ones you read about in those faraway books, holding my breath and swimming beneath the waves in search of treasures. But there were monsters in the water, lurking in shadows and hiding behind rocks. Monsters with tentacles that grabbed me around my bare ankles and pulled me down towards their mouths, mouths filled with sharp teeth and long tongues that wrapped around my legs and crawled between my thighs. The tentacles and the tongues poked and sucked in areas that to be honest, being a good girl, I'd never had poked or sucked before. It wasn't an entirely unpleasant experience, I must admit, and small ripples of pleasure and shame resonated through my naked body. If it wasn't for the fact that I was underwater and was desperately holding my breath, I think I could have quite happily floated away with the caressing water currents and allowed the tentacles and the tongues to have their wicked way with poor old me. But I couldn't breathe, I was drowning, my body a battlefield between pleasure and pain. I wanted to stay and be embraced by the monsters, but I had to escape if I wanted to live. I struggled to free myself from the grip of the monsters, tried to swim back to the surface, but the tentacles and the tongues held me fast, exploring my body, pulling me deeper, and I knew that I was going to drown in the deep blue ocean or succumb entirely to the pleasure of my body's climax or both.

I woke with a start and didn't know where I was. My first thought was that I was at home, with my mam and daddy asleep in the next room. Then my surroundings came into focus and reality slowly dawned. It was clearly morning as a single, small shaft of light was penetrating between the heavy black drapes that the girls had pulled across the bedroom window. I looked around the room and noticed two more mattresses on the floor with bodies asleep upon them. So the girls must have returned from their hunt during the night as I slept. It was apparent that not all of them slept in the same room, which of course made sense; the house, for saying it was a crumbling terrace, was large enough for all the girls to share the rooms between them in ones and twos.

I knew from experience that sunlight was bad and that daytime was for sleeping. Just looking at the thin shaft of light arrogantly poking between the drapes stung my eyes and made them water. Although the room was bathed in darkness, my vampire senses were now keen and I could make out most of the room's details. A dressing table, a chair, a bowl filled with water standing on a stool, a collection of pretty dresses hanging on a clothes rail.

My stomach grumbled and I felt incredibly hungry. Poppy had said that she would find some food for me. I wished she would wake up and come to see how I was, but it was daytime. Would she sleep all day? I was so hungry that I didn't think I could wait until evening fell once more.

As I lay in my bed, a figure on one of the other mattresses stirred and sat up. It was Little Red, her curly red hair falling over her shoulders and half way down her back. She pulled back her sheets and stood up, and I noticed to my horror and fascination that she was naked. I pulled my sheets up to the bridge of my nose, fearful that she would catch me staring at her but unable to look away. The swelling of her large breasts and the curves of her hips held me mesmerised. I'd never seen anyone, not even my own mam, fully, completely naked before. Beneath the sheets I felt my fangs extending and saliva began to fill my mouth. My body gently trembled, a combination of fear, desire and hunger.

Sounds from the outside daylight world filtered through into this darkened doss house bedroom. Horses' hooves on cobblestones, a child singing, a newspaper boy selling *the Strand*, a market trader hawking his wares.

Little Red walked on bare feet across the floor of the bedroom, as graceful and as artful as a fox sneaking up on a chicken coop. She stopped at the second mattress and knelt down beside it. She pulled back the covers to reveal Poppy laying on her back, head turned away from me, as naked as Little Red. I saw Poppy's breasts and her shoulders and her exposed neck, the brutal short cut of her blonde hair a bewilderingly sharp contrast to the elegance of her lithe body. Little Red placed a hand on one of Poppy's breasts and began to slowly caress it. Then she stopped and looked at me. She had seen me, had seen me staring at her, and yet still I could not drag my gaze away. I held my breath like a pearl diver, not daring to move. Little Red smiled craftily and blew me the smallest of kisses. Under the covers my fangs ached and my body trembled. Little Red laid down next to Poppy and began to kiss her neck, her own fangs exposed and nipping playfully at Poppy's vulnerable skin. Poppy stirred into wakefulness and moaned gently.

One thing I quickly learned as a vampire: our hearts still beat and our blood still circulates, else how would a wooden stake kill us so readily if our hearts were merely dead pieces of meat? No, our hearts beat all right, and there on that mattress my heart beat hard and fast enough to make me think that all the girls in the house must be able to hear it.

As she awoke, Poppy placed her arms around Little Red's back and turned her head to kiss Little Red on the lips. They kissed deep and long, and began to make a low, guttural moaning noise, the likes of which I'd never heard before, not even when, through the thin walls of my home, my *old* home, I had heard mam and daddy having *marital relations*. Whatever they did when daddy rolled on top of mam, I'm sure, I'm positive, it was nothing like this. Both of the girls flashed extended fangs and playfully bit each other. Little Red was on top of Poppy and it dawned on me that Poppy was allowing Little Red to ride her, to kiss her, to suck at her nipples and lick at her lips, as a form of worship, of adulation; a way of acknowledging that Poppy was the boss, the pack mistress if you like. Poppy laid back and allowed Little Red to have full and complete knowledge of her mistress's body.

I moaned a little myself, I couldn't help it, and discovered that I had placed a hand quite subconsciously between my thighs and was gently rubbing at myself in a most indecent manner. Another first in what was proving to be, over the last few days, a succession of firsts. But as my eyes could not move away from staring at the naked forms copulating in front of me, so my hand steadfastly refused to move away from between my legs. My body had betrayed me. I surrendered to its demands and continued to rub, sometimes gently, sometimes with more urgency. My fingers found the hole and entered, and I thought to myself, 'Well, Katie, that's it. If God's watching, you're bound for hell now and no mistake.' Funny how after being turned into a vampire and killing and drinking the blood of a cat, it was the sexual act that I thought of as offering eternal damnation. But I was beyond caring and besides, the thought of God watching and disapproving only served to add extra spice to this most intoxicating of dishes.

Poppy and Little Red's love-making became ever more violent and I noticed that some of the play bites were beginning to draw blood. They growled and moaned and cried, a sound like a dozen cats on heat, baying before the moon. Little Red was bigger and more forceful than Poppy, and she tossed the blonde girl over onto her tummy and clamped her jaws around her exposed neck, fixing her in position. I suppose Poppy allowed this to happen, the ultimate demonstration of faith and trust in one of her lieutenants. With Poppy secured and unable to escape, Little Red placed three fingers into the blonde girl's hole and began to thrust violently.

Poppy cried and moaned and wailed and writhed as though attempting escape, but it was no good. Little Red's jaws bit deeper, over-mastering the smaller vampire, and her fingers thrust with more urgency, harder and faster. Eventually Poppy could resist no longer, and in a terrifying struggle she reached orgasm with such a-wailing and a-shrieking that I thought the walls would crumble around us and the police burst in to discover who'd been murdered. To see this beautiful blonde vampire, the leader of this pack, pinned to the mattress and helplessly forced into orgasm was too much. My own body surrendered and juices the likes of which I'd never experienced flowed from inside me.

As I reached my own crescendo, I saw Little Red staring at me, her eyes glowing as red as her hair. She'd known all along that I was watching. Was this display for my benefit? A way of marking her territory, of showing me where she, Little Red, stood in the hierarchy of this group? Or did the knowledge of my presence excite Little Red, the thought of being on display adding extra eagerness to her already significant lust.

I didn't have to wait long for my answer. Averting her eyes back to Poppy, Little Red flipped her over onto her back and climbed on top of her. The red haired vampire slithered up Poppy's body, eventually placing her knees over Poppy's arms like a schoolboy pinning down a rival in a school yard fight. Sitting up, she placed Poppy's mouth between her legs and began to thrust. I could see Poppy's tongue flicking backwards and forwards, backwards and forwards, and before long Little Red was writhing like some Arabian belly dancer from the Tales of a Thousand and One Nights, sweat making her body glisten and her hair stick to her forehead and her cheeks. She held her own breasts, caressed her own nipples, as she rocked to and fro, flinging her head back to address the heavens with her sobs and her sighs; her curly hair falling down her back, and her fangs flashing like twin daggers in the night.

Little Red's climax was quieter and more self-contained than Poppy's. She bit down on her own lips and blood trickled down her chin. But all the time she fixed me with a red eyed stare, daring me to look, to witness her during her most vulnerable and exposed moment, but daring me also to look away. I watched and I whimpered and I cried and I bit down on my own lip and sucked my own blood because I was so hungry and so evil and so lost.

At some point I must have dropped back off to sleep, and in sleep came again strange dreams. This time there was a dragon or giant serpent in my stomach, writhing around and pulling me apart from the inside. In my dream I wailed, for it felt as though the dragon was feasting on my stomach and the agony was too much to bear. I was nothing more than food to this dragon, this serpent that lived inside me, and I screamed "Food!" at the top of my voice so as to warn others of the monster and to call anyone to my side who might aid me. "Food!"

I awoke and was still lying on the mattress in the bedroom. I was still screaming "Food!" and could not stop myself, and though awake I could still feel the dragon writhing within my stomach. "Food!"

Poppy, and behind her Little Red, came swiftly to me, pulling silk gowns across their shoulders to hide their nakedness.

"What's wrong with her?" asked Little Red.

"She's starving to death," said Poppy. "Her body has started to consume itself. God! I was so stupid. I thought she'd last till tonight."

The thin shaft of daylight still protruded from the gap in the drapes, although its intensity has waned a little.

"Can we not go out and feed now?" asked Little Red. "Is the day still too bright?"

Poppy looked behind her at the drapes. "Still too bright I fear," she said. "If there'd been a pea-souper we could have gone out, but not with the afternoon still being so bright as this. There's nothing else for it." Poppy lifted a wrist to her mouth and I saw her fangs extend.

"No!" said Little Red. "Not that."

"There's nothing else for it," said Poppy. "If I don't, she'll die. I won't have her dying on us, Little Red, not after saving her just yesterday. I couldn't bear it." She raised her wrist again to her lips.

"Please," said Little Red, placing a hand on Poppy's arm and looking into her eyes. "Please don't. It wouldn't be fair. It wouldn't be fair on me, and it wouldn't be fair on her. Please, don't."

Poppy met Little Red's gaze but ignored her pleas. Her fangs penetrated the exposed flesh of her wrist and immediately Poppy's bright red blood flowed. She placed her wrist between my lips and the blood ran into my mouth like water from a tap. Instinctively I grabbed her wrist with both my hands and pulled it closer, my lips clamping around the torn flesh, my tongue licking at the wound furiously, and my own fangs extended. Poppy's blood entered me and I fell into a swoon.

I saw Poppy again as an angel dressed in white, but she was a fallen angel, an angel refused admittance to Heaven and cursed to walk the Earth for all eternity. Her pretty white dress was smeared in red blood and blood poured from her mouth and fangs and ran down her chin. Her short hair was golden and almost too bright to look at. "Bless you my dearest Snow," she said, and her fangs caused her to lisp slightly in a way that was at once incredibly attractive and heart-rendingly pitiful. She held out her hands and I noticed blood pouring from both her wrists. Taking hold of her hands in my own, I suddenly found myself in the middle of a green field on a beautiful summer's day. Poppy was there though she looked somehow younger and her blonde, golden, hair was long. She laughed with unbridled joy as we ran across the field hand in hand. We came to a small brook and there we stopped. A cloud passed over the sun and the once bright day turned dark and sinister. "This is where it happened," said Poppy. "This is where it found me and bit me and turned me into a vampire." And she started to cry and her tears were blood.

I embraced her and pulled her close to me. She was naked now and I felt her breasts press up against my dress. "It's all right," I comforted her. "I'm here now. I'll look after you." "Will you?" asked Poppy. "Will you really?" "Yes," I said. "Of course I will."

Poppy smiled again and the sun came out from behind the cloud. "Come," she said, "the sun will burn us. We must run."

We were in a dark alleyway, both naked now and feral and covered in blood. A young, well-dressed couple came strolling along the cobble-stones and Poppy and I jumped out on them and ripped out their throats. Poppy looked up at me and said, "This is how I lived for so long. A monster. A creature. Thank you for saving me from all this. It is an act of love that I will not soon forget." "Oh Poppy," I said. "I do love you. I do! I hereby swear that my heart belongs to you and no other." Poppy smiled and a dark shadow seemed to pass, momentarily, across her eyes.

On the mattress, Poppy pulled her wrist away and I slipped out of the blood-induced euphoria. "I love you," I whispered to Poppy and I meant it. I did love her. I always had and I always would. Poppy was my world, of course.

"I fucking knew it," hissed Little Red and she stormed out of the room, still wearing nothing more than the silk robe, slamming the door behind her with such fury that a crack appeared in the wood, and the door would never quite fit the frame properly afterwards.

My belly full at last, I laid my head back against the pillow and looked up at the ceiling. "Thank you," I said.

"Dearest Snow," said Poppy and she stroked my hair while I looked at her through adoring eyes.

Thirty minutes later Little Red returned and finding that she could not close the bedroom door properly, she flung her purse across the room and sat sulking in a corner. Poppy ignored the outburst. Indeed, she ignored Little Red altogether and remained sitting at my side.

"Tonight is your first night with us," she said, holding my hands in hers. "This calls for a celebration. I shall collect the other girls and we shall all be properly introduced. Then we'll head up West. There's sure to be some tasty toff blood up there for us to feast on. A treat for us all – it is Saturday night after all. I think we deserve something a little special."

With that she stood from my mattress and skipped out of the room, my sweet fallen angel, leaving me alone with Little Red.

Little Red looked up at me with tear stained eyes. "She's mine, you know," she said. "Whatever you think you feel for her, it's just her blood talking."

"I love her," I said without shame. "I can't help how I feel." "Yes, but you only love her because you've drunk her blood.

You don't understand do you? When one vampire drinks another's blood, it creates an unbreakable bond of devotion. You're tied to her forever now, because you drank her blood. But remember, I was here first and if you try to take her away from me I will kill you."

I was silent. What could I say? At length I whispered, "I love her. But perhaps I should go home? To my mam and my daddy? Get a good night's sleep in my own bed and see where things stand when I'm properly rested?"

Little Red laughed; a spiteful, futile, angry noise that bore no resemblance to any laughter I'd heard before.

"Listen to me," she said. "You can never, ever go home. Remember how you felt when you killed that cat? Remember how the hunger took a hold of you? Remember just now? How your body began to consume itself through hunger? You cannot trust yourself around humans any more. If the hunger takes you, you would gladly eat your parents and do so willingly. You are a vampire, little girl. Your life has changed more than you can possibly imagine. You may, in time, come to wish that you had died in that alleyway after all, rather than be turned.

"And as for Poppy, well, do you think you are the first to drink her blood and fall in love, totally and absolutely, with her? Do you not imagine that I too drank of her blood in the same way as you did, and do you not think that I adore her with every fibre, every last, tiny fibre, of my being? And do you think I will sit idly by while someone new walks into our house and tries to steal her away?

"You saw me making love to her last night. Did you not see the passion and adoration in my actions? Did I not demonstrate to you my love for her? Did my passion for her not manifest itself before your very eyes? Do you not think that I, like you, can never, ever go home again to my own parents? And that Poppy is all that I have now? That Poppy is my mother and my father and my sister and my lover and my whole world? Can you imagine for one moment that I would sit back and let you, *you*, come into our home, into our *bedroom*, and steal all of that away from me? Can you?

"She calls you Snow after Snow White. Fifty years ago she named me Little Red after Little Red Riding Hood. You see how history repeats itself? Are you so vain as to think yourself the first, little girl? Poppy walked the earth when the Romans founded London. She can speak Latin and name all of the Caesars, and she made them and their consorts her lovers. She is an *old* vampire, perhaps as old as civilisation itself. She is my world and my stars and my past and my future, and for fifty years, *fifty years*, I have loved her and worshipped her and been at her side. I have fought alongside her, killed alongside her, and worshipped her body as only a lover who has truly surrendered themselves can. As long as there is a moon in the sky and passion in my heart I will continue to adore her. I will kill you, Kate. I will fucking kill you."

And she was crying now and convulsing, and the words that she spoke broke my heart, and I wanted to tell her it was all right, and hug her and caress her, but I couldn't. And I couldn't because it would be a lie. It would be a lie because I hated her and I loved Poppy. If she was my rival, then fair game. I was an East End girl and I'd had a few scraps in my time. Poppy was, without doubt, the one thing in my life that now I was willing to fight for. I had lost my parents; I understood that instinctively and painful as it was, I thought I understood it completely. I had changed beyond all recognition. I had become a vampire, I had masturbated for the first time, I had fallen in love with a girl. I was, apparently, a lesbian. I was beyond redemption.

Well, fair enough. Fair play. But if unredeemable I was, then unredeemable I would be. I would fight for Poppy's love. I would destroy Little Red's world. Kill or be killed. That was me now, and no mistake. I thought all this but simply said, "Been with you's not done her no favours then, has it? If she was, like you say, a lover of the Caesars and a lover of their wives, then what's she doing now living in a poky doss house on Flower and Dean Street having your scruffy fingers thrust inside her? You've brought her down to your own level. Let me free her, and take her back up to the place where she belongs." And I smiled because I was just a general shop girl who had worked in a hat shop, and yet look at the fancy words that love had placed into my mouth. I smirked at my own cleverness and turned my head away from Little Red as Poppy and the other girls walked into the bedroom.

"Playing nicely?" asked Poppy knowingly.

"Perfectly!" I said, as Little Red hid in the shadows and wiped away her tears of blood and said nothing.

I was introduced to the other girls, and they were very nice to me, full of smiles and kisses on cheeks and hugs, and they made me feel more welcome than I could have hoped for. It became apparent that none of the other girls had drunk from Poppy's blood, for although they all adored her and obviously loved her, none of them looked at her with swooning eyes and devotion as I did. It made me happy to know that my only competition was Little Red, who seemed to be retreating further and further into herself with the passing of each minute.

Poppy introduced each girl to me in turn. There was the pretty Irish girl Mary Jane, Abigail with the short curly black hair, Catherine who appeared to be a little older than the other girls, maybe in her mid-thirties, and finally sweet, dear Holly with the stutter ("D-d-delighted t-t-to m-m-meet you K-K-K-Kate"), a re-sult, Poppy said, of the traumatic manner in which she was turned by a brute of a vampire back in the 1830s.

Something dawned on me then that perhaps I should have no-ticed before, but with all that had been going on I'm sure I could be forgiven for being a little slow realising, namely that the leg-ends were right. Becoming a vampire really did stop the ageing process. In human terms these girls were old ladies at best, and in some cases positively ancient, and yet here they were, still more or less in the first flush of youth. It was a remarkable revelation, made all the more remarkable by the realisation that I too would be young forever. Forever. I was immortal. Or so I thought.

Chapter Three

Have you ever been up the West End on a Saturday night? How jolly and gay it is! The bright lights turn the darkest of nights into a rainbow tinged playground, with people of all shapes, sizes, nationalities and persuasions rubbing shoulders with each other. Here a toff in a top hat, here a shop boy dressed up for the night in his best bowler. A soldier in a red tunic next to a Chinaman with a long pipe sticking out of his mouth. And the ladies! How beautiful and sweetly perfumed they are, dressed in their finest silks and bows and parasols. The very air seems intoxicating and you cannot help but be swept along by the revelry and the joy of it all.

Poppy and myself stopped by the statue of Shakespeare in Leicester Square and took in the sweet night air. The girls had split up into smaller groups, the better to hunt in. Poppy said that a large group of girls would only draw undue attention to themselves. Better to slip unnoticed through the mass of humanity in twos and threes. Poppy had invited Little Red to come with the two of us, but she'd said no, saying that she was going out by herself and had stormed out of the house in a right old sulk before us. And so, on foot and by hansom, we had made the three-or-so mile journey from Spitalfields, along Clerkenwell, to the West End.

"You haven't mentioned your parents or your old home once since I found you," said Poppy. "You must be thinking of them."

"I talked to Little Red about them," I replied. "She told me to forget them. That I couldn't trust myself around them, for if the hunger took me I might do something terrible."

"She's a wild one, that girl," said Poppy in a tone that put me in mind of a doting parent who cannot scold their child without there being an overtone of love in their voice. A pang of jealousy bit at my heart. "But she's right. Dearest Snow, as awful as it may sound, and as flippant and heartless, you must let your old life fade and die now. But fear not, for you are surrounded by friends and you know that I love you and will protect you always."

She placed a gloved hand to my cheek and I felt desire and passion rising within me. I longed to hold her in my arms and kiss her as passionately as I had seen Little Red kissing her the previous night. And I believe that there in Leicester Square, surrounded by toffs and dandies, mashers and Mohammedans, black men, white men, and yellow men, and all over-looked by the statue of old Shakespeare who I'm told wrote of forbidden love and secret passions, that if I had taken Poppy in my arms and kissed her with all the infatuation that burned in my heart, on that Saturday night, in that wondrous place, no eyebrows would have been raised. But I was afraid. Afraid of rejection, afraid that she would push me away, afraid that my heart would be broken. So no, I told myself, I would play the waiting game, for better to slowly win her passion than to scare her away through acting too rashly. So I held my gloved hand to hers and simply said, "Thank you."

Before leaving the house, the girls and I had all washed with a big tin bath of water placed in front of the fire in the drawing room downstairs. None of the girls seemed to feel remotely self- conscious about their nakedness and gaily paraded around in front of each other without a stitch of clothing on them. I was filthy still, with caked blood in my ears and the creases of my neck, and my hair muddy and dirty. 'In for a penny, in for a pound, my girl' I thought and stripped my clothes off and with a bar of carbolic soap I began to scrub and rub as I'd never scrubbed and rubbed before. Then Poppy lent me lip balm and eye paint and I felt like a princess, never having used such things before, my dear old mother believing that girls who painted their faces were no better than Jezebels. And sweet Holly, blessed Holly, sat behind me and braided my hair while telling me how beautiful I was in that sorry stuttering voice of hers. I longed to know more of Holly, to hear her story, the story of her turning and her stutter, but that would have to wait. For now, it was enough to know that Holly seemed to like me and I knew that I liked her.

Throughout all this Little Red sat upstairs in the bedroom, falling deeper into a sulk until as we were dressing we heard her thunder downstairs and slam the front door on her way out.

"Silly girl," said Poppy, and we did not mention her again until we stood in the shadow of Shakespeare's statue.

Poppy had found me out a black dress that she said I should wear. I worried that it was too funereal and would make me look too dour, but Poppy and the other girls all agreed that the dress suited my complexion perfectly, and it was such a pretty dress trimmed in exquisite lace that I had to agree. I noticed that the other girls as they put on their dresses were wearing no under-garments at all. Nothing. When I questioned this, they laughed and said that undergarments were for humans. They preferred to go naked beneath their dresses. "Al fresco!" laughed one. "Al dente!" laughed another. "Nudos!" said Poppy, and though we didn't know what it meant, we knew that she was right. And so there we stood in Leicester Square, me in black and Poppy in her usual white, looking like two squares on a chess board. But soon enough there would be plenty of the old red stuff being splashed around, enough to add more than a dash of colour.

Poppy noticed her first, moving effortlessly through the crowds, confidently navigating the street, alone and with a bounce in her step. "She's pretty," said Poppy, "and she's on her own. A show-girl probably, from out of town. Family only hear from her once a week in a quick letter if they're lucky. Won't be missed for a while. Perhaps she has a beau who will assume that she's eloped with someone else, a theatre manager who will tut-tut about the youth of today and hire another girl when she fails to appear for tomorrow's performance. She should be yours, dearest Snow. She should be your first kill."

And so she was.

We followed at a polite distance as she weaved her merry way along Charing Cross Road before she ducked down a poorly lit side street. Perhaps this was to be a short cut to her destination, a route she had taken a hundred times before and the thought of danger or mishap had never crossed her mind, just as it had never crossed my mind as I wandered up that darkened alleyway not forty-eight hours earlier. Sadly for her, this was to be the last time she took this particular short cut, and indeed it was to be the last time she did anything much at all.

"Excuse me, my darling?" called out Poppy as we turned into the side road and saw the girl walking alone a little way ahead. From the hustle and bustle of Charing Cross Road, suddenly we were in a deserted spot without a soul to be seen save the three of us.

The girl turned and upon seeing Poppy and myself, smiled a little. Nothing here to concern her. Just two girls, out for a promenade on a Saturday night, probably lost or looking for a road that they cannot locate.

"Can I help you?" she asked, edging towards us. I saw that her pretty clothes were worn in places, and darned in others. Working in the theatres did not pay so well, especially for those in the chorus line or with a small walk-on part. I felt a little sorry for her, clutching her purse and with her white lace gloves that were now more grey than white, and with her ready smile. But my hunger began to rise at the sight of the naked cleavage on display and at the nape of her neck, her skin creamy and warm.

"My friend," said Poppy indicating me, "appears to have done something. I think she's hurt. Can you help?"

The girl walked towards me. "What's happened? Did you trip?"

"No," I said and was stuck for a reply. Poppy and I had not rehearsed this. I had no idea I was to be called upon to play out a role. "I think I have twisted my ankle," I managed to say, "or something."

"Well I'm sorry for your troubles, I'm sure," said the girl, coming within touching distance. I could smell her now. She smelled of lavender with an undercurrent of gin, "but I ain't sure how's I can help, to be honest."

I pretended to stumble. The girl reached for me. I reached for her and grabbed her with both my hands. She was no match for my vampire strength and speed. With a little "Oh!" I had spun her around, placed a hand across her mouth, and bitten deep and mortally into her neck. She struggled for a moment, but only a moment, and I dragged her across the pavement and into a small space between two buildings, wide enough only for me and the girl. It was dark in here and safe. I consumed the girl's blood and felt her soul entering my body.

The ecstasy was not as intense as with Poppy's blood and I had not expected it to be. Still, spasms of pleasure rippled through my body as I felt the girl die and felt her blood satisfying the hunger within me. There were flashes of images too, pieces of her life entering my mind. A provincial girl dreaming of being on the stage in London, her worried parents waving her off, the early successes and later the disappointments of not becoming an overnight star. She was thinking of going back home to her parents. She even had a sort-of beau back home. He was waiting for her, waiting for her to get this theatre nonsense out of her system before she came home to marry him. Home. Where I could never go again, and now neither could she. Her soul entered me and merged with my own soul. We were now both greater than we had been before. She had now become a part of me in a very real sense. I knew her memories, I shared her triumphs and her tragedies. I would honour her in everything I did. She had not died that night; she was reborn within me. I drained her dry and pulled my fangs clear of her throat and I laughed raucously. "Oh Jesus fucking Christ!" I shouted at Poppy.

Poppy ran over to me telling me to shush and to hurry, but she was smiling too and trying not to laugh, like we were two school boys riffling through the teacher's desk during playtime. I managed to twist around in the narrow gap and gave the girl, Maria, her name had entered me with her blood, she was Maria, a hefty push. Her body fell in a heap several feet inside the gap, deep in darkness where no-one would find her for days. The rats would find her first, and the cats. That thought did not please me, but what could I do? Her spirit was no longer inside her body at any rate, it was now inside me. I looked down and saw her purse on the floor. It was red with a rose embroidered on it. Embroidered in gold thread above the rose were the words 'Merry Christmas

1885 from Mummy & Daddy'. I instinctively kicked it into the gap to come to a rest besides her body. "Get the money out of the purse," said Poppy but it was too late. The purse was out of reach and besides, I had no desire to rob Maria. I turned to Poppy and shrugged, then laughed hysterically and mouthed 'thank you' to the dark space where Maria's body now lay. We ran back along Charing Cross Road with wings on our feet, knocking people out of our way and being pursued by cries of, "Oi!" and "Watch it!"

We came to a rest in Soho Square, panting and laughing, taking some cover behind the trees. Our vampire strength meant that we were hardly out of breath with the exertion, but we laughed so loudly and were so excited that it was difficult to breath. "Maria!" I said. "Her name was Maria and she came from out of town. Her purse said Merry Christmas from Mummy and Daddy on it, but it's not to be fretted over because she's inside me now, I can feel her inside me, she didn't die, not really, she's with me now."

"Dearest Snow," said Poppy, hugging me close, "how sweet it is to see you this way. I have been a vampire for so long that all of this I take for granted. You give me back my youth, make me glad to be alive. As much as I saved you in that alleyway, I am beginning to think that you may have saved me also."

And I fair swooned at her words. My love and devotion for Poppy knew no bounds. I wanted to hold her and kiss her and caress her naked body, but still, even now, I feared rejection, so I merely gave her a peck on her cheek and left behind a smear of Maria's blood. I had not realised it, but I was covered, dripping, with blood.

Poppy pulled a kerchief from her bag and wiped the blood tenderly from my face, although in all honesty it would take another bath in front of the fire to clean it all away. As she fussed over me a young soldier, smart and neat as a new pin in his red tunic and tight black trousers, strolled into the centre of the square and proceeded to light a cigarette. "Watch this," whispered Poppy and she walked out from behind the tree and approached the soldier.

"Evening soldier boy," I heard her say, a confident swagger in her voice. "Fancy a quick kiss? On the house, as it were. By ways of saying thank you for your bravery overseas?"

She was going to kiss this soldier? Again jealousy was quick to rise in my gut, but I need not have worried. It was a ruse. Of course, it was just a ruse.

"A kiss?" said the soldier, blowing smoke from his mouth and tossing the cigarette aside. "Be my pleasure, ma'am."

Poppy put her arms around his neck and pulled him close. But her lips did not go to meet the puckering lips of the soldier. Instead they moved swiftly to the side and latched onto his neck. The soldier struggled and seemed to shake, a look of wild disbelief in his eyes, but soon enough he went limp in her arms. It took a full two minutes for her to drain him, right there, out in the open, for all to see. During that time several couples walked past, arm in arm, and even a policeman – how my heart leapt at the sight of him – but none took any notice of this couple, perhaps after a few too many gins, kissing in the park. After all, he was a soldier, and if a soldier cannot partake of a few gins and then kiss a pretty girl on a Saturday night, then when can he?

With the soldier quite drained, Poppy let his body slump to the floor. Two elderly ladies were walking through the park and noticed the soldier fall. "Bloody drunk," said Poppy to them. "Men, eh? Not to be trusted with the demon drink."

But what she did not know was that she had blood over her lips and her chin and down the front of her sweet white dress. The old ladies screamed and looked fit to faint. Discretion being the better part of valour, Poppy legged it over to me, grabbed me by my arm, and pulled me away onto Soho Street and from there onto Oxford Street. Poppy wrapped her shawl around her shoulders and the bottom part of her face, and with such deceptions in place were we able to hail a cab and be transported away, back to Flower and Dean Street, two dark Cinderellas returning home from the kind of ball you don't read about in Hans Christian Anderson.

"Frank," said Poppy at last of the soldier, as we entered the house and closed the door behind us. "His name was Frank and he was a bastard. We need not mourn him. To be honest I rather hope that his soul did not merge with mine, although I have had so many souls enter me that it's getting quite crowded in there and difficult to tell just who is who."

As soon as we entered the house we noticed the gas lamps burning in the lounge and found all of the girls there save for Little Red. They were laughing and talking loudly, and at the sight of us they let out a small cheer and bid us welcome. All the girls had blood about their faces and their clothes, and it seemed that this Saturday night had proven itself to be a most successful hunt.

Vampires of course are unable to partake of human food or drink without convulsing into fits of nausea. But all the girls smoked cigarettes, and upon our return Poppy held up a lit cigarette and said, "A toast! A toast to our newest member who this evening took her first live human prey with aplomb, discretion, well," she winked over at me, "almost discretion," and everyone laughed, "and certainly with modesty, understanding and a good heart! To dearest Snow! Our dearest Snow!"

And all the girls raised their cigarettes as humans might raise glasses filled with champagne, and they rushed over to kiss me on the cheek and tell me how well I had done.

It was perhaps two or three o'clock in the morning with plenty of darkness left in the night, and so we sat up chatting, swapping stories of the evening's adventures, and I found myself warming to each and every one of the girls. Mary Jane told us the story of her life in Ireland and how she had ended up in London. I dragged on my cigarette, closed my eyes, and listened to the sweet melody of her voice.

Chapter Four

"I fell in love," said Mary Jane. "I fell in love with a fucking stupid human boy. Can you believe it?

"I used to share a house in Belfast with a few other girls, all vampires you understand, a little like the set up here. Except we had no-one like Poppy to look after us. We were all just young and silly and didn't really understand what being a vampire meant. So we used to go out walking in the parks of Belfast after sunset, and the boys would be drawn to us like flies to shite. Oh, the boys! They couldn't get enough of us. There must be some kind of attraction that we have on human boys, a bit like moths to candle flames. So anyways, there was this one boy, Johnny was his name, a labourer up in Belfast to work on the ships. He came from Londonderry originally but had arrived in Belfast to find his fame and fortune, or so he joked. And he was human. So awfully human.

"Anyways, silly girl that I was, when he starts to chatting me up like, I takes his arm and agrees to go for a walk with him through the park, to take in the evening air.

"My two friends, the vampire girls, giggled and winked at me, and I giggled and winked back at them, and off I set for a fine old romantic walk. He was a perfect gentleman, to say he was just an uneducated boy from Londonderry. He didn't try any funny business, just let me hook my arm around his and we walked for an hour or more talking about nothing much in particular. I had a wonderful time. I don't think he realised I was a vampire. I think he just thought I was a bit different. A bit different? Yes, I was a bit different all right. The only thing he did seemed concerned with was whether I was protestant or catholic. Well I'd been brought up protestant, so that's what I told him. That seemed to please him well enough as he just smiled and nodded his head, so I can only guess that he was protestant too, although to be honest even then I thought it something of a moot point – I was pretty sure that as a vampire I was operating well outside the grace of God! But I didn't say anything and we genuinely had a nice time, so we agreed to meet again the next night. 'Oh it's love at first sight!' laughed my silly friends, but I smiled too because I kind of thought it was as well. I don't know what it is, but since I became a vampire I find I make emotional attachments a lot quicker than I did when I was human."

I smiled and stole a glance at Poppy.

"Oh, it's all so stupid," said Mary Jane, blowing cigarette smoke into the air. "I know that now. But at the time it just seemed really nice. It reminded me of my days before I was turned, you know? The days before I was a vampire. The days when I had a family and a brother and played in the streets with the other kids and wasn't afraid of the sun. Somehow just walking with Johnny on that evening took me back to those days, and for a few minutes I wasn't a vampire any more, I was plain old human Mary Jane Kelly and I was allowed to give my heart to a boy from Londonderry.

"We stopped walking and took a seat on a bench, looking out across the duck pond. It must have been about 7 o'clock at night, not particularly late. The path was lit up with gas-lamps and there were a few other couples around, love-birds like me and Johnny." A sad smile seemed to form on Mary Jane's lips, and she fell silent for a moment.

"Anyways," she continued, "he puts his arms around my shoulders and I lean into him. He looks me in the eye and I think to myself 'I could fall head over heels in love for a boy like you Johnny', and then suddenly we're kissing. Kissing passionately. More passionately than I'd ever kissed anyone before. I wanted him so badly that the desire burned inside me. I wanted him, all of him. I wanted to devour him.

"Then I hear screams and I look up. There's a group of girls and boys and they're looking at me and Johnny and they're screaming. I wonder why they're making such a fuss – after all, haven't they ever seen a couple of love-birds smooching before? But then I notice that my face is wet and Johnny's kind of slumped and he's all wet too and I can't understand it. But my fangs are extended and slowly it dawns on me. The girls and boys are pointing and screaming and it all makes sense. I've just fed on him. It wasn't love. It was hunger. I'm a fucking vampire and he was my prey. What a stupid little girl I was, trying to hang on to being human, to the daylight, to family and friends. Stupid, stupid girl.

"He was dead of course. I'd drained him dry, more or less. Some of the braver boys are edging closer by now and they've picked up tree branches to use as clubs and one boy even has a knife. What was he carrying a knife for? What mischief was he planning? Anyways, now he's pointing it at me, so I suppose now he's being the big hero. So I stands up, looks at poor Johnny's body, and I tanks it away into the trees. The human boys can't keep up of course and I soon lose them. I make it back home and I begin to calm down and the other girls are comforting me and telling me it's all going to be all right, but then an hour later there's a banging on the door and it's the police. Stupid, stupid, stupid. I'd told Johnny where I lived the night before, hadn't seen the harm in it, and he must've told his pals, and now they're all outside our front door.

"Me and my two friends climbed out the bedroom window and made our getaway along the roofs. It was my fault. My stupidity had brought the fucking Royal Irish Constabulary to our front door. The two vampire girls saw me head one way, and then they headed the other way. I'd let them down, and they dumped me, just like that.

"Well," Mary Jane smiled to us all, "let that be a lesson to yous all. Don't fall in love with a human as like it or not you'll end up eating them, and when you find yourself in a tight squeeze, that's when you'll discover who your friends really are." She shrugged her shoulders. "From Belfast I got a ferry to Liverpool, then a train to London; all the time keeping out of the sunlight, sleeping anywhere I could find shelter, till I ended up in Whitechapel and Poppy rescued me. So count your blessings girls, you're lucky to have a mentor like Poppy to keep you on the straight and narrow, ain't that so Poppy?"

"Amen, my sweet," said Poppy, and everyone smiled.

"I always thought vampires had no soul," I said hesitantly. "Seems to me that we have more soul than a dozen humans."

"The Romanians used to call us *Cei Singuri*, literally the lonely ones...," began Poppy when the front door crashed open and in walked Little Red.

On her head she was wearing a man's boater hat, her face was smeared in blood, and in her left hand she carried two severed men's heads by the hair, their eyes rolled up, tongues hanging from the open mouths, and blood and gore dripping everywhere. "Ho ho, sisters!" she cried as she stumbled into the lounge holding up her gruesome trophies. "If you want to get ahead, get a hat!" and with her right hand she lifted the boater in mock salute. One or two of the girls giggled, but in the main we sat frozen. "What's wrong, you boring old tarts? If you want to get ahead, get a hat! Get it? It's a joke. You're all pretty slow on the uptake tonight."

Poppy stood up. "Get those fucking heads out of here, you stupid little girl," she said, calmly in a way that terrified me even more than if she had screamed the words. "Do you wish to call every copper in the capital down upon us? Take those heads, and throw them in the river. Do it now and do it quickly."

Little Red stood staring at Poppy for a moment, as though weighing up her options. Then she said, "You used to find me funny. You used to like me and my little jokes. I used to make you laugh. I used to make you happy. What's wrong now? Don't you love me anymore? I love you so fucking much, Poppy! I would die for you, again and again and for all eternity if it just meant that you would be happy for one more second, that you would smile at me one more time. What now? Are you suddenly pretending to be refined and dignified for our new friend?" Little Red turned her gaze on me. "There was a time when she would have laughed at my joke, Kate," she never called me Snow, ever, "and then she would have kicked the heads around the street just for the jolly of it and played cricket with them. Don't let her fool you. She's a fucking brutal piece of shit at heart." And with that Little Red turned around and walked out of the house, carrying the severed heads with her. There was silence for a few moments, and in those few moments I smiled inwardly. Poppy didn't like Little Red any more. Now she liked me.

Suddenly Holly piped up, "S-s-s-stupid c-c-c-cow." And everyone laughed, not at Holly, not at her stutter, but at the sentiment and because the tension had been broken and we could smile again.

But we couldn't smile again, not really. The time for smiling and laughing had passed, and when Little Red returned, without the heads but still wearing the boater in a defiant gesture, all the girls started to make their excuses and retired to their rooms.

I went upstairs to the top bedroom with Poppy and we began undressing. Little Red burst into the room, eyed us both suspiciously, and said, "I can't sleep in here. There's a bad smell." And she picked up her mattress and dragged it out of the room. "I'm sleeping with Holly tonight," she said and slammed the door behind her. The door rattled in the frame, then slowly swung open again.

"Ignore her," said Poppy. "Things have been a little stale around here for a long time. It's good that you're here. We must change or we slowly decay. It seems to me that Little Red is having problems adapting to the changes, but in time I'm sure she'll settle down again. She's a good girl at heart, just a little reckless at times."

I smiled in reply, but my soul was on fire. I hardly heard the words that Poppy was saying and could now care less about Little Red, for here in front of me, taking off her dress and revealing herself in her nakedness was the object of my passions, my dreams, my masturbations. The dress slipped down her lithe legs and she stepped elegantly over it and towards me.

"You still have a little blood around your mouth," she said, and rubbed a forefinger across my lips. I stood, frozen. Should I throw my arms around her? Should I try to kiss her? I was, in case you haven't already fathomed it, a virgin. I had no idea what I was supposed to do. I wasn't sure I even knew how to do the things that I had seen Little Red doing to Poppy. I would be awkward and fumbling, I just knew it, and I would do it all wrong. And then Poppy would laugh at me, or worse, simply sigh and run back to Little Red's mattress. So I did nothing. I turned my back, took my dress off quickly, and jumped beneath the covers on top of my mattress. "Well, good night," I said, trembling.

"Yes, good night," said Poppy. "You did very well tonight." There was a moment's silence, and then she blew out the candle, allowing darkness to hide my confusion, my shame, and my self-loathing.

"Thank you," I whispered into the darkness.

Of course the darkness was no match for my vampire eyesight, and I could see Poppy lying on her mattress close to me. Throughout the day and the night, the mattresses tended to get kicked around the room, and Poppy's had ended up perilously close to mine. She was lying with her back to me. If I reached out, I could touch her.

My hand strived forward, half an inch from her naked back, half an inch from those delightful little blonde hairs on the nape of her neck. But then I pulled my hand back. It was too late. The moment was lost.

Downstairs there came much wailing and moaning, and Holly in rapture cried out, "Ooooh!" It appeared that the poor girl's stammer did not encroach on her declarations of pleasure.

"She's not calling Little Red a stupid cow now," I said to the back of Poppy's head.

Silence.

"Good night."

Silence.

Chapter Five

Over the following week we settled into a kind of routine. I learned that a vampire doesn't need to kill every night. That as long as I had a whole human to myself, I needed only to go out to hunt every third or fourth day. This we mainly did around Whitechapel and Spitalfields and the surrounding areas where life was cheap and the hunt was easy. Once we had devoured our prey we tended to, if at all possible, haul their bodies down to the Thames and throw them into the river, allowing time and the water and the fishes to dispose of the evidence. Poppy explained that our jaunt up West was a special treat, and that they weren't normally so careless. "I think I was showing off to you," she said of the soldier. "Trying to make you think I was something special." "Oh but you are special," I said earnestly and she smiled at me, a little sadly I thought.

Little Red was still in her melancholy, and spent each night with a different girl. Despite what they thought of her as a person, it seemed that none could resist her sexual advances, and she certainly seemed to have the Midas touch when it came to bringing the girls to pleasure.

As for Poppy and myself, we were no closer to consummating our love than we had been on the previous Saturday. I despised myself for my own inaction, and with the passing of each day it seemed even harder for me to make any amorous moves towards her. A kind of invisible wall was being built up between us and with every hour the wall seemed higher and more impossible to climb. I was terrified that Poppy regretted her decision to save me, to let me drink her blood, to let me fall in love with her. When I loved her so much and lusted after her so vehemently, damn my inaction and my fear.

Of Little Red, I said to Poppy one evening, "Well, she's certainly doing the rounds." But Poppy did not reply, nor even smile, and it seemed that as Little Red retreated more into melancholy and sexual adventure and the brutal slaying of mortals just for the wheeze of it, so Poppy was retreating into an elementary form of sadness that was all the worse for its purity and simplicity. This was all my fault.

August had turned into September, and the newspapers were full of murder. Not ones committed by our little troupe I'm pleased to report (or at least I don't think any of them were ours, although, as you will see, I cannot vouch for Little Red in those days), but the work of some mass murderer named Jack who was stalking the same streets that we stalked, killing girls and ripping out their innards. The Ripper, they called him. However, he was a little less careful than what we was, leaving his bodies where they fell with no attempt made at hiding them. Poppy said that it troubled her somewhat, though she wouldn't elaborate, but she also said that it could be a boon. If there was a human murderer on the prowl, then any bodies found that we had butchered would likely be attributed to this Jack character.

"We must be careful," she concluded, "but no more than that. He is, after all, just a human. No threat to us."

On the Saturday, Poppy and myself decided we needed to eat and headed out into Whitechapel, to the gin houses, to catch a prostitute or maybe some sodden old bloke made incapable by drink. What a change from a week ago and our glamorous trip to the West End, with all the laughter and shrieks and running that had entailed. Now we walked in silence through the dirty streets, hardly glancing at each other. My stomach churned with sadness, for I loved Poppy more than life but could not express this love. What had started a week ago as a fear of rejection had become over the passing days just fear, plain and simple, but fear writ large with capital letters and underlined for good measure. As we walked, I left my hand dangling by my side in the hope that she might grab hold of it with her hand, squeeze it tightly, pull it up to her lips and kiss it. Oh, just the thought made me warm inside, but no such action took place. We simply walked and in my head I could hear Little Red laughing at me and mocking me. A week ago I had thought that I had won the battle. That Poppy was mine and Little Red was beaten. Now all I could think was that Poppy regretted what had happened to Little Red, and wished that she had left me to die in that stinking alleyway.

Why couldn't I say all this to her? Why couldn't I turn to her, look her in the eye and explain? Why? Because I loved her with all my heart, that's why. And to have her by my side in sorrow was better than losing her altogether. It made no sense, I understand that now. But then, pray tell, when has love ever made an ounce of sense?

We were walking a side road with a gin house situated just ahead of us, when Poppy suddenly stopped. "Sssh," she hissed at me. I stopped moving and looked at her. She raised her eyebrows and nodded her head behind her. I looked where her head indicated, and saw standing 20 yards behind us a man in shadow. He appeared to be wearing a black cape and a hat of some kind. His face was in darkness. As we stopped walking, so he too had stopped. Poppy turned to face him and I followed suit.

There followed a kind of stand-off, with the man staring at us (or at least I think he was staring at us, with his face in darkness it was difficult to tell) and the two of us staring back at him. Heat flushed my cheeks, my vampire senses became alert and vibrant, and I instinctively knew that from out of nowhere Poppy and I had found ourselves in a life or death situation. Who was this man? I had no idea. But he did not fear us, he was not cowed by our stare, and he clearly was not beyond his own attempts at intimidation.

Deliberately he began to walk towards us, one step at a time, like time had slowed and he was the master of it. In his hand he held a. . . what? A knife? A sword? No. A stake. A wooden stake. And around his neck? A crucifix and a dog collar.

"Run," said Poppy. "Run with me."

We turned and we ran, Poppy taking the lead and me following. Through streets, over walls, down alleyways, we ran and ran, all the way down through Whitechapel and to the banks of the Thames. We flitted amongst the boats moored for the night, taking to the darkness by the walls, until we found sanctuary in an alcove deep in shadow. Overhead the quarter moon shone and clouds sped across the night sky.

We rested on our knees in silence, our vampire ears keen to pick up any sound. A minute passed, two, then three. The only sound was the lapping of the Thames and the clanging of an occasional bell aboard a boat. I found I had no voice. Again. Like the whole week that had just passed, fear had stolen the words from my throat. But this time not from fear of love, but from fear of the unknown. What was it that could make Poppy, beautiful, eternal Poppy, turn and run so?

I swallowed hard and said simply, "What?"

Poppy gave me a hard stare and put a finger to her lips, telling me in no uncertain terms to shut the fuck up.

Another minute, two, three, four, five. Slowly I sensed Poppy relaxing a little. She turned to me and smiled. Placing a hand on my cheek, she whispered, "Sorry. I'll explain."

"Since the time of the Holy Roman Empire, there have been warrior priests, sanctioned and trained by the Vatican and under the jurisdiction of the Pope, whose role it is to hunt down and kill all manner of 'unnatural' creatures. Sadly that includes us, the vampires. They are highly skilled in the fighting arts, they are remorseless and relentless in the pursuit of their prey, believing that their task is a holy one. They are promised by the Pope himself a place in Heaven by God's right hand for the work that they do. They are, of course, devout believers in their Christian God, and so to be told that they are doing this God's work makes them dangerous and pitiless.

"The Vatican also uses ancients magicks from Babylonian times to enhance the strength and fortitude of their warriors. A combination of prayers and rituals and herbal concoctions that turn a normal human into a beast with strength and stamina to match our own. Make no mistake, they are very dangerous creatures, and retreat is always the sane option to take if you ever find yourself confronted with one.

"I haven't heard of one being in London for over to twenty years. I had hoped they'd gone forever or had decided to leave me, *us*, alone. I don't think any of the other girls will have come across one. In medieval times of course they were prevalent, their tentacles spreading throughout Europe, burning and hanging witches, vampires, and anyone who didn't share their particular religious viewpoints. Those were awful, fearful times, and I thought them behind us. But when I heard of this Jack the Ripper, something just made me suspicious. There was something about it that had echoes of an earlier more barbaric time. It seems my suspicions were sadly correct."

"Those girls who were killed," I asked. "Were they vampires then?"

"I don't think so," said Poppy. "When we vampires die, well, we don't die like humans do, and the drawings and photographs in the newspapers seemed to show very human corpses. However, it's very possible that they were humans that this priest mistook for vampires or even witches. The killer priests are not known for their restraint, and if they should kill you in error they would say that they have done you a favour, and if you are innocent you will find a place in God's paradise. Their reasoning and beliefs are evil and confused, and self-justification is something that they are very good at. We used to have a name for them, we used to call them the Vatican Man. And a rhyme we used to sing."

Poppy grinned at me, and yes there was love in her eyes, I was sure of it.

"Would you like me to sing it for you?" "Oh, yes please," I said.

Poppy smiled bashfully, and then in a voice no louder than a whisper, she sang:

> *"Watch out, watch out for the Vatican Man*
> *With rosaries, beads, and a stake in his hand*
> *He'll cut out your heart and chop off your head*
> *And then you'll know what it's like to be dead."*

"A few hundred years ago, some vampires thought it was all just a myth, a legend, that the Vatican Man was just a story used to scare gullible vampires. Well, they were the ones who ended up with a stake in their heart or their head chopped off. The Vatican Man is real all right, and we must now be vigilant until he moves off to persecute some other poor souls in another corner of the globe. Come, the coast appears clear. Let us make our way home and warn the girls."

Poppy emerged from the alcove with me close behind her. There was a blur of movement and the man in the cape and the hat, the Vatican Man was upon us. Poppy tumbled to the floor, tripping over the folds of her dress. The man had a hold of my arms and threw me across the cobble-stoned walkway, coming to a rest by a thick rope that was being used to tether a boat. He turned his back on me and approached Poppy who was struggling to get to her feet. In his hand he held the wooden stake, raising it up to strike at the love of my life.

"No!" I screamed at him and launched myself, full pelt, at him. I barged into his back sending him arse over tit. As he sprawled on the ground, I leapt again at him but he was faster than I imagined and twisted out of my way. I lost my balance and found myself tumbling into the filthy water of the River Thames.

My black dress with the pretty lace frills was dragging me down. The dark, dirty waters of the Thames clung to me and refused to relinquish its hold. Like the monsters of my dreams, I felt things in the black waters reach for me, claw out at me, pull me deeper, the better to hasten my doom. My mind whirred and panicked, and as I struggling in the wet darkness, not knowing which way was up and which way was down, I fancied that these monsters had not tentacles and long tongues, but arms and legs and eyes; the victims that I had thrown into these very waters myself this past week. Now they sought to wreak their terrible revenge.

It was my dress that was pulling me down, not the hands of dead men. A sensible mind, so different from my own, spoke to me in calming tones. Take off the dress and save yourself. With the dress on, you are doomed. There are no monsters here, only your own panic.

This was not the voice I was used to hearing in my head. Kate's voice was always full of fanciful ideas ('away with the fairies' the teachers had said), too afraid to touch the love of her life, mas-turbating quietly in the dark, dreaming of tentacles and corpses in the water. Who now was this sensible voice telling me to take off the dress, to dismiss thoughts of monsters, to save myself?

Maria. Of course.

Sweet Maria from Charing Cross Road who was my first kill, whose soul I had physically felt merge with mine. I killed her, and now here was her voice in my head, saving my life.

'Take off the dress and swim to the surface.'

I tore at the fabric of the dress, pulling and yanking until it began to rip and come away from my body. 'That's it girl,' said the voice in my head, the voice of Maria, 'now look up, see the moon, and swim up to it. Swim for the moon.' And I swam upwards even as the hands of the dead dragged my pretty black dress down into the depths.

I burst through the surface of the water, naked now, and looked around desperately. There was no sign of Poppy or that bastard Vatican Man. I swam as best I could towards to river's edge and dragged myself back onto the cobblestones from whence I had tumbled just minutes before.

I sagged into a heap and scanned the river's edge for any sign of Poppy. I saw a figure a hundred yards from me, staring at me. Even from this distance, with my vampire eyes I could see her pretty dress, worn in places and darned, her purse clutched close to her bosom on which was embroidered a rose and the heart- breaking dedication. She looked at me and I fancied she smiled, before she walked around a corner and was gone.

A coughing fit engulfed me for a minute. Like a feral cat, on all fours, I coughed and spluttered until at last a small amount of blood coloured vomit flopped from my mouth and onto the cobblestones. Not my blood, you understand.

And then I knew I needed to get home, to Flower and Dean Street. It was not safe for me here, out in the open, naked, with the Vatican Man somewhere, perhaps somewhere close, observing me even now with the dead body of Poppy lying at his feet. No! There was no point thinking in such a fashion. Now was not the time to get lost in flights of fancy. Now was the time for action, for movement, to get away from the banks of the Thames and up into Spitalfields where the girls were. Safety in numbers. No matter how tough this Vatican Man fancied himself, he would surely be no match for half a dozen or more vampires. The thought of him coming face to face with Little Red and having his arse kicked all the way back to jolly old Rome brought a glimmer of a smile to my face.

I stood up, and began to move.

It was early in the morning, perhaps one or two o'clock, and the only signs of life I encountered were centred around the gin houses and therefore easily by-passed. Couple that with my vampire senses and speed, and though I was naked, the journey up to Spitalfields was less eventful that you might have imagined. But what a sight I must have looked. I fancied myself to look like some character from a fairy tale; a cat, perhaps, thrown down a well by a mean boy and turned into a girl by a kindly god-mother, thereby allowing me to climb out of the well and return to my master's home, a wild-eyed naked girl covered in dirt and river water, with filthy feet and fingers.

Being a vampire, the cold did not affect me so much, but still the September wind blew and pockets of goosebumps formed on my skin, on my arms and on my breasts, and my nipples stood prouder than a couple of guardsmen on duty outside Buckingham Palace.

I arrived on Flower and Dean Street and silently padded along, keeping to the shadows and away from the small pools of yellow light created by the gas lamps. Then I saw her approaching from the other direction, her dress torn and a slight stagger in her walk.

Poppy. She was alive.

could not help myself. I ran down the road towards her, and seeing me she began to run in my direction. Like Shakespeare's star-crossed lovers, we met beneath a gas lamp outside our house and fell into each other's arms. "I thought I'd lost you!" I cried. "I thought I'd lost you! I thought I'd lost you!" And I kissed her full on the lips, passionately, intensely, joyfully for being given this second chance when I'd thought her, deep in my heart, to be dead, a victim of the Vatican Man.

"I love you!" I hissed between kisses, my fangs now fully extended. "I love you! I love you!"

"Oh Snow," said Poppy, her own fangs extended, "do you? I was so scared that you found me bland and uninteresting and not worthy of your affections. You never tried to touch me or kiss me. In the bedroom you turned your back on me, and never crawled under the covers to visit me while I slept. I thought you regretted meeting me."

"No!" I wailed. "Oh no! I was so shy, so terribly shy and scared of being rejected. I'm so sorry. But I love you, I really, truly do love you."

"And I love you my dearest Snow."

We kissed again and began to snarl. The snarling was something I did quite instinctively and with no feelings of self-consciousness, another little detail of being a vampire I suppose.

After kissing and declaring our love for what seemed like hours –
and oh what blissful hours – Poppy placed a hand on my breast
and said, "My dear, you appear to be quite naked."

"And filthy," I replied. "I need a bath."

"Oh no," said Poppy. "I'm quite the admirer of this street urchin
look. I shall take you, if you please, muck and all."

"Oh I do please," I smiled, and was this not the greatest night
of my life? And had not the Vatican Man, who had meant to kill
us both and chop off our heads, actually placed me in the arms
of my beloved? How sickened would he be to know it, I thought.
And how clever we were to have out-smarted him. And how hollow
those words would ring but a few short days later. But for now, I
was in the loving arms of my Poppy and it seemed that nothing
could ever be wrong again.

We kissed once more, and then before any coppers could come
a-wandering by and happened upon a pair of vampire lesbos hard
at it beneath a gas lamp, we trotted up the few steps to our front
door and popped our saucy little selves inside.

I vaguely noticed the gaslights burning in the lounge, but paid
the fact no heed. We climbed up the stairs as fast as our legs
would carry us and closed the bedroom door. Of course it wouldn't
stay closed, so Poppy hastily thrust a chair behind it and then
turned to look at me, her fangs exposed and her sweet nose wrinkled in a snarl.

"I'm still a virgin," I said. "Please don't be cross if I don't do
it right."

"Lay down on the mattress," said Poppy. "You'll not be virgin
for long."

Her lips and her tongue.

Her lips and her tongue were relentless.

Chapter Six

I laid back on the mattress, as naked and as dirty as I had been when I'd crawled out of the Thames. No sooner had I lain back than Poppy was upon me. Her lips and her tongue ran over my neck, my ears, my shoulders. Kissing, licking and nipping at my collarbone and my chin and then around my breasts, carefully avoiding my nipples at first for fear of rushing and spoiling the fun.

Her tongue followed the contours of my breasts, looping circles that went around and around and around. I moaned gently in an ecstasy that was different to that of drinking her blood. This was somehow more personal, more intimate. This was an ecstasy that only I would know of. As Poppy was an ancient vampire, I knew (though I hated to think of it) that many vampires would have loved her through the ages and would have eagerly partaken of her blood. But here, on this night, the pleasure she gave freely to me was individual, was for me and me alone.

When at last her lips and her tongue and her teeth found my nipples, the first wave of climax came over me. As a virgin, I was powerless beneath her touch, and my orgasm was easily found. My back arched, pushing my nipple further into her mouth, begging her to suck harder, nip just a little deeper.

I heard a voice far away moaning and crying. The voice came nearer, and in my ecstasy I strained to understand who it was or where the sound was coming from. I writhed on the bed, my hips pushing skywards, harder and harder, and with time I came to realise that the voice was mine; the moans, the cries, the pitiful sobs, all were mine. What a place this ecstasy was, within her arms, within her embrace. What a place of wonders.

Her tongue moved down my body, down towards my navel which it circled and teased and finally ambushed. As my back arched once more, and now it was becoming difficult to tell where one climax ended and a new one began, I felt my juices squirt across her breasts which hung between my legs and gently rocked against my womanhood. She let out a little sigh of surprise, and sat back to rub my juices into her breasts and across her erect nipples. Smiling craftily, she lay back upon me and slowly moved her tongue down, across my thighs, and finally penetrated me.

The bedroom, that dingy top floor room within a doss house in the shittest part of London, became a palace of marvels. Brightly coloured lights flashed in my vision, a rainbow of shades and hues, and I felt myself rise out of my body. What miracles I felt taking place within my body; miracles so powerful that they forced my very soul to rise from out of me and float up to the bedroom ceiling. There I looked down upon Poppy and myself, making love. From my vantage point, Poppy was bathed in a golden light, like some soon-to-be-damned goddess from the Garden of Eden. Her shoulders and legs moved in rhythm with my own body as her tongue penetrated one moment, and licked around the edges the next. She found the tip of my womanhood, the very pinnacle of my joy, and as she did I felt so much pleasure that I think I may have fainted. I awoke, opening my eyes, back within my body. My face was tear streaked and my body was quivering, and all I could say was, "Oh, oh, oh," and then, "Thank you," and then, "I love you."

Poppy looked down at me and kissed my lips, and on her I could taste myself, the perfumed brine of my passions. "Love me more," she said. "Love me more than life itself." "I will," I replied. "I do." Without answering me, she bit deep into her own wrist and dripped her warm sweet blood once more into my mouth.

My back arched again and I knew pleasures such as no creature that walks this earth was ever intended to know. If what was to follow in later days was terrible, it was only terrible as payment for the pleasures I knew that night.

The walls of the room fell away and I found myself in a field at night-time. I was naked but felt no cold. Overhead a full moon bathed me, and by my side stood Poppy, naked also and bearing her now trademark short blonde hair. "What fun we shall have tonight, ma chérie!" she whispered at me, and together we crept across the grass and between trees until we came to an encampment of tents and open fires. Soldiers in smart blue uniforms wandered nonchalantly around the perimeter of the camp. The breighing of horses and the shouts of men's voices filled the air.

We crept closer to the camp, swiftly, undetected, until we found the tent we were looking for. A sentry walked lazily by us and Poppy in an instant was upon him, dragging him to the ground before he could make a sound, and tearing out his throat. With the sentry dead, we advanced upon the tent. Within the tent lay our victim, the man we had been sent to kill.

All at once I was floating in the night sky, surrounded by stars. The stars vibrated in unison, and their vibrating created a humming noise, the song of the universe. For a hundred years or more I floated amongst the stars, being lamented by their eternal music, and eventually, too soon, I descended back inside the tent and found myself making love to Poppy. We kissed, caressed, and licked each other's naked forms amongst the half dozen slaughtered bodies of men. Blood, flesh and limbs surrounded us as we writhed and thrust ourselves upon each other, the remnants of blue uniforms and discarded swords laying hither and thither.

Instinctively I seemed aware that we were in a field in Europe (France? Belgium?) and the slain soldiers around us were French. But more than that I did not know. All I was certain of was Poppy and her lust and my love. I closed my eyes and kissed her.

When I opened my eyes I was back in the London bedroom. "Oh my angel, what a life you have led," I said to her. "What a wonderful, terrible life."

And with that blood tears welled in her eyes and she placed her head upon my breast. I wrapped my arms around her and "shushed" her gently as one might a child who has been awoken by demon-filled nightmares, and I wondered how it was possible that my heart now held even more love for her than it had done previously.

As day broke behind the heavy black drapes, we dozed happily with our arms around each other. Eventually I spoke.

"The memory that I saw when you gave me your blood, you were in France or somewhere, killing French soldiers?"

Poppy was silent for a moment, her eyes buried beneath an arm that I had draped around her slender shoulders. At last she murmured, "Belgium." And then she was silent again.

We lay in silence for two minutes, three minutes, and then she murmured again, "Belgium," and sat up to look down at me.

"It was the Napoleonic Wars. They paid me very well, the British army, and well, king and country and all that. Oh Snow! Please don't judge me! Please don't hate me! I've done some terrible things, some really awful things! But I couldn't stand it if you hated me for it! Can't we just be together now, and let the past be hanged?"

"Oh Poppy," I said pulling her close. "How could I possibly hate you or judge you? I love you more than anything, more than life itself. I love you so much that my heart feels fit to burst, so it does. I've never met anyone like you before. If I could just stay here in this room with you, on this mattress, and never go anywhere else for all eternity, then I would be the happiest girl who ever lived, ever."

This seemed to please her, and she relaxed into me. "I should hope you never have met anyone like me," she said. "After all, I'm the nearest thing to a living god that London has known in a very long time." And she snuggled into me and fell asleep. Lying awake on the mattress, I remembered what Little Red had told me; that Poppy had been alive when the Romans had founded London, and she had been a lover of the Caesars. And my reply haunted me that morning: what was she doing now living in a doss house in Spitalfields?

Later that evening, Poppy gathered all the girls round, including Little Red who sat sulking in a corner, and, I fancied, eyeing me with a look of seething hatred, and told them about the Vatican Man. She told them that I had only survived because I'd fallen in the Thames (there was some muffled sniggering when this fact was pointed out), and that Poppy herself had managed to escape purely by running and running until she'd lost him around the docks. The girls all looked worried and concerned, and promised to be vigilant. "This isn't a joke or something to be taken lightly,"

Poppy told the girls. "The Vatican Man is real and very dangerous. If you come across him, don't try to fight. Better just to run. And of course, make sure you've lost him before returning here to our home. The last thing, the very last thing, we want is him knowing where we live."

I never told anyone that it was Maria who saved me from the waters of the Thames, or that I'd seen her at the riverside.

Despite the worries about the Vatican Man, the following week proved to be a perfectly blissful one. Poppy and myself indulged in our passions for each other at every available moment, a fact that was not missed by our house-mates who giggled and winked conspiratorially whenever we entered a room together or were caught holding hands as we strolled along a street. It was all good natured, of course, and dear Holly came to me one evening during that week and said, "I-I-I'm r-r-really g-glad you're w-w-with P-Poppy now and n-n-not th-that c-c-cow." And I gave her a big hug and said "Thank you."

I walked around with my head in the clouds, forever humming some merry tune or other. True, the atmosphere when Little Red was in the room was a little strained to say the least, but she seemed to be spending less and less time in the house, and would always go off hunting by herself. My secret wish was that she'd disappear altogether, a wish which seemed to come true on the Friday when it was noted that nobody had seen her since Thursday.

Ah yes. Thursday. The one day during that week that had proved to be less than blissful.

Most of the girls, including Poppy and myself, had hunted on the Wednesday, and so on Thursday evening our appetites, for blood at least, were sated. On those evenings when hunting was not a priority, we would sit around the house playing cards and smoking cigarettes (all the girls smoked – it was quite the thing), or we would go for a walk simply to take in the night air. This evening, while the girls were sitting in the parlour, playing cards, teasing each other, and smoking, Poppy and I sat outside on the steps that led down to the street below. I had my head on her shoulder and was enjoying the simple pleasure of just sitting in her company. There came a sudden shrill peel of laughter from within the parlour, and I raised my head to hear better. Some of the girls were laughing raucously, and I was intrigued as to what had amused them so.

"What's going on in there?" I asked Poppy, and stood up. "I'll go and take a gander."

With a merry hop and a skip, I bounded up the stairs, walked through the front door which stood ajar, and entered the parlour. There was nothing sensational to report, just silly young girls playing at being silly young girls. Apparently Catherine had stolen Abigail's cigarettes and had put them down the neck of her dress, between her breasts. Abigail had managed to pin Catherine to the floor and had recovered her cigarettes in a rather lusty fashion. At this, Catherine had kissed Abigail full on the lips, and everybody in the room, believing this to be the sauciest, funniest thing they had seen in the last, oh, ten minutes, fell about screaming and laughing.

As they recounted the story to me, I laughed and shared in their joy. Such simple joy.

Once the story had been told (and re-told as apparently some elements had been omitted in the first telling and this warranted a second performance), the girls then asked when Poppy and I would join them for a game of cards. "Oh, in a minute or two I suppose," I replied. "Let me go and ask her if she fancies a game."

I walked back to the front door and saw immediately that Little Red was sat on the step next to Poppy. Only she wasn't really seated, she was more crumpled in a position half-way between sitting and laying.

I stood on the doorstep, hardly daring to breathe, watching the whole awful scene unfold before me. Earlier in the evening, as soon as the sun had set, Little Red has left the house by herself. This had become her routine all week, and I imagine, having returned and found Poppy sitting by herself, she had decided to seize the opportunity.

"Please," Little Red was saying to Poppy, "please, let's just run away. You and me. Let's leave this house and start anew, somewhere else. No-one has ever loved you like me, you know that. No-one else knows how to love you like I can. I know I can make you happy, keep you satisfied. I've drunk so much of your blood that I can't even imagine a future without you. I would die, simply die, without you. Even now I can feel myself withering away. Without your love, without your touch, without your affection, I'm dying inside.

"Let's leave, you and me, and find happiness elsewhere. It's this house, this damned house, that's turning your head away from me, making you want to experiment with that stupid girl. Do you think she can love you like I can? Of course she can't! How could she? She doesn't know you like I do. I can make you happy again, I can change, I can love you even more. Let me drink some more of your blood and let me show you how I can change, how I can love you even more than before. Please!"

Little Red lunged forward, trying to grab hold of one of Poppy's wrists, trying to bite it and release Poppy's blood into her mouth. There was a pitiful struggle, with Little Red desperately reaching out at Poppy, and Poppy batting her away with ease. After thirty seconds, Little Red gave up the assault, and let her arms flop down by her side.

Poppy hardly looked at Little Red. She simply said coldly and without emotion, "I'm with Snow now."

At this Little Red wailed and I fancied I really did hear her heart break, literally break, in that moment. She stood up, still not even noticing me behind her, and staggered down the steps like a scarecrow, bereft of bones and managing to stay upright only through the questionable strength of the straw stuffed roughly inside her. She staggered down the road, falling onto all fours occasionally, and eventually disappeared into the night.

"I'm sorry you had to see that," said Poppy without turning to look at me. She had known I was there all along. And there was a part of me, an evil, selfish, ungrateful part of me, that wondered how many years it would be before it was me staggering off down the road, and a new beau sitting on Poppy's arm.

I had seen Little Red as my adversary in the war for Poppy's love and affection. I had wanted to beat her, to subjugate her, to be her better. But now, when the war was won, all I could feel for Little Red was sorrow. That was all to change of course, with what was to happen over the following days. But at that moment at least, I felt sorry for the girl.

I leapt down the step and fell at Poppy's side, kissing her neck with little kisses, one, two, three, four, five. "Never leave me," I said. "Never let that be me staggering down the road utterly destroyed. Say you'll never leave me."

Poppy looked at me and a warmth re-entered her eyes and her voice. "Dearest Snow," she said, "I will never leave you." And she picked me up and carried me into the house, up the stairs, and into our bedroom.

Now, when I'm in a particularly dark or cynical mood, I look upon that night and wonder how many times in Poppy's past had that exact same scene been played out? How many broken hearted girls sent packing, how many new lovers welcomed with promises of forever? But that night I believed her, and in my brighter moments I believe her still. She had meant us to be together. Forever.

Chapter Seven

Saturday night came around, and with Little Red no longer lurking in the corners like the Harbinger of Doom, and with us having seen neither hide nor hair of the Vatican Man all week, the mood in the house was decidedly giddy and excitable. Poppy picked up on the atmosphere, and thought that we ought to do something special. Perhaps not West End special, but special none-the-less.

"We shall all stick together this time," she said. "None of this breaking up into little groups nonsense. Let's all stick together and have a little fun, and if the humans don't like it, well, they can just jolly well lump it, can't they?"

And all the girls laughed and applauded and thought this was the most wonderful idea. I thought it was a wonderful idea too, I really did, but there was a small part of me that just wanted to hold Poppy near to me, to monopolise her time and her affections, and not share her with the others. But that was me just being mean and silly, and of course love can do that to you if you let it, turn you mean and silly. I clapped my hands along with the other girls and declared it to be a great idea. All of us together, one big gang of swells.

With September by now beginning to come to a close, thick pea-souper fogs had started to roll in off the Thames, immersing whole swathes of London in a thick grey-green mist that erased the light from gas lamps and blotted out the sun. The girls loved the pea-soupers for it meant that they were safe to walk once more in daylight, the destructive power of the sun negated by the fog. So it was that Saturday; a pea-souper had blown in and turned the vibrant streets around us into a kind of eerie ghost town. Most humans stayed indoors during the fogs if it was at all possible for them to do so, chest infections and killer flu becoming prevalent during the fog season. Looking out of our parlour window, I could barely see past the steps where two nights previously Little Red had had her heart broken. I fancied I could hear a cab clip-clopping along, but I could see, even with my vampire eyes, precious little of it. Perhaps the flicker of the flame of his lamp, but nothing more.

"I used to hate the old pea and ham soups," I said. "But now, how wonderful they are. To think that I have not seen daylight for two weeks or more!"

"Two weeks?" laughed Mary Jane in her beautiful Irish lilt. "Were it not for these fogs, I wouldn't have seen daylight for twenty years."

"You're all babies, of course," said Poppy. "I can't begin to think of how many *centuries* it is since I last stepped out on a proper summer's day. We must thank London's polluted air for salvaging our sanity and allowing at least a peek of daylight to enter our otherwise frightfully morbid and dark lives." And with that she laughed at her own sense of drama and made a self- deprecating bow, and the other girls laughed also and applauded her as if she were a drama queen upon the stage. "So this *afternoon*," and at the word everyone oohed, "we shall promenade along the Embankment alongside old Mother Thames, and see what tasty morsels should come stumbling our way out of the desolate fog."

And we cheered and dragged out the tin bath and started to ready ourselves for another night on the tiles.

How queer it must be to hear me speak of the beauty of the pea-souper fog, and yet, as a vampire, that was how I viewed it. Even now, all these years later, when a good thick fog descends upon my world, my pulse quickens, my spirit soars, and I find myself rushing out into the streets to poke fun at the impotent sun and celebrate my ability to, all too briefly, walk the daylight world unscathed. So it was that Saturday afternoon. The six of us strolling along the Embankment, arm in arm, singing silly songs, daring to bare our fangs and reveal our true nature, protected and concealed by the wonderful fog.

Occasional humans would emerge from the fog in ones or twos, and if they happened to notice us, happened to notice our fangs or the singular redness of our eyes, they quickly shuffled off, heads down, to fade away back into the fog from whence they'd emerged. Perhaps they hurried home to tell their loved ones of the darnedest thing they had witnessed in the fog, although of course, they would quickly add, it was quite obviously just the peculiar light within the fog playing tricks on their eyes, for six women walking arm in arm, and all of them displaying fangs (for want of a better word) for teeth, was quite a preposterous thought, after all, wasn't it?

At that point in my new life as a vampire, I had killed seven humans. Only seven! How many more would I send to the mortuary or the murky depths of the Thames over the coming years! But at that point, my tally was a mere seven, starting with Maria, my first, who broke my duck and saved my life. It is true that with each kill, a part of the victim's soul intertwines with the vampire's own, so that following the kill no vampire is *quite* the same person that they were before. But with each kill that change becomes more subtle, less obvious even to the vampire, until, as Poppy had pointed out to me, after several thousand kills (and if Poppy had been a vampire since Roman times, then her personal tally must have been in the thousands), the changes brought about by the addition of yet another new soul could be barely perceived, their names and life-stories quickly forgotten.

But Maria, my first, will stay with me forever. She lives inside me in a way that is difficult to describe to those who can't have no understanding of what it means to rely on mortals for food when you was mortal yourself, so desperately mortal, not so long ago.

I had killed and eaten seven. By the end of this night, on the fog-shrouded Embankment, that tally would be eight.

They came out of the fog towards us in ones and twos, until in a matter of seconds a gang of six young men (six, just like us, it must have been fate) were stood in front of us. I knew their kind, having encountered more than my fair share of them when I was human. They're the kind of boys who are as sweet as pie if you catch them on their own, and probably still live at home with their mammies and their daddies, but once you put a few of them together they start acting like regular lotharios, eyeing up the ladies, even following them down the road, trying to chat them up, and generally being a right royal pain in the backside.

"A bunch of ladybirds!" exclaimed one of the boys, which wasn't particularly nice considering none of us were prostitutes. But then, I suppose, being a houseful of prostitutes was our alibi, so you can't blame the poor chap for thinking so. "Perhaps we gentlemen can escort you to your destination? Seeing as it's such a foggy evening? Or maybe you'd prefer a leisurely stroll along the river in the company of gentlemen such as we?" He turned and winked at his friends, his hands sticking out of his pockets like he was a proper Jack the Lad, and a certain swagger in his voice.

I half expected Poppy to leap onto this boy (really, he was little more than a boy, perhaps in his later teen years) and rip out his throat. But she seemed game for a bit of sport, it being Saturday and all.

"Come here darling," she said, turning on the East End accent like she had done when she'd taken the soldier that night in the West End, "and let me whisper sweet nothings in your shell-like." This slutty approach was obviously her party piece, her Saturday night special. It made me cross for reasons I couldn't quite put my finger on.

The boy smirked round at his friends, and then stepped forward. Even though I knew it was all part of her game, that this boy would be dead within the next few short seconds, I still couldn't resist that demon envy from gnawing away at my heart with teeth every bit as sharp as my own. As the boy moved towards my beloved, I leapt on him, clamping my jaws around his throat, and dragged him away into the fog.

I heard behind me screams, first of shock and then of terror as the girls laid into the remaining lotharios. 'Not much swagger left in them by now I'll wager,' I thought as I hauled my prey up against the Embankment wall.

Although his neck was a right old mess, he was still alive. Blood gurgled from a huge gash that spread almost from ear to ear. Miraculously he was conscious, and he stared at me through big saucer eyes. He moved his mouth up and down, producing a strange wheezing noise. I looked at him quizzically. What was he doing? Why, he was trying to speak.

I knelt down next to where he sat with his back against the Embankment wall, and noticed that he had spoiled his trousers, both front and back, if you see what I mean. There was quite a pong in the air. I tilted my head to one side and held my breath, the better to hear what he was saying. In a low, rasping whisper he was muttering, "Mummy. I want my mummy. I want to go home now."

Home. I was surrounded by people who wanted to go home and now never could, and there in the centre of this merry-go- round of impossible wishes stood me, the Queen of Can't Go Home. I put a gloved finger to the boy's cheek. "Oh no, my dearest boy,"

I said. "You can't never go home, not no more" A look of terror dimmed the faltering light in his eyes, and all at once I regretted the cruelty of my words. So I put both hands to his cheeks, one either side, and said, "It's me, your mummy. I'm here now. All's well, my sweet boy." And instantly, I swear to you, *instantly*, a look of peace replaced the fear in his eyes. He kind of smiled at me, and then gurgled, and blood poured from his mouth. "Mummy?" he managed to cough. "Yes, my dearest son," I said, "here I am." And then I went at his neck with mixed emotions, part of me wanting to kill this brute who thought that he could lay a hand on my beautiful Poppy, and part of me simply wanting to end this, to put the poor lad out of his misery.

His last thoughts had been of home and of his mother, and as I drank his blood, visions and images of both his mother and his home (yes, as predicted, he lived at home with his parents) flooded my mind. A rotund mother bustling around in a large floral dress and apron, baking in a kitchen that was always too warm, with bread and cakes in the oven, big wet kisses at bedtime, bone-crushing hugs, and love; so much love, and baking, and cleaning, and scrubbing the front doorstep, and nipping to the lav out back, and yet more love. Home. His home had been a real home, like mine had been.

I finished his blood, picked up his body, and threw it as far out into the Thames as my strength could muster. The fog was too thick for me to see how far out the body had landed, but it did so with a wet 'sploosh', so at least I knew I hadn't inadvertently thrown it onto a passing coal barge or something. "There you go, silly boy," I whispered. "Back home with you." And through the elation of the feed, I also felt a little melancholy. I leant against the wall and decided that I, myself, had to go home one more time. Just to see my mam and my daddy. Just one more time.

I was in trouble with Poppy. Why hadn't I let her kill the lead boy? Why had I jumped in like that? It was terribly untidy and Mary Jane had had to chase one boy for a quarter of a mile before she caught him, and all the while he'd been screaming blue murder and could have brought the coppers or worse, the Vatican

Man, down on us. I should learn to be patient and act on her command.

But she didn't stay cross with me for long, and when we got home we made love as intensely as we ever had. Until, that is, the morning when I told her I wanted to visit my home (my *old* home, I corrected myself) one last time. Then I was in trouble all over again.

I knew the arguments of course, and I understood them. It wasn't safe for me to visit my parents in case I killed them, plain and simple. They could never welcome me back into their home once they knew what had happened to me, and in all likelihood they'd report me to the authorities and I'd be carted off to some insane asylum or worse, handed over to the Vatican for extermination. I understood that a visit to my old home, to meet my parents, to reassure them that I was all right and not actually, in the strictest sense, dead, was a folly. But even though I knew and understood all this, still I could not shake off the desire to do exactly that – to run up to them, throw my arms around them and kiss them. Damn that stupid boy last night. It was his blood putting these ideas into my head. Poppy was right, I'd been stupid to jump on him, letting my emotions cloud my judgement. Typical Katie.

"A quick kill, that's the way," Poppy had lectured me. "Letting them live long enough to realise what's happening to them, to allow time for remorse and regret to cloud their minds as you drink their blood, that's the sure path to distress, dearest Snow. If nothing else, I hope you have now learned the lesson of why the kill should be quick."

I lay in bed all that morning with my back turned to Poppy. I couldn't sleep and I know that she couldn't either. Eventually she relented, but she insisted that I did not approach my parents, but merely observed them from a distance, just to satisfy my own curiosity, just so I would know they were doing well, or at least as well as could be expected of an ageing couple whose only daughter had mysteriously disappeared only a few weeks since.

My mam was a housewife, cooking, cleaning, looking after the house. My old daddy was a porter down at Kings Cross Station, and they lived in a two-up two-down in Camden. Daddy never got back home from the station much before ten o'clock at night, so that suited me just fine, being a creature of the night and all. Of course, Poppy insisted that she come with me too, just to make sure I didn't get into any bother, and I didn't mind her company one little bit. My only regret was that I wasn't allowed to hold her hand in public or kiss her occasionally on the neck and the cheek as we walked. The fog had lifted somewhat, and Poppy said that people would look and stare if we were too amorous with each other. It would attract undue attention. I think thoughts of the Vatican Man still played on her mind, and this is what she meant by 'undue attention'. So we walked along arm-in-arm like we were sisters, acting perfectly prim and proper. Though as we walked I felt awfully proud, to see how handsome she was, how she drew admiring glances from men and women alike, how she was the most incredible creature to ever walk along those roads between Spitalfields and Camden, and to marvel at the fact that I, little old me from the hat shop, was walking by her side as her vampire lover.

"Sod this for a game of soldiers," I whispered into her ear. "Let's just go home and fuck." I think the influence of the boy's blood was beginning to wear off. I was also feeling a little anxious about seeing my parents now that the thought of doing so had become a reality, and retreating back up Flower and Dean Street had suddenly become something of a welcome proposition. What if they were beside themselves with woe? Or had moved out of what had been our home and had gone to live elsewhere? Or what if they'd both died of a broken heart? Or worse, what if they were happy that I'd disappeared? What if they were all laughs and smiles? Oh, Poppy had been right. No good could come of this. Fucking Poppy was by far the more sensible option.

"Tut, tut!" said Poppy with a dark twinkle in her eye. "Absolutely not. Let us see this thing through to its end. We shall let you see your dearest parents one last time, and then, when you are

satisfied, we shall rush home and you may ravage me then. Till then, dearest Snow, put your fangs away, you're starting to drool."

I hadn't noticed that my fangs had extended. I giggled like a schoolgirl and squeezed her arm. The boy's blood was most definitely wearing off.

But oh! Not for long!

Poppy and myself walked along the street where my old house had been, and there, right there, was my mam, on her hands and knees, scrubbing at the pavement outside the house with a bucket of water and a wire brush. She looked so small and frail, and the task of cleaning the filthy pavement so huge and pointless, that I just crumpled to my knees. What was she doing? Scrubbing the pavement? At gone ten o'clock at night? I thought of my new home; a place of decadence and sex and blood. The girls there would rather poke their eyes out with blunt knives than scrub and clean. Their lives were a whirl of passions, desires and appetites. Yet here was my mam, who saw it as her duty to clean the pavement outside her home so that strangers could walk over it with their muddy boots and make it filthy again, scrubbing her fingers down to the bone.

She looked up from her toil and saw me, or rather she looked straight through me as though I wasn't really there. Her eyes had dark circles around them and she looked older than I remembered her just a little over two weeks previously. I realised, to my horror, that she was deep in mourning for my absence and presumed death. All this talk of Jack the Ripper in the newspapers, and then my own disappearance. It wasn't hard to imagine the thoughts that must have been going through the poor woman's mind as she scrubbed. "Oh no," I whispered and started to crawl towards her on all fours.

"Snow, Katie, stop," said Poppy, pulling me back by my shoulder. She never called me Katie, it was always Snow, so I knew she was worried. I shrugged her off, and staggered to my feet, still walking towards mam. As I got closer I started to run. She must have heard my footsteps and looked up at me. "Mam!" I wailed. She looked at me but there was no recognition in her eyes. "Mam!"

I fell down at her side, on the pavement, still wet from her scrubbing. "Mam, it's me!"

Mam shrank away from me. "I'm sorry, madam," she said. "I think you must have me mistaken for somebody else."

I looked at her, confused. "Mam? It's me. Katie. It's Katie."

Mam shrank back further and shouted, "Father!" She always called daddy 'father'. "Father! Come here at once!" Then she looked back at me with venom in her eyes, "I don't know what your game is, young lady, but my daughter has been missing these past two weeks. I don't know if this is your idea of a joke, but I ain't laughing. Did you think I would mistake you for my own poor angel? Whoever you are, you ain't my daughter."

As those words left her mouth, and instantly froze my heart, daddy came out of the front door, carrying with him his heavy walking cane.

"What is it, love?" daddy asked of mam.

"This, this *trollop* has been trying to tell me that she's Katie," she started to weep. "She's had the gall to come up to me and call me 'mam'."

"Has she now?" said daddy.

"Daddy?" I looked up at him. "It's me. Katie."

"No it ain't," said daddy and he raised his cane and smacked me around the head.

Darkness. Then Poppy's face slowly coming into focus. And more blood, mine by ways of a change, running over my forehead and down into my eyes.

"I didn't kill them," said Poppy, gently, almost sweetly. "I should have done, but I didn't. I just dragged you away."

"What happened?" I asked. My head hurt, but already my vampire strength was combating wounds that in a mortal could very well have proven fatal.

"What I knew would happen," said Poppy, but there was no malice in her voice. "I'm so sorry, dearest Snow. I tried to save you from this. I know how awful it is."

There is, Poppy later explained as we lay on our backs in Regent's Park looking up at the stars, something quite remarkable that happens to a human body when it is transformed into a vampire. Well, I thought to myself, that's stating the bleeding obvious, but she went on to explain. There are the palpable physical changes that take place; the hunger for blood, the amplification of the senses, the increase in strength and speed, the halting of the ageing process. Everyone knows all about them. But there is a change that happens that is for the most part imperceptible, but to those who are family to a human who is turned, the change is devastating. Put quite simply, they fail to recognise their kith and kin. A brother, a sister, a mother, a father; if they are turned into vampires, the rest of the family will simply not recognise them. It is as though a mesmeric fog descends, confusing the recollection of what the person they had once loved looks like, so they may, as in the case of my own mam and daddy, look straight into the face of the family member and claim, swear, believe that the person standing before them is not in actual fact their loved one.

Poppy said that she thought it was some kind of self- preservation tactic triggered in the human mind, a way for humans to protect themselves from, and even kill, loved ones who have been turned into vampires, and do so without remorse. "I can believe that," I said, rubbing the lump on my head. It was still a little sore.

"Oh my dearest," said Poppy, rolling over to look at me and resting her head upon her upturned hand, "does it hurt awfully?"

I told her that it did, feeling more than a little sorry for myself, and allowed her to kiss my poor forehead better with her luscious lips of ruby red.

Naked as usual beneath my dress, I felt her hand navigate its way up my stockinged legs towards what my mother used to describe as my 'foof', and what Poppy called my 'cunt'.

"You promise you didn't kill them?" I asked between passionate kisses.

"I promise, my dearest," said Poppy impatiently. "Now unless you're moaning in delight, I don't want to hear another word."

I never visited my parents again of course, and in a strange way, after that night I never really thought of them to any great degree. Something had changed in them, *everything* had changed in me, and our lives were now destined for completely different paths. Never the twain shall meet, as they say, and a blooming good job too as I really didn't fancy another whack around the head from a weighted walking stick.

Did Poppy kill them that night? I don't know. She said she didn't, but then Poppy used to say a lot of things. If she did kill them, perhaps it was for the best. Perhaps it would have put them out of their grief, a little like me putting that boy on the Embankment, the boy who had inspired this whole sorry adventure, out of his misery just the night before. Just the night before? As I lay on my back on the grass of Regent's Park, with the stars twinkling majestically overhead and Poppy's fingers playing deep within me, that night on the Embankment seemed a hundred years ago. Funny how time plays tricks on the mind when you're immortal.

And listen to me, listen to the little monster I had become, contemplating my own parents being murdered by my lover as being perhaps 'for the best'. Please don't ever confuse me for a human. I wasn't that no more. I was by now something else entirely.

Chapter Eight

She stood before me in our bedroom, the heavy black drapes drawn against the angry sun. Outside, a thousand mortals in a thousand homes rose from their slumber to work, to slave, to exist. But inside this room such obligations were meaningless. In here existed only carnal desires, love and lust.

I stood behind Poppy and gently kissed the nape of her neck. She let out a sigh. With fingers that trembled with anticipation, I undid her white dress and allowed it to fall to the floor. She turned and stood before me naked, save for her white stockings and her black leather ankle boots. I was naked and barefoot, and the heels of her boots allowed the shorter Poppy to look me directly in the eye. "Worship me," she said. "Oh yes," I replied, entranced.

I laid her down upon the mattress and caressed her with my kisses. I started with her fingers, such delicate little things that had caused so much death, their grip as strong as a python's coils when they had cause to be, but now subdued and soft as my lips pressed against them, on the tips, then the knuckles. I turned her hand over and kissed her palm, then allowed my tongue to trace her lifeline, the line where fortune tellers and gypsies alike gaze in the hope of seeing the past, the present and the future. My tongue caressed this line, attempting to erase her past, and place only thoughts of me and my love in her present and in her future.

Along her arm I moved, savouring every sweet touch of my lips against her pearly white skin. Her shoulders, her neck, her breasts, down to her stomach and then slowly across to her thighs, protected as they were from the attentions of my kisses by white cotton stockings.

I pulled down the stocking of her right leg, all the way down to the top of the boot, revealing her soft skin; white with hints of blue around the thigh and a sweet redness around the knee. I kissed gently and lovingly, careful not to allow my fangs to penetrate her skin just yet.

As my lips reached the top of the black boot, I felt the softness of the leather against my skin. Taking the boot in my hands, I knelt up and lifted her leg to my mouth, kissing the boot once before untying the laces. The boot came away from her stockinged feet easily and fell to the floor. I removed the stocking completely and once more lifted her foot, now naked, to my mouth, caressing her toes with my lips.

She lay before me, naked save for the stocking and boot still on her left leg, and I wondered at the beauty of her. How was it possible that this enchanting, wanton creature was mine? What could I possibly have down to warrant such a treasure? My fangs were fully extended and ached with desire. I took one more lingering look at her as she writhed before me, her eyes closed and with a curled hand tentatively brushing at her lips, before I revisited her naked thigh and allowed my fangs to penetrate the flesh. I sucked at her blood, and placed fingers within her. The pleasure and the pain. Tiny explosions flashed in my mind as her blood came into me, and the lights were accompanied by the sound of Poppy's lust; moaning, sighing, screaming high above me.

I pulled my fangs away and licked the blood from her wound, then lay marvelling as the tiny puncture wounds healed themselves. I stroked the flesh with one hand as the fingers of my other hand continued to pleasure her. Once the marks had healed completely, which took but a miraculous few moments, my fangs once more broke the skin, causing a spasm to ripple through her body, and I drank of her blood again.

The memories that entered me as a result of her blood were this time vague and confusing. I saw pyramids illuminated by moonlight and a thousand stars in a deep blue sky, and I felt a dry, acrid heat pressing upon my face. This imagery, at that time in my life, made no sense to me. I did not recognise these impressive structures as the Great Pyramids of Giza, for although they were at that point well known to those moving in archaeological circles, as a poor shop girl I had never seen a picture or certainly a photograph of them. It was only years later that I saw a postcard in a shop and my blood froze, knowing that I had seen such things once before, as I drank Poppy's blood on that fateful evening. I also fancy that I saw the River Nile while in that blood induced stupor, though at that moment I did not, of course, recognise it, and mistook it rather for London's own Thames.

Poppy was there; sometimes she floated in the sky with the stars, other times she was at my side, holding my hand, and always smiling. Yes, she was there, but she looked different somehow. Her eyes were heavily decorated with black eye paint, so much so that I hardly recognised her at times as she passed in and out of my visions. She was always naked but her skin shone like gold. "Are you a god?" I asked her. She simply smiled, as one would smile at a small child who had asked a question more profound than it realised.

I drank her blood and fingered her cunt, and high above me she writhed and moaned and screamed. But then the screaming seemed to be coming from all around me, and there were more voices now, not just Poppy's. I saw pyramids and stars and heard screams. I drank blood and gave pleasure and heard yet more screams. And the screams were trying to tell me something.

"Poppy! Snow! Please! Mary Jane is dead!"

It was Catherine, standing in the bedroom doorway, supporting herself on the frame, crying out to us. Behind her stood the distraught figures of Holly and Abigail. It was evening now. How long had I been fucking on the mattress with Poppy? All day and into the evening?

I rolled onto my back and moaned, images of stars and pyramids continuing to fog my mind. Behind me Poppy jumped to her feet, still wearing only one boot and one stocking, and wrapped her silk gown around herself.

"Tell me what's happened," she asked of Catherine.

"I saw it with my own eyes," she said, blood tears smudging her cheeks. "Oh Poppy, it was awful."

The three girls stumbled into the bedroom, leaning on one another for support.

"We was going to tell you Poppy, really we was," said Abigail.

"Tell me what?" asked Poppy. "What's going on?"

"While you and Snow was busy up here," said Catherine, "Little Red came round. She was sweet as pie and said we should take a stroll round to her new crib for a bit of a laugh and maybe, if we fancied it, go out hunting. She wanted to show us where she was living, like, so we said all right, and she wrote down her address for us and told us she'd see us later as she had some business to attend to. We were supposed to meet up with her tonight around midnight at her place."

"Midnight?" I said. "What time is it now?"

"Around two in the morning," said Catherine. Two in the morning? Me and Poppy had been hard at it for around eighteen hours.

Blimey. You could've blown me down with a feather. Time flies and all that.

"Only we changed our mind," said Abigail. "We thought it weren't right going round her place after all, not after everything what had gone on."

"I-I-I w-would never have g-g-gone anyway," said Holly. "I h-hate h-her."

"But Mary Jane said she was going," said Abigail. "She said she missed Little Red and was just going for a natter and that. Nothing special."

"So she went, on her own. But then about one o'clock we got to wondering if Mary Jane was all right and if she'd got to Little Red's new digs safely, and, to be honest, we got to thinking that maybe a bit of a parley might have been just the thing, you know, to see if we couldn't settle any differences, make the peace and all," said Catherine. "So me and Abigail took a stroll down to Little Red's digs, it's only down the road a ways, in Whitechapel, to see what was going on."

"I-I-I stayed here," said Holly.

"When we got there," said Catherine, "there was no sign of life, no candles burning, nothing. We knocked on the door but there was no reply. The window had a curtain drawn across it, but the window was open a touch so I reached in and pulled the curtain back a little way, you know, just to make sure the girls weren't in there, hiding and giggling and having a bit of a wheeze at our expense. So I pulls the curtain back, and oh. . . ." Catherine put a gloved hand to her mouth and seemed unable to speak.

"It was awful," said Abigail, taking up the story. "Mary Jane had sort of, I don't know, sort of imploded. It looked like her body and her face was inside out. The bits what should be on the inside were now on the outside, and everything had collapsed, her chest, her stomach, her head. You couldn't see her face, it had just sort of disintegrated."

With that Poppy started to get dressed quickly, but she demanded more details from the girls. How exactly had Mary Jane's body looked? How could they be sure that it was Mary Jane? Had they seen Little Red? Had they seen anyone else hanging around? The girls attempted to compose themselves and further describe the state of Mary Jane's body. It was, they said, as though she'd been decomposing for six months and not just an hour or so. Poppy just nodded at this and muttered, "Right you are." They knew it was Mary Jane because of the jewellery on her fingers and wrists, and the shoes she was wearing. There'd been no sign of Little Red or anyone else. "It was as quiet as a grave," said Abigail, shivering.

"If Little Red comes back here," said Poppy as she laced up the boot that earlier I had relieved her of in the throes of passion, "make sure she stays here. Don't let her disappear again. But be careful – she may not be all she seems. If anyone else comes to the house, scarper. Just leg it. Don't take no chances, even if it means letting Little Red get away again. Anyone knocks on the door, leg it. Any signs of a priest or any kind of bloke hanging around in the shadows, leg it. In fact, anything happens at all, just leg it."

"The Vatican Man?" I asked.

"I reckon so," said Poppy. "Sounds like he got Mary Jane good and proper."

"What you going to do?" asked Abigail.

"What I should have done a very long time ago," said Poppy. "Sort this sorry mess out once and for all."

"I'll come with you," I said.

"No you won't my girl," said Poppy. "I need you to be safe. And besides, you girls should all stick together now, safety in numbers and all that. Don't worry about me. I've dealt with some rough bastards before in my time. This'll be a stroll in the park by comparison. I'll catch up with you later, even if you do have to leg it. I'll find you, don't you worry about that."

She smiled, kissed me on the cheek and whispered, "Dearest Snow." I was filled all at once with a sense of dread. "Don't go," I said. "Stay with me."

"I have to go," said Poppy, "and you know I do. I have to sort this out. I can't let that bastard kill anyone else."

"You're going to die," I said, and I knew it, just knew it, to be true.

"Now don't be silly," said Poppy, though her voice was strained. "Take more than that old fucker to get the better of me." She smiled and I tried to smile but couldn't, and then she kissed me on the forehead.

"I love you," she said.

"Thank you," I replied. "I love you too, more than you know."

And then she was gone. Wearing her boots and her stockings and her pretty white dress with her short blonde hair, she was gone.

Holly, Abigail, Catherine and me stood in the top bedroom, hardly daring to move. I forced myself to get dressed, for although I'd managed to throw a robe around my shoulders when the girls had crashed in, I was still naked and covered in blood and other such bodily fluids. Then once I was dressed, though still stained with blood around the mouth and teeth, we stood in a sort of circle, holding hands, and waiting.

How long we waited, I don't know. Half an hour, maybe more. I felt myself starting to rock gently, an involuntary reaction to standing so long on the same spot. Slowly the other girls began to rock gently too, until all four of us were rocking backwards and forwards in unison. It felt comforting, this easy rocking motion, and I began to hum, a tuneless noise, but again comforting. The other girls picked up on this and we produced, the four of us, a humming sound, a vibration almost, that reminded me of the visions I'd seen after drinking Poppy's blood; the sound of the universe, the sound the stars make. *Hummmmm...*

The front door crashed in, startling us out of our reverie. There was a moaning on the stairs and then erratic footsteps. "What is it?" hissed Catherine.

I opened the door, stepped out of the bedroom and I saw her, two steps below me, reaching out with a bloodied hand. It was Poppy. Her face, her pretty, beautiful face, was cut and grazed and looked like it had been burnt on one side. There were streaks of deep red in her blonde hair that spoke of damage to her skull. "Snow?" she whispered and fell into my arms.

Oh, even now it pains me to even think of the scene. I held her in my arms, me on my knees and her laying on the floor. Sticking out of her chest was a ruddy awful wooden stake that protruded perhaps twelve inches. It had pierced her ribs and entered her heart, and her pretty white dress was, as was quite usual, smeared in the red stuff. But this time it was her own blood. I looked at the stake and it didn't seem real. I remember thinking that it had torn the dress and how were we ever going to darn it back together again? Such silly thoughts. "Poppy?" I cried. "Can you hear me."

"Snow, it was Little Red," she said, although the effort seemed too much. More blood gurgled from her mouth and I noticed that the wound around the stake was pouring blood, like a standpipe left dribbling away in the street. There was blood everywhere, so much blood, it didn't seem possible. "She grassed us up to the Vatican Man, Snow. Told him where we are. He'll be coming here. You have to run."

"No!" I said. "I'm not leaving you. Let him come. Let him kill me. I can't leave you. I can't live without you, not now, not after all this."

"I've lived for a long time Snow. Too long. I think it's time I went to sleep. Hold me tightly my darling. I need to close my eyes now. Hold me and rock me to sleep, like I was your baby."

So I did. I rocked her and I hummed a tuneless song again, like me and the girls had done just a few minutes before. I made the sound of the universe and Poppy died in my arms. The other girls cried and snivelled behind me, but I didn't. I sang my song because I wanted to be sure that if her soul was making the journey to heaven or, in all honesty more likely, hell, I wanted her to still be able to hear me as she went, to know that I was still with her, every step of the way.

Have you ever seen a vampire die? No, of course, probably not. Let me explain it to you then.

The body kind of slumps, like the insides have shrunk all of a sudden, leaving nothing to support the skin on the outside. The hair falls out of the head, and the skull folds in on itself. Parts of the body turn to dust and crumble, while others turn to liquid and drip. It is as though time has finally caught up with them, and all the years that they have lived, defying the natural order of things, of life and of death, those years finally wrap their tentacles around them and exact a terrible revenge. The body is ravaged, torn asunder, and ripped into oblivion. So it was with Poppy. She fell apart in my arms. My beautiful, wonderful Poppy. She fell apart in my arms.

There was no time to mourn. From the bottom of the stairs came a gruff voice shouting, "Are you there, whores? Are you ready to die? I've come in the name of the Father, the Son, and the Holy Spirit. Time for judgement!"

What happened next I cannot, in all honesty, recall in much detail. My heart was breaking for Poppy, and if I had died in the moments that followed I would not have argued or felt aggrieved. I would have welcomed it. I did not, at that point, want to live in a world that did not have Poppy in it.

I remember Holly throwing her arms around me and dragging me backwards. I remember what was left of Poppy falling apart in my arms; dust, liquid, bone, all just tumbling to the ground as Holly pulled me away and towards the window. I remember falling through the window and spiralling over the roof top, falling down, down until I landed on my back on the cobblestones, Holly next to me.

Still I would have happily laid there, not moving, waiting for death to visit me, if it weren't for Holly who dragged me to my feet and pulled me along, forcing me to run down the street. I may have been crying or wailing or silent. I do not know. I was in a black daze, and it was only Holly's stubbornness that saved me from the Vatican Man.

I took a second to look behind me and saw Abigail and the priest rolling around on the floor, slashing, biting, stabbing. I never saw

Abigail again after that glimpse, and the last I ever saw of Catherine was up in the bedroom as Poppy died.

Holly dragged me along, through Spitalfields, down side roads, through Clerkenwell, down yet more side streets and alleyways, and only after what felt like an hour, did we slow and stop and hide in a dark alleyway. Another alleyway. Where else, eh?

"Oh P-Poppy," said Holly. "W-whatever shall w-w-we do?" There was a footstep behind us. We turned. He'd found us. Oh, he'd found us all right.

When I was ten years old, I had a fight with a boy who lived next door to us in Camden. He was eleven years old, a big fat lad, a lot bigger than me. He laughed at me and mocked me as he slapped me around the head with his great fat hands, and eventually he pinned me to the cobblestones and punched me in the eye, just once. I got a beautiful shiner from that punch and no mistake, and had to go to school every day with a big black eye and listen to the other kids laughing at me and saying how I'd been given a right royal thrashing and wasn't it jolly funny.

So a week later I hid around a corner with an old cricket bat I'd found down by the Thames. A lot of the wood had crumbled away with age and decay, but the handle was firm enough and there was enough wood still attached to it to cause some serious damage to someone's head.

The boy next door came a-wandering down the road (his name was William, Fat William they called him, in case you're wondering) and as he rounded the corner, I mustered up all my strength and all my bravery, took a deep breath and caved his head in with the bat. Bosh. That was that. He never came near me again, and neither did any of the other kids at school. They stopped their laughing and didn't dare look at me. With William laid out on the cobble-stones, a huge black lump forming on his forehead, I walked home, laid down on my bed, and read a book of fairy stories, about princesses kept in high towers by wicked witches, and brave knights that came to rescue them.

There was a right old fuss. The boy didn't die of course, otherwise I'd have been hanging from a rope or shipped off to Australia or whatever it is they do to children who murder, but he was in a bit of a state for a few days, walked around with his head tilted at a jaunty angle, and his parents weren't too happy with me or my mam and daddy. There was shouting and cursing on the street outside our house, and the next door neighbours never spoke to us again. I was taken out of school as well, and had to go and work as a maid-of-all-work in a big house a mile or so away. I worked there for a few years before getting that job in the hat shop.

But I read the fairy stories, about the princesses, the witches, and the knights, and I thought to myself that I'd never need to worry about some stupid old knight coming to rescue me. If any witches come near me, I thought, I'll just crack them around the head with a cricket bat. Done it before, was easy enough, and if push ever came to shove, I told myself, I'd do it again.

My jaws were clamped around the Vatican Man's neck as quick as a flash. He weren't expecting that. I bit down hard, as hard as I could, and not been particularly interested in knowing his life story, I did my best not to drink too much of his manky blood. I heard and felt bone and sinew being crushed beneath my bite. I rammed him up against the wall, and continued to bite. His struggling lessened as the seconds passed, and then Holly was there beside me. She clamped her jaws around the top of his head and ripped off the dome of his skull, revealing his brain. We dragged him to the floor between us, and then we tore him apart like a pair of stray dogs tearing apart a cat.

Chapter Nine

There was perhaps an hour left of darkness before the sun would rise and fry us alive. We could of course take our chances in the alleyway, keep to the shadows, and hope to make it through the day, but the prospect didn't seem appealing, particularly with the arms and legs and torso of the Vatican Man scattered hither and thither. So we made the decision to try and make the journey to Highgate Cemetery and find some accommodation there more befitting two lost children of the night.

We hurried along the streets of Islington and up the Holloway Road. As dawn came closer, the roads and pavements became busier with mortals starting their working day. We ignored them and hurried along, and for the most part they ignored us. A couple of prostitutes smeared in blood was, perhaps, not an uncommon sight for these early birds to witness.

Once at Highgate Cemetery, we clambered over the railings (not a difficult proposition for a vampire, but one that was not helped by our voluminous dresses) and wandered along the road there called Lebanon Circle. Here we found a vault with a great iron door slightly open. Our combined vampire strength opened up the door, and in we walked, pulling the door tightly shut behind us.

In the middle of the vault lay a stone tomb. I sat down and rested my back against the cold granite. Holly stood in front of me, not moving. With her dress in tatters, her dirty hair falling over her face, and her mouth covered in drying blood, she looked like nothing more than a vengeful spirit, haunting this vault.

"Some human walks in here, he's going to get the shock of his bleeding life," I said, trying to brighten the mood. Brighten the mood? What a stupid thing to try and do. Holly started to cry, her chest heaving up and down in the darkness, and she tried to speak, "H-h-h-h-h-h-h-h-h. . . ," but no words would come. Only her sweet, terrible stutter.

I held out my hands to her. "Come here darling," I said. She knelt down beside me and placed her head in my lap, and there I gently stroked her matted hair and whispered nonsenses to her about how everything was going to be all right, until finally she fell asleep. And only when she had fallen asleep was I able to mourn my own loss, the loss of Poppy. There in the darkness of that crypt, with Holly's head on my lap, I cried and I cried and I cried.

We hid in the vault until night fell once more and then we made our way onto the streets surrounding the cemetery. On Swain's Lane we happened across two couples out for an evening stroll. Food and clean new dresses were thus gratefully received, and feeling much revived we were able to continue our journey back to Spitalfields.

The house was a complete tip. The front door was kicked in, Poppy's blood was all over the stairs, and then in the upstairs bedroom we found what was left of both dear Poppy and Catherine. Again I felt like I couldn't continue and fell to my knees weeping. This time Holly comforted me and stroked my hair. In the days that followed, Holly and me leaned on each other for constant support. Every time a kind word was needed, every time a small smile was required, every time an attentive ear was called for, we were there for each other. I don't think either one of us would have survived those first dark days and nights had it not been for the support we gave each other.

It wasn't easy, and it wouldn't be easy for a good while yet, but somehow we made it through. We found ourselves a new door. Well, I say 'found'. Purloined would have been more like it, and we even talked a passing couple of likely lads into fixing it to the door frame for us. Their reward? We didn't kill them. Not quite the reward I'm sure they were hoping for, but reward none the less.

Holly scrubbed the stairs although the blood (*Poppy's* blood) never really came out, while I swept and mopped out the top bedroom. What was left of Poppy I placed into a china vase, and did likewise with the remains of Catherine. Then we walked back up to Highgate Cemetery (it was a bleeding long walk but due to the nature of our task, quite therapeutic) and placed their vases besides the vault on Lebanon Circle where me and Holly had hid that first night. It seemed a fitting resting place for them both, being a location that was, and continues to be, beautiful and Gothic and dark.

And of Little Red, nothing was seen for a couple of years. But I would meet her once more, and there would be a reckoning. There was a debt to be paid, and to be paid in blood.

Part Two: "Holly"

Chapter Ten

"I never used to go with girls," said Holly as we lay in bed together. "Before I was a vampire I mean. Before I was a vampire, I used to like boys well enough. But soon as I got turned, well, girls just seemed more, I don't know, appealing somehow."

That was us, me and Holly lying in bed together on Christmas morning, a year later. And yes, lying in an actual bed and not on a mattress dropped on the floor. Didn't take her long, I can hear you say, between her having the love of her life die in her arms and then finding herself in bed with another girl. Well, if that's what you're thinking, you can take a long walk off a short plank.

There wasn't a day went by, and there still isn't a day goes by, when I don't think of Poppy. And at the beginning, in those first dark days and nights after her death, there wasn't a minute that went by when I didn't think about her. How we survived those early days, me and Holly, I still don't rightly know. How we managed to force ourselves off those stinking mattresses to walk the streets of Spitalfields looking for food is beyond me. We were in mourning, we were in shock, and with every breath that we took me and Holly cursed the fact that we had lived when they, all of them, not just Poppy, when all of them had died.

As the nights turned into weeks, and then into months, the tightness around my chest relented the smallest amount, allowing me to take a modicum of pleasure in the things around me that I should be grateful for. The way that Holly's stutter got better when it was just her and me sitting in the candlelight, talking. The way that when I woke up screaming after another nightmare in which the tentacles were dragging Poppy away from me and down into the dark teeth-infested depths, Holly would hold me close and tell me it was all right. The way that when we hunted, she would never want us to have a human each but would insist that we share. And the way that neither of us could fall asleep without the other laying close by, some part of our body touching, the same way that wolf packs sleep, in touch with each other so that if one springs from their slumber, the next is immediately aware. These were the things that kept me alive, and kept her alive, in those first months.

The mattresses were the first to go, once the door had been repaired. "Cheers lads!" we'd cried merrily at the boys who'd fixed our door, and smiled and waved at them as they walked down the road. But once the door was closed on the outside world, we both hugged each other and started to cry for no apparent reason. I patted the door with my palm and said, "Nice door. Good strong door." And it all seemed so sad that we cried and agreed that it was a nice strong door, and that if ever there had been a nice strong door it was this one. And then I'd laughed, and Holly laughed too, until we weren't sure if we were laughing or crying or why we were doing either.

A few days later we threw out the mattresses. We chucked them into the road and thirty minutes later they were gone, some other poor bastard had taken them away, no doubt to furnish another house further along the road. I saw our mattress lying in the road, the one that me and Poppy had shared. It was dirty and stained with blood and sex juices, the most foul looking thing you're likely to see, but it was my blood and her blood and my sex juices and her sex juices that stained it. I ran out into the road and threw myself onto the mattress and started to wail like a baby, and Holly had to drag me back inside and lock our nice strong door behind us until someone came along and removed it from the road. "But it was our mattress!" I wailed, and Holly shushed me and told me that it stank something horrible and I should be glad to see the back of it.

We stole ourselves a nice bed, a proper wooden bed with a new feather mattress and clean sheets. We'd 'found' it in the home of a sweet young couple we'd happened upon in Hoxton. It was early evening and it looked like they'd been out doing a spot of shopping. They were walking arm-in-arm, all smiles and giggles, him carrying the shopping bag like he was Sir Galahad or something. We followed them to their home, stalked them really, keeping to the shadows, as slippery as eels. When he turned the key in the lock and opened the door, we pulled a trick right out of Poppy's book; we pretended we'd just been set upon by a gang of thugs and were in need of assistance. They were very kind, let us inside their home, got chairs for us to sit on, poured us a small glass of gin to help steady our poor nerves (which we had to pretend to drink), and then asked if there was anything else they could do for us. There was just one more thing they could do, of course. Die.

We fed on them, Holly taking the man at first and me the gentle lady, but then we swapped around half way through, just so we both experienced the same sweet delights of their blood.

The lady was small and petite like a little doll, with blonde hair in ringlets and sweet dimples in her cheeks. I remember her because she kind of cried as I pinned her to the floor and drained her blood, kind of cried and whispered her husband's name, "Joseph, Joseph, Joseph. . . " Isn't it funny how I still remember the name? The shopping bag had fallen over. I remember seeing eggs, a cauliflower, some dates and apples spilled out onto the floor. I'd never tasted dates, and still haven't of course. But her blood tasted of strawberries and summer meadows and all those things that I could no longer know. I growled and forced my fangs deeper into her sweet neck.

By the time Holly and I swapped meals, he, *Joseph*, was already close to death. He had no struggle left in him. He looked at me through milky eyes and kind of smiled. He was probably hallucinating. Or perhaps he could see angels, coming to deliver him from the cruelty of this world? Who knows what goes through their heads in those final seconds?

I preferred her, of course. With her dimples and her strawberry blood.

With the feeding at an end, we helped ourselves to their bed, sheets and all, and Holly, spying some of the lady's pretty dresses, decided to take them too and threw them on top of the bed.

We must have looked a right old sight, the two of us, me and Holly, walking through the streets of the East End, lugging a great bed between us. But, you see, the East End was full of all manner of weird and wonderful sights so that in the main you could get away with just about anything – so long as the rozzers never spotted you.

Oh, we thought we were a couple of princesses on that first night, laying down in the bed with that deliciously soft mattress beneath us. "Ooh," I said. "Ooh," said Holly. And we lay back and wrapped our arms around each other and slept all the way till nightfall.

Holly and I became lovers the following night. Our newly acquired bed creaked and rocked and finally broke, two of the legs snapping off under the exertion. "Ain't that just fine and dandy?" I said. "Our lovely new bed only twenty-four hours old and we broke it already." The next morning, I snapped off the other two legs so that it could lay flat on the floor, and it served us well thereafter for the next few years.

Holly. What can I tell you about Holly?

Where Poppy was beautiful, Holly was plain. Where Poppy's hair was brilliant blonde and short, Holly's hair was long, brown, bordering on ginger. Where Poppy's skin was white and pure, Holly's was freckled. Where Poppy was a goddess from the dawn of civilisation, Holly was a girl who had been lost for half a century, had never come to terms with becoming a vampire, and the loss that this transformation had entailed.

For a long time I would not drink her blood. I looked upon that ritual as something that I had shared with Poppy and would only ever share with Poppy. It was to me a sacred communion, and to betray Poppy by partaking in this communion with someone else was something that I could not and would not contemplate. But Holly wanted me to drink her blood, and my refusal started to become a wall between us, a wall which, in its turn, reminded me of the wall that I had built up between myself and Poppy in those early days when I dared not declare my love.

Holly and myself lived entirely in each other's company in those days. We had no visitors or friends. There was only the two of us. We lived together, hunted together, slept together. As the days and the weeks and the months wore on, as we replaced the door and acquired our bed and became lovers, so her stutter got better. At first it wasn't noticeable, then the occasional sentence would pass through her lips and it would strike me that she hadn't stuttered on a single word. And then those perfect sentences increased in frequency, until at last, when she did stutter, it was the stutter that attracted my attention and not the lack of it.

"It's you!" she would cry in delight. "You've cured me! I love you, Snow. Drink my blood, please, and let our souls be united."

And I would turn my head away and say that I could not, and the more that I said I could not, the more her stutter returned and the more she pulled her brown almost ginger hair across her face and began to retreat once more inside herself. She mistook my reticence for a lack of love. It wasn't that at all, really, but I can see, with the benefit of hindsight, how she might have perceived it as such. It was just that, oh, it was just that I missed Poppy so.

Vampires do not get drunk. Or at least, they do not get drunk in human terms. That is, they cannot consume alcohol, and therefore alcohol cannot befuddle their senses and make them act foolishly. However sometimes when a vampire drinks the rich blood of a young mortal that the vampire may find sexually attractive, that blood may have an intoxicating effect on the vampire. There is also the matter of cigarettes. Vampires can smoke cigarettes with no ill effects, and indeed back in the late 1800s it was quite the fashionable thing. Of course not all cigarettes are as they seem. Apart from tobacco, other ingredients of a more intoxicating nature may be added, and in turn this can have an effect on the vampire, the equivalent I suppose of a human being drunk on gin or steamed on hashish. So it was on that night in the Christmas season of 1889, over a year since we lost all those dear to us, and several weeks into the 'Snow won't drink Holly's blood' drama.

It was Christmas Eve. We decided to get dressed in our best dresses, do our hair nicely, put on our most impressive jewellery and find ourselves a smart Christmas ball to gatecrash. To be honest we weren't really speaking in the friendliest of terms; we had rowed in the afternoon when during our love-making Holly had offered me her neck and asked me to drink her blood and I, as usual, had declined. "I know I'm not Poppy!" she had screamed at me. "I c-c-c-can't help that!"

It was a bitterly cold night, and even though vampires do not feel the cold in the same way that mortals do, still I wondered exactly why we were stepping out on such an evening when we weren't even on the friendliest of terms. But out we stepped, found ourselves a cab, and headed up West.

Up West. Even the destination reminded me, of course, of Poppy. There was no escape from her memory. She was haunting me and destroying my relationship with Holly. And if I was to be completely honest, I didn't care. Holly was nice, but she wasn't Poppy. She had been correct that afternoon when she had screamed those accusations at me. She wasn't Poppy, she never would be, and I held it against her. Oh, what a beast I am, for if I am to be absolutely frank with you, the thought that kept entering my mind, the one thought I could not escape from, was the one that asked why Poppy had died when Holly had lived? Wouldn't it have been better, more preferable, if Holly had perished and Poppy had survived? How cruel I am, and how little I deserved the happiness that I was later to find at dear, sweet Holly's side.

Arriving in the West End, we lingered for a while in Leicester Square, taking in the atmosphere of the Christmas crowds as they made their way to the various theatres, operas, and music halls that populated the area. My own eyes kept been drawn towards the park and the statue of Shakespeare, as though I expected to see Poppy standing there, waiting for me, smiling, telling me to hurry up, perhaps a dead soldier in her arms. But she wasn't there, of course. She was gone and my heart still ached at the thought of it.

We stood before the Empire Theatre gazing at the posters on display. A production of Charles Dickens' *A Christmas Carol* was attracting much attention, and crowds thronged around us. A small Christmas tree stood by the side of the steps that led into the theatre, and at its twinkling my heart, perhaps like that of Mr. Scrooge himself, melted. "Oh Holly," I said. "It is Christmas Eve. Let us not argue tonight, of all nights."

Holly turned to me and said," It's m-my birthday."

I was taken aback by her pronouncement. "Really?" I asked. "How splendid! You never said!"

"It's why I'm c-called Holly. B-because of, you know, the holly and the ivy."

"Oh look," I said. "shouldn't we perhaps go and see the perfor-mance of A Christmas Carol? It starts in a quarter of an hour. It seems quite apt and, by the attention it is attracting, I am sure it is rather good."

I held her hands in mine and reached over and kissed her on the lips. I had wanted to win her over, to spend an enjoyable night with her, for us both to forget this blood drinking nonsense. But, although she returned my kiss and held it full on the lips for sev-eral seconds (prompting one old duffer walking passed to raise his monocle and pronounce, "I say!"), I could tell that she was holding back. She was still mad with me. I tried to force my lips on her, to make her relent, relax, and enjoy this evening that was both Christmas Eve and her birthday. But she started to withdraw and placed her hands against my chest as to push me away.

At that moment we heard from behind us, "Ahem," and we both span around.

It was a girl, a woman really, perhaps in her mid-twenties. And oh! What a sight she was! She looked quite the scandal, for she was wearing nothing less than a full riding outfit. On her head was placed a topper complete with a black veil that fell over her face, she wore a full length crimson riding jacket beneath which could be seen a starched white shirt and black bow tie, and then she wore a black riding dress hitched up to reveal black boots. In a world of pretty dresses and demure ladies, she stood out like the proverbial.

"What ho, ladies," she winked, raising a hand to the tip of her topper. Her accent was posh, cosmopolitan, from the other side of town to us poor East End girls. "Season's greetings, and all that."

I found myself instinctively curtsying, the old shop girl in me suddenly coming to the fore, and Holly did likewise beside me. "Evening, ma'am," I said, "and season's greetings to you too." I couldn't help myself. Although inside I was screaming at myself to stop fawning over this woman, an instinct within me, nurtured from birth, was forcing me to be subservient. Me! Me who had killed dozens, including may I add the blooming Vatican Man, and had been the lover of a vampire goddess who, quite possibly, had walked the Earth before Jesus Christ himself! And all because of her accent, her demeanour, and her riding suit, which I'll admit was quite as becoming as it was scandalous. The sight of her made my heart race a little faster. I felt my fangs stretching within my mouth and realised that me behaving like the good subservient shop girl probably wouldn't last long. If there was an internal battle taking place between the old shop girl and the new vampire, the new vampire, with the passing of each second, was beginning to regain the upper hand.

"Now look here," said the lady. "I couldn't help but notice you two behaving like quite the love birds, if you'll pardon the expression. I'm on my way to my club. It's a rather special club, open only to females of a certain persuasion, if you catch my drift? A club where love birds such as we may stretch our wings in safety and without fear of being judged by the masses. Comprenez-vous?"

Holly, it appeared, did neither *comprenez* nor *vous*. "So are you human? Or are you like us?" she whispered, at which the lady laughed.

"Well I hardly think I'm one of Mr. Darwin's blessed monkeys!" she exclaimed. "What a question to ask. We are, I can assure you, quite human, although we are all in favour of ladies enjoying each other's company. And we are always on the lookout for fresh, er, recruits."

"Oh, you mean you like girls?" said Holly.

"Quite so," said the lady.

"Well, let's go then," said Holly, rather too lustfully for my liking.

And before I knew it, Holly and the lady were walking arm-in- arm, leaving me trailing in their wake. Clearly I was in more bother with Holly than I'd realised, and no mistake. I trudged behind them, the shop girl once more with my fangs shrunken and impotent. What a turn up for the books.

The club, it transpired, was on the Strand, so a quick hop, skip and a jump down Charing Cross Road and we were there. It lay behind an unassuming grey door, the only indication that any-thing of note lay behind it being a discreet bronze plate screwed to the wall and engraved with the words, '*Lieu de Rencontre pour les Dames*'. I thought I knew what 'dames' meant, but apart from that I was lost.

The lady in the riding clothes (whose name was Veronica) opened the door and we entered. After climbing a short flight of stairs, we came to a reception area, decorated, like the rest of the club, in a most luxurious manner. The carpets were deep and cream, bronze gas lamps burned brightly, all the tables had golden silk cloths thrown over them, the walls were decorated with burgundy paper, and on each wall had been placed huge mirrors decorated with golden cherubs and angels and bunches of stylised grapes. On each table flickered candles, and dominating the entire room was a giant chandelier in which candles twinkled and shone.

"I couldn't help notice," said Veronica as she handed over her coat and signed us into the club as her guests, "that neither of you girls are wearing coats? And on such a chill night too?"

"We h-have our passions to keep us warm," said Holly, flirting.

"Oh bravo!" said Veronica. "Quite right too!"

We entered the club proper and I felt a hundred or more pairs of eyes turn to examine us. Veronica waved and smiled and said 'hallo' to perhaps a dozen people as we walked to a table, and it seemed to me that she was quite revelling in the attention that our presence was generating.

"Don't mind the staring," she said once we were seated. "We don't get too many new recruits, hence why your arrival has caused quite the stir."

A waiter (a girl waiter dressed as a male waiter! I must admit, it took me a few moments to clock that it was a girl!) came to take our drinks order. Veronica asked for a glass of champagne (or 'cham' as she called it), but of course Holly and myself had to politely decline, unless they wanted to see us on all fours puking our guts up, because that's what happens if a vampire takes human food. And of course they had no idea that they'd let two vampires into their little den! They all merely took us for a couple of sapphists like them, which of course we were, but with our own very special little quirk – namely the fangs and the blood and the death.

"Well," said Veronica, "if I can't interest you girls in a glass of cham, how about a cigarette?" Now that was more like it. We both took a cigarette from Veronica's silver cigarette case. "I must warn you," she said as she offered us a light from a match, "that they're quite an exotic blend, and nicely perfumed too." And she smirked knowingly at us.

What I didn't realise at the time, and didn't realise for quite a time after, was that her 'exotic blend' of 'perfumed' cigarettes were in fact hashish. When you hear what happened next, please bear that fact in mind. Me and Holly had smoked a hashish cigarette each for the first time. So you see, all that was to transpire wasn't entirely our fault.

As we puffed away on our cigarettes and, it must be said, started to smile and relax, Veronica asked Holly about her stutter. Had she had it from birth? Was she taking any medication for it? Opium, she had heard, was good for conditions of the nerves.

"Oh miss, it was awful, so it was" said Holly. She was laying the East End accent on a bit thick, I thought. "It was my father, he used to beat me awful, and one day he knocked me quite sense-less. When I woke up on the kitchen floor, I found I cun't speak proper no more. He'd hit me so hard, you see? Said he was going to knock some sense into me. Knocked some out of me, more like, that's what I've always said."

Her speech was becoming slurred and she was leaning forward to Veronica and gazing at her earnestly.

"Is that true?" I asked. I'd always wondered about her stutter but had never found the right moment to bring the subject up. Now she was revealing all of this to Veronica, just an hour since meeting her on the streets. Charming. "Is that really how you got your stutter?" The waiter delivered a second glass of cham to Veronica, who slurped it down greedily.

"Nah!" laughed Holly. "Only yanking your chain! It was the killer flu! Oh, the doctors all thought I was going to die. My fever was so high, my own dear mother couldn't bear to put her hand to my face. And if they put a damp cloth to my brow, it hissed and spat and steam rose from it. That's how high the fever was. But I survived, and the doctor said it was a blooming medical miracle and that he ought to write a book about me. About me! Imagine that? The only sign that I was ever so ill is this stutter. Which I don't appear to have at the moment. Tell me Veronica, what's in them blooming cigarettes? 'Cause I ain't stuttering no more."

"Is that true?" I asked. "Is that really how you got your stutter?"

A third glass of cham arrived at the table and was scooped up greedily by Veronica.

"Nah! Course not!" laughed Holly. "You know your problem Snow? You're too gullible. Not like me, I'm as wise as the street. Not catch me out. Not in a month of Sundays."

"Snow?" asked Veronica. "Is that your name? How quaint. Is it a common name amongst the working classes?"

"It ain't her real name," said Holly, gripping Veronica by the arm. "It's a nickname given to her by her one-time lover who is now deceased, no more, gone the way of the angels, if you catch my drift. She was named after Snow White, no less. Now ain't that a reputation to live up to? Being named after Snow bleeding

White. I, of course, was one of the ugly dwarves what found her. Says it all really. She's the bleeding princess and I'm a bleeding dwarf. No wonder she don't love me!"

And with that Holly began to pretend to cry in quite the most dramatic fashion.

"More cham over here!" Veronica called to the waiter. "Make it a bottle!"

"And what's more," said Holly through phoney sniffles, "she refuses to drink my blood on account of it."

"Drink your blood?" asked Veronica. "I say, what's that all about? Do tell."

"I'll do better than tell you," said Holly, suddenly brightening up. "I'll show you if you like?"

"Holly, no," I said. "Don't."

"Oh hark at her, Veronica. First it was my bleeding father knocking me about, now it's her trying to tell me what to do. Well, me and Veronica will do what we bleeding well like and it ain't none of your pigging business. My blood might not be good enough for you, your royal highness, but I bet it's good enough for Veronica here, ain't I right Miss Veronica?"

"Oh, well I must say," said Veronica, "it does all sound rather intriguing."

"Intriguing ain't the half of it, miss," said Holly.

"Holly," I said, "we should go."

"I ain't going fucking nowhere," she hissed back at me, baring her fangs.

"Now, now, girls," said Veronica. "No need to fight. We're all friends here."

"Abso-bloody-lutely!" agreed Holly, patting Veronica on the shoulder. "Ain't we all good chums here, Snow?"

"Call me Kate if you like," I snapped. "If the name 'Snow' upsets you so much."

"It don't upset me darling," said Holly. "If you want to go around being named after some blooming fairy tale, that's your preroga-bleeding-tive. Listen here, Veronica, we got anywhere more private we can go? I can show you the blood thing, if you like and all?"

"Well we can move to one of the boxes up there, if you prefer," said Veronica, indicating fixed tables and chairs that lined the perimeter of the room, each with a small booth surrounding them and thereby affording the occupants a modicum of privacy.

"I'm going to the rest room," I said as Holly and Veronica gathered themselves to move to a box. "I'll be back shortly. Holly, try to be sensible."

She looked at me and stuck out her tongue in quite the nastiest fashion that I've ever seen, then she threw her arms around Veronica and was escorted to the perimeter of the room.

I made my way to the rest room and relieved myself. As you can imagine, the rest room was quite as impressive as the rest of the club, all deep carpets and bronze gas lamps and ornate mirrors. I stood before the mirror feeling quite wobbly from the exotic cigarette, and hardly recognised the reflection that stared back at me. My eyes seemed darker somehow and cat-like, and my skin white and smooth, while my lips had a deep red tinge to them, like they'd been stained by all the blood that had passed their way over the last year.

There was somebody standing in the corner of the rest room. I could see their dark form in the mirror, lurking in the shadows. At first I thought it was one of the club's patrons, but after a moment I realised who it was. It was Maria, my first kill. She stepped out of the shadow, just one step, and regarded me with kind eyes. Now out of the darkness, she looked just like she had that fateful night when our paths had crossed.

I didn't turn to look at her, but merely continued to stare at her reflection in the mirror.

"Oh Maria," I said, "what has become of us all?"

She merely smiled by way of an answer. There was silence for a moment or two, and then I said it. "I'm sorry. I'm sorry I took you. But I had to, I would've died otherwise."

Maria raised a finger to her lips to shush me. "You are what you are," she said, and I do not know to this day whether that was forgiveness or accusation. I closed my eyes and took a deep breath. When I opened my eyes again she was gone.

I straightened my hair with a touch of water, smoothed down my dress and made my way back into the club.

I noticed the box where Holly was sitting. She had her back to the rest of the club but I couldn't see Veronica. I assumed that Holly's back was hiding her, and that she and Holly were deep in conversation, inspired no doubt by the cigarettes and the cham, or worse yet, that Holly and Veronica (and oh, my heart gave a little flip of jealousy at the thought) were kissing. However, as I approached the box, I quickly saw the truth.

Hidden by Holly's back, Veronica was sucking on Holly's wrist. Holly must have bitten into the flesh herself and then offered the bleeding wrist to Veronica. Veronica was sucking enthusiastically, her eyes glazed. Occasionally she would stop, and with blood dripping from between her lips, she would say something like, "Oh I can see the moon and the stars and the trees and the lakes and the mountains," and "Oh you are monsters, such beautiful, devilish little monsters".

I sat down on the seat opposite them. "Holly, stop it," I said. "You're going to kill the poor woman."

"What do you care," said Holly, "if she lives or dies? Don't we kill enough of them already?"

"Yes," I said, trying to remain calm and reasonable, "but not here, not with all these people around, not like this."

"Like what?"

"With your blood. Humans aren't meant to drink our blood."

"Why not? You've been a vampire for what? A year? Suddenly you're the expert?"

"Stop it," I said. "Stop giving her your blood." "Why?"

"Why? Because it's not right, that's why."

"Veronica ain't complaining, are you darling? She thinks it's all right."

"Monsters, my beautiful monsters," said Veronica.

"See? She adores it," said Holly. "She's quite got her wind up."

"Stop it," I said.

"No."

"Stop it."

"Why?"

"Does there have to be a reason?" I snapped and tried to wrestle her arm away from Veronica. Veronica tried to cling onto it, and the three of us began tugging and pulling at each other's arms over the top of the table, with Holly's blood dripping here and there, splashing onto a near-by mirror and plopping into Veronica's glass of cham.

"Give me your arm!" I screamed, and pulled Holly's wrist towards me. "It's mine!" And I thrust my lips upon the wound and began to drink.

It was the sweetest, richest blood and it made me all a-quiver, so much so that I wondered why I'd never drunk it before. There had been a reason, I was sure, but for the moment it quite escaped me. The walls of the club fell away and I found myself within Holly. I became Holly. This is her story.

Chapter Eleven

My baby was going to die. Of that much I am certain. You could see it in the midwives' eyes. They'd smile and cluck and talk about 'best foot forward', but they knew and I knew that the poor little thing was too small and wasn't feeding. She only had a few days left in her, then they'd have taken her from me and put her into a wooden box and that would have been that. Poor mite. She really was very small and steadfastly refused to take my breast, like she just wanted to get it over and done with. To stop the pain of being alive.

On the night when it happened, when so many people including my baby died, I remember holding her in my arms and looking out of the hospital window at London, at all the gas lamps and the fog rolling in off the Thames, and I remember thinking that it all felt like a dream.

My baby was dying in my arms and before me lay London, sparkling like some faerie city enveloped in mist. It felt surreal and I had what may almost be described as a religious experience. I ain't one to hold much truck with God and Heaven and all that, especially with all that happened to me in the days that were to follow, but I can't think of any better way of describing it than as a religious experience; I felt myself rise out of my body, float all the way up to the ceiling, and look back down at myself and my baby. I hardly recognised myself. I looked frail and beaten, and like I wouldn't be long for this world either. I'd been bleeding since the birth of my baby, and they were having the devil of a time trying to make it stop. I was dying too, I suppose. Slowly bleeding to death. A coffin for the two of us, me and my baby. Maybe that wouldn't have been so bad.

I was floating out of my body, somewhere up near the ceiling, and was wondering quietly to myself as to whether this was all a dream or whether it was actually happening, whether I'd discovered some new talent in me for floating around out of my body, when suddenly the screaming brought me back down to earth with a jolt. Half a dozen midwives from other wards came running and screaming onto our ward. They slammed the big wooden doors behind them and started to pull spare beds and chairs across in an attempt to make a barricade.

"What's going on?" we asked. The other mothers had woken up and some of the babies were crying.

"Monsters!" one of the midwives replied.

"They're mad dogs," shouted another, "or men with rabies or some such! They're killing everybody!"

Killing everybody? It sounded barmy. But they were clearly scared out of their wits, and some of the mothers on the ward started to cry and wail too. They all picked up their babies and held them in their arms, coo-cooing and shush-shushing.

"Hide!" shouted one of the midwives. "For the love of God, don't just stand there! Hide and pray for your babies!"

Then there came a-banging and a-crashing upon the doors, and within a matter of moments they flung open, splintering like kindling, and in walked the mad dogs, the men with rabies, the monsters.

There were about six of them, vampires of course although I didn't know it at the time. They looked, I'll admit even now, like the stuff of nightmares. Blood and gore covered their faces and their clothes and their hands, and their eyes wild and crazed. To see these creatures approaching me and knowing that they were about to kill me, I think I must have gone into shock. While the other mothers and the midwives hid under beds or beneath desks or cowered in corners, I just stood there, holding my baby, as they advanced upon me.

They took my baby from me. I tried to hold on to her, but it was like trying to hold on to water. I screamed, "My baby!" but they just took her and killed her and fed upon her. I stood there and I wailed. Just wailed.

Then I watched as they killed all the other babies and the mothers and the midwives. They killed them all, every one. They even killed them when they no longer needed to feed. They killed them just for the sport of it.

After they had killed everyone on the ward, they laughed and joked with each other, throwing tiny baby corpses to one another, like it was all a jolly wheeze, like they were all fine fellows taking supper at their club. But they didn't kill me. They simply ignored me, like I wasn't there, like I was a ghost. I was dying, you see. I was still bleeding, haemorrhaging the nurses had called it, and they could sense that. There was no sport in me. So they left me, and started to walk out of the ward, leaving me alone, barefoot, amongst the bodies and the blood, and I just screamed. I don't know where the idea or the notion came from, but I screamed, "Take me, you bastards!"

Even now, I don't know why or how those words formed in my mouth. Maybe years of being downtrodden, of being beaten by my father and then by my husband, years of working as a skivvy, as a maid-of-all-work, and then finally, after all that, to have my baby taken from me and butchered in front of my own eyes, maybe it was all just too much. I was tired of being the victim, tired of this life of drudgery and work, tired of being bullied by everyone.

"Take me!" I don't know whether I meant 'take me with you' or 'kill me'. Either would have done I suppose. Just don't leave me here!

One of the vampires stopped and turned to look at me. A smile broke on his face and he walked back towards me. I must have looked like the most pathetic little specimen he'd ever examined. Small, hunched, broken, weak. He reached a hand out and stroked my hair.

"What's your name?" he asked.

"Holly," I said, "as in the holly and the ivy."

"Holly, you're dying," he said, and those words, spoken from the mouth of the monster who had just killed my baby, were the most reassuring words I had ever heard spoken.

He looked into my eyes and he understood me. How strange this must sound to anyone who is not vampire, who knows nothing of the majesty and poetry of the darkness. I can only tell you how it felt, all those years ago now and yet the memory still so fresh. He knew me, he understood me, and the touch of his bloodied hand upon my cheek took away all of the pain.

"I can give you a gift, Holly," he said. "Use it how you will. Die, if you wish. Or live like you've never lived before. A gift for you, in exchange for the little one." He pointed to the body, what was left of it, of my little baby girl. It was all I could do to whisper, "Yes please."

And then he was upon me, his teeth biting ferociously into my neck. The pain was intense and yet it was a good pain. It was a pain that washed away all the sorrow, all the wasted years, all the insults, all the dirt and the grime. The pain became a fire inside me and in it I was cleansed.

I awoke several hours later. It must have been sometime after midnight. I was lying on the floor, soaked in blood, and around me more blood and the bodies of the midwives, the mothers, the babies, their lifeless eyes staring at me and passing no judgement. I dragged myself through the flesh and the gore, and pulled myself onto my legs with the aid of a desk at the end of the ward.

Then I heard something whimpering, a small voice, "Are you still alive? Have they gone? Oh God, have they gone?"

The voice was coming from beneath the desk. I knelt down and looked. It was a young trainee midwife, younger even than me, her eyes wide in terror and her face streaked with tears. "Help me," she whispered. "Help me get out of here. I have to go home. Mama will be wondering where I have got to." She was clearly in shock, traumatised by all she had witnessed.

A sharp pain erupted across my teeth and my mouth filled with saliva. My fangs, of course. My fangs and my hunger. All the rest was instinct. I didn't think. I just acted. My senses were ten, twenty times heightened, I felt strong, alive, like I could take on the world by myself and win. I pulled the young midwife out from under the desk and threw her on top of it, back down, eyes up to the heavens, arms and legs flailing, and I took her.

I ripped out her throat and gorged myself on her blood. I took too much at first. I was eager. It was my first time feeding. The warm blood hit my empty stomach and I vomited it back up. So I slowed down, and took her at a more gentle pace, sucking the blood from the wound in her neck and feeling the life-force drain from her body and into mine. This was the gift given to me in exchange for my baby's life. To be reborn as a vampire.

I looked down at my baby's body, ripped apart now and torn to pieces. I tried to say that I was sorry, tried to explain that I couldn't save her, could never have saved her, but my voice wouldn't work properly. The words got stuck in my throat.

"I'm s-s-s-s-s-s," I stuttered, trying to form the word 'sorry', but it wouldn't come.

I stumbled out of the hospital ward, my bare feet slipping occasionally on the blood. The hallway outside was scattered with more corpses, more torn limbs, more blood. I made my way down the cold steps and out into the street, and I started to scream.

Then she was standing by me. "Come with me quickly," she said, "or you'll be dead before the night is over." She put her arm around me and I knew instinctively to trust her.

"W-w-will th-they l-l-look after m-m-my b-b-baby now?" I asked. I was frightened, lost, traumatised.

"Of course they will," she said. "They'll look after your baby for you, and I'll look after you."

It was Poppy of course and she saved my life, although for a long time I didn't thank her. I just wanted to die. I hadn't been able to say sorry to my baby. My stupid voice hadn't worked on the one occasion when I needed it to. My stupid fucking voice. I wanted to die for a long time, but instead I just shut my trap.

Then Katie, Snow, arrived and I watched her in the tin bath on that first night and I braided her hair and I thought that perhaps I could live again now, knowing that she was in my world. It was love at first sight, or so I told myself. But like all good love stories, it was embroiled with woe for the object of my affections was in love, of course, with another. She loved Poppy and she loved her so much, and she never looked at me, except out of politeness or when passing the time of day. Perhaps, I thought, that was enough to let me live again; knowing that even though she was barely aware that I existed, I could still secretly love her and that love, albeit unrequited, would be enough to breath fresh life into my lungs.

I started to try to speak again. I hadn't said a blinking word in fifty years, not since I'd stuttered and blubbered to Poppy outside of the hospital, but if Snow was ever to know me, I needed to start speaking again. So I tried, but it was hard.

"D-d-d-d-delighted t-t-t-t-t-to m-m-m-m-meet you K-K-K-K-Kate."

Chapter Twelve

Imagine, if you can, the scene there in that lesbian club on Christmas Eve. There's me sucking on Holly's wrist. There's Holly sucking on Veronica's neck. There's Veronica all pushed up in the corner going, "Oh oh oh," as the blood is being drained out of her. And all around us there's blood, Veronica's blood, Holly's blood, on the table, on us, on the floor, on the mirrors. So far we haven't been noticed by the other party goers, but really, it's only a matter of time before the screaming starts, ain't it?

I dropped Holly's wrist and looked at her. She dropped Veronica's head (which smashed down with a bang onto the table) and looked at me. "Oh my sweetness," I said. "I'm so sorry. I love you so much. So, so much." She looked at me and she smiled and then we kissed across the table. "Let's go home," I said. "Let's go to our home."

We stood up from the table and started to walk out of the club. We didn't notice, being so much in love and all, that we were quite literally drenched in the old red stuff, and as we walked we sort of squelched and left behind us red footprints on the cream carpet. All eyes turned to us in a kind of stunned silence. Every sapphist in the room stopped talking and just stared. Then one of them screamed – perhaps they'd discovered poor old Veronica laying quite dead upon the table in the box – and then two of them screamed, and then four and eight and sixteen and on and on until the whole room was full of screams, with girls and ladies running here and there and getting nowhere fast.

Me and Holly just laughed, because after all what were they going to do to us? We laughed and strolled out hand-in-hand. "Merry Christmas!" I said to the woman on reception, and we skipped down the stairs like love's first bloom and walked out into the night air. It was almost midnight now, almost Christmas Day, and would you believe it? It was snowing and had been doing so, judging by the depth of the stuff on the cobblestones, for the past hour or so.

We held hands and span around in circles with our tongues out, letting the snow fall into our mouths and around our mouths and into our eyes.

"I love you!" I said at the top of my voice to Holly. "I'm so sorry I didn't see it before. Your blood is so sweet. It's beautiful, like you!"

"I love you too," said Holly. "I always did. And you needn't worry. This doesn't mean you've forsaken Poppy. It just means that she says it's all right for you to be happy again."

And at that moment in time, that sounded like the most profound thing I'd ever heard. And did you notice? No stuttering. Bless her.

Behind us we heard screaming. Dozens of terrified ladies came flooding out of the club doorway and into the night, and upon seeing us standing there, started screaming afresh and legged it back into the club. I imagine there was quite a crush in the club's reception area, what with some people trying to get down the stairs while others were trying to get back up. We left them to it and went home.

With the weather being so festive and wintry, there were no cabs to be found, so we followed the route of the Thames so far before cutting back up towards Spitalfields. It was the perfect Christmas Eve, it really was. Like something from a Christmas card or a tin of biscuits.

"It's been a mad year," I said to Holly as we looked over the Thames, snow falling, with the dome of St. Paul's in the distance.

"It's been a mad fifty years," said Holly.

"I suppose it rather has," I agreed, squeezing her hand. "Here's to the future and to us. We'll make things better."

"I suppose you might not have seen it, when you drank my blood," said Holly, "but I had a name for my baby daughter. She never got christened or nothing, not with everything that happened, but I gave her a name and they put it on the birth certificate."

"It wasn't Kate, was it?" I asked.

"Nah, you daft brush!" she laughed. "But I wish it was. In my heart it was."

I gave her a big hug. Somewhere a bell rang for midnight. "It's not your birthday anymore!" I said. "What a shame!"

"Oh don't worry about that," said Holly. "Birthdays are all right I suppose, but Christmas Day is better!"

And she was right. It was.

Chapter Thirteen

I lay her down upon the bed and flipped her over onto her tummy. My fingers, as swift and as nimble as thieves in the night, quickly unbuttoned her dress. I pulled the dress apart to reveal a thin sliver of her precious white skin. My hands entered the dress and caressed the skin, pulling the dress further apart to reveal her shoulder blades. My tongue found her spine and chartered its course, sending a shiver of pleasure down her back. I pulled the dress further apart still. It resisted, but I was not to be denied. I ripped the dress and it surrendered her shoulders, white skin, slender, freckled. I kissed her shoulders, brushed away her hair and kissed the back of her neck, and let my tongue caress her ear. "Oh my sweetness," I whispered, "my dearest Holly."

With a sudden turn of speed and strength, I threw her over onto her back. She giggled nervously and smiled broadly at me, her thin lips revealing her teeth and her fangs.

"You have no idea," she began, "how long..." I put a finger to her lips and shushed her.

I pulled the dress down and away from her, revealing first her collar bone, then her breasts, her large nipples blooming and erect, her stomach, her slender hips and her beautiful long legs, hidden cruelly up until now inside the long dresses that society insisted she wore. Her breath was shallow and quick, and she trembled gently. Vampires do not feel the cold. She trembled at my touch.

Freckles lay over her forehead, her cheeks, her nose, and across her shoulders and the tops of her breasts. My lips touched each and every one. How had I not seen this before? Her freckles were beautiful, adorable. I placed a nipple in my mouth, sucking and then biting gently, playfully with my fangs. She thrust her hips up to me eagerly. Placing a hand between her legs, I found her wet, hungry, impatient. There was a heat between her legs that my fingers tried to quell, but it was not my fingers that were required. She gripped my hair forcefully and thrust my head down.

How long I devoured her I do not remember, nor could I count the number of times she reached her ecstasy. There is a clever little trick that a cunt can perform, when it is in the mood of course and when it is playing with a tongue or with fingers that it is particularly enamoured with, a trick whereby one orgasm follows another with barely a second to separate them. They tumble onto each other, like the game children play with dominoes where the wooden pieces are stood on end and then topple over, one knocking over the next and then the next and then the next. So it can be with a clever little cunt and its orgasms. One into the other, tumbling, tumbling, ecstasy upon ecstasy, tumbling, crashing, exploding, until the poor girl has nothing left inside her, no energy, no juices, and still the cunt says 'one more' and crash! The hips thrust and the girl moans for she is spent, and even the slightest touch, a kiss, a caress, can cause one more wave, the pleasure now so profound that it hurts, and yet, just once more. . .

So it was with Holly. I was a virgin when I met Poppy, so perhaps I am not the most experienced love-maker. But all I can say is this: Poppy never came this hard, so many times, to the point where her orgasms became a beast in their own right, a demon that possessed Holly's slender little freckled body and used it as a whore for its own infernal pleasure.

As she lay on the bed, half asleep, moaning gently to herself, her skin glistening with sweat and her sex juices, I lay beside her and watched. Her tiny eyelashes, the small bags beneath her eyes that puffed up if she squinted, the nose that wrinkled like a child's when she laughed. 'Oh poor girl,' I thought. 'They killed your baby, and what a struggle it must have been for such a slight thing to have carried a baby to full term. Of course it was tiny, for your hips are so slim that anything else would have killed you as sure as daylight now would kill you.'

I brushed her hair away from her face, where sweat had made it stick to her cheeks and her forehead. At my touch, she moaned once more and gripped my hand and held it tight against her cheek.

"What I said in the club," she whispered, "about me dad punching me and knocking me sparko in the kitchen. It were true. And he did other things to me as well, Snow. Awful things."

"I know," I said. And I swore that if I ever found her father or her husband, who her blood had revealed to me as a wife-beater, I would kill them both slowly with my bare hands. And if I ever found the vampire who turned her, I would kneel before him, kiss his hand, and thank him for delivering to me such a precious, darling jewel.

Chapter Fourteen

There is, of course, just one loose end to be tied up in this tale of lust and love, betrayal and salvation. And that is whatever happened to the bitch whore Little Red? Well now, settle down and let me tell you.

In 1891 they came to knock down Flower and Dean Street, our home. Following the hoo-ha of the so-called Jack the Ripper murders (which in reality were all to do with the Vatican Man and others – as was later revealed to me, and will also be shortly revealed to you), the powers-that-be, and by that I mean the mortals, decided that the best way to deal with all this unpleasantness – the prostitution, the gin houses, the murdering – was to knock down the slums and start again. Well, as I heard my mam say to my daddy once when they thought I wasn't listening, "You can't polish a turd." But they tried it anyway.

Now they claimed that they'd posted bills up and down Flower and Dean Street giving residents notice of eviction, and they claimed that they'd pushed letters under the door of every house notifying us of where we should go to be given new accommodation. That's what they claimed. But, to be honest, me and Holly existed in our own little bubble, quite oblivious to what was going on in the mortal world. It simply didn't interest us, and we thought that it was nothing to do with us. We weren't mortal, we were vampire. We never let what happened in their world intrude on our little vampire world. In fact, if the Great War had started in 1890 rather than 1914, and the Kaiser and all his German and Austrian soldier boys had come a-marching up the Strand to the sounds of an oompah band, and Queen Victoria had declared that we all had to start cackling in German, I genuinely believe that me and Holly would have been remained blissfully unaware. So, as you can imagine, when the workmen knocked on our nice strong front door to check there was no-one at home before they started with the demolition, it came as something of a shock.

We were sleeping at the time (it being in the daylight hours) and at first I thought I was dreaming. There came such a-banging and a-crashing on the front door, and cries of, "Hello? Anyone in there?" that I thought I was dreaming about the Vatican Man breaking in again. But as I sat up in bed, and as Holly started to stir next me, the banging and the shouting continued. Clearly it wasn't a dream.

"What is it?" mumbled Holly. "Who there?" She was still half asleep.

"Sssh," I said. "I think someone's at the door."

"But nobody ever comes to our door. We don't have visitors." This wasn't entirely true. Mr. Baginski came once a week, every Friday evening, to collect his rent. We never let him inside, not that he seemed overly interested in coming in anyway. We just stood on the doorstep and handed over the cash. He would look at it, count it, sniff, and then mumble, "Same time next week, ladies." Then he'd touch the brow of his bowler, and off he'd jolly well pop. That was the extent of the visitors we had appearing on our doorstep, and hence why when the workmen came a-knocking we were all at sixes and sevens.

"Who can it be?" I whispered, jumping naked out of bed and throwing a gown around me.

"It ain't that Vatican bloke is it?" said Holly, pulling the covers up to her chin.

"I don't think he'd knock, my sweet," I replied. "Come on, let's sneak down and see."

Holly put a gown on also, and the two of us crept down the stairs like two little mice, holding onto each other's arms. It was daytime, but we were always careful to pull tight the black drapes that hung over every window, and so we were able to creep through the house as it lay in twilight.

There came another banging on the door, which made both of us jump. "We're vampires!" I hissed. "Why are we acting so scared?"

"I dunno," said Holly, gripping my arm even tighter.

We crept up to the door and listened, our vampire hearing becoming very useful. Outside we could hear men's voices.

"Well I don't know, I'm sure. All these houses are supposed to be empty by now."

"We can't go knocking anything down until we're sure there's no-one in. Ain'tcha got a key for the door?"

"I've got a key that's supposed to fit, but it don't. I reckon they've had a new door fitted or somefink. And look, curtains pulled tight at each window. I reckon someone's still living here."

"Well they ain't ruddy well supposed to be. Knock again. See if they answer."

Bang bang bang!

"We can't do anything till we get inside to check. I ain't asking my boys to start knocking down the walls when they could be some poor bugger still inside."

"Course not, nobody wants to do that. We'll have to get a locksmith over here and get him to open up this door for us. Never bleeding easy, is it?"

"Well we won't get nobody to look at the lock till tomorrow now. Look at the time. Gone four, already. Listen, tell the boys to go home, have an early one. But tell them to be here all the earlier tomorrow. We'll get a locksmith first thing, sort this house out, then they get to work on the entire row."

"They wanted these all knocked down by the end of the week."
"Well that ain't going to happen, is it?"
"No."

And the voices faded away as they left our doorstep and walked away. Our good strong door had saved the day! Without it, those workmen would have been in and would have found us, two vampires, asleep. If they'd opened up the curtains, well, that would have been curtains for me and Holly I suppose, if you'll excuse the pun.

"Oh Holly," I said. "I think they want to knock down our house!"

"Well they can just blooming well coco!" said Holly. "The cheek of it!"

228

We ran back upstairs and huddled on the bed until darkness fell. As soon as the sun's head dipped beneath the horizon, we threw on overcoats and stumbled out into the street. It was utterly deserted. There were no cabs, no carts, no people. Just me and Holly standing there, looking around, and trying to fathom out what was going on. At a near-by junction we saw why the street was so empty. Barriers had been placed across the road with candles in lamps hanging from them. Notices read: Demolition in Progress – Do Not Enter.

We ran back up the street and noticed that none of the boarding houses had gas lamps or candles burning inside. None of the curtains were closed. Some of the houses even had doors swinging open, flapping gently in the breeze.

"This isn't good, Holly," I said.

We looked in a few houses, all of them 'bed and breakfasts', near to ours. They were empty, not only of occupants but of contents. No chairs, no rugs, no pictures on the wall. Quite, quite empty. Then we saw a bill poster on a near-by wall. Notice to Quit. Planned Slum Demolition.

"Who they calling a slum?" asked Holly. "I like it round here."
"I think it all got too much for them," I said. "Us, the killings, the Vatican Man, Jack the blinking Ripper, the whole shooting match. I think they finally got fed up with us." "So what happens now?"
"We have to leave."

"Leave? But where would we go?"

"I don't know," I said, "but we can't stay. If the workmen arrive tomorrow and break into our house, they're going to find us lying there and then what will happen?"

"I'll rip out their blinking throats!"

"Exactly," I said. "And then more men will come, and the police, and they'll pull back the curtains, they'll have daylight on their side. We wouldn't survive such an encounter. We have to leave."

Holly saw the truth of my words, and so we walked in silence the short distance to our home. There we got dressed, and gathered together a few things, spare dresses mainly, hanging up on the rail that had been there since that first night I'd arrived, and had watched breathlessly as Poppy and Little Red had made love. Had sex. Whatever you want to call it. The memory brought back emotions that I didn't know what to do with, so I put them out of my mind. There were more important things to deal with right now.

Me and Holly dressed, and a more productive thought entered my mind; about where we should go.

"Highgate Cemetery," I said. "That's where we'll go. We can spend the night there, be nice and safe, and gather our thoughts. Ultimately we're going to want to get a new house, but I've no idea right now about how to start organising that. For now, we need somewhere that we know is good and safe, and that's the only place that springs to mind."

"Wish we could take our bed," said Holly, looking wistfully at the bed where we'd slept every day since we became lovers. "Do you remember that Christmas Day after you first drank my blood? Struth, but we was evil."

"I do remember," I said, smiling, as I pushed a dress into a carpet bag. "You were," I shook my head, "unbelievable."

"Bless you," said Holly. "You say the sweetest things."

"Listen here, we'll take blankets and sheets. Make it as cosy as we can."

Once we were dressed and had packed several large bags with dresses, blankets, sheets, a few hair brushes, spare boots, and whatever else we could gather up and thought we might need, we opened up the good strong door for the last time and headed out into the night. Holly started to cry, and I felt like crying too. I put an arm around her, two big bags hanging from my other arm (thank you vampire strength!), and she buried her head into my shoulder. "It's not fair," she sobbed. "That was our lovely home."

And she was right. It was our lovely home, and now we were having to leave. It wasn't fair, not fair at all. But what could we do?

We walked along Flower and Dean Street for a little way, before reaching Brick Lane. Here life carried on as normal, pedestrians walked the pavements, horses and carts and cabs clip- clopped along the road. We hailed a cab and set off for Highgate Cemetery.

"Good night, little road," said Holly as the cab pulled away. "Sleep tight." What a dear girl she truly was.

The cab dropped us off at the gates, and once it was safely out of sight, we ducked around a corner, threw the bags over a wall, and clambered over ourselves. The cemetery lay still in pitch blackness. Of course, this meant nothing to us with our vampire senses, but I could imagine how to a mortal the graveyard would have appeared foreboding, intimidating, and so, so, dark that they would have to walk with their arms outstretched before them so as to avoid bumping into tombs, crypts and trees that over-hung the pathways. This was the perfect hiding place for a vampire. Humans would have to be insane to come a-stumbling around here after nightfall.

We had intended to find the vault that had been our refuge on *that* night, the night that Poppy, Mary Jane, Abigail and Catherine had died. The vault outside of which we'd placed the vases containing the last earthly remains of Poppy and Catherine, but we never made it that far. As we walked along the path, I suddenly stopped in my tracks and shivered like someone had just stepped over my grave.

"Well fuck me sideways!" a voice exclaimed behind us. "You are positively, absolutely, the last couple of tarts I ever expected to see wandering around here."

I span around, fangs bared. It was Little Red. It was fucking Little Red.

Chapter Fifteen

"So what happened?" asked Little Red. "The Vatican finally catch up with you?" She had an aren't-I-so-clever smirk about her face and standing behind her was a young girl, probably about the same age as me I guessed, a vampire though she looked demonic and somehow out of place. Her fangs weren't on show, but she had eyes that burned red and pointed ears, like a little elf. She clearly had no idea who me and Holly were. She stood barefoot I noticed, and looked dirty, lost.

"The Vatican?" said Holly. "Me and Snow killed him, or didn't you hear? And we know it was you what grassed us up, you bitch blower!"

"It speaks!" said Little Red, smirking. "How comes you're talking now, Holly? You're not even s-s-s-s-stuttering. What happened? Let me guess, Kate fucked you better?"

"Leave her alone," I said.

"Or what, Kate? You going to kill me? I'd like to see it, really, I would. And anyway, I've no argument with you. What happened with the Vatican Man, believe it or not, had absolutely nothing to do with you. Sorry to shatter any illusions you might have had about the importance of your role in proceedings."

"So you just thought you'd get Poppy killed for the hell of it, then?" I said. "It had nothing to do with the fact that she'd broken off with you in favour of me?"

I was quite happy to stick that little knife into the bitch's belly.

"Oh Kate, you really have no comprehension of who or what Poppy really was, do you? To be honest, you have no idea who I am, or even who poor voiceless Holly is. Does she Holly? She doesn't know much about you, does she? She doesn't know you like I do, does she?"

Little Red spoke to Holly like she was talking to a slow child. Holly fumed, bared her fangs, but said nothing.

"Tell me Kate, has she told you how me and Poppy used to fuck her? Oh, *how* we used to fuck her! She used to beg for it! Not with words of course, because she never spoke, not in those days. But she used to beg for it with actions. That made it all the more fun, all the more exciting. She wouldn't ask to be fucked, but she'd come to us naked and start rubbing herself up against us. Caught us quite by surprise the first time it happened, and no mistake. But we got used to it. It used to be quite a thrill really, this little mute girl rubbing her cunt up against my leg and pleading with me to fuck her with her big eyes. And I'll admit it, she really is quite the passionate one when she gets going, isn't she? Me and Poppy used to wind her up like a clockwork monkey and then

232

just watch her go! Bet she never told you about those passionate encounters. Ha! Of course she never.

"And how about," she continued, warming to the subject by now, "the whole blood drinking fetish she has. Oh, lordy, how she used to beg and plead for me and Poppy, or *anyone*, to drink her sodding blood. We wouldn't do it, of course. Well, I for one didn't want infecting with anything manky that might make me, you know, lose my own voice. And Poppy had more sense. How about you, Kate? Bet she asked you to drink her blood, didn't she? Bet she went on and on about it. She used to bite her wrist, then follow me around trying to get me to drink it. I do hope you've had more sense, Kate, than to do as she asked? I do hope?"

"Yes, I've drunk her blood," I said, "and I love her and I don't care a fig about what might or might not have happened in the past. I love the girl and if you carry on like this Little Red, I swear I will kill you."

"Oh Kate! No!" said Little Red. "Not the blood thing! Don't you see how destructive that is? You say you love Holly, but you don't, not really. It's just the blood talking. It clouds your judgement, makes you see things that aren't there, it's a fucking trick that vampires have used since time immemorial to gather around them loyal, devoted bodyguards. It's why Poppy had me drink her blood. To protect her, to keep her safe. It made me love her, it made me love her so much that it physically hurt.

"And yes, I'll admit that she took a shine to you as soon as she saw you. The little waif in the alleyway. She fancied having a bit of a crack on you, and that's fair enough 'cause in case you ain't gathered it yet, we was all at it with each other like a clowder of street cats, but what was the first thing the bitch did? She made you, *made* you, drink her blood. Just to make sure that you fancied her more than she fancied you. But it wasn't your fault, Kate. You didn't know. You were dying. She was playing her blooming head games and she nearly killed you as a result. She made us enemies from the off. We could have been pals, you and me. But Poppy wouldn't have it, would she? She had to set us up as enemies. Rivals for her love. It was more fun for her that way.

She loved to play with people's minds. She played with my mind and she played with yours and look where it's got us all.

"So you've drunk Holly's blood? Well, that's all right I suppose, if it makes you happy. Look Kate, I've no argument with you. We all made mistakes. We were all victims in our own way. We should call a truce. If we can't be friends, we can at least agree to keep out of each other's way?"

"It wasn't just Poppy you got killed." I said. "That bastard killed Mary Jane, Abigail and Catherine too. You got them all killed."

Little Red fell silent and looked at the floor. The girl behind her shuffled her bare feet and wiped her nose on the back of her hand, clearly feeling self-conscious about being caught up in all this drama that she had no comprehension of.

"All right, Kate. I'll tell you everything. But not here. Not like this." Little Red glanced at her friend and Holly.

"Holly," I said, "take Little Red's friend for a walk will you? Look after her, keep her safe, she's not our enemy. Me and Little Red are just going to, I don't know, go somewhere for a chat."

"In here," said Little Red pulling back the entrance to a vault. "This is where we live."

Bedding was scattered around the inside of the vault, even a mattress, which reminded me of the old house on Flower and Dean Street. A few candles were scattered here and there, which Little Red took a moment to light with a pack of Lucifers, and in the corner of the vault lay a fresh human corpse, a female, probably a prostitute; a stark and timely reminder, amongst all this talk of love and lust, of our true nature.

I meant what I had said. I did love Holly. I loved Holly in a manner that in some unfathomable fashion seemed more honest and more down-to-earth than the sheer adoration I had felt for Poppy. I didn't care what they'd all been up to before I'd arrived. Yes, of course, when Little Red had told me they'd been fucking each other like alley-cats, I'd known she was telling the truth, and yes, it had made my stomach and my heart flip with jealousy, I couldn't help that, but I knew that it wouldn't affect how I felt about Holly. I knew that Holly was a good, decent, sweet girl who had been dealt a gammy hand in life, and had spent most of her years looking for love and having it snatched away from her. Well I would always stand by her. I would always be there for her. I truly loved her, and if that was her blood speaking, so be it. I didn't care. It was how I felt and I didn't care how that feeling had got there in the first place.

"She ripped off the top of his skull with her bare teeth," I said of Holly and the Vatican Man. "I wouldn't cross her if I was you. She's not the idiot you think she is."

Little Red just smiled, as you might smile at a small child who came to tell you there was a giant purple snake in their bedroom. I wanted to knock her block off. She knelt down by the mortal woman and gently brushed her hair away from her face. "Bag of blood," cooed Little Red. "Pretty, pretty bag of blood." I saw several wounds in the woman's neck. The woman let out a shallow moan. Still alive. What monsters we were.

"Do you know who Poppy was?" asked Little Red looking up at me. "I mean, really know who she was?"

I stood in silence.

"Well," said Little Red, "let me tell you. Poppy was very old; as old as the hills, as they say. Her real name, of course, wasn't Poppy, any more than your real name is Snow or mine is Little Red. Her real name, if I recall correctly, was Popillia. Ain't that sweet? It's some kind of Roman or Latin name, or some such. It's also the name of a kind of beetle, which is quite apt as I think she may have originally come from Egypt and they always worshipped beetles there, didn't they? I'm talking about a long time ago here, certainly as far back as the birth of Jesus. So when she died, as heartbreaking as it must have been for you, and for me, you have to bear in mind that she'd had a good innings. Two thousand and odd before being given out to a Vatican spinner!

"It seems a little odd, doesn't it, that Poppy came from Egypt but was so fair of face and hair? I'm not what you might call a genius with my geography and what-not, but I'm pretty certain that people from Egypt tend to be quite dark. So how come Poppy was blonde and fair? Oh, there are more mysteries surrounding that girl than I dare to think. Perhaps she was an angel from heaven? Or perhaps she really was a goddess like she always joked?

"Anyway, she came over to England with the Romans. She really did! Fancy that! I'm pretty sure she must have already been a vampire by then, and I think the Romans used her as a kind of secret assassin, to kill their enemies as they slept in their bed. Oh, how exciting it all must have been for her! I'm sure she was very good at her job. When the Romans left again, she stayed here and worked for whatever baron or king or whoever could pay her the most, and I'm sure she'd have been fucking them all too, or at least fucking their wives and daughters! She was a saucy little minx that one, and no doubt.

"I suppose the trouble really started for her last century. She started to piss off the Holy Roman Empire and the Pope. Whenever there was a war, she always seemed to find herself fighting for the side that was opposed to the Pope. This carried on to the Napoleonic Wars when the British Army sent her to kill old Boney himself. She didn't get him, but she got most of his lieutenants," and at that point I remembered my blood dream, "and that really got the Pope mad. She'd been fucking with the Vatican and the Holy Roman Empire and their favoured little despots for too long. So they issued a decree. Whosoever kills the vampire Popillia will be assured a place in heaven! So assassins came, and she sent them all back across the English Channel a lot deader than when they'd arrived! No human assassin could get near her. She was a tough old boot, after all.

"So they started to train special assassins, holy warrior monks, who were both highly religious, and also trained in the fighting arts. They also used special magicks that they'd had stashed away from the times of Babylon – special spells and prayers and amulets and things that could make a human as powerful as a vampire. They sent them, one after the other, to kill her. They were a lot harder to knock off than the first lot of assassins, so Poppy had to go into hiding, in Spitalfields. Live the life of a mortal prostitute, and gather around her a small gang of vampires, to help keep her safe. Oh, what a come down it must have been

236

for her. From fucking kings and queens and princesses, to living with us East End girls in Spitalfields. But still, needs must, eh?

"But they found her, as you know only too well. They found her and then they killed her."

"And then me and Holly killed him, the Vatican man," I said.

"Yes," said Little Red, "but don't get too up yourself about that. All the spells and incantations and magic amulets that he'd been blessed with in order to make him some kind of super warrior, they'd all been conjured with the intention of killing Poppy. He was only a super warrior when it came to Poppy. To the rest of us, he was a formidable opponent, and one-on-one he would probably have bettered you. You were lucky that there were two of you, it gave you the edge. So he killed Abigail and Catherine too? Shame. They were nice girls. They never liked me, mind. Then again I don't think any of them really did."

"Mary Jane liked you," I said. "And he killed her as well."

"No he didn't," she said. "I did."

My mouth fell open and I must have looked like I'd been slapped with a wet fish. "You did? But why? For God's sake, Little Red, she was your friend!"

"God's got nothing to do with it, you drippy cow!" she snapped. "I told you what I'd do if you took Poppy away from me. Turns out I was wrong to threaten you, I realise that now. It wasn't your fault. It was hers. She was the one who gave you her blood while I begged her not to. It was her who looked at me and smirked while she did it. I loved her, oh yes, I loved her, but she was a heartless bitch when she wanted to be.

"Remember how she just abandoned me, with my heart break-ing, to sit by myself, to cry in the dark, while she ran off hand-in-hand with you? Was that what I really deserved after fifty years of love and devotion? Was it? So when I heard that the Vatican Man was in town looking for her, I saw my opportunity to get my own back. Inside, it felt like she'd killed me, like she'd stuck a stake in my heart and then laughed as she watched me wither and die. So I found the Vatican Man, tracked him down, told him I could get her out in the open for him. I killed Mary Jane, made it look like the Vatican Man, and that brought Poppy out of the house, running right into the trap. He threw holy water into her face, put a sack over her head, and stuck a wooden stake in her heart. She wasn't laughing then, was she? She didn't look much like a goddess when he'd finished with her."

"She always looked like a goddess," I said. "She died in my arms and she never looked more like a goddess than in those last few seconds of her life."

"Oh, how sweet," said Little Red.

I threw myself at her, nails scratching at her eyes, fangs searching for her neck. My sudden lunge had caught her by surprise and she fell backwards onto the floor of the crypt with me on top of her. I grabbed her hair and yanked great clumps of her curly red locks out of her scalp. I pushed my mouth towards her neck, trying to get close enough so that my teeth and fangs could get to work on her throat, but she began to regain her composure. She grabbed my wrists and forced my hands away from her face and head. She gripped my wrists tightly. Very tightly. Her nails dug in and sliced my flesh. Blood began to stream down my wrists and into the palms of my hands. At the last moment she realised what was about to happen and twisted her head away, but it was too late. My blood dripped from my palms and into her mouth. "No," she managed to protest. Such a futile little word.

She let go of my wrists and let her arms fall above her head as she lay spread-eagled on the floor. Her eyes glazed over and she looked at me with adoration. "Oh my sweetheart," she sighed. I seized the opportunity and thrust one of my wrists into her mouth, allowing more blood to be swallowed. Her back arched and I felt the warmth between her legs thrust up against my thigh.

I lay down on top of her and began to gently kiss her neck. She was helpless beneath me now. I could do with her what I wanted. I could have fucked her all night long and she would have thanked me for it. I kissed and nipped at her neck, then kissed her full on the lips. Her passions were rising and she squirmed beneath me. "I love you," she whispered. "I always did." She didn't and never had, of course. It was my blood talking. I had no idea what scenes from my past life were being flashed through her mind, and didn't rightly care. All I knew was that I had her, as harmless as a little kitten, purring beneath my touch.

I rubbed more of my blood over her face, the wounds were quickly healing now, and then licked it off, feeling the sweet tang of my own life force.

"Will you do anything for me?" I asked, as gently as a lover might.

"Anything my sweetheart," she replied. "Anything you ask."

I kissed her on the forehead and remembered her fucking Poppy and remembered the sound of her fucking Holly. She was my rival.

"Oh my darling," I said, "would you die for me?" "Oh yes, gladly."

"Good," I said and ripped out her throat.

Her body went into a spasm. I sat up, half of Little Red's neck hanging from my mouth, and watched as her body collapsed in on itself, her precious red hair falling out, her face caving in, her breasts withering and turning to dust. I spat her neck out onto the rest of her fast decomposing remains and wiped my mouth with the back of my hand. I was covered in blood again. No surprises there then.

I watched for a moment, just to make sure she was gone. She was. She really was gone. There was nothing left. Then I left the crypt, pushed the door tightly closed behind me and found Holly and Little Red's friend standing in the darkness amongst the crypts, looking for all the world like Hansel and Gretel, lost in the woods.

"What happened?" asked Holly, running over to me and throwing her arms around my shoulders.

"It's finished, done with," I said. "She won't bother us again."

"Oh did she say awful things about me, Snow? I promise I'll be good from now on. You know I love you."

"Holly," I said, "it was Little Red. She said nasty things about everyone."

Holly buried her head into my shoulder and whispered, "You're so brave. So brave."

"I was lucky more like," I said. "Being brave had nothing to do with it."

"You were lucky then!" she smiled, looking me in the face. "Lucky in love!"

I heard a shuffling behind us. It was the young barefoot vampire girl with the pointy ears. What to do with her?

The girl looked demurely to the floor. I noticed that she was filthy, not just her feet, but her clothes, her hair, her face.

"Don't be scared, sweets," I said to her.

"Oh, I ain't scared, treacle," she said defiantly. "Don't worry your pretty little head about that."

"She's a Dolly Biter!" whispered Holly, loud enough for all to hear, like this was supposed to mean something to me. "I thought they'd all been killed, but look at her. She's one of the old Chicksand mob for sure!"

"That's right," said the barefoot girl, "I'm the last of the Biters. Is that a problem for you fine ladies?"

"It's no problem for me," I said. "I don't even know what a blinkin' Dolly Biter is! But we're all vampires here, and we should try and help each other out. That's how I sees it, anyways. Me and Holly are going to pretend to be prostitutes and get a crib up Whitechapel. You're welcome to join us, if you likes?"

"All right, I s'pose," said the girl a little hesitantly. "Where's Little Red gone?"

"She's dead," I said. "I killed her. Me and her, well, we had what you might call 'history'."

"I only met her a few days ago," said this strange little creature. "Been on me own for a long time."

"What's your name, darling?" I asked.

"Moran," she replied. "That's all. Just Moran."

"Then you're more than welcome to come along with us, Moran," I said.

"You girls," she said, "you all wear shoes. I ain't never worn shoes, not since I got turned." I smiled at her quizzically. "Maybe I should start wearing shoes again, like I used to before I was turned," she continued, "and get myself an 'aircut?"

"You do whatever you want, darling," I said.

So off we walked, the three of us, a fresh vibrancy and purpose in our step. We'd head up to Whitechapel, get some digs, and start again. We'd make it nice for ourselves and for this demonic little vampire called Moran. We'd look after her, show her the ropes (although I had a sneaking suspicion that it would be *her* who ended up showing *us* the ropes), and hope that the rest of the world, the mortal world, the Vatican, would leave us in peace.

I clambered over the cemetery wall first, followed by Holly and finally Moran. As me and Holly stood by the side of the road, waiting for Moran, Holly whispered, "If you let her drink your blood I'll fucking kill you." And do you know what, I think she meant it. Charming.

"It's a good job I love you," I said, "or I might have to put you over my knee and tan your arse."

"Oh," said Holly. "Promises."

So later that day, I did exactly that.

A new home, and a new girl in tow. A new story. And yet as the 20th Century barrelled towards us, the more things changed, the more they stayed the same.

Epilogue

Excerpt from *A Very Bohemian Slaughterhouse*, Edwin Wallace, first published 1923.

She moves with an effortless ease through the crowd of ladies in the bar area of Lieu de Rencontre pour les Dames. She is the perfect little Tom, with her hair cut short and parted to one side, combed to perfection, Brylcreem giving it an immaculate shine. She is wearing a man's black dinner jacket and trousers, a white shirt with starched collar and a black dickie-bow. She looks for all the world like a sixteen-year-old boy rather than the eighteen-year-old lesbian vampire that she really is, and of course it is this fe-male element that has all the old dears at the club slavering at the chops. They run their hands over her arse, they touch her cheek, they beg to be engaged in conversation, to have her whisper into their ear, to maybe, perhaps, kiss them on the cheek and, who knows, if they're lucky, to let them fuck her with their old tongues and their wrinkled fingers in exchange for their money.

She is a tart, a prostitute, a slag. They pay her the kind of money that would feed a working class family for a week, and in exchange for this they are permitted to lick her body from lips to toes, and be reminded of their own youth, now long gone. And after the fucking has ceased they will usually cry. It is all part of the game, all part of the trade.

They will say that they do not know why they find themselves in tears, but deep down they will know the awful truth. That they are old, the years slipping away, heading for the grave and the

242

cold earth and neither their money nor their influence can do a damned thing to stop it. But she, *she*, in her youth and in her beauty is perfection. Untainted by time, untouched by the years; her breasts pert, her stomach flat, her thighs smooth and her legs lithe. Her perfection reduces them to tears, not of joy but of loss. Youth, once lost, can never be found.

There are some, of course, for whom the terrible ravages of the years are simply too much to bear. And on their last night on this cruel earth, they may drink of the best champagne, gaze upon her most perfect body, caress her lips, her breasts, her thighs, and then politely ask for blessed release in her arms. And so she will extend her terrible fangs, and as gently as a sweetheart, she will bite at their neck and allow their soul to enter her body and become part of her perfection.

Oh, this vampire lesbian, this forever-eighteen-year-old Tom, dressed in her immaculate male clothes, is as kind and as considerate as any lover has ever been.

See her move through the crowd, smiling, winking, smoking on her expensive cigarettes. They ask her, "My darling, what is your name?" She smiles sweetly with a smile that breaks the heart. "Moran," she says. "They call me Moran."

The End

Interlude

When a brave, young (if not slightly naïve) Salvation Army girl by the name of Eloise Bacon ventured into Spitalfields one November evening in 1866, little could she have imagined the tragic chain of events that her spirited actions would set in motion.

Eighteen-year-old Eloise was the daughter of a Methodist minister, a devout Christian, and one of the Salvation Army's first recruits, one of the first to don the famous scarlet uniform and venture into London's East End in order to spread the word of the Lord. Her death at the hands of a vampire, a 'Dolly Biter', and the knowledge that her beloved Bible, ripped from her dying hands, had subsequently been sold to a Whitechapel fence for a few coppers, caused outrage amongst the population of London and beyond, and the newspapers of the day demanded that *something be done* about these vampires. The London Times, describing Eloise as a 'sweet, innocent Christian rose' and her vampiric assailant a 'despicable agent of the night', called for a cull of the vampires of the East End, and when the guilty vampire, the woman who struck down this sweet, innocent Christian rose, was revealed to be none other than the missing daughter of shipping magnate Sir Adler, turned into a despicable agent of the night by a foreign vampire of royal descent, the howls of outrage and the calls for a 'final solution' grew ever louder.

The net result of the turning of Miss Adler and the murder of Miss Bacon was what has become known as the Battle of Brick Lane; the establishment's attempt to eradicate the East

End vampires once and for all. As a cure to the night-time ills of Whitechapel and Spitalfields, it was only partially successful.

High Born vampires, those born of vampire parents and blessed with lineage, titles, money, and stately homes, had been an integral part of European society for many centuries. The High Borns (or *natural borns* as many mortals referred to them) often held positions of great power, many being involved in politics or having even attained royal standing thanks to centuries of political manoeuvring, cleverly arranged marriages, and the occasional war.

The 'East End problem' first began to emerge in the mid-18th Century when the city of London started to grow at an exponential rate thanks to the ever expanding British Empire, and young people were drawn in from the surrounding countryside in large numbers to service the needs of the capital. Young female prostitutes soon caught the eye of male High Borns, and the ensuing trysts, thanks to vampire saliva and semen infecting the human female, created the first documented 'turned' vampires. Urban myth tells us that the very first woman to be turned in the East End was a young scullery maid kidnapped by a visiting European High Born in the mid-1700s, who, having escaped from her captor, was hunted down and turned vampire as punishment.

As far as we are able to ascertain, only females were capable of being turned. Males, it would appear, always succumbed to their wounds; the only explanation therefore for any bloody attacks on mortals by gangs of male vampires is that they were High Borns, perhaps letting off a little steam and hunting humans for fun, as distasteful and unsavoury as that sounds. Which leads us to the question of the sexual orientation of the female turned vampires. From all accounts (the main ones which are, of course, contained within this tome), the turning process had the side-effect are making most females lesbian. This was not always the case, there are one or two accounts within this book of female vampires falling in love with or having sexual relations with men; but *in the main* the female vampires were lesbian and any tales of relationships with human males are told almost exclusively as tales of warning, for it seems such relations rarely ended well for the human male.

Regarding the two main accounts held within these pages, the accounts of Irene Adler and the account of Katie Bell, we are left with the inescapable conclusion that the vampire infection mutates and changes with every outbreak, perhaps in a similar way to the behaviour of influenza and the common cold, where the genetic make-up of the virus is continuously evolving (what is known as *antigenic drift*). When we compare the 'Dolly Biters' of Miss Adler's account with Miss Bell's girls of Flower & Dean Street, there are some striking differences.

The Dolly Biters certainly seem a darker incarnation than the girls of Flower & Dean Street who would follow some twenty years later. With pointed ears, red eyes, long fingernails, elongated (and occasionally forked) tongues, the Dolly Biters found it difficult to traverse the human world without being spotted and recognised. Compare that with the girls of Flower & Dean Street who seemed able to wander mortal society without fear of recognition. The Dolly Biters also needed to feed on a nightly basis, which led to many of the younger girls literally starving to death, while the later incarnations needed only to feed every three nights. Perhaps this is a case of the vampire virus mutating and evolving in order to aid its proliferation – a vampire that needs to feed only every three nights will have a better chance of survival than one who needs to feed every night.

The later vampire incarnations, as read about in Katie Bell's accounts, seemed to have a predilection for drinking each other's blood; an occupation that seems in many ways to be a vampiric counter-part to the opium dens of Victorian human society. Drinking of another vampire's blood produced feelings of euphoria, gave the vampire visions and intense dreams, and produced huge amounts of endorphins in the brain so as to create an over-whelming sense of love and adoration in the vampire. This practice was unheard of as recently as the 1860s, although in Irene Adler's account vampire blood was drunk as a means of communicating telepathically. Another case, perhaps, of the vampire virus mutating, constantly changing, never being exactly the same in any two outbreaks.

There has often been, in vampire society, the myth that the blood of a virgin mortal holds intoxicating properties. This has been, in the main, seen as little more than a legend and a story told half in jest between vampires. However, throughout the early and mid-19th Century (let us say pre-battle of Brick Lane), there were stories of High Borns coercing, one way or another, mortals to partake of opium in order for the opium to be in the mortals' blood when they feasted upon them. This blood-opium mix produced in the vampire much the same effects as the opium had on the human. In *homage* to the urban myth, this was known as 'Virgin Blood' amongst High Borns engaged in this dubious and despicable practice. There can be little doubt that the author of The Vampire Alice was describing the exploits of a High Born girl in his narrative, and that Alice's adventure through the looking glass was inspired by having partaken of 'Virgin Blood'.

Prior to the Battle of Brick Lane, much was made of the distinction between High Borns and the 'turned'. This is perhaps not surprising in a Victorian Britain that was obsessed with class and social standing. However, following the dreadful events of New Year's Day 1867, this distinction between the High Born and the turned seems to have become somewhat blurred. By the time Katie Bell was transformed, it appears to be no longer such a thorny and contentious issue. If we look at Poppy (or 'Poppillia') in Miss Bell's account, if she was not a true High Born then she had certainly been walking the Earth long enough to be considered one, and yet she happily lived in the East End with a group of young women, most of whom were, at the time, only recently turned. It seems almost as though the terrible events that occurred during the Battle of Brick Lane made the vampires who survived look at themselves and realise that if their kind were to survive, they would have to put aside petty differences and work together as a single species.

It would appear that the Vatican had been at war with vampires, on some level or other, for many centuries. An uneasy alliance seems to have been formed with the High Born, and the full weight of the Vatican's rage seems primarily to have been focused on turned vampires. In Katie Bell's account we hear of the 'Vatican Man', the name given to the assassins sent by Rome to kill vampires (and in this instance, to kill Poppy in particular). The Holmes brothers of Irene Adler's account are also empowered by Rome, and it is not too much of a stretch to imagine that the Holmes brothers of the Baskerville rookery were indeed the 'Vatican Man' of the 1860s.

By the turn of the 20th Century, vampire numbers were in steep decline. Mortal society, following the Battle of Brick Lane, was no longer in awe of vampires, no longer afraid of these creatures that lived in darkness and scuttled about in the shadows. January 1st 1867 had shown the humans that, if need be, they could fight back and they could beat the 'despicable agents of the night'. No longer was a blind eye turned to the crimes of the High Borns, no longer was the problem of the working class vampires in the east End brushed under the carpet and ignored in the hope of it going away. Now mortal society showed an appetite to track down and prosecute vampires who fed on humans, and records show a steep increase in the number of vampires convicted of murder and burned at the stake. These executions normally took place in Holloway prison in London, in a special courtyard constructed specifically for this purpose.

Due to this crackdown, vampires were encouraged to take up residence in 'hives'. Hives were large houses, often donated by wealthy High Borns, where vampires could live together for the safety and protection both of themselves and the surrounding human population. Since drinking human blood was illegal, and offenders now being prosecuted to the fullest extent of the law by a reinvigorated human judicial system, vampires were forced to exist on pigs' blood; hundreds of the animals being delivered to the Hives' kitchens to be prepared for consumption. An all-too brief glimpse into the world of the vampire hive is given in the short story that follows this interlude. Originally published in the Christmas 1926 edition of the Strand magazine, it serves both as a cautionary tale and as an endorsement of the hive system.

It was hoped that the hive system would ensure the safe and continued survival of the vampire race, but as an experiment it failed – not least due to the intransigent and bloody-minded (*sic*) attitude of many vampires who steadfastly refused to enter a hive, believing that the hive system infringed on their independent nature. A brief cult, the Order of the Black Dawn, rose up in the 1920s, comprising vampires who believed it to be their God-given right to hunt humans.

The last British vampire was executed in Holloway prison in 1931. Or so we are led to believe. Whatever the truth of that official statement, let us hope that in some way it allows the soul of Eloise Bacon, the girl who ventured into Spitalfields on that cold night in 1866 with the intention of saving the vampires but who inadvertently brought about their doom, some relief and that she may now rest in peace.

Book 3
Joan Dark is Lost – a Cautionary Tale

Paul Voodini

First published in the Christmas 1926 edition of The Strand magazine

by
Paul Voodini

251

Hyde Park, Winter, 1926

Following the tragedies surrounding the Battle of Brick Lane, the outrages of the so-called Jack the Ripper murders, and the subsequent bulldozing of large parts of London's East End, all vampires residing within Great Britain were enthusiastically encouraged to join a registered 'hive'. Any rogue vampires found not to be a member of such a hive could be arrested by the human authorities on suspicion of 'vagrancy' and placed into the care of a local hive. Hives existed to protect humans from vampires, and vampires from humans.

London, being the epicentre of all vampire activity in Britain, had several established hives. So-called 'High Born' vampires donated large houses within which their 'fallen' cousins could reside in relative peace and security. One such hive is Apsley House. Situated at Hyde Park Corner, Apsley House is an impressive neo-classical mansion, built in the late 18th Century and owned by the High Born Duke of Wellington. Even amongst the capital's vampires, the Apsley House hive is regarded as conservative, dark, and Gothic, ruled over by their ancient High Born queen, the redoubtable Mme. Weisner. The mansion perfectly reflects these values, with its impressive pillars, archways and leaded windows. On a dark and stormy night it resembles no less than the traditional haunted mansion of a hysterical human's fevered imagination.

Joan Dark is a member of the Apsley House hive.

Having been given the immortal kiss at the age of 18 (back in 1801, or so she thinks, maybe it was 1802), she is one of the younger members of the hive; forever frozen at the age of 18, never ageing, never maturing, her head forever full of the thoughts of an 18-year-old girl. To the vampires of North London, the hive and the house offer security, sanctuary and an ordered existence. Since the Battle of Brick Lane, it has been illegal for a vampire to kill a human. In the human world, of course, it has always been illegal for a vampire to kill a human; but vampires have rarely, if ever, paid much notice to human laws. Now, however, it is illegal under vampire law. So the hive provides food, pigs mainly, slaughtered in the kitchens and the blood served, still warm, in the dining hall during the many grand banquets. Yes, the hive and the house are a rock upon which the vampires of North London may comfortably cling. But to Joan Dark, 18-year-old vampire girl, the hive and the house were, this last year, becoming increasingly stifling.

On late Saturday afternoons, as the burning sun sank into twilight, Joan Dark and her two best friends Magnolia and Lillian, would take a short walk from Apsley House to Hyde Park. There they would promenade along the pathways; three vampire girls taking in the evening air, gossiping, and regarding with a mixture of amusement and fascination the human boys who sat on the park benches and watched the girls as they walked by. Magnolia and Lillian were also young when they had been turned, and the sight of three young, attractive vampires was too much for some of the local boys to resist.

Fraternising with humans was not illegal, however it was frowned upon. It was not seen as proper, in the dark eyes of Mme. Weisner, for a vampire to lower herself to the level of the human. But this did not stop Joan or her friends from delighting in the attention they were given by the local human boys. It seemed that the vampires were as intriguing to the humans as the humans were to the vampires.

So they would walk along the paths of the gardens, surrounded by grass and flowers and trees and boys, the fast-fading sun falling onto their pale skin and making it tingle sensually. And during one such perfect late afternoon, Joan met Billy. Billy was a builder's labourer from Tooting Bec, south of the River Thames, working in North London on some building development or other. Following the end of the Great War, London was once more an expanding centre of industry and commerce, the centre of the Empire, and a transient working population had arrived from throughout Great Britain and Ireland, finding work and money and, in some instances, love. South London Billy was funny and handsome, with a glint in his eye and curly blonde hair. He was the mortal summer to Joan's eternal winter, and over the following month they met whenever possible, walking hand in hand, laughing, giggling, and gazing into each other's eyes. When Joan looked into Billy's eyes, she saw a soul looking back at her. It made her hungry, but not for blood. It made her hungry for a past she could barely remember. For a past when she could play in the sun, when her parents still protected her, when she splashed in the stream at the bottom of the garden and swung from ropes tied by her father to the branches of trees. It made her hungry for the days before she was turned, before her parents died, and before the hive. Billy reminded her of those bright mortal days and she could not help but fall hopelessly, foolishly, in love.

But fate, it seems, has never been fond of young love and spitefully attempts to extinguish its flame whenever it is in its power to do so. So it was that one evening Billy broke the news to Joan. He was to return to South London, to Tooting Bec. His work here in North London was finished, and he had been promised new work in his home borough. Billy was sad and downcast, and Joan, her undead heart breaking, sobbed tears of blood and asked what now was to become of her? Was she forever to be a prisoner behind the walls of the hive? Was she never to know happiness? Was she doomed to spend eternity as a spinster, never loving, never marrying, never bearing children or walking again in the sun?

Oh, what fools love can make of the young.

"Come with me!" said Billy suddenly as they sat on the park bench, the moon gazing down silently upon them. "I'm shipping out south of the river tomorrow afternoon, but you could travel down later, when it's dark and when you've made arrangements, and come and live with me!"

Joan looked up, blood tears still streaking her cheeks. "What's that, Billy? You mean we should be married?"

"No, silly," smiled Billy. "But we could live together in my digs. The foreman's sorted us all out digs in Tooting and we could live there, you and me. It'd be like we were married and we'd be together."

"But isn't that, you know, a sin?" asked Joan.

Billy smiled. "Didn't know your kind believed in sin and God and stuff? I know I don't, though it's probably wicked to say so.

All I know is that I'm going to miss you something awful Miss Joan, and the only way I can think of us being together is if you join me in Tooting."

Joan fell silent, her mind racing. She wanted to scream 'yes!' at the top of her voice, but it all felt wrong. To leave the hive? To live in sin? God and the Vampire Nation between them battled for Joan's conscience while all poor Joan wanted to be was happy.

"Yes," she whispered at last. "Yes Billy, I'll do it. Tomorrow night I'll pack my things and sneak out of the hive and catch the Tube, if there is a Tube station in Tooting? I'm not sure but there probably is, and I'll meet you in Tooting! South London! Is it as grand as it sounds? It sounds awfully grand and I'm sure we shall be terribly happy! Oh Billy, yes, I'll do it!"

Joan gave Billy a hug and Billy hugged her back. He quickly scrawled down his new address on a piece of paper, and Joan secreted it away into her handbag. Then they kissed passionately and Billy wiped away the red tears from Joan's ivory cheeks.

The next day, while Joan slept within the walls of the hive, Billy departed south of the river. And the following evening, as the sun set, Joan dressed herself in her best dress, put on her best hat, packed a few belongings into her best handbag, and without a word to anyone, not even to Magnolia or Lillian, she slipped noise-lessly out of the door and walked the few streets that led to the Tube station.

There was indeed an underground train station in Tooting, the newly-opened Trinity Road station, with a train departing in that direction at 9.30pm. Joan purchased a single ticket, her best cream lace gloves dipping into her purse to locate the not insub-stantial fee, and took her seat in the carriage.

The journey across London took a little less than an hour, dur-ing which time Joan allowed her imagination to get the better of her. She wondered what Tooting Bec was like. It sounded very grand, and she imagined a gleaming borough with high towers and impressive turrets, all surrounded by castle walls. She imag-ined cobble-stoned streets with bustling markets and friendly lo-cals. And most of all she imagined Billy and her walking hand-in-hand, looking in shop windows and smiling, while their children, two of them, a boy and a girl probably, played merrily at their feet.

Arriving at Trinity Road tube station at 10.30pm, Joan found herself standing alone on the platform with no idea of how to get to the address scribbled on the piece of paper. The first seed of doubt and worry made a little knot in her tummy, but she disregarded it and attempted to stride purposefully out of the station. A kindly guard answered her query, looking at the address on the piece of paper and pointing Joan in the general direction that she should be walking. Joan thanked him kindly and set off walking. "Best foot forward, my girl," she told herself.

She walked for ten minutes, for twenty minutes, through dark streets and along gloomy roads, hoping to stumble, by some marvellous accident, upon the correct road, but such a miracle continued to elude her. What she did find was a dozen pubs with drunken men on the streets who leered after her and shouted obscenities. Those who recognised her vampiric state shouted insults such as "dirty vampire whore", while those who were too far in their drink to notice the fact that she was a vampire expressed a desire to have carnal knowledge of her. This was not the South London that she had dreamed of. This was the real world, the dirty human world that the hive had sought to protect her from.

Joan approached a woman on a street corner, a prostitute she assumed judging by her attire and her manner, and asked her if she knew the road she was looking for. The prostitute looked Joan up and down, observing her best shoes, her best dress, and her best hat. Then the prostitute took hold of Joan's piece of paper, upon which Billy had written his address what seemed like a lifetime ago, and spat into it. The prostitute, stinking of cheap gin and early death, smiled a toothless grin, placed the crumpled, wet piece of paper back into Joan's gloved hand and sauntered up the road.

"Oh Billy," whispered Joan in a quivering voice, "what have I done?"

The pencil written address on the piece of paper was beginning to smudge and become difficult to discern. Joan could remember the address, she thought at least. 24a Dixon Lane. Or was it Dixon Street? Oh, it was difficult to see now. Dixon Lane, it was, it had to be. 24a, or 22a? 24a! Definitely.

"Calm down girl," Joan whispered to herself. "Let's not get in a tizzy."

Joan leant with her back against the brick wall, the sound of jeering and laughing and singing coming from the public house down the road, and attempted to construct a plan. She was lost, that much was obvious. What were her choices? To head back to the tube station and catch a train back across the river, or to carry on looking for Billy on Dixon Lane or Dixon Street or wherever the Dickens it had been. But she no more knew the way back to the tube station than she did to Dixon Lane. She needed a policeman, or Billy, or Magnolia or Lillian, or anyone who could tell her what she should do.

Suddenly there were five of them. Men, humans, in their early 20's, and they were standing in front of her.

"Hello my little pigeon!" said one of the men, the ring-leader judging by how he acted and how the others looked up to him. "Bit lost are we? Don't worry pet, we'll look after you, won't we boys?" His inquiry was met by sniggers and snorts. "We can be right friendly, we can, when we wants to be. But only if you're friendly back to us, ain't that right boys?" More sniggers and snorts.

"Please," said Mary, "I'm trying to find a gentleman friend. His name is Billy and he lives on Dixon Lane. Perhaps you know him or could kindly direct me to Dixon Lane?"

"A gentleman friend?" mocked the ring-leader. "But I'll be your gentleman friend if you want, petal, and you can call me Billy if it'll make you feel any better."

"Look!" said another member of the gang, peering intently through the darkness at Joan. "She's a blooming vampire, so she is!"

"A vampire?" leered the ring-leader. "Never had a vampire before! Been told you're dirty whores, though!" More laughing and snorting. "Ain't that right, petal? Would you like me to kiss you? Little vampire whore."

The ring-leader stepped forward and put a hand on Joan's breast. To the outside observer what happened next happened in the blink of an eye, but for Joan time slowed to a crawl and a second could last a minute, an hour, a day. . .

There was her mother and her father and the garden and the sunshine and the loss and the grieving as the vampire killed them and turned her at just 18. There was Billy who brought back the sunshine and the love but was now gone, swallowed up by these South London streets and the evil and the stinking gin prostitutes and the leering humans with their hands on her breasts. There was the hive and the night and the protection of her kind, and she knew, for the first time ever perhaps, what she was. She was a vampire. Not a silly human girl playing in the sunshine and swimming in the stream, getting married and having babies, and sitting in pink and blue nurseries singing lullabies. She was a vampire, she was the night, she was the wolf and the hunter and the moon and the reason children cried in the dead of night for the unseen demons lurking in the shadows. Joan, at last, acknowledged who she was. She was terrible, fearful, and demonic. The little girl had died, for the second time, but in her place came majesty and power and the poetry of the kill.

With fangs extended, she ripped out the throat of the ringleader and dragging his still breathing corpse behind her, she moved through the gang like a terrible ballerina, breaking necks, crushing skulls, and ripping flesh. It took less than five seconds, and once it was over Joan was drenched in blood and surrounded by human corpses. She dropped to her knees and screamed, and soon her screams were met by the screams of others until there was a harmony of screams in the night, singing to the moon.

The police came and she put up no resistance as they placed her in a straight-jacket and threw her into the back of the paddy wagon.

She was placed in a cell still in the straight-jacket, dried blood caking her face and her hair, and felt no hope for ever being released. But then, an hour or maybe two later, the sergeant unlocked her cell and in walked three vampires. Magnolia, Lillian, and behind them the imposing figure of Mme. Weisner, the queen of the Apsley House hive.

Magnolia and Lillian moved aside like the Red Sea to allow Mme. Weisner to enter the small cell.

"On your feet my girl," commanded the ancient female vampire, "and stop that snivelling."

Waves of relief crashed over Joan. Here was familiarity, an authority she could rely on. She knew that she was going to be in a world of trouble, but at least it was trouble that she understood. Mme. Weisner would make everything right.

Mme. Weisner clicked her fingers and the police sergeant scurried into the cell and proceeded to remove the straight-jacket that restrained Joan.

"Lesson learned?" asked Mme. Weisner in clipped, nasal tones.

"Yes, my lady," replied Joan.

"Good," snapped Mme. Weisner, but then her tone softened infinitesimally. "You're not the first, Joan, and you won't be the last. All that I ask is that it doesn't happen again."

"It won't, my lady," said Joan.

"There is a reason we live in the hive, Joan. Humans are not decent, like we are. They are animals. It has long been noted that the walls of a hive are built not to keep us in, but to keep them," she gave the police sergeant a disdained look, "out."

"Now," continued the hive queen, "I have sorted out the necessary paperwork. You are to be placed into the care of the hive, and no further action will be taken. This means that you are now my personal responsibility. You will not let me down, do you understand?"

"Of course, my lady," replied Joan.

"Good," said Mme. Weisner. She turned on her heels and left the cell, clapping her hands twice as an instruction for the three female vampires to follow her. To follow her out of the police station and into the carriage that awaited them on the street outside, from there on to North London and Apsley House, the sanctuary and safety of the hive.

And there Joan lives to this day, an ivory princess in a dark tower, no longer waiting for a prince to rescue her and lead her back into the daylight. For mortal princes are weak, their bodies feeble, and like Billy, the simple labourer from the tenements of Tooting, they succumb before long to tuberculosis or small pox, while the vampire princesses live forever, eternity stretching before them in all its darkness and in all its wonder.

Book 4
The Vampire Alice Through the Looking Glass

by
Paul Voodini via Lewis Carroll

Ancient child of Vampire brow
And dreaming eyes of wonder!
Thy time be eternal, yet I and thou
Are half a life asunder,
Yet thy smiling fangs will surely hail
This love-gift of a fairy tale.

Chapter I
Looking Glass House

One thing was certain, that the girl with the blonde hair had nothing to do with it – it was the girl with the black hair's fault entirely. For the blonde girl had been having her blood sucked out of her by the old Mistress Vampire for the last quarter of an hour (and bearing it pretty well, considering); so you see that she couldn't have had any hand in the mischief.

The way the Mistress sucked a mortal's blood was this: first she held the poor thing down by its hair with one mighty hand, and then with the other hand she twisted the head to one side, revealing the juicy flesh of the neck, into which her bright white fangs bit and onto which her lips attached like terrible suckers; and just now, as I had said, she was hard at work on the blonde girl, who was lying quite still and trying not to moan – no doubt feeling confused as to why the act of dying should feel at once so terrifying and yet so erotic.

But the girl with the black hair had been tied up all afternoon, and was meant to be Alice's meal. But Alice was feeling both restless and tired and not in the slightest bit hungry, and so she was sitting curled up in a corner of the great armchair, half talking to herself and half asleep. However, the black haired girl kept trying to escape, and occasionally managed to free herself of the ropes that bound her, so that Alice had to climb out of the chair and sleepily slap her around a bit before tying her back up.

"Oh you wicked little thing!" cried Alice, catching up with the girl, and giving her a kiss to make her understand that she was in disgrace. "Really, you ought to have better manners. You must be eighteen winters old by now, and I would have thought that your parents would have taught you to behave more appropriately in civilised company!" she added, looking reproachfully at the girl, and speaking in as cross a voice as she could manage – and then she scrambled back into the chair, this time taking the girl with her, and deciding that perhaps she was hungry after all, she started to lick the girl's neck. But she didn't get on very fast, as she was talking all the time, sometimes to the girl, and sometimes to herself. The girl sat very demurely on her knee, pretending not to look at Alice, and now and then putting out one hand towards her blonde haired friend, as if she could help her in the slightest.

"Do you know what tomorrow is, Kitty?" Alice began. The black haired girl's name, apparently, was Kitty and Alice thought this a fit and proper name for a human pet whose hours were numbered. "Tomorrow they're going to burn a giant werewolf at the stake! I was watching the boys collecting sticks for the bonfire, and they're going to need plenty of sticks, Kitty! Only it got so cold, and it snowed so, that they had to leave off. Never mind, Kitty, I'll go and see the burning tomorrow. But, oh dear, you probably won't be around to see it! I will probably have eaten you by then, you poor thing. It is such a shame." Here Alice wound Kitty's long black hair once or twice around her hand, made a fist, and pulled the girl's head back painfully just to see how it would look. This led to Kitty moaning and crying and whispering, "Please, please, please."

"Do you know, I was so angry, Kitty," Alice went on, "when I saw you trying to escape earlier, I was very nearly opening the window, and putting you out into the snow! And you'd have deserved it, you little mischievous darling! What have you got to say for yourself?" At this Kitty could only whimper. "Now don't interrupt me!"

Alice went on, holding up a finger. "I'm going to tell you all your faults. Number one: you moan and wail and cry too much. Now you can't deny it, Kitty, I can hear you! What's that you say?" (pretending that Kitty was speaking). "My teeth are too sharp and I'm going to kill you and drink your blood? Well, that's *your* fault, for being so awfully pretty. If you were an ugly old thing, this would never have happened. Now don't make any more excuses, but listen! Number two: you tried to encourage your little golden haired friend to escape. Now, how do you know she wanted to escape? Perhaps she is enjoying the attentions of the Mistress? Now for number three: you've tried to escape yourself several times this afternoon while I wasn't looking!

"That's three faults, Kitty, and you've not been punished for any of them yet. You know I'm saving up all your punishments for a little later today. Suppose the humans catch me and have been saving up all *my* punishments?" she went on, talking more to herself than the girl. "What *would* they do once they catch me? I should be sent to prison, I suppose, and tortured. Perhaps they would pull out my toenails and fingernails and force me to sign a full confession, admitting to being in league with Satan and all his minions, and then perhaps they would burn me at the stake or chop off my head. I think I shall prefer to be beheaded than burnt at the stake like that smelly old werewolf! Oh what a day that shall be, Kitty! But they haven't caught me yet, and I don't think they will for a very long time, so you don't have to fret about that, you poor darling, worrying for my welfare so.

"Do you hear the snow against the window panes, Kitty? How nice and soft it sounds! Just as if someone was kissing the window all over outside. I wonder if you would like to be kissed all over, Kitty? By the twinkle in your eye, I do suspect that the thought of being kissed all over rather excites you! Well, perhaps I shall kiss you all over a little later today, and then I shall cover you up with a white quilt, and perhaps I shall say, "Go to sleep, my darling, till the summer comes again." Oh, when you look at me like that, Kitty, you are so very pretty!" cried Alice, letting go of her grip on the human girl's hair, and stroking affectionately at her cheeks. "I do so hope that you'll let me kiss you all over, just before I make you go to sleep, and by sleep I do of course mean the sleep of death."

At this poor Kitty began to wail and cry, and so to punish her Alice lifted her up in front of the large looking glass that stood above the fireplace, so that Kitty might see how sulky she was. "And if you don't stop whimpering this instant," Alice added, "I'll put you through the looking glass and into Looking Glass House. How would you like *that*?

"Now, if you'll only attend, Kitty, and not blub so much, I'll tell you all my ideas about Looking Glass House." And Alice looked into the mirror and ran her finger over the glass. "First, there's the room you can see in the mirror – that's just the same as our drawing room, only the things go the other way. I can see all of it if I stand on my tippy-toes – all but the bit just behind the fireplace. Oh! I do so wish I could see *that* bit! I want so much to know whether they've a fire in the winter: you never *can* tell, you know, unless our fire smokes, and then smoke comes up in that room too – but that may be only pretence, just to make it look as if they had a fire. Well then, the books are something like our books, only the words go the wrong way: I know *that*, because I've held up one of our books to the glass, and then *she* holds up one in the other room. And by *she* I mean, of course, the vampire girl who looks just like me but lives in the Looking Glass House. I don't think she's quite as pretty as me, well, how could she be? But I suppose she may be considered pretty in her own plain kind of way.

"Oh Kitty, how would you like to live in Looking Glass House with that duller yet still quite pretty vampire girl? Now do say you prefer it here with me, or I shall be quite jealous! I wonder if vampires drink blood in Looking Glass House? Perhaps looking glass blood isn't good to drink – but oh, Kitty! Now we come to the passage. You can just see a little *peep* of the passage in Looking Glass House, if you leave the door of our drawing room open: and it's very like our passage as far as you can see, only you know it may be quite different beyond. Oh, Kitty, how nice it would be if we could only get through into Looking Glass House! I'm sure it's got, oh, such beautiful things in it! Let's pretend there's a way of getting through into it, somehow, Kitty. Let's pretend the glass has got all soft like gauze, so that we can get through. Why, it's turning into a sort of mist now, I declare! It'll be easy enough to get through." She was up on the chimney-piece while she said this, though she hardly knew how she had got there, and she hardly noticed the black haired Kitty crawling away, trying to reach the door despite the fact that her ankles (such shapely ankles) and her wrists (such dainty wrists) were roughly tied with ropes. No, Alice was by now fully preoccupied by the looking glass, and certainly the glass *was* beginning to melt away, just like a bright silvery mist.

In another moment Alice was through the glass, and had jumped lightly down into the looking glass room. The very first thing she did was to look whether there was a fire in the fireplace, and she was quite pleased to find that there was a real one, blazing away as brightly as the one she had left behind. "So I shall be warm here as I was in the old room," thought Alice, "warmer, in fact, because there's no old Mistress here to scold me away from the fire. Oh, what fun it'll be, when she sees me through the glass in here, and she can't get at me!"

Then she began looking about, and noticed that what could be seen from the old room was quite common and uninteresting, but that all the rest was as different as possible. For instance, the pictures on the wall next to the fire seemed to be all alive, and the very clock on the chimney-piece (you know you can only see the back of it in the looking glass) had got Roman numerals rather than the more ordinary numbers that you might have to write down in school, and the clock also appeared to be ticking backwards.

"They don't keep this room so tidy as the other," Alice thought to herself. "Mistress would punish our housemaid most severely if she ever found *our* room in such a state!" And for a moment, Alice amused herself by imagining all the torments that Mistress would inflict upon the housemaid (her name, in case you were wondering, was Zena – quite an extravagant name for a housemaid thought Alice, and Alice fancied that Zena didn't much care for her which made her imaginings of the girl being punished all the more pleasurable) – a poke in the eye, a tug of the hair, a fang to the neck, just nipping, just by ways of a warning. "Oh I do hope that Mistress will punish nasty Zena most cruelly one day, when I'm in the room to witness it," thought Alice.

There was a book lying near Alice on the table so, being an inquisitive kind of girl, she took a seat in a near-by chair and picked up the book. She turned over the leaves, trying to find some part that she could read, "For it's all in some language I don't know," she said to herself. The words made no sense and appeared to be written backwards. She puzzled over this for some time, but at last a bright thought struck her. "Why, it's a looking glass book, of course! And, if I hold it up to a mirror, the words will all go the right way again."

This was the poem that Alice read.

LYCANTHROPE!

Twas brassik night with brass balls on
Too nesh for hope nor love:
Scared witless were the villagers
And the moon mocked from above.

"Beware the Werewolf, my son!
The jaws that bite, the claws that catch!
Beware the Lycanthrope and shun
The limbo cast Wolfman!"

He took his silver sword in hand:
Long time the canine foe he sought -
So rested he by the hanging tree
And stood awhile in thought.

And, as in sleepish thought, he stood,
The Werewolf, with eyes of flame,
Came sniffing through the tangled wood,
and growled as it came!

One, two! One, two! And through and through
The silver blade went snicker-snack!
He left it dead, and with its head,
He went a-trotting back.

"And hast thou slain the Werewolf?
Come to arms, my clever boy!
O rejoiceful day! Hurrah! Hurray!"
he chortled in his joy.

Twas brassik night with brass balls on
Too nesh for hope nor love:
Scared witless were the villagers,
And the moon mocked from above.

"It seems very dark," Alice said when she had finished it, "but a little difficult to understand!" (You see she didn't like to confess, even to herself, that she could hardly make it out at all.) "Somehow it fills my head with portents and omens – only I don't exactly know what they mean! However, somebody killed a werewolf, that's clear, at any rate."

"But oh!" thought Alice, suddenly jumping up, "if I don't make haste, I shall have to go back through the looking glass. They are burning our werewolf tomorrow – and how funny that the poem, if a poem it really is, should talk of werewolves too – and of course I must eat poor delightful Kitty before then. I shall have to hurry, and perhaps explore the garden now that evening has fallen, before I must return home!"

She was out of the room in a moment, and ran down stairs – or, at least, it wasn't exactly running, but a new invention for getting down stairs quickly and easily, as Alice said to herself. She just kept the tips of her fingers on the hand-rail, and floated gently down without even touching the stairs with her feet: then she floated on through the hall, and would have gone straight out at the door in the same way, if she hadn't caught hold of the door-post. She was getting a little giddy with so much floating in the air, and was rather glad to find herself walking again in the natural way.

Chapter II
The Garden of
Carnivorous
Flowers

"I should see the garden far better," said Alice to herself, "if I could get to the top of that wall: and here's a path that leads straight to it – at least, no, it doesn't do *that*," (after going a few yards along the path, and turning several sharp corners), "but I suppose it will at last. But how curiously it twists! It's more like a corkscrew than a path! Well, *this* turn must go to the wall, I suppose – no, it doesn't! This goes straight back to the house! Well then, I'll try it the other way."

And so she did: wandering up and down, and trying turn after turn, but always coming back to the house, do what she would. Indeed, once, when she turned a corner rather more quickly than usual, she ran against the house before she could stop herself. And all the while, a plump full moon gazed down upon her and said not a word, though, Alice observed, it did look as though it might be smirking slightly. "How rude!" thought Alice, and stuck her tongue out at the moon.

"It's no use talking about it," Alice said, looking up at the house and pretending it was arguing with her. "I'm *not* going in again yet.

I know I should have to get through the looking glass again – back into the old room – and there'd be an end of all my adventures!"

So, resolutely turning her back upon the house, she set out once more down the path, determined to keep straight on till she got to the wall. For a few minutes all went well, and she was just saying "I really *shall* do it this time," when the path gave a sudden twist and shook itself (rather like a dog, or a wolf, might shake itself), and the next moment she found herself actually walking in at the door.

"Oh, it's too bad" she cried. "I never saw such a house for getting in the way! Never!"

However, there was the wall full in sight, so there was nothing to be done but start again. This time she came upon a large carnivorous flower-bed, with a border of Venus Fly Traps and Butterworts, and a gigantic Pitcher Plant growing in the middle.

"Oh Venus!" said Alice, addressing herself to one of the plants that was weaving and bobbing menacingly. "I wish you could talk!"

"We can talk," said the Venus Fly Trap, "when we haven't got our mouths full of flies and frogs!"

Alice was so astonished that she couldn't speak for a minute, almost as though *her* mouth were full of flies and frogs. At length, as the Venus Fly Trap went on weaving about, she spoke again almost in a whisper. "And can all the flowers here talk?"

"As well as you can," said the Venus Fly Trap, "and a good deal louder."

"It isn't manners for us to begin," said a nearby Butterwort, its shiny, sticky glands twinkling in the moonlight, "and I really was wondering when you'd speak! Said I to myself, 'Her face has got *some* sense in it, though it's not a clever one!' Still you've at least got some sharp teeth, and that goes a long way around here."

"I don't care about her teeth," said the Venus Fly Trap. "If only her mouth snapped shut a little faster, she'd be all right."

Alice didn't like being criticised, so she began asking questions. "Aren't you sometimes frightened at being planted out here, with nobody to take care of you?"

"There's the Pitcher Plant in the middle," said the Butterwort. "What else is it good for?"

"But what could it do, if any danger came?" Alice asked.

"It would eat anything that came near," said the Butterwort.

"Yes, anything that comes within grabbing distance, it's picks them up and pitches them in!" cried the Venus Fly Trap. "That's why it's called a Pitcher Plant!"

"Didn't you know *that*?" cried another Butterwort.

"We had a werewolf here once," laughed the first Butterwort. "He didn't last long! Picked him up and pitched him in! The smell was quite intoxicating after a day or two!"

And at the mention of the rotting werewolf they all began shouting together with excitement, like children remembering a particularly splendid Christmas Day, till the air seemed quite full of little shrill voices.

"Will you all be quiet for a moment?!" snapped Alice. "I'm trying to think straight, and your chattering is making me feel quite confused."

"Oh dear, you should not have shouted so!" cried the Venus Fly Trap. "Now you've awoken the Pitcher Plant, and it will be after you and will gobble you up just like it did the werewolf. I'd do the job myself, but my roots go too deep and I can't get at you!"

And with that the ground began to rumble, and the large Pitcher Plant (it really was quite huge) appeared to be rousing itself, and preparing itself for the task of walking.

"Pick her up and pitch her in!" cried the Butterworts, working themselves up into an ecstasy. "Pick her up and pitch her in!"

The Pitcher Plant attempted to walk a step or two, but seemed to be struggling somewhat, like an old woman, thought Alice, who'd spent too long dozing in a chair and whose body had grown stiff and stupid. "Why I shall simply walk away from this so-called Pitcher Plant," said Alice. "Have you not noticed that I am a vampire and therefore rather nimble on my feet?"

"Quite right too, my dear!" exclaimed a voice behind Alice. All of the plants let out a scream, and drooped down apologetically, and

Alice turned to come face to face with a stately looking vampire lady, dressed all in black, and wearing a crown.

"Ignore those silly plants," said the black garbed lady. "They are feeling rather tetchy due to the fact that I haven't fed them in a day or two. And if they aren't careful I shall not feed them again!" The lady vampire gave the plants a cold hard stare, and they withered visibly before her. The Pitcher Plant quickly buried its roots once more beneath the earth and tried to pretend that it hadn't been attempting to walk.

"Now then," said Queen Victoria (for upon closer inspection it became apparent that this vampire lady was no less than Queen Victoria herself – a thought that at first confused poor Alice, "I'd never thought that our own dear Queen was herself a vampire!" - but then reasoned Alice, it would explain how she managed to live for so very long!), "who are you and where do you come from? I know all of the vampires around here, and you aren't one of them. Come along, look up, speak nicely, and don't twiddle your fingers all the time."

Alice attended to all these directions, and explained, as well as she could, that she had lost her way.

"I don't know what you mean by *your* way," said the Queen: "all the ways about here belong to *me* – but why did you come out here at all?" she added in a kinder tone. "Curtsey while you're thinking what to say. It saves time."

Alice wondered a little at this, but she was too much in awe of the Queen to disbelieve it. "I'll try it when I go home," she thought to herself, "the next time I'm a little late for the dinner that Mistress has brought home."

"It's time for you to answer now," the Queen said, looking at her watch: "open your mouth a *little* wider when you speak, and always say 'your Majesty.'"

"I only wanted to see what the garden was like, your Majesty."

"That's right," said the Queen, patting her on the head, which Alice didn't like at all. A flash of rage rushed through her body and she felt her fangs extending. "Now, now," she told herself, "One mustn't eat the Queen. It is probably terribly bad manners."

"Though," continued the Queen, "when you say 'garden' – *I've* seen gardens, compared with which this would be a wilderness."

Alice thought better of arguing the point, but went on: " - and I thought I'd try and find my way to the top of that wall."

"When you say wall," the Queen interrupted, "*I* could show you walls, in comparison with which you'd call that a cellar."

"No, I shouldn't," said Alice, surprised into contradicting her at last: "a wall *can't* be a cellar, you know. That would be nonsense."

The Queen shook her head. "You may call it 'nonsense' if you like," she said, "but *I've* heard nonsense, compared with which that would be as sensible as a dictionary!"

Alice curtseyed again, as she was a little afraid from the Queen's tone that she was a *little* offended, and Alice had noticed the flash of the Queen's own fangs and they did look rather long and sharp. The Queen and Alice walked for a few minutes until in silence they reached the wall and climbed to the top of it.

Alice stood without speaking, looking out in all directions across the country – and a most curious country it was. It seemed to be entirely made up of a dark, dark woods, with giant trees wrapping their branches, like arms, around each other for support. Beneath the giant trees lay smaller trees, and bushes, and hedges, and brambles – and all so shrouded in darkness and mist.

"I declare it is the most wonderful place I have ever seen!" exclaimed Alice. Her heart began to beat with excitement. "It's a giant dark wood! What fun! Oh how I would love to hunt in there if only I might?"

She glanced rather shyly at the Queen as she said this, but her companion only smiled pleasantly, and said, "That's easily managed. You can hunt all you like in the dark wood, but you must know this one thing: the woods are also the home to a giant werewolf, and he will gobble you up if he can! The most important thing for you, young vampire girl, is to get to the other side of the wood without being eaten by Monsieur Wolf! That's how you play the game! Don't get eaten!" Just at this moment, somehow or other, they began to run.

Alice could never quite make out, in thinking it over afterwards, how it was that they began: all she remembers is that they were running hand in hand, and the Queen went so fast that it was all she could do to keep up with her: and still the Queen kept crying "Faster! Faster!", but Alice felt she *could not* go faster, though she had no breath left to say so.

The most curious part of the thing was, that the trees and the other things round them never changed their places at all: however fast they went, they never seemed to pass anything. "I wonder if all the things move along with us?" thought poor puzzled Alice. And the Queen seemed to guess her thoughts, for she cried "Faster! Don't try to talk!"

Not that Alice had any idea of doing *that*. She felt as if she would never be able to talk again, she was getting so much out of breath: and still the Queen cried "Faster! Faster!", and dragged her along. "Are we nearly there?" Alice managed to pant out at last.

"Nearly there!" the Queen repeated. "Why, we passed it ten minutes ago! Faster!" And they ran on for a time in silence, with the wind whistling in Alice's ears, and almost blowing her hair off her head, she fancied.

"Now! Now!" cried the Queen. "Faster! Faster!" And they went so fast that at last they seemed to skim through the air, hardly touching the ground with their feet, till suddenly, just as Alice was getting quite exhausted, they stopped, and she found herself sitting on the ground, breathless and giddy.

The Queen propped her up against a tree, and said kindly, "You may rest a little, now."

Alice looked round her in great surprise. "Why, I do believe we've been under this tree the whole time! Everything's just as it was!"

"Of course it is," said the Queen. "What would you have it?"

"Well, in *our* country," said Alice, still panting a little, "you'd generally get to somewhere else – if you ran very fast for a long time as we've been doing."

"A slow sort of country!" said the Queen. "Now, *here*, you see, it takes all the running *you* can do, to keep in the same place.

If you want to get somewhere else, you must run at least twice as fast as that!"

"I'd rather not try, please!" said Alice. "I'm quite content to stay here – only I *am* so hot and hungry!

"I know what *you'd* like!" the Queen said good-naturedly, taking a little piglet out of her pocket. "Have a piglet?"

Alice thought it would not be civil to say "No," though it wasn't at all what she wanted. What she really wanted was pretty, warm young Kitty, not this squealing, wriggling piglet. But she took it, and drank its blood as well as she could: and it was *very* bitter, not nearly as sweet as she knew Kitty would taste: and she thought she had never been so nearly choked in all her life.

"Hunger sated, I hope?" said the Queen.

Alice merely nodded politely by ways of an answer.

"Remember now," said the Queen, "that you must make your way across the dark forest without being eaten by the werewolf. That is how you play this game. And do you not have a remark to make?"

"I – I didn't know I had to make a remark," Alice faltered out, pig's blood adding extra rouge to her plump lips.

"You *should* have said," the Queen went on in a tone of grave reproof, " 'it's extremely kind of you to tell me this' – however, we'll suppose it said. I do hope we shall meet again once you make it through the dark woods. If you do make it safely, do come visit me at Buckingham Palace, won't you?"

Alice got up and curtseyed, and sat down again.

"And remember," said the Queen, "speak in French when you can't think of the English for a thing – turn your toes out as you walk – and remember who you are!" She did not wait for Alice to curtsey, this time, but walked away quickly.

How it happened, Alice never knew, but as she was walking away, the Queen was suddenly gone. Whether she vanished into the air, or whether she ran quickly into the wood ("and she *can* run very fast!" thought Alice), there was no way of guessing, but she was gone, and Alice began to remember that there was a werewolf in the woods and she was going to have to make her way through it without finding herself eaten alive.

Chapter III
Looking Glass
Spectres

Quite how it happened, Alice was never sure. But the fact of the matter was that one moment she was surveying the great wood, and planning what may or may not have been the easiest route through to the other side, and the very next moment she found herself sitting in a train carriage.

"Tickets please!" said the Guard, putting his head in at the window. In a moment everybody was holding out a ticket: they were about the same size as the people, and quite seemed to fill the carriage.

"Now then! Show your ticket, girl!" the Guard went on, looking angrily at Alice. And a great many voices all said together ("like the wailing of ghosts in an abandoned church," thought Alice) "Don't keep him waiting, girl! Why his time is worth a thousand pounds a minute!"

"I'm afraid I haven't got one," Alice said in a frightened tone: "there wasn't a ticket office where I came from." And again the chorus of wails went on. "There wasn't room for one where she came from. The land there is worth a thousand pounds an inch!"

"Don't make excuses," said the Guard: "You should have bought one from the engine driver." And once more the chorus of wails went on with "The man that drives the engine. Why, the smoke alone is worth a thousand pounds a puff!"

Alice thought to herself, "Then there's no use in speaking." The wails didn't join in, *this* time, as she hadn't spoken, but, to her great surprise, they all *thought* in chorus (I hope you understand what *thinking in chorus* means – for I must confess that I don't), "Better say nothing at all. Language is worth a thousand pounds a word!"

"I shall have nightmares about a thousand pounds when I'm back in my coffin, I know I shall!" thought Alice.

All this time the Guard was looking at her, first through a telescope, then through a microscope, and then through an opera glass. At last he said "You're travelling the wrong way," and shut up the window, and went away.

"So nasty a vampire as you," said the ugly witch sitting opposite her, (she was dressed in a pointy hat and was carrying a broom,) "ought to know which way it's going, even if it doesn't know its own name!"

A wizard that was sitting next to the witch, shut his eyes and said in a loud voice, "It ought to know its way to the ticket office, even if it doesn't know its manners!"

There was a magician in a cloak and top hat sitting next to the wizard (it was a very queer carriage – full of passengers altogether), and, as the rule seemed to be that they should all take it in turns to be rude about poor Alice and to call her 'it', *he* went on with "It'll have to go back from here as luggage!"

Alice couldn't see who was sitting beyond the magician, but a hoarse voice spoke next. "Change engines. . . " it said, and there it choked and was obliged to leave off.

"It sounds like a horse," Alice thought to herself. And an extremely small voice, close to her ear, whispered, "You might make a joke on that – something about 'horse' and 'hoarse', you know."

Then a voice in the distance said, "It must be labelled 'Vampire, With Care'!"

And after that other voices cried out ("What a number of people there are in the carriage!" thought Alice), saying "Chop off its head and send it by post!" "Burn her at the stake and send her by smoke signal!" "Tie her up and put a harness on her and get her to pull the train herself!" and so on.

But the witch leaned forward and whispered in her ear, "Never mind what they all say, my dear. I shall make you into a soup when we arrive at our destination. That shall teach you to be so wicked and not purchase a ticket for the journey. What do you think of that?"

"I don't think very much of it at all!" said Alice rather impatiently. "I shall not be turned into soup, you old hag! Indeed, I do not even belong to this train journey. I was in the wood just now, and I wish I could get back there!"

"You might make a joke on that," said the little voice close to her ear: "something about 'you *wood* if you *could*', you know."

"Don't tease so," said Alice, looking about in vain to see where the voice came from. "If you're so anxious to have a joke made, why don't you make one yourself?"

The little voice sighed deeply. It was *very* unhappy, evidently, and Alice would have said something pitying to comfort it, "if it would only sigh like other people!" she thought. But this was such a wonderfully small sigh, that she wouldn't have heard it at all, if it hadn't come *quite* close to her ear. The consequence of this was that it tickled her ear very much, and quite took off her thoughts from the unhappiness of the poor little creature.

"I know you are a friend," the little voice went on: "a dear friend, and an old friend. And you won't hurt me, though I *am* a ghost."

"What kind of ghost?" Alice inquired, a little anxiously. Alice had never trusted ghosts and what she really wanted to know was, whether it was a poltergeist or not and whether it was going to start throwing things around the carriage, but she thought this wouldn't be quite a civil question to ask.

"What, then you don't. . . " the little voice began, when it was drowned by a shrill scream from the engine, and everybody jumped up in alarm, Alice among the rest.

The magician, who had put his head out of the window, drew it in and shouted, "Zombies! Zombies on the track! We are under attack!" Everybody started to scream, and in the next moment Alice felt the carriage come off the tracks and rise straight up in the air. In her fright Alice caught at the nearest thing to her hand, which happened to be the wizard's beard.

* * *

But the beard seemed to melt away as she touched it, and she found herself sitting quietly under a gnarled old tree – while the ghost was floating just over her head, and fanning her gently with its ectoplasmic presence.

"Then you don't like ghosts?" the ghost went on, as quietly as if nothing had happened.

"I like them when they can talk in a civilised manner," Alice said. "None of them are particularly civilised where I come from."

"What kind of ghosts do you rejoice in, where *you* come from?" the ghost inquired.

"I don't *rejoice* in ghosts at all," Alice explained, "because I'm rather afraid of them – at the least the angry kind. But I can tell you the names of some of them."

"Very well," said the Ghost, "go on with your list of ghost names."

"Well, there's the poltergeist," Alice began, counting off the names on her fingers. "I don't like them at all. Altogether too noisy and bothersome. They throw things, don't you know? We once, and by *we* I do of course mean Mistress, nasty Zena the maid, and myself, we once had a poltergeist in our house. Apparently it was the poor unhappy soul of some drippy girl we'd eaten once. *Apparently* we were supposed to feel sorry for it and show remorse for our actions, and all this while the tiresome thing threw chairs around the room and made the curtains flutter. A hairbrush flew through the air and bashed me on the forehead, which stung awfully, and in the end Mistress was forced to send Zena, being human, into the village to steal some holy water from the church. When Zena came back she hurled the holy water around the room in which the poltergeist had set up residence, and that seemed to do the trick. The nasty creature disappeared, although some of the holy water splashed on to me and did burn awfully. I'm sure spiteful Zena did that on purpose, just made sure that a little holy water landed on me, just to hurt me for fun."

And with that, Alice folded her arms and pouted.

"Goodness me," said the ghost. "All that from a poltergeist? There's no wonder you don't like them! Well, pray, do go on."

"Well," said Alice, still pouting and feeling sorry for herself, "then there are spirits."

"Ah, spirits!" sighed the ghost. "I remember spirits well! Gin, in particular, was a favourite. And a sherry or two on Christmas Day!"

"Not those kind of spirits!" snapped Alice, and she would have stamped her feet had she not been sitting down in a sulk. "The spirits I'm talking about are, I believe, human souls that have moved on to heaven or hell or somewhere like that, but have chosen to return to the earthly plain (or is it *plane*?) to communicate with the living, or haunt them, or some-such. Not having a soul myself, I am certain that once I am dead, and that probably won't be for many centuries as I am quite immortal, I shall never return to haunt anyone!"

"Quite immortal?" asked the Ghost. "Are you sure about that? What should happen if a great werewolf should clamp your pretty little head between its giant jaws and separate it from your body? You would be quite dead then, wouldn't you? And with no soul to go to heaven or hell or even to haunt the living, you should truly be dead. As dead as a dodo and quite as extinct. But, dear vampire, you are already dead, are you not? How can something die *twice*? That's the conundrum about you undead creatures that continues to perplex me!"

"Oh dear," said Alice, more to herself that to anyone in particular. "I do wish you hadn't said that, for now I am pondering it also. How can someone who is dead, namely myself, die again if a werewolf separates my head from my shoulders? What a puzzle! Perhaps I shouldn't die. Perhaps I should wander around, a body with no head, bumping into things and giving people a frightful scare. Or perhaps I should just be a head! A head with no body, and Mistress shall be forced to place me on the mantelpiece above the fire, and when no-one's looking nasty Zena shall stick her tongue out at me and flick holy water into my eyes! Oh woe! I shall have to make sure that no werewolf ever gets his filthy paws on me! For I have no desire to be dead and yet undead, with Zena pestering me for all eternity!"

Then she let out a melancholy sigh and when Alice looked up, the ghost appeared to have vanished entirely. And as she was getting quite fed up with sitting in the damp grass for so long, she got up and walked on.

She very soon came to an open field, with a wood on the other side of it: it looked much darker than the last wood, and Alice felt a *little* timid about going into it. However, on second thoughts, she made up her mind to go on: "for I certainly can't go back," she thought to herself.

"This must be the wood," she said thoughtfully to herself, "where the werewolf lives. Well, it is very late at night, and perhaps the old wolf is asleep, curled up in his nest or den or wherever it is that he lives, snoring his great head off, and I shall pass through without incident, and will not get captured and eaten and die or not die as the case may be."

"For anyway," she rambled on, "if I am dead anyway, what fear should I have for dying again? I did it once, it wasn't *that* awful, and if I should die again, perhaps I should not think that too awful either!"

She stood silent for a minute, thinking: then she suddenly began again. "Has all this really happened? For just a minute ago, or perhaps it was an hour, I was in the drawing room. Or maybe it was the living room of our house, and I was about to eat that delightful girl, whatever *her* name was, and now I am here, in a strange wood, with the prospect of being eaten or not being eaten by a giant werewolf."

Just then a fawn came wandering by: it looked at Alice with its large gentle eyes, but didn't seem at all frightened. "Here then! Here then!" Alice said, as she held out her hand and tried to stroke it; but it only started back a little, and then stood looking at her again.

"What kind of creature are you?" the fawn said at last. "It's very dark beneath the trees and I cannot quite make you out." Such a soft sweet voice it had!

"Oh, I'm just a girl," said Alice, not wanting to scare the fawn with the awful truth.

"I'm rather afraid of the night," the fawn said. "There is a were-wolf in this wood, and I am scared that he will find me. Will you walk awhile with me?"

So they walked on together through the wood, Alice with her arms clasped lovingly round the neck of the fawn, till they came out into another open field and the full moon shone down brightly upon them. Here the fawn gave a sudden bound into the air, and shook itself free from Alice's arm. "I'm a fawn!" it cried out. "And, dear me! You're a vampire girl!" A sudden look of alarm came into its beautiful brown eyes, and in another moment it had darted away at full speed.

Alice stood looking after it, almost ready to cry with vexation at having lost her dear little fellow traveller so suddenly. "It needn't have been quite so startled," she almost sobbed. "I might not have eaten it! Such a silly creature! But now, look, which of these sign-posts ought I to follow?"

It was not a very difficult question to answer, as there was only one road through the wood, and the two signposts both pointed the same way along it. "I'll decide which one to follow," Alice said to herself, "when the road divides and they point different ways."

But this did not seem likely to happen. She went on and on, a long way, but, wherever the road divided, there were sure to be two signposts pointing the same way, one marked 'TO Dr. JEKYLL'S HOUSE', and the other 'TO Mr. HYDE'S HOUSE'.

"I do believe," said Alice at last, "that they live in the *same* house! Well, I can't stay there long. I'll just call and say 'How d'ye do?' and ask them the way out of the wood. I certainly need to get out of the wood and home again before the sun comes up and I'm fried alive. Or fried dead. Or whatever."

So she wandered on, talking to herself as she went, till, on turning a sharp corner, she came upon two strange men, so suddenly that she could not help starting back, but in another moment she recovered herself, feeling sure that they must be. . .

Chapter IV
Dr Jekyll and Mr Hyde

They were standing under a tree, each with an arm around the other, and Alice knew which was which in a moment, because one of them was carrying a doctor's bag in his free hand and around his neck hung a stethoscope. "So you must be the doctor," said Alice thoughtfully. "Dr Jekyll, if I recall what the signposts said correctly." The doctor, if indeed he was a doctor, said nothing, but stood quite motionless. Alice turned to the second man, a larger chap altogether, with wide shoulders and a hump on his back, wearing a top hat and cape, and in his free hand he held a silver tipped walking cane. "And you," mused Alice, "must be Mr Hyde! Delighted to make you acquaintance." And remembering her manners (perhaps the words of Queen Victoria were still ringing in her ears), Alice gave a little curtsey.

"If you think we're hiding," said Mr Hyde in a gravelly kind of voice, "you'd be correct!"

"Oh no," said Dr Jekyll, "we're not hiding as such. Just taking the necessary precautions, so to speak."

"I'm sure I don't understand," said Alice. "Hiding? Necessary precautions?"

"You don't fool us," said Mr Hyde. "We know what you're thinking. You're thinking about dobbing us in and saving your own hide!"

"On the contrary," said Alice as politely as she could in the circumstances, "I was merely wondering which is the best way out of this wood: it will be dawn soon. Would you tell me please?"

But the two odd fellows only looked at each other and grinned. This infuriated Alice so much that she bared her terrible fangs and growled at the men. Both Dr Jekyll and Mr Hyde shrieked in terror, and clung to each other even tighter. "Don't make so much noise!" said Mr Hyde. "Don't be making a commotion!" said Dr Jekyll. "Let's all just settle down, shake hands, and agree to be friends."

Alice did not like shaking hands with either of them at first, for fear of it being a trap of some kind, that they would grab her by the hand and tie her up. But the two men made no such advances, and before long the three of them were seated around the tree, chatting quite amicably.

"Pray tell," said Alice once she felt the formal introductions had been dispensed with, "what is it that makes two such fine gentlemen as yourselves so afraid that they find themselves cowering beneath a tree, jumping at shadows?"

"Shall I tell her?" Mr Hyde asked of Dr Jekyll, looking at him with great solemn eyes.

"Tell her the poem," agreed Dr Jekyll. "You know the one. The message is hidden in there."

"*The Werewolf and the Pied Piper*?" asked Mr Hyde.

"The very same," agreed Dr Jekyll.

Mr Hyde began: "The sun was shining..."

Here Alice ventured to interrupt him. "If it's *very* long," she said, as politely as she could, "would you not rather please just tell me which road I should take, and save us all a lot of bother?"

Mr Hyde smiled sadly, and began again:

The sun was shining on the streets,
Shining with all its might:
He did his very best to make
The cobblestones shine bright -
And this was odd, because it was
The middle of the night.

The moon was shining sulkily,
Because she thought the sun
Had got no business to be there
After the day was done -
'It's very rude of him,' she said,
'To come and spoil the fun!'

The streets were wet as wet could be,
The cobblestones wept and cried.
You could not see a cloud, because
No cloud was in the sky:
No crows were flying overhead -
There were no crows to fly.

The Werewolf and the Pied Piper
Were walking hand in hand:
They complained angrily to see
Cobblestones cover the land:
'If they were only cleared away,'
They said, 'it would be so grand!'

'If seven men with seven axes
Chopped for half a year,
Do you suppose,' the Werewolf said,
'That they could get it clear?'
'I doubt it,' said the Pied Piper,
And shed a bitter tear.

'Oh Vampire children, walk with us!'
The Werewolf did beseech.
'A pleasant walk, a pleasant talk,
Along these London streets:
We cannot do with more than four,
To give a hand to each.'

The eldest Vampire looked at him,
But never a word she said:
The eldest vampire winked her eye,
And shook her pretty head -
Meaning to say she did not choose
To leave the vampire nest.

But four young Vampires hurried up,
All eager for the treat:
Their coats were brushed, their faces washed,
Their shoes were clean and neat,
Their hair was curled into ringlets
For an evening on the streets.

Four other Vampires followed them,
And yet another four;
And thick and fast they came at last,
And more, and more, and more -
Young Vampires dancing in the hallway
And scrambling through the door.

The Werewolf and the Pied Piper
Walked on a mile or so,
And then they rested on a wall
Conveniently low:
And all the little Vampires stood
And waited in a row.

'The time has come,' the Werewolf said,
'To talk of many things:
Of ghosts and goblins and wicked witches,
Of knights and queens and kings.
And why the moon is silver bright,
And whether fairies really do have wings.'

'A loaf of bread,' the Pied Piper said,
'Is what we chiefly need:
Pepper and vinegar besides
Are very good indeed -
Now if you're ready, Vampires dear,
We can begin to feed.'

'But not on us!' the Vampires cried,
Turning a little blue.
'After such kindness, that would be
A dismal thing to do!'
'The night is fine,' the Werewolf said.
'Do you like the view?'

'It was so kind of you to come!
And you are oh so nice!'
The Pied Piper said nothing but
'Cut us another slice.
I wish you were not quite so deaf -
I've had to ask you twice!'

'It seems a shame,' the Werewolf said,
'To play them such a trick.
After we've brought them out so far,
And made them walk so quick!'
The Pied Piper said nothing but
'The butter's spread too thick!'

'I weep for you,' the Werewolf said:
'I deeply sympathise.'
With sobs and tears he sorted out
Those of the largest size,
Holding his pocket-handkerchief
Before his streaming eyes.

'Oh Vampires,' said the Pied Piper,
'You've had a pleasant run!
Shall we be walking home again?'
But answers came there none -
And this was scarcely odd, because
They'd eaten every one.

"I like the werewolf best," said Alice: "because at least he was a *little* sorry for those poor vampire children."

"He ate more than the Pied Piper, though," said Dr Jekyll.

"Well then I like the Pied Piper best, if he didn't eat as much as the werewolf," said Alice.

"But he ate as many as he could get," said Mr Hyde.

"Well then they are *both* very unpleasant characters and I don't care for either of them." Here Alice checked herself in some alarm, at hearing something that sounded to her like the puffing of a large steam engine in the wood near them, though she feared it was more likely to be a wild beast. "Are there any lions or tigers about here?" she asked timidly, although her words sounded foolish the moment they left her mouth.

"It's the werewolf!" cried Dr Jekyll. "He's here! We must flee!" And with that the good doctor picked up his bag, and disappeared into the wood. There came, mere moments later, a terrible shrill scream as though the doctor was being ripped apart. And then a second shrill scream as though his throat was being sliced from ear to ear. And then there came a third shrill scream which ended, thought Alice, all too suddenly.

"Do I look very pale?" asked Mr Hyde timidly.

"Well, yes, a *little*," Alice replied gently.

"I'm very brave, generally," he went on in a low voice: "only today I happen to have a headache."

"Then perhaps you ought to go and hide," said Alice kindly, "and wait until the werewolf, if it is indeed the werewolf, has passed by?"

"Yes," agreed Mr Hyde. "I shall hide." And Alice fancied that a very quiet little ghost-like voice whispered in her ear, "You could make a joke on that, I suppose. *Hyde* and *hide*, you know, that kind of thing." But now was not the time to be entertaining ghosts and their stupid jokes. Now was a time for running and hiding from giant werewolves.

Alice glanced around and noticed that Mr Hyde had disappeared into the woods. She took a hard look at the road, and then began to run along it as fast as her vampire legs could carry her. Behind her she heard more screams. Mr Hyde this time, three terrible screams, the last of which seemed again somehow too short and too sad.

"Don't look back!" gasped Alice to herself. "Just run!"

Chapter V
Fairy Tales

Alice ran for what felt like a long time, and eventually she came to a quaint little hamlet, nestled in the woods. "I suppose humans live here," said Alice as she wandered into the village square, surrounded by houses and shops, and there in the middle of the square was a well, with a wooden bucket attached to a piece of rope. The village was shrouded in darkness; no candles burned in any of the windows, and Alice thought that all the humans must be fast asleep, tucked up in their beds, clutching their crucifixes to ward off evil.

"And who would they see as being the most evil?" Alice wondered as she approached the well. "Me or that brutish werewolf? As protection against which of us do they clutch so tightly to their baubles and trinkets? Or maybe they see the werewolf and I as being as bad as each other? Well, I would certainly be most offended if that were to be the case! Imagine those stupid humans comparing *me* to a filthy old werewolf! The very thought!" And feeling quite annoyed by what the humans might or might not think of her, Alice stamped her foot on the cobblestones, leant against the well with her arms crossed, and decided that she might very soon have a tantrum.

Only she didn't have a tantrum as she suddenly noticed a black kitten crawling out of the well. The kitten was soaking wet and looked very sorry for itself. Around its neck was tied a red ribbon, and attached to the ribbon was a silver bell that jingled sweetly as it teetered on the edge of the well.

"Oh you poor dear thing!" gasped Alice, and she scooped up the kitten in her hands. "Who ever threw you down the well? What a nasty thing for anyone to do! Or did you fall? Were you chasing a mouse and perhaps tumbled over your own feet in all the excitement and then splash! You found yourself trapped down a dark, smelly well? I know myself how easy it is to become clumsy when one is enthralled by the thrill of the hunt. Why, once when I was chasing a pretty girl down a country lane, I got so carried away that I ended up in a hawthorn bush and my tasty little treat got plain away. So I do understand, little kitten, how easy it is to find oneself in peril. How easy it is to change from a fearless hunter to a stupid girl trapped in a hawthorn bush, or, indeed, a pussy down a well."

Alice lent forward to give the kitten a small kiss on its black nose, but at that instant the cat shrieked loudly and lashed out with its claws, cutting Alice on the cheek. "Why you spiteful creature!" cried Alice, and she threw the cat across the village square. It landed on its feet (as cats have an annoying tendency to) and then walked off as calmly as you like, its little silver bell tinkling merrily in the night.

"You brute!" Alice hissed after it, and then she placed a hand to her cheek and began to cry. She'd had quite enough of this stupid looking glass world where everyone and everything was being awful to her. She tenderly touched at her cheek. The scratch was almost healed already, but it did feel sore, and besides, perhaps it was the shock of the kitten lashing out like that that had upset Alice more than the actual physical attack. "I want to go home," she whispered, "to Mistress and yes, even to silly Zena. I want to go home, eat that girl, whatever her name was, and then rest by the fire until they execute that damnable werewolf in the morning!"

At that point Alice noticed a lamp burning in one of the shops near-by. Intrigued to discover a human shop still open at this late hour, Alice decided to go and take a look, "More out of curiosity," she told herself. "After all, I have no money on me, and besides, what could a human shopkeeper have that I could possibly want? Well, apart from directions out of these blessed woods. And blood coursing through their mortal veins."

Alice had just decided to march across the village square, put on her bravest face, and ask the shopkeeper which was the best way out of the woods, when she heard a growl and a snarl behind her. "Oh dear," she managed to whisper, more to herself than anyone else.

Slowly she turned around to come face to face with the giant drooling werewolf. It was eight feet tall, its fur was filthy and matted, and its snout was curled up in a terrible growl. Its teeth were dirty and it smelt of rotting flesh and hanging from its mouth was a large lump of flesh that might, or might not, have once been part of poor Dr Jekyll or the lamentable Mr Hyde.

"Vampire!" said the Werewolf, although he didn't say it in a manner that you or I would recognise as speech. Rather he sort of growled it and sort of yawned it, and his eyes blazed red in anger and hunger and malice.

At that point Alice decided that she'd just about had enough. She stamped her feet and crossed her arms and pouted her lips at the wolf. "Now just look here!" she snapped. "My name is Alice and I don't belong here! I come from a world that exists on the other side of the looking glass. In my world I live with Mistress who is a very old and very powerful vampire, more powerful even than you I'd wager, so if you know what's good for you, you will turn around and leave me alone. I refuse to be your dinner, or, indeed, your dessert."

The werewolf looked at Alice in a confused kind of way for a moment or two, and then it leapt at the poor vampire girl, its mouth gaping and its teeth snapping. Little Alice was nimble on her feet and managed to duck and roll out of the way of the werewolf's attack, and then, as quick as a flash, she was across the village square and up a side road, the werewolf but a hair's breath away in dogged (there's a pun in there, somewhere) pursuit.

Oh, up roads and down roads, across gardens and paths, over fences and hedges until they were both quite out of breath, ran

Alice and the werewolf. "I shall never out run him!" thought Alice in desperation. "He is just too strong and relentless." But just at that moment, just as that thought had entered her head, the werewolf vanished. Alice looked behind her and he simply was not there.

"How odd!" said Alice, stopping and looking around. "I could have sworn I was being chased by a giant werewolf, and yet now he has gone! Still I shouldn't complain, even if it is rather rude of him to abscond without even so much as a cheerio!"

Alice had arrived, thanks to the running and chasing, back in the village square. In fact, she was standing right in front of the shop where a candle burned brightly in the window. "Right," said Alice, quickly straightening her hair and tidying up her dress, "now would seem to be the perfect moment to discover a quick and easy way out of here." And so she popped herself into the shop.

* * *

Once inside, Alice noticed that there appeared to be a sheep sitting behind the shop's counter. She rubbed her eyes, and looked again. Yes, that really was a sheep sitting on the other side of the counter. Rub as she would, she could make nothing more of it: she was in a little shop, leaning with her elbows on the counter, and opposite to her was an old sheep, sitting in an armchair, knitting, and every now and then leaving off to look at her through a great pair of spectacles.

"What is it you want to buy?" the sheep said at last, looking up for a moment from her knitting.

"I don't *quite* know yet," Alice said very gently. "I should like to look all round me first, if I might."

"You may look in front of you, and on both sides, if you like," said the sheep, "but you can't look *all* round you – unless you've got eyes in the back of your head."

But these, as it happened, Alice had *not* got: so she contented herself with turning round, looking at the shelves as she came to them.

The shop seemed to be full of all manner of curious things – curious things that made Alice's eyes sting and water simply to look at. For instance, there was a Holy Bible, and a silver crucifix, and a garland of garlic, a revolver-type gun (the type that a handsome captain in the army might have, Alice supposed) with silver bullets, and a flask of holy water.

"What awful things!" observed Alice after a moment or two. But then her attention was drawn by a book entitled 'The Wolf Prince and the Vampire Princess'. Alice picked up the book. It was most delightful to hold, being petite in size and bound in leather. "I think I should like to read this story," said Alice, but when she opened the pages she found that the words appeared to make no sense.

"Ah yes," said the sheep from behind the counter. "My lady has made a wise choice. For in that book are all the answers that I feel you are looking for."

"Oh I do hope so!" sighed Alice. "But really, the words inside make no sense to me. I'm sure they aren't written in English, or even French, or Russian. Not that I can read French or Russian, you understand, it's just that I'm sure I would recognise the writing should I see it. But this writing, well, it is all wrong! It is upside down, inside out, and altogether the wrong way around."

"That," said the sheep, "is because it is written in wolf language. A very old and ancient language understood only by wolves. Some dogs *claim* to be able to read it, but really they can't, apart from perhaps the odd word such a 'ball' and 'fetch' and 'dinnertime'. Luckily though," continued the sheep, "I speak fluent wolf and will happily translate for you."

"Oh goody!" smiled Alice, and it felt like this was the first time she'd properly smiled for a very long time.

"But not here," said the sheep. "Stories, I find, are best told while meandering down a gentle stream in a small row-boat, don't you agree?"

"I'm sure I wouldn't know," Alice said: "and besides, how are we to get aboard a row-boat or indeed find a gentle stream?" Just as Alice was saying these very words, she found that both her and the sheep were indeed in a little boat, gliding along a stream. So *many* strange things had happened to her during her time in looking glass world, that Alice decided not to question how or why she found herself in a boat upon a stream, but rather to simply lie back and enjoy the journey. Above her the moon glowed full and bright, and dark clouds rushed by overhead, but on the horizon came tinges of red and Alice was sure there was something she must do and that the tinges of red on the horizon meant something awfully important. But her head ached a little from where the kitten had scratched her, and all this thinking was only making the pain worse. So she decided not to think at all, but simply listen to the voice of the sheep as it read from the book.

* * *

"In the old times," began the sheep, "when it was still of some use to wish for the things one wanted, there lived a vampire king whose daughters were all beautiful, but the youngest was so beautiful that the moon herself was outshone in her presence.

"Near the royal castle there was a great dark wood, and in the wood there lay a deep and wide pond. On long summer's nights the king's daughter would go forth into the wood and sit by the edge of the pond, and if she wished to amuse herself she would take out a golden ball, and throw it up and catch it again, and this was her favourite pastime.

"Now it happened one day that the golden ball, instead of falling back into the vampire's little hand which had sent it aloft, dropped into the pond and floated away to the middle of the wa-ter. The king's daughter followed it with her eye, but the pond was so wide and so deep that she could never hope of wading out to retrieve it. Then she began to weep, and she wept and wept as if she could never be comforted. And in the midst of her weeping she heard a voice saying to her, 'What ails thee, king's daughter? Thy tears would melt a heart of stone!'

"And when she looked to see where the voice came from, there was nothing there but a wolf laying by the side of the pond.

"'Oh, is it you, old growler?' said she, for as a vampire she had been taught never to fear a wolf but to be its master. 'I weep because my golden ball has fallen into the pond.'

"'Never mind, do not weep,' answered the wolf. 'I can help you, but what will you give me if I fetch your ball back for you?'

"'Whatever you like, dear wolf,' said she, 'any of my clothes, my pearls and jewels, or even the golden crown that I wear.'

"'Thy clothes, thy pearls and jewels, and thy golden crown are not for me,' answered the wolf, 'but if thou wouldst love me, and have me for thy companion and playfellow, and let me sit by thee at table, and drink blood from thy cup, and lie with thee in thy bed – if thou wouldst promise all this, then would I swim out into the water and fetch thee thy golden ball.'

"'Oh yes,' she answered, 'I will promise it all, whatever you want, if only you would fetch me my ball.'

"But she thought to herself, 'What nonsense he talks! As if he could do anything other than live out in the wood and cry out to the moon! As if he could ever be a vampire princess's companion!'

"The wolf, as soon as he heard her promise, leapt into the water and swam out to the centre of the pond. There he caught the ball in his jaws and he returned to the princess, dropping the golden ball at her feet.

"The king's daughter was overjoyed to see her pretty plaything again, and she caught it up and ran off with it.

"'Stop! Stop!' cried the wolf. 'Take me with you!'

"But it was no use, for howl after her as he might, she would not listen to him, but made haste home, and very soon she forgot all about the poor wolf.

"The next evening, when the king's daughter was sitting at table with the king and all the court, and eating blood from her golden goblet, there came a pitter-patter of pads up the marble stairs, and then there came a knocking at the door, and a voice crying, 'Youngest king's daughter, let me in!'

"And she got up and ran to see who it could be, but when she opened the door there was the wolf sitting outside. The princess shut the door hastily and went back to her seat, feeling very uneasy.

"The king's vampire senses could not help but notice how quickly his daughter's heart was beating, and said, 'My child, what are you afraid of? Is there a troll at the door ready to carry you away?'

"'Oh no,' answered she, 'not a troll, but a horrid wolf.'

"'And what does the wolf want?' asked the king.

"'Oh dear father,' answered she, 'when I was sitting by the pond last night, and playing with my golden ball, it fell into the water, and while I was crying for the loss of it, the wolf came and got it for me on the condition that I would let him be my companion, but I never thought that he would come after me and follow me to the castle. But now he is outside the door, and he wants to come in to me.'

"And then they all heard him knocking a second time and howling:

"Youngest king's daughter,
Open to me!
By the pond water
What promised you me?
Youngest king's daughter
Now open to me!"

"'That which thou hast promised, must thou perform,' said the king, 'so go now and let him in.'

"So she went and opened the door, and the wolf trotted in, following at her heels, till she reached her chair. Then he stopped and cried, 'Lift me up to sit with you.'

"But she delayed doing so until the king ordered her. When the wolf was on the chair, he wanted to get to the table, and there he sat and said, 'Now push your golden goblet a little nearer, so that we may eat blood together.'

"And so she did, but everybody could see how unwilling she was, and the wolf lapped the blood heartily, but every drop seemed to stick in her throat.

"'I have had enough now,' said the wolf at last, 'and as I am tired, you must carry me to your room, and make ready your silken bed, and we will lie down together.'

"Then the king's daughter began to weep, and was afraid of the wolf, that nothing would satisfy him but that she must lie with him.

"Now the king grew angry with her, saying, 'That which thou hast promised in thy time of necessity, must thou now perform.'

"So she led the wolf away from the table and escorted him upstairs and put him in a corner. When she laid down to rest in her bed, the wolf came creeping up, saying, 'I am tired and want sleep as much as you. But first I would couple with you. Let me into your bed or I shall tell your father.'

"So the princess pulled back her silken sheets and allowed the wolf to climb on top of her. But once they had coupled, the wolf turned into a handsome human prince with beautiful kind eyes and a smiling mouth.

"And it came to pass that, with the king's consent, they became bride and bridegroom. And he told her how a wicked witch had bound him to be a wolf with her spells, and how the only way he could be released from the witch's spell was to mate with a princess.

"The prince and the princess lived happily enough and had many children. But here is the curious thing; each of their children was cursed to transform into a wolf on the full moon. This then is how the first werewolves were created, and why their fates are so often bound up with the fates of vampires."

* * *

The sheep closed the book and looked at Alice. Alice felt very sleepy and as she laid back in the boat she whispered, "Well I certainly would *not* have let that smelly old wolf climb into *my* bed! The very thought! I should have killed him and fed his carcass to the crows."

"Why you insolent little vampire!" cried the Sheep angrily in a manner that made Alice jump and stirred her from her reverie. Before her she saw the Sheep beginning to tear and claw at itself, pulling wool from its body, until from within the sheep began to emerge the giant werewolf!

"A disguise!" said Alice. "You wily old wolf!"

"Wily?" growled the werewolf, now fully emerged from within the sheep's carcass. "Wily enough to trap you, little vampire whore! For dawn breaks even as I speak," and it was true, the red on the horizon had grown and increased and in parts was now more yellow and golden than red, "and our boat sails on a river of holy water!" Alice looked over the side of the boat and her eyes began to cry to be so close to so much blessed water. "And so here you are, trapped in this boat with me! Now which way to kill you? Should I let the sun rise and burn you to a cinder? Should I tip over the boat and let you be dissolved? Or perhaps I should prefer to rip you apart with my own teeth?"

A flock of bluebirds alighted from a near-by tree and fluttered overhead, and they sang a merry song:-

"To the Looking Glass world it was Alice that said
'I've a Werewolf chasing me who wants me dead.
Let the Looking Glass creatures, whatever they be
Come and dine with dear Queen Victoria and me!"

And hundreds more bluebirds flew close and joined in the chorus:-

"Then fill up the glasses with lashings of blood
And rid the world of anything good
Put cats in the wells and ghosts in the trees
And welcome dear Alice, a vampire, you see?"

" '*Oh Looking Glass creatures,*' *quoth Alice,* '*draw near!*
'*Tis an honour to see me, a favour to hear:*
'*Tis a privilege high to have dinner and tea*
With my friend Queen Victoria and me!'"

Then came the chorus again:-

"*Then fill up the glasses with blood and with ink*
Or anything else that is pleasant to drink:
Mix fur with the gin and wool with the wine -
And welcome dear Alice, a vampire out of time!"

A ray of pure sunlight burst across the heavens and stung poor Alice's eyes. Her flesh began to scream and she knew she would soon begin to burn. This was too much. Too, too much. If Alice was going to die, she decided, she was going to do it while having a tantrum. She was *not* going to go quietly.

Chapter VI
Shaking & Waking

She threw herself across the boat and at the werewolf, and grabbed him around the neck and shook and shook and shook. "This is all your fault!" she screamed into his face, and with a strength that surprised even her, she continued to shake the wolf backwards and forwards with all her might.

The werewolf made no resistance whatever: only his face grew smaller, and his eyes became softer and green: and still, as Alice went on shaking him, he kept growing smaller – and less hairy – and softer – and sweeter – and...

... and the werewolf was really the human girl Kitty, after all.

"Sweet little human girls shouldn't moan so much," Alice said, rubbing her eyes, and addressing Kitty, respectfully, yet with some severity. "You woke me out of oh! Such a nice dream! And you've been along with me, Kitty – although you were a werewolf! Or at least I think that was you. Or perhaps you were the kitten thrown down the well?"

It is a very inconvenient habit of human girls (Alice had once made the remark) that, whatever you say to them, they *always* scream, or moan, and say the word 'please'. "If they would only occasionally say 'yes' or 'no' so that one could keep up a conversation! But how *can* you talk with a person if they *always* say the same thing?"

"The question is, dear Kitty," continued Alice, "whose dream was it that I entered? Was it my dream or perhaps yours?" Alice looked across the room, to the Mistress as she pinned the blonde haired girl to the floor and drained the last of her blood. "Or perhaps it was the Mistress's dream? Does the Mistress still dream?" she pondered. "She is so old that perhaps she never dreams at all these days? How awful would that be, Kitty? To never dream? But enough of these musings, sweet girl, for my nap has aroused in me a fierce hunger. Now don't be scared and don't struggle so, I shall be as gentle as a lover with you."

And with that, Alice's fangs pierced the soft, creamy skin of the human girl Kitty's neck and began to suck. Kitty did not struggle, not much, but she did make a sound not unlike a cat mewing, and Alice decided that Kitty probably hadn't been the werewolf at all but rather the kitten from the well. "In that case," thought Alice, "I shall punish you most severely for scratching at my cheek."

And she did, for Alice could really be quite cruel when she put her mind to it.

A house, beneath a night-time sky
Dreaming sweetly as clouds pass by
In the dark month of December.

Two girls by the fire nestled near
One the hunter, the other her dear
A dance not unlike that of love.

Long has brightened that moonlit sky
Echoes fade and memories die
Summer sun has melted the snow.

Still they haunt me, as phantoms may
Alice and Kitty and their tender ways
Never seen by waking eyes.

In a Wonderland now they lie
Dreaming as the nights go by
Neither realising that both of them died.

Ever living within that room
Lingering eternally in twilight's gloom
Life and death, what are they but a dream?

THE END

The Nail in the Coffin
a Final Word

"Is that it, then?" asks Katie as I lean back against the chair and stretch my arms. "You finished with me now?"

"Thanks, Katie," I smile sleepily. It's been an exhausting two weeks, listening to Katie speak, transcribing her stories, trying the make sense of the amazing, terrible things she has confessed to me. "I really appreciate it."

Katie leans back against her chair also, and a half smile breaks on her face. I notice her fangs peeking out from behind her lips, and perhaps for the first time I fear for my safety. Now that the story is told, what is to stop her from killing me and drinking my blood in the manner she has described so vividly in her stories?

She seems to instinctively know of my concerns. "Don't worry sweetie," she says. "I ain't hungry. Besides, you and me, we're muckers now, ain't we?"

"Of course," I reply, forcing a smile to break on my face against its will.

I walk her to the door of my office, located on the ground floor of a building that was, once upon a time, a brewery. These days the building is a very trendy shopping arcade, full of independent record stores, hippy jewellery retailers, tattoo parlours, and coffee shops. But still, above the main entrance, words carved into

308

the brick archway read 'Black Eagle Brewery 1846'. A reminder, perhaps, that lately I seem to have been spending more time, as it were, in the 19th Century than the 21st.

"So long, sweetie," says Katie as she slips from the entrance and into the late evening throngs heading down Petticoat Lane. "It's been fun, ain't it?"

"Yes," I say, feeling relieved that the interview is finally over and that I have escaped my contact with a genuine vampire with my life still intact. "It's been fun. And interesting. Listen, *thank you.*"

She pats my cheek with a hand ensconced in an old lace glove. "Don't mention it, petal," she says, and with that she turns and is gone, vanishing almost instantly into the crowds.

We are in the middle of the East End of London, and yet on this November evening I swear I can smell bonfires and autumn leaves on the air. I stand there, on the threshold, for a full ten minutes. Then, when Katie has gone, properly, totally gone, I turn around and walk back in to my office. I lock the door behind me and sit down at my desk. Before me, on its shiny screen, my computer proudly displays the transcript of Katie's words. I read a sentence or two, and then the enormity of it all, and all that I have heard, dawns on me. "Fucking hell!" I laugh out loud, and bury my head in my hands.

Katie Bell will, by now, be half way down Petticoat Lane, eyeing up the humans around her, selecting her prey, deciding whether, this fine evening, she fancies eating or fucking or perhaps both? I remember something that she said to me, after I had asked her whether she felt guilty about causing the death of so many humans. Rather than give me some glib reply about cattle and survival of the fittest and whether the lion feels guilty about killing an antelope, she had said, "We lived each night in the shadow of death, darling; it was our constant companion. I thought about death all the time, didn't I? But not like it was an enemy or something to be feared. Death was a friend, by and large. It rode alongside us, it stepped beside us, it opened our doors and it closed them behind us. We vampires, we was immersed in death as much as we were immersed in life, and the two, death and life, were given as easily as it was to speak the words out loud. Guilty never entered into it. Such talk is human talk, you understand?"

Vampires are aberrations, make no mistake about that. They simply should never have existed. They were one of nature's more extravagant mistakes, an evolutionary dead-end that by now is all but spent. Katie Bell, of course, in typical Katie Bell style, refuses to surrender to the inevitable and holds on to existence like a deadly siren clinging to a rock while the waves of humanity crash around her and threaten to submerge her. She may very well be the last of her kind, or there may yet be others secreted away (Miss Adler in the secret laboratory for example). But the fact of the matter is that the vampire race is by now all but extinct. I, for one, cannot decide whether that thought fills me with relief or fills me with remorse.

There. That seems a fitting place to stop. Let us take our leave there, while we are filled with thoughts of life and death and relief and remorse. Let us take our leave there.

Fin

9 781034 468608